DANCER IN THE FLAMES

DANCER IN THE FLAMES

Stephen Solomita

This first world edition published 2012
in Great Britain and 2013 in the USA by
SEVERN HOUSE PUBLISHERS LTD of
19 Cedar Road, Sutton, Surrey, England, SM2 5DA.

British Library Cataloguing in Publication Data

Solomita, Stephen.
  Dancer in the flames.
  1. Police--New York (State)--New York--Fiction.
  2. Police murders--New York (State)--New York--Fiction.
  3. Police corruption--New York (State)--New York--
  Fiction. 4. Brooklyn (New York, N.Y.)--Fiction.
  5. Suspense fiction.
  I. Title
  813.5'4-dc23

ISBN-13: 978-0-7278-8228-8 (cased)

All Severn House titles are printed on acid-free paper.

Severn House Publishers support The Forest Stewardship Council [FSC],
the leading international forest certification organisation. All our titles that
are printed on Greenpeace-approved FSC-certified paper carry the FSC logo.

Typeset by Palimpsest Book Production Ltd.,
Falkirk, Stirlingshire, Scotland.
Printed and bound in Great Britain by
MPG Books Ltd., Bodmin, Cornwall.

I'm not big on philosophy, Boots.
In fact, as far as I'm concerned,
The examined life's not worth living.
Crazy Jill Kelly

ONE

D etective Boots Littlewood shook out a handful of Tic Tacs and popped them into his mouth. He sucked on them for a moment, intending to savor the flavor, as he liked to say. But on this particular night, what with the disagreeable job at hand and the unusually cold April weather, he quickly grew impatient. Very deliberately, he straightened the lapels of his overcoat before crunching down hard enough to produce an explosion of spearmint that saturated his entire mouth, from his lips to his tonsils. Finally, he rang the doorbell.

The outdoor light came on a moment later and a face appeared in the door's small window, a round face made rounder by the window's beveled glass. Then the door opened to reveal Frankie Drago, the man Littlewood had come to see.

'Gimme a break, Boots,' Drago said. 'It's after ten o'clock.'

Detective Littlewood stepped into the house, forcing Drago aside. As he passed, he pulled a transistor radio from his overcoat and held it up for Drago's inspection.

'Batteries went dead on me,' he explained. 'I don't wanna miss the end of the Yankee game. Plus, I'm killin' two birds with one stone. The autopsy's complete and you asked me to stop by, let you know how it went.'

Passing through the foyer and into the living room, Boots placed himself in front of a gigantic flat-screen television. He watched the Yankee reliever, Joba Chamberlain, deliver a high outside fastball that David Ortiz, the Red Sox batter, was taking all the way. Then he said, 'You don't mind, I'm gonna keep an eye on the game while we talk. I got a bet down, if you remember.'

Boots shrugged off his overcoat, folded it across the back of an armchair, finally settled himself on the couch, only pausing to tug at the crease in his trousers and press the remote's mute button.

'You think I don't know you got a bet down?' Drago followed Boots into the room. 'I'm your goddamned bookie.'

'Hey, do me a favor, Frankie. Lay off. I got a thing about takin' the Lord's name in vain. Which you already know.'

Drago was about to respond when Chamberlain began his wind-up and the Yankee catcher stepped to the left, setting a target on the inside corner, a target Joba missed by eight inches when the ball sailed away from Ortiz before centering itself, belt-high, over the heart of the plate.

'You mother-fucker,' Boots shouted as the bat of David Ortiz ripped through the hitting zone.

'Boots,' Frankie Drago said, 'you can open your eyes. He popped it up.'

Littlewood followed instructions, regaining his sight in time to watch the ball drop into Bret Gardner's glove. The score was tied six–six and the Yankees were coming up to start the tenth inning.

'Chamberlain,' Boots complained, 'that prick. You see him walkin' around out there? This is a guy, lemme tell ya, he'd rather be takin' a shower.'

'Cut the man some slack,' Drago objected. 'It's thirty degrees and he's tryin' to grip a goddamned baseball.'

'Frankie, what'd I just say about blasphemy? Have some consideration here.'

Drago raised a meaty hand to scratch his left ear. He was a short man, grossly overweight, and his movements were slow enough to appear grave. 'Didn't you just call Chamberlain a prick and a mother-fucker?' he asked.

'That's different.' Boots turned far enough to look up at the bookie. 'The Commandment only says you can't take the Lord's name in vain.'

Drago sat down in a massive rocking chair to Littlewood's left. For a long moment, he stared at the side of the detective's head. Drago had known Boots for more than twenty years – their relationship went all the way back to high school. And that was the wonder of it, because he still couldn't peg the big cop. The gray three-piece suit? The baby-blue tie? The gleaming ankle-high boots? The nearly transparent silver socks? The coarse iron-gray hair that hugged the top of his head as though afraid to move?

'Bullshit' was the word that popped into Drago's mind. Just like the rest of the cop's life. Here was a man who went to mass every Sunday, but tolerated Frankie Drago because he needed a place to lay down his bets. Here was a man who called himself Boots because his real name, Irwin, didn't square with his image. You couldn't be a hard-ass cop in a suit too expensive for your paycheck and have a name like Irwin Littlewood. Impossible. So, whatta ya do? You make up a name that fits your image like the handmade Italian boots on your feet. Then, as if that wasn't phony enough, you swear that you only spend that kinda money on shoes because you got bad wheels.

Drago ran a hand across the top of his nearly bald head. It came back slick with sweat and he wiped it on his pants. 'You wanna tell me what happened?' he asked.

'Wait a second, Frankie.'

The requested second stretched on for a full two minutes as the Red Sox pitcher, Alfredo Aceves, walked the Yankee center fielder, Curtis Granderson, on four straight pitches. The Red Sox manager, Bobby Valentine, was out of the dugout before the catcher reached into his mitt for the ball, his head shaking in disgust as he signaled for Tim Wakefield, the last available pitcher in the Red Sox bullpen.

Boots crossed his legs and let his gaze drift over to Frankie Drago as the network cut to a commercial. 'It's a question here of how much you wanna know, Frankie,' he said. 'Bein' as we're talkin' about your sister.'

When Drago shook his head, his many chins slogged from side to side like water in a bathtub. 'It can't be no worse,' he insisted, 'than what I already imagined.'

'OK, then let me get this part over with. Angie was naked when we found her body, with her arms tied behind her back and a thin rope tied around her neck. There was an unused condom next to her leg, still in its wrapper, a ribbed Trojan. Keep in mind, Frankie, this was a disposal site. She wasn't killed in Prospect Park.'

Drago thought it over for a moment, then said, 'Angie, she was forty-nine years old and looked every day of it. Why would . . .?'

'That part doesn't matter. Some of these perverts specialize in older women, and some of them just grab whoever's available. Anyway, we at least determined when her body was put in the park.'

'How's that?'

'You remember March fifteenth? The blizzard?'

'Of course. I didn't get my car out for a week.'

'Well, we found a little snow beneath Angie's body and we're certain there wasn't any snow on the ground before the storm hit. That means the blizzard started right before she was dumped, two days after your mom reported her missing.'

'You think she was held somewhere?'

'There's no other possibility.'

'Was she . . .'

'Dead or alive?'

'Yeah.'

'She was dead, Frankie.'

'And you can tell how long?'

'Thirty-six to forty-eight hours, accordin' to the pathologist who did the autopsy. That's how long the perp held on to her body.'

Boots's attention returned to the television as Tim Wakefield threw his last warm-up pitch. 'Valentine's gotta be pissing his pants,' he told Frankie.

'He ain't the only one,' Drago replied. 'I took a lotta Yankee action this afternoon. They win, I'm up shit creek.'

'You didn't lay it off?'

'Sometimes in life you gotta take a chance, Boots. With Beckett goin' against Freddy Garcia, I figured I had an edge.'

Boots shook his head. 'The way I saw it, with all the injuries to the Red Sox bullpen, after the Yanks got past Beckett, they'd be the ones with the edge.'

An instant later, the Red Sox pitcher took an important step toward neutralizing whatever edge the Yankees may have had when he picked off Curtis Granderson. Boots's mouth dropped open and his eyes widened as he absorbed the extent of his misfortune. He started to speak, stopped, then started again. Still, no words came out.

Flashing a wolf's grin, Drago took a pack of cigarettes from his shirt pocket. He lit one up, then blew a narrow line of smoke at the ceiling. 'So,' he asked, 'how's the quittin' goin'? You still nicotine-free? It's been, what, a month now?'

Boots drew his arms over his chest, but didn't respond. Wakefield's knuckleball was dancing out of the strike zone and Mark Teixeira, the Yankee's first baseman, was flailing away. It came as no surprise when he struck out on the fourth pitch.

'Could we get back to Angie?' Drago asked. 'The game's liable to go on for another two hours.'

'Angie's been dead for more than three weeks. She'll keep.'

'That's pretty hard, Boots. It's not like we're talkin' about a stranger. You grew up with Angie and you might wanna consider her last hours.'

'Right, her last hours. How do you figure they went? What do ya think happened to Angie?' Boots let his eyes dart from the screen to Drago, then back to the screen. 'Don't worry,' he said as Alex Rodriguez stepped to the plate, 'I'm listenin'.'

Drago rocked back and forth for a moment before responding. 'This kinda pervert, Boots, he oughta be shot down like a dog. Forget the handcuffs, forget the lawyers. Shoot him down. Leave him to rot where he falls.'

'Yeah,' Boots finally said, 'but what do you think actually happened? Was she on her way someplace? Did he drag her out of the house without your mom noticing? And where did he take her? And why did he hang on to the body for two days? And why didn't she put up a fight? I mean, Angie never backed away from anyone, not that I ever noticed. Meanwhile, she doesn't have a bruise on her body.'

'What if he had a gun? You put a gun to someone's head, they tend to get very docile.'

'And then what?'

'He forces her into a car and takes her wherever.'

'And who does the drivin'?'

Drago thought this over for a moment, then said, 'It'd make more sense if there was two of them.'

'Yeah, that's possible, but what I'm thinkin', it's most likely she was killed by someone who knew her. A scumbag who lives in the neighborhood. Somebody who could take her by surprise.'

Tim Wakefield finally made a mistake on the fifth pitch he threw to Alex Rodriguez. His knuckleball failed to knuckle and the ball rolled over the outside half of the plate, waist-high, at seventy miles an hour. A few seconds later, it came to rest in the center-field seats, five hundred feet away.

Boots jumped up and did a little dance. 'Patience,' he told Drago as he spun around. 'That's what it's all about. That's the lesson here. A-Rod took four straight pitches, didn't move the bat an inch. That's because he knows that hitters are always overmatched. They gotta wait for the pitcher to make a mistake. Hitters hit mistakes.'

'Yeah? What about Vladimir Guerrero? He hits whatever's thrown up there.'

'Fuck Vladimir Guerrero.'

'And what about Alfonso Soriano?'

'Fuck him, too.'

Littlewood retrieved his Tic Tacs, shoveled a few into his mouth and crunched down. At the same time, he inhaled deeply, taking the smoky air down into his lungs. 'So, who do you think it could have been?' he asked as Nick Swisher stepped up to the plate.

Again, Drago took his time, sucking thoughtfully on his cigarette while he regarded the detective. 'How about one of the freaks down the fuckin' block,' he finally asked.

Drago was referring to a bohemian enclave centered around the subway stop at Bedford Avenue and North Seventh Street, but the cop wasn't buying. 'Angie hated those people,' Boots said. 'She was strictly old school when it came to preserving her neighborhood. If she asked me, which she didn't, I would've told her the truth. The neighborhood moved out to the burbs thirty years ago. There's nothin' left to preserve.'

Boots continued to stare at the television as Wakefield threw one knuckleball after another to Nick Swisher. As usual, Swisher's attitude was intense. When he swung, as he did on three of the five pitches thrown to him, his bat tore across the plate as though reaching into another dimension. Fortunately for the Red Sox, ball and bat never came within a foot of each other and Swisher slammed his bat into the dirt when he finally struck out to end the inning. The camera lingered on his features for a moment, then cut to the Yankee's ace reliever, Mariano Rivera, as he trotted across the outfield. Up a run, the Yankees were going with their best.

Boots watched Drago grind the stub of his cigarette into an aluminum ashtray stamped into the shape of a mermaid. His eyes lingered on the butt for a moment before he spoke.

'What we're thinkin' now,' he told Frankie Drago, 'is that Angie's dump site was staged. We're not thinkin' her killer was sexually motivated.'

'You're sure?' Drago asked.

Littlewood's grin was as quick as A-Rod's bat, here and gone, a blur. 'First thing is the cause of death, which I'm surprised you didn't ask me about sooner. Most times, the family asks right away. They wanna know how their loved one died.'

With Boots staring straight into his eyes, Drago had to struggle for words. He could smell the sour stink of his own sweat as it wafted up from his crotch and his armpits. He knew that Boots smelled it, too.

'So,' he asked, his voice weaker than he would have liked, 'you gonna tell me or not?'

'Blunt force trauma to the back of her head. See, that's not the way sexual predators kill. I know because I checked with this profiler who works downtown. Stabbing and strangulation, those are the most common methods. True, you also find thrill killers who batter the faces of their victims, but Angie's face was untouched.'

'Wait a minute,' Drago interrupted, 'didn't you tell me she had a rope around her neck?'

'Yeah, I did. But it was put there after she was dead. Likewise for the ligatures on her wrists. That's what I meant when I said the scene was staged.'

TWO

D rago lit another cigarette and immediately felt better when Boots looked away. He told himself to take the advice he'd given Boots a few minutes before. Calm down. Relax.

'You spent the last twenty minutes tellin' me what didn't happen,' he finally said. 'Why don't you tell me what *did* happen. So we'll both know.'

Boots glanced at the television as the Red Sox lead-off hitter, Dustin Pedroia, approached the plate. 'I think the perp grabbed Angie by the hair,' he said, 'then slammed her head into a concrete wall or a concrete floor. Probably once, but no more than twice. I think the killing was impulsive and I think he wished he could take it back afterward.'

Pedroia was batting from the right side against the right-handed Rivera. Strictly old school, he was a dirty-uniform second baseman with a tendency to hit clutch home runs even though he was by far the smallest player on the field.

'I hate this guy,' Boots said. 'He doesn't give an inch.'

'Boots . . .'

'Hang on, Frankie.'

Rivera's first two pitches, both cutters, started in the center of the strike zone, then broke to the outside, clipping the front corner of the plate. Pedroia took both and both were called strikes. Rivera came inside with his third pitch, uncorking a head-high fastball that put the little second baseman on his back.

Littlewood turned away in disgust. 'So, what were you sayin', Frankie?'

'Nothin'. I don't know what to say. I'm kinda stunned.'

'OK, then let me ask you this. You remember I told you the killer hung on to Angie's body for two days, right? And I asked why he'd do something like that? I mean, if it wasn't a sex killing?'

'Yeah?'

'So now I'm askin' you again. Why did he keep the body for two days?'

'How am I supposed to know?'

'Don't get your balls in an uproar. I'm just askin' what you think might've happened. I'm askin' you to put it together. Your sister's killed in a moment of rage by someone who knows her. After the deed is done, he stashes her body for a couple of days, then dumps her in the woods in Prospect Park. Why do you think he waited?' Boots turned his attention back to the game. 'Don't worry,' he advised, 'I'm listenin' to every word.'

'All right,' Drago said as Pedroia took a practice swing, 'you know what I'm thinkin'? I'm thinkin' Angie had a lover, somebody in the neighborhood. You remember the way she carried on about loose morals, like she thought the sky was fallin' when Janet Jackson showed her tit at the Super Bowl? Well, if Angie was doin' the nasty out of wedlock, she woulda definitely kept it to herself.'

Boots made a little gimme gesture with his hand. 'Go on. Why would Angie's lover hold on to her body for two days?'

Drago began to speak as Rivera threw his next pitch, a high fastball that Pedroia took. The count was now two balls and two strikes.

'Ya gotta figure like this, Boots. If Angie had a boyfriend, he wasn't no mover and shaker. He had to be an ordinary guy. Remember, you said he killed Angie in a moment of rage, which I could understand, Angie havin' such a big mouth. But that means he didn't have a plan goin' in. So, what can he do? He's not a killer. He can't get on the phone, call in a disposal expert like in that movie. But he's gotta do somethin', right? And he's gotta do it pretty quick. Then he hears there's gonna be a blizzard in a couple of days and he figures the snow will cover her up.'

'And what happens when the snow melts, like it finally did?'

Drago stared at the side of Littlewood's head for a moment, then laid his hands on the arms of the chair and began to rock back and forth. 'That's why he made it look like a sex crime. He probably thought her body would be in bad shape and you wouldn't be able to tell what really happened.'

'Pretty good, Frankie. Credit where credit is due.' Boots nodded approval. 'And it mighta happened exactly that way, except for one little thing. Angie didn't have a lover.'

Drago's mouth opened, then snapped shut. 'You're positive?'

'Absolutely.'

'How . . .'

'How can I be positive?'

'Yeah.'

'Because Angie was a virgin when she died. Because she never had a lover in her life.'

Mariano Rivera's fourth pitch took a sharp break to the outside about twenty feet away from the plate. Well back on his heels after two inside pitches, the best Pedroia could do was flick the bat out there and pray for contact, a prayer that would certainly have gone unanswered if the pitch had been perfect. But the ball traveled across several inches of the plate and Pedroia managed to catch it on the end of the bat, lifting a soft flare that sailed over the head of a leaping Derek Jeter. A moment later, Pedroia was standing on first base and the Boston fans were again on their feet.

'Did you see that?' Boots slammed his fist into his palm. 'The little prick couldn't hit that pitch again if his fuckin' life depended on it.'

'Boots . . .'

'What?'

'Can we talk about this for a minute?'

'Talk about what?'

'Angie.'

'Frankie, there's nothing to say. We're gettin' a search warrant for the house. The Crime Scene Unit will be here in an hour.'

'For my house?'

'Yeah, the whole house, includin' your mother's apartment. The ME recovered concrete dust and paint chips from Angie's wound. If we match that paint to paint on a surface in this house, you're gonna have a lot of explainin' to do. Unless, of course, you wanna pin it on your mom.'

Unable to contain himself, Drago rocked forward until his bulk was centered over his knees, then pushed himself to his feet. Boots paid the bookie no mind, his attention returning to the game. For the next several minutes, while Drago loomed, unmoving, above him, Boots watched Rivera obliterate Adrian Gonzalez on four pitches, the last a borderline, chest-high fastball that the umpire, Dan Eddings, called a strike.

'One out,' Littlewood said, rubbing his hands together.

'Fuck you, Boots. I don't give a damn about the game and neither do you.'

Littlewood's eyes widened and he smiled. 'You pissed off, Frankie?'

'Yeah, now that you mention it. If you wanted to make an accusation, you should've done it up front. It's not like we're strangers.'

'OK, you're right. I've been fuckin' with your head. But look at it from my point of view. You've been lyin' to me from day one, you and your mother both, and I've been runnin' around in circles when I could've been solvin' crimes. No more, though. This is where all the circles intersect. We're not only gonna find that paint, we're gonna find traces of blood and tissue. I don't care if you cleaned up with bleach.'

With his teammate safe in the dugout, Kevin Youkilis stepped to the plate. All hustle and determination, Youkilis was the kind of player Boots most feared, a guy who personified the scruffy, working-class image Red Sox players cultivated.

'Here's another one,' Boots said, 'who don't give an inch.'

Rivera's first pitch was a cutter that missed the strike zone by a foot. Though Youkilis leaned across the plate, he didn't offer. Rivera's second pitch was a thigh-high fastball over the outer third of the plate – a gift. Youkilis jumped on it, but made a grave error when he tried to pull the ball into left field. The pitch was too far outside and his weight was too far back on his heels. Inevitably, he topped a weak grounder to Derek Jeter, who did everything right. He charged the ball, caught it gently in the web of his glove and shoveled it over to the second baseman. Already spinning toward first, Robinson Cano leaped high in the air to avoid the sliding Pedroia as he uncorked a perfect throw. Ball and runner arrived at first virtually at the same time, but the umpire didn't hesitate. His arms traced a wide arc away from his body. Kevin Youkilis was now on first base.

Boots watched the replays in disbelief, replays from every angle that clearly showed the ball in the first baseman's glove while Youkilis's foot was above the bag. Meanwhile, it was tough shit. Baseball had no instant replay rule and the umpire's call stood, despite Joe Girardi's passionate argument.

'I got a bad feelin' here,' Boots announced as the Red Sox catcher, Kelly Shoppach, settled into the batter's box. 'Like, what's next? Rivera pitched great, but these scumbags don't give up.'

Boots glanced up at Frankie Drago who stood above him, hands balled into fists, jaw rigid, nostrils flared. 'You got somethin' you wanna say, Frankie?'

'I don't want my mother hassled.' Drago managed to put a little menace in his tone, but the detective only turned back to the television.

'Frankie, your mother told me that Angie never came home that afternoon. I don't care if she lied because she loves you. I don't care that you were always her favorite. Unless you tell me the truth, she's fair game.'

'So, you're puttin' the squeeze on me?'

'I'm a cop. Squeezin' criminals is what I get paid for.'

'I know what you do for a livin', but I can't have my mother hassled.'

'Then you gotta step up. You gotta tell me the truth.'

Drago's immense torso quivered, the tension rippling through his body, from his shoulders to his knees. He wasn't afraid of Boots Littlewood, not exactly, but there was something about Littlewood's attitude as he watched Mariano throw a fastball that Shoppach fouled into the seats. Like Frankie Drago was no threat. Like Boots knew he'd already won.

*   *   *

'All right, Boots, you want the truth,' Drago said, 'here it is. Like you figured, it happened on March thirteenth. Ma was sleepin', so Angie came downstairs to watch *Law and Order*, which we both love, and which we been watchin' together for years. Anyway, Angie went into the kitchen. I think she said she was gonna nuke some popcorn, but I can't remember exactly. What I do remember is that I called to her just before the show started and she didn't answer, so I put the DVR on pause and went to look. Boots, she was lyin' at the bottom of the cellar steps, curled into a heap, and there was blood all around her head. I couldn't believe it, couldn't get my mind around it, that she could just be gone, that she . . .'

'If you were standin' at the top of the stairs,' Littlewood interrupted, 'how'd ya know she was dead?'

Boots waved off Drago's reply as Rivera threw a cutter into the dirt. Instinctively, Youkilis took a few steps toward second, then quickly reversed field when Martin came up with the ball and fired to first. Again, ball and runner arrived at the same time, again the ump called the runner safe, again the replays proved the ump wrong, again Joe Girardi came flying out of the dugout. The only difference this time was that Girardi got himself tossed out of the game.

As the Yankee's manager walked off the field, Boots finally rose to his feet. He watched the umpires resume their positions, watched Rivera lean in for a sign. 'C'mon, Mariano,' he whispered. 'Just do this one thing for me. Never again will I say you choked in the playoffs. And if someone else says it, I promise I'll defend you. Just do this one thing.'

'Boots?'

Littlewood's eyes snapped open. 'What, Frankie? What the fuck do you want?'

'I just told you.'

'Told me what?'

'I just told you I went down the stairs. I mean, her eyes were open and I knew she wasn't seein' anythin', but I checked Angie's pulse anyway.'

Rivera threw a knee-high fastball over the outside corner that Shoppach fouled off behind third base. A-Rod made a run for it, but the ball dropped several rows back in the stands.

'So why didn't you call nine-one-one?'

'I thought about it, Boots. I swear. But I couldn't seem to do anythin'. I kept tryin' to figure out how I was gonna tell Ma. And I was afraid you'd accuse me the way you're accusin' me right now. I mean, I spent the whole night goin' back and forth. What am I gonna do? What am I gonna do? It was like I went crazy. And then it was too late. It was the next morning and I knew if I called the cops, I'd never be able to explain why I waited.'

Boots considered this for a moment, then said, 'Tell me something, Frankie. When you laid your sister out nude in the snow, did you think about how she'd look to the person who found her? How she'd look to the cops who came to investigate? This was Angie, who was never naked with a man in her entire life.'

'Boots, please . . .'

'And by the way, Frankie. I lied to you before. When I said that Angie didn't have any bruises on her body. She had two bruises on her chest, parallel to each other. These bruises were almost identical, a pair of crescents about five inches across. The pathologist who did the autopsy says they were made with the heels of her killer's hands and I agree with him. Now, ya wanna hear something funny? About how amateurs always fuck up, about how they hang themselves in the end? If she died right away, like you claim, those bruises would've been very faint. But they weren't. They were deep purple and that means Angie was alive for at least two hours after you broke her head open.'

Drago's teeth ground together as he made a feeble attempt to process the information, including the possibility that Boots was still lying, that every single word was a lie. The bookie felt as though he was opening doors in some gigantic house, looking for a way out, a complete waste of time because there was only one door left. Drago opened it as the ball left Mariano Rivera's hand.

'I want a lawyer, Boots,' he said. 'It's my right.'

Rivera's cutter was ankle-high over the outer half of the plate when the batter's upper-cut swing interrupted its downward arc. The fly ball that resulted would have been a routine out in almost any other stadium. But this was Fenway Park and the foul pole in right field was only 302 feet away. Boots felt his heart jump as Nick Swisher raced toward the warning track.

'Gimme a break here,' Boots said, pumping his fist. 'Gimme a fuckin' break.'

But there was no break to be had. The ball traced a gentle, rainbow arc that finally dropped it into the seats one row beyond Swisher's outstretched glove. The game was over.

Initially, Boots froze, his body rigid, his mouth open, staring straight ahead. Then a gurgling sound issued from the back of his throat, as though he were choking on his own phlegm. He watched Shoppach circle the bases, watched him leap into the arms of his jubilant teammates while the Yankee players walked off the field. A close-up of Mariano Rivera revealed an anguish that bordered on despair. He could not have pitched better and he knew it.

Suddenly, Boots whirled in a half-circle and kicked Drago's legs out from under him. Frankie threw out his hands as he crashed to the floor, but he wasn't strong enough to break his fall. His face slammed into the carpet hard enough to bounce. An instant later, Boots Littlewood dropped on to his back.

'Gimme your hand,' Boots shouted. 'Gimme your hand.'

Boots jerked Drago's right arm behind his back and fastened one end of a pair of cuffs to his wrist. Then he reached for Drago's other hand, still shouting, 'Gimme your hand. Gimme your hand.' But Drago's back was very broad and he was carrying an extra hundred pounds as well. Though he didn't resist, his hands wouldn't come together, no matter how hard Boots yanked. Still Boots persisted, until finally he grew tired, until finally he heard Frankie Drago's plea.

'Boots, it was an accident. I swear. An accident.'

'Shut up, Frankie.' Boots had zero interest in hearing another version of the same event, a version guaranteed to be as self-serving as all the others. He jumped to his feet, yanked out a roll of bills, counted off two hundred dollars in tens and twenties, finally dropped to his knees and shoved the money into Drago's pocket.

'There, ya fuck,' he said. 'Now we're even.'

THREE

An hour later, Boots Littlewood entered Angie Drago's kitchen to find Officer Enrique Torres seated across from Frankie Drago at a table in the center of the room. The table was covered with a plastic tablecloth depicting scenes from Ancient Rome, the eruption of Vesuvius being the most prominent. Drago's coffee mug sat dead center over the rim of the volcano and Boots had to wonder if he'd placed it there deliberately, perhaps to contain the explosion that threatened to engulf him.

'Hank,' Boots said, 'you mind givin' us a little privacy?'

'No problem.'

Boots waited for the door to close behind the uniformed cop, then crossed to the sink. He found a mug in the drain basket, filled it with coffee from a gleaming percolator, added milk and sugar, finally took Torres's seat at the table. Drago watched Boots carefully, knowing that his own future was on the line. Make a mistake here and a series of very bad things would happen to him. Drago had spent four years upstate in the 1990s following a conviction for armed robbery and assault. In fact, prison was where he'd finally wised up, where he'd stopped dreaming those crime-czar dreams. Neighborhood bookie, he'd admitted to himself, far better suited his talents and his nerve.

'You asked for a lawyer,' Boots said. 'Are you takin' that back, Frankie?'

'Yeah, I am.'

'So, what do ya want?'

Drago took a deep breath as he sucked up every molecule of courage from his small reservoir. 'Ya know, Boots,' he finally said, 'you been placin' bets with me for a long time. If that should come out . . .'

Disappointed, Boots glanced around the kitchen, at what he knew to be Angie Drago's creation: the yellow walls and counter tops, the pale red curtains over the windows, the dark green cabinets, an off-white linoleum floor speckled with mica. Behind Drago's head, a religious calendar displayed the risen Christ. No more than a yard away, a wall clock bore the portrait of a smiling Minnie Mouse.

'You sealed your own fate,' Boots told Drago, 'when you arranged your sister's body the way you did. You can't fix something like that, not after the media gets wind of it. In addition to the Crime Scene Unit, there's an inspector from Borough Command and a prosecutor downstairs. They're gonna hold a press conference later on, after you've been arrested.'

Boots sipped at his coffee, trying to cool it down even as he took it into his mouth. Still, it was too hot and he burned his tongue. 'Shit,' he said.

'What's that supposed to mean?'

'It means,' Boots explained as he set down the mug, 'that I wouldn't save your ass even if I could. It means you have to pay for what you did to Angie, before and after her death.' Boots flashed his here-and-gone smile as he pushed the chair away and stood up. 'That's just the way it is,' he said. 'No hard feelings.'

Drago motioned for Boots to sit back down. 'Awright, forget about the threat, which I didn't mean anyway. I'm not gonna rat you out. I got somethin' much bigger to trade.' The bookie welcomed Littlewood's scrutiny. He'd finally gotten the bastard's attention. 'I'm not gonna beat around the bush. I have information – which I am willin' to share under the right conditions – regardin' Christopher Parker, the cop who got killed down by the bridge three weeks ago.'

Drago lit a cigarette, then blew a stream of smoke over the cop's head. Boots inhaled as it went by, sucking the air down into his lungs. 'Are you tellin' me,' he asked, 'that you know the identity of the shooter? And think twice before you answer. You lie about somethin' like this, you're gonna think you were sightseein' in Hiroshima on the day they dropped the bomb.'

'Boots, do I look like a schmuck?' Drago scrutinized the detective's features, one by one, finally deciding that the guy was such a hard read because he was so ordinary. The nose just a little too short, the mouth a little too pinched, the blue eyes a little too narrow, the chin a little too prominent – Boots was neither ugly nor handsome, nor remarkable in any way.

'I don't know who pulled the trigger,' Drago finally admitted. 'I'm not makin' that claim. But I do know somebody who watched the hit go down. And that's what it was, Boots. A hit.'

Boots nodded once, then rose to his feet. 'OK,' he said, 'I'll relay the message. But I've got one piece of advice, which you should really take to heart.'

'What's that?'

'When the time comes, show remorse.'

Boots set the wheels in motion by reporting Drago's gambit to his immediate superior, Lieutenant Carl Levine, commander of the Sixty-Fourth Precinct's detective squad. Levine took the offer to Inspector Mack Corcoran, who commanded all of Brooklyn's detectives. Corcoran huddled briefly with a pair of Homicide detectives, Artie Farrahan and Thelonius Tolliver, before approaching Assistant District Attorney Thelma Blount. Another discussion followed, after which Blount, Corcoran, Farrahan and Tolliver went upstairs to interview Frankie Drago.

Boots watched the posse mount the stairs before wandering into the living room where he found his boss sitting on the couch. Lieutenant Carl Levine was a short man with a thick neck that ran straight up into his round skull. His bony jaw was large and his broad nose short, leaving his mouth an isolated slash of pink midway between these two landmarks. In his mid-fifties, Levine was fast coming to the end of a long career. Under ordinary circumstances, he might have been proud of that career – the Detective Bureau was a prestige assignment for any lieutenant. But Levine's wife had deserted him more than a decade before and his two children were grown and gone. With no replacements in sight and no significant hobbies, retirement was little more than a black hole into which he would pour the remainder of his days. Levine's wistful eyes reflected this truth. Among the detectives at the Six-Four, his nickname was Lieutenant Sorrowful.

'Don't worry,' Boots said after a moment. 'I'll have a confession out of Frankie Drago within an hour.'

'You?'

'Frankie will never talk to Corcoran.'

'And why is that?'

'Because Frankie's been around the block. It'd be different, of course, if he knew the name of the shooter. Then he'd have to testify and the state would have to be nice to him. But the way it is, once he reveals the name of this witness, the criminal justice system will no longer need his services. That's why Frankie's gonna want some-body in the room he can trust.'

For once, Levine's eyes grew merry as a deep chuckle rumbled up from somewhere in his gut. He and Boots had been working together for many years.

'And that somebody he can trust would be you?'

'What can I say, boss? By now, the poor jerk's gotta be desperate.'

Fifteen minutes later, Boots heard the posse's footsteps on the stairs. He turned in time to watch Inspector Mack Corcoran, with Blount and the two detectives bringing up the rear, march into the living room.

'He'll only talk to you,' Corcoran announced. 'He thinks you're his friend.'

Corcoran was in his mid-forties, a rising star who'd jumped from captain to inspector as if the rank of deputy inspector didn't exist. Boots let his gaze travel past Corcoran's slash of a mouth, past the cold, suspicious eyes behind the wire-rimmed glasses, to the full head of brown hair that crowned his scalp. Dye job or a top-of-the-line rug? Boots couldn't decide.

'Don't test my patience, Detective.'

'If you want the name of the witness,' Boots finally said, 'I can get it for you. No problem. And while I'm at it, I'll have Frankie confess to whatever he actually did to his sister.'

Corcoran glanced at his two Homicide detectives, but they remained impassive. Both were acquainted with Boots Littlewood, having made use of him from time to time when searching for a witness or a suspect in the Six-Four. Boots knew everybody, had enough snitches to fill a high school gym and was generally cooperative. Alienating his affections was not on their agenda.

Halfway up the flight of stairs separating the apartments of Frankie Drago and his mother, Assistant District Attorney Thelma Blount abruptly sat down, turning to face Boots Littlewood in the process. She rummaged in her bag for a moment, then removed a thin silver flask and unscrewed the top before taking a quick chug. Finally, she thrust the flask at Boots.

'You have a bet on the game?' she asked.

'Don't remind me. The last thing I need is to get aggravated again.'

'Boots, I'm trying to be sympathetic.'

'I don't want sympathy. I want the umpires to get the calls right. I won that game twice over.'

Boots took the tiniest of sips, barely enough to wet his tongue. Shortly after Blount's divorce became final two years before, he and Thelma had passed a frenzied weekend at a honeymoon resort in the Pocono Mountains, virtually all of it on a heart-shaped water bed. They'd emerged from their tryst good friends, though neither had expressed a desire to repeat the experience.

'So what do you think?' Blount finally asked.

'About Frankie or about the witness?'

'Start with the witness.'

Boots squatted down until he was face to face with the ADA. 'Frankie's tellin' the truth. Somebody he knows claimed to witness Parker's murder. But was that individual also tellin' the truth? Frankie Drago's a bookmaker. His deadbeat customers have lied to him so many times that he's developed a cop's nose for horseshit. On the other hand, Frankie has every reason to exaggerate. We'll just have to see.'

FOUR

B oots positioned himself with his back to the sink, leaving the arena of the kitchen table to Drago and Blount. By mutual agreement, Littlewood's role in the proceedings would be limited to that of honest broker.

'Mr Drago, are we ready now?'

'Yeah, let's do it.' When Frankie Drago swallowed, his bobbing Adam's apple created a series of ripples that flowed through his jowls to finally meet at the back of his neck. Game time, he told himself. Do or die.

'You claim that you have personal knowledge of a witness to the murder of Captain Christopher Parker,' Blount continued. 'Is that correct?'

'Yeah, personal knowledge. As in the witness described the circumstances under which he did his witnessin' in great detail. My guess, he was coked up that night because he usually keeps his lip buttoned.'

'Did he recognize the shooter?'

'I asked him, but he wouldn't say.' Drago looked over at Boots. 'You know this guy, Boots. You and him have crossed paths many times.'

Boots nodded. 'Any chance he pulled off the hit?'

'None. And when I say his name, you're gonna know why.' Drago turned back to Thelma Blount. 'Now,' he said, 'it's your turn. What's in it for me?'

Thelma stared at him for a moment. She was a small woman, in her late thirties, with a thick head of extremely curly hair that tended to pull away from her scalp as the day progressed. It was very late, well past midnight, and her dark red hair now surrounded her face like a halo.

'Given the totality of the circumstances,' she said, 'I'm not willing to make any deal with you until I know exactly what happened on the night your sister died. It's that simple.' Thelma paused long enough to let the message sink in. According to Boots, Drago wanted nothing more than to unburden his guilty conscience. 'If you wish, Mr Drago, we'll keep it off the record for the present. But I won't go in blind, not with the media already alerted.'

Frankie again looked over at Boots, and again Boots nodded once. For just a moment, Drago was puzzled, but then he recalled the detective's parting advice: Show remorse.

'With Angie, it was always the weight,' Drago said, 'the weight and my health. I got high blood pressure to the point where I get chest pain, adult-onset diabetes, and my ankles and knees hurt so bad on rainy days I need a cane to get around. This is my fault, accordin' to Angie, because I'm a fat slob, because I don't have any self-discipline, because I'm weak. All through dinner she went at me – the soup, the salad, the pasta, the dessert – I was talkin' too much, eatin' too fast, chewin' with my mouth open. Finally, I told her, "If I wanted a wife, I woulda married one. Leave me the fuck alone."'

As his story progressed, Drago's eyes gradually dropped to the tablecloth, until he was finally staring at a crude representation of the Roman Colosseum that included a leaping leopard and a fallen gladiator. 'The point I'm makin' here is that Angie had these times when she just got mean. Myself, I think her hormones were outta whack, and I told her so, too, but she never got tested. That's because she liked being nasty. I swear to God. The way some guys like to hurt people with their fists, Angie liked to hurt people with her words. And I wasn't the only target. When Angie was in one of her moods, Ma took a beatin', too, along with the grocer, the butcher and the girls at the beauty parlor. Even Father Ryan got his share and everybody knows he's a fuckin' saint.'

Boots tuned out when Drago began a detailed account of the two hours before Angie came downstairs to watch *Law and Order*. Turning toward the sink, he found his box of Tic Tacs and shoved a few into his mouth. For the past month, he'd been hoping for a grace period, even five minutes, without wanting a smoke. Meanwhile, he couldn't find ten seconds of peace in an entire day.

Boots refocused as Drago wound up for the big finale. By then, tears were flowing in intermittent drops from the inside corners of both eyes.

'Angie came down at ten o'clock and right away she went off on me,' he said. 'Only this time she started in about my business. I was too soft, too weak. My customers didn't pay when they lost. This guy owes me this much. That guy owes me that much. Meanwhile, Ma's dishwasher leaks and her apartment needs paintin' and the toilet don't flush right and the stair railing's been loose for the last fuckin' year. After a while, I couldn't stand it no more. I felt like I was on fire, like if I didn't do somethin' I'd burst into flames. So, I jumped up and ran into the kitchen.'

Drago's head rose slightly, though his eyes never left the table. His tears were coming faster now.

'Angie followed me. It's unbelievable, right? I'm tryin' to get away, to create a little space, but she won't let me go. Boots, then and there, I knew she'd follow me even if I left the house, even if I got on a rocket ship and flew to the moon. There was no gettin' away, no place to hide. And her words were like bullets, the way they came out of her mouth – she was spittin' razor blades at me. I remember spinnin' around, tryin' to keep my back to her, but she just kept followin' me until I finally stopped. Then she said, "What, ya wanna hit me? Huh? Well, go ahead, ya fat slob. I dare ya."'

By the time Drago raised his head to look at Boots, he'd turned the jets up to full. Tears streamed from his eyes, a thin trail of snot ran from his nose to his quivering upper lip, sobs erupted from deep in his chest.

'I pushed her, Boots. I did it. Just like you said. I slammed her chest with the palms of my hands and she went flyin' backwards. But I swear on my soul that I never even thought about the basement stairs. I never thought for one second that she was gonna die.'

Boots rummaged in the cabinets until he found a roll of paper towels. He stripped away the plastic sheeting, then tossed the roll to Drago. The bookie tore off several sheets and wiped his face before continuing.

'What you said, Boots, about Angie bein' alive for two hours? That can't be right. It just can't be. She didn't have any pulse and her eyes . . . I'm tellin' you that Angie was gone before I got down the stairs. If I thought for one second she was alive, I would've definitely called nine-one-one. This was Angie, my sister. I don't care how pissed off I was, I loved her, too. You know that Boots. You know I loved her.'

In fact, the forensic evidence Boots reviewed before coming to Drago's home revealed Angie's cause of death to be a cerebral hemorrhage that killed her within seconds. And while a pair of contusions had been found on her chest, they were extremely faint.

'Mr Drago,' Thelma said after a moment, 'you need to finish.'

Though Frankie continued to stare at the tabletop, he felt his mind slowly rotate, felt every emotion, felt even the possibility of emotion spill out. All along, he'd believed that confession would be good for his soul, that he'd be somehow restored. Now he was left as shriveled and empty as a punctured balloon. He wondered how many times Boots had done this over the years, and to how many people.

'When I ran down the stairs and saw that she was dead, it was like I went crazy, like all my thoughts were crazy thoughts and I couldn't do a fuckin' thing about it. I kept tryin' to imagine myself explainin' to Ma, explainin' to the cops, but I couldn't get it straight in my mind. All I knew was that it was my fault Angie was dead and I had to make sure nobody found out. So when I heard about the snowstorm, I just figured . . .'

Suddenly, Drago leaned back in his chair. He laid his hands on the back of his knees and drew out his lower lip. Though his eyes were red and swollen, they were now dry.

'I'm done,' he declared. 'I gave you what you wanted. I told you the truth.'

Boots watched Thelma's full lips compress and her eyes narrow. Time for the bad news, time to put the squeeze on Frankie Drago. The sad part was that what Drago did to his sister, assuming his confession was truthful, amounted to no more than second-degree manslaughter, and maybe not even that. Meanwhile, Blount was set to lower the hammer.

'We're going to charge you with first-degree manslaughter,' she said, 'with a recommendation for bail. That's if you cooperate on the cop killing. If you don't, the charge will be second-degree murder and you'll be remanded without bail until the time of your trial.' Blount straightened in the chair. She was staring directly into Drago's eyes. 'You understand, Mr Drago, that you're going to get the fifteen minutes of fame that naturally follows dumping your sister's naked body in a public park. And you might also want to consider that every judge is a hanging judge when the media's looking over her shoulder. The maximum sentence for second-degree murder is twenty-five to life and that's exactly what you'll get if you're convicted.'

Drago shook his head as though trying to rid himself of an insect that had crawled into his ear canal. 'I didn't mean to kill her. I didn't even mean to hurt her. I just wanted to get her away from me.' He looked over at Boots. 'This ain't right, what you're doin' here. You know it happened the way I said. You know that—'

'Mr Drago,' Blount interrupted, 'the statement you just gave is off the record. If you refuse my offer, it ceases to exist. That leaves the prosecution with the series of lies you told Detective Littlewood, with the forty-eight hours between when your sister died and when you disposed of her body, and with the way you chose to display her. Trust me on this, when a jury sees the photos taken at the crime scene, they'll want to tear the flesh from your bones.'

Drago let his eyes drop to his hands as he dealt with Blount's threat. I should wait, he told himself. I should get a lawyer and let the lawyer bargain with the DA.

But he would have to find that lawyer first, then sit in jail until the deal was cut, all the while hoping the payoff would be more generous than the deal he'd already been offered. Drago finally raised his head to look at Boots.

'Don't be a jerk, Frankie,' Boots said. 'Nobody's askin' you to plead guilty. You can fight the manslaughter charge, just like you can fight the murder charge. The only difference is that if you take the state's offer, you'll be fightin' from the comfort of your own home, instead of Rikers Island.'

Drago stared into Littlewood's eyes for a moment, then broke into the first genuine smile he'd displayed since Boots turned up at his door. The recommendation for bail was an offer that could not be refused.

'Vinnie Booster,' he said. 'Vinnie Booster saw the whole thing.'

Some two hours later, Boots made his way to the Six-Four's squad room. There he accessed the squad's single computer, blundering through several databases before uncovering a borough-wide list of vehicles stolen during the month of March. He ran his finger down this list until he reached March 20th, the night of Christopher Parker's murder. Sure enough, a 2005 Nissan Altima had been reported stolen by its owner, a man named Rajiv Visnawana, at one thirty a.m. At the time, the vehicle was parked opposite 411 Berry Street, less than a block from where Parker was killed. Boots signed off, then crossed the room to pull the case file. He noted a few additional details, including the odd fact that Visnawana, rather than call 911, had filed his complaint at the precinct. Then he replaced the file and closed the drawer.

Boots crossed the room to his desk. Frankie Drago had been right when he predicted that Boots would recognize the name of the witness. Boots had known Vinnie Palermo, aka Vinnie Booster, almost as long as he'd known Frankie Drago, long enough to be certain that Vinnie's monicker aptly described the entirety of his adult life. Vinnie Booster was a car thief. As far as Boots knew, he'd never been anything else, his dedication to the craft undiminished by overlapping cycles of probation, prison and parole. Executing cops was not his bag.

Boots wrote out Frankie Drago's story, his intention to record the details while they were still fresh in his mind. According to Drago, Vinnie had been inside the Altima, jimmying the car's steering column, when a vehicle entered Berry Street, traveling away from the Williamsburg Bridge. As interruptions of this sort were commonplace in his world, Palermo simply hunkered down on the front seat and waited. But then the car remained stopped for an extended period of time and he cautiously lifted his head to peer through the Nissan's windshield.

Over the next twenty seconds, Palermo observed a white male exit this vehicle, then circle it to step on to the sidewalk and light a cigarette. At that point, a second male stepped out of a doorway and shot the first male twice, once in the back and once in the head.

'Blew his fuckin' brains out,' was how Palermo had described it to Drago.

For the next few seconds, the shooter had remained motionless, staring down at his victim. Then he shoved his weapon into the pocket of his coat before taking off along South Fourth Street in the direction of the East River. Vinnie Booster, having finally started the Nissan, made his own getaway fifteen seconds later.

FIVE

The rising sun was still below the eastern horizon when Boots entered the two-family home he shared with his father, Andy. Eager for bed, he climbed the stairs to his apartment. He was fishing for his keys, when the door opened ahead of him.

'Boots, *que passa*, man?'

'I think I should be asking you that question, being as it's so early,' Boots said.

Joaquin Rivera looked into his father's eyes and grinned. Boots was busting balls, as usual. 'You up for coffee?'

'Caffeine is the last thing I need.'

'Then how 'bout a hit of Jim Beam?'

'Great.'

Boots followed his son into the kitchen. At age twenty, Joaquin had a round face, a small pursed mouth and incipient jowls that would inevitably lengthen as the years went by. People commonly took him for soft, which was a mistake. Joaquin's early years were as hard as years can get for a child and he'd learned his lessons well.

Joaquin poured out Boots's drink. 'Here ya go, Boots,' he said as he laid it on the kitchen table. Boots raised the glass to his mouth and sipped. The bourbon slid down into his stomach, then curled up, warm as a kitten. 'You broke again?' he asked.

'I'm fucked,' Joaquin said. 'I can't make the rent.'

Even with the Pell Grants and the loans and his part-time job and Boots paying most of his tuition, Joaquin's struggle to meet the costs of an education at New York University was ongoing. The rat-trap studio apartment he shared with his girlfriend rented for fifteen hundred dollars a month.

Boots finished his drink, then went into his bedroom. When he returned, he had five hundred dollars in his hand. Joaquin took the money and put in his pocket.

'You know I hate this,' he said.

'I do,' Boots said. 'That's why I'm keepin' track of every penny. Somewhere down the line, after you get rich, you can expect a bill.'

The joke fell flat. 'By the time I graduate,' Joaquin said, his expression grave, 'I'll owe thirty-five thousand dollars to various banks. If I go on to graduate school – which is the only way I can make enough money to pay off my debt – the bottom line could double. When I think about it hard, which I try not to do, I feel like a sucker. I feel like I stumbled into a con game.' Joaquin shifted forward on his chair. 'See, that first loan, the one you get before you understand the system, it locks you in. You think, if I quit, how the hell can I pay it off? That's how long cons work, marks throwing good money after bad.'

Boots nodded as Joaquin went along. He was listening to an old story. 'Not to change the subject,' he said, 'but are you still doin' computer research for that private investigator?'

'Galligan? Yeah, three afternoons a week.'

'Does that mean you have access to Lexis/Nexis?'

'And a dozen other data collection agencies.' A smile, as suspicious as it was broad, spread across Joaquin's face, revealing a pair of shadowy dimples. In Boots Littlewood's universe, no favor was freely given.

'Well, I want you to check someone out for me. A police captain named Christopher Parker. He was murdered a while back.'

Joaquin nodded once as he recognized the name. 'What do you want to know about him?'

'Whatever's out there.'

'That's gonna cost.'

'Cost?'

'You're talking about a hundred databases. Galligan would never agree to do it on the cuff. Now, if you're willing to settle for a local media search, I could probably run it in my spare time. No harm, no foul.'

Boots nodded. 'Just do the media, Jackie. If something turns up, we'll go from there.'

Boots was fast asleep when his phone rang at nine thirty on the following morning. Nevertheless, as he'd been expecting a call, he rose to a sitting position and picked up.

'Yeah?'

'Boots, did I wake you?' The apologetic tone belonged to Littlewood's commander, Lieutenant Carl Levine. 'I was gonna call you earlier, but I figured you were asleep.'

'It's OK, boss. What's up?'

'I need you in my office at noon. You're now working for the Parker task force.'

'Oh, are you telling me that Vinnie wasn't home when the task force raided Connie Palermo's house?'

Levine sighed. There were times when Boots was a total prick and this was one of them. 'Let's hear it,' he said.

'Vinnie wasn't at his aunt's because Vinnie doesn't live there. Connie provides her nephew with an address for his parole officer, takes his phone calls and warns him if there's trouble. Myself—'

'Wait a second, Boots. Are you sayin' that you knew Vinnie wasn't living with Connie Palermo?'

'Yeah.'

'But you didn't tell anyone – also right?'

'Nobody asked me, boss. They kicked me right to the curb.'

Levine could barely contain his anger. 'Ya know, Boots, the way you strut around, you're a fuckin' peacock.'

'Sue me.'

'In my office, Boots, at noon.'

Boots shook his head as the smell of the proverbial rat finally reached his nostrils. 'Wait a second. If I'm being assigned to the task force, why am I reporting to your office?'

'To meet your new partner, son. Her name's Jill Kelly. You'll like her.'

*   *   *

When Boots arrived at the precinct ninety minutes before his appointment with Carl Levine, he was wearing sweats beneath his pearl-gray overcoat. His suit, also pearl gray, was draped over a padded wooden hanger, along with a jet-black shirt, a silver tie and his vest.

Boots headed down the stairs to the weight room in the basement after greeting the desk officer. As he entered the poorly ventilated room, he drew in the familiar odor of human sweat, sharp and salty, then announced, 'Yo, Boots is in the house.'

There were only two men present when Boots made his appearance, both members of an Anti-Crime unit attached to the Six-Four. Though the older of the pair, John Rimple, was a decade younger than Boots, he apparently had no respect for his elders.

'Who gives a shit,' he replied evenly.

Littlewood's gaze rested momentarily on a scraggly beard that failed to cover the ravages of Rimple's teenage acne. Like all Anti-Crime cops, Rimple worked the streets in plain clothes, mingling with the demons who haunted those streets in an effort to prevent crime before it happened.

'I don't get no respect,' Boots finally said as he hung his working clothes on a hook and began to loosen up. 'It must be a charisma thing.'

'Yeah, that's right,' Antoine Crudup interjected. 'Without the suit, you're just another chubby, middle-aged white man.'

A year on the wrong side of forty, Boots was coming to accept his middle-aged status. But the chubby part hurt. At six-three, two-twenty, he was proud of the body he'd worked so hard to maintain. Maybe his belly was somewhat rounded, but there was barely enough fat around his middle to pinch.

Though Boots worked non-stop for the next thirty minutes, he was only a third of the way through his usual routine when he called it quits. Rimple and Crudup were coming out of the shower room. Time to go to work.

'Guys,' Boots said, 'hang out a second.'

Crudup sat on one of several weight benches spread across the center of the room. 'What's up, Boots?'

'Vinnie Booster. I need to find him in a hurry.'

'That man is a complete asshole,' Crudup observed. 'He ain't two months outta the joint and he's back to stealin' cars. Swear to

God, Boots, if I had a dog that couldn't learn from his mistakes, no matter how many times he got punished, I'd take him out in the backyard and shoot him.'

'Much as I respect the sentiment, Antoine, I need Vinnie alive and talkin'. Now if I remember right, he was partnered up with a thief named Pete Karakovich before he went away last time. I was wonderin' if they got back together since Vinnie made parole?'

Crudup and Rimple exchanged glances as they searched their memories. That Boots was requesting their assistance came as no surprise to either.

'Didn't we see Vinnie with Peter Polack at Gentleman Johnny's last Friday night?' Rimple asked Crudup, naming a topless club on Kent Avenue.

'That's right. Vinnie was tryin' to slip a dollar bill into Candy Heart's G-string, but she wasn't havin' it. She shook her ass at him and went off to hustle somebody more generous.' Crudup rose to his feet. He was wearing a Fubu hoodie beneath an Avirex bomber jacket. 'I gotta get home,' he announced. 'Mama's waitin'.'

'One more thing,' Boots said. 'You ever hear of a cop named Jill Kelly? She's gonna be my new partner.'

Crudup's mouth opened in amazement. 'Bro,' he said, 'I'm not disrespectin' you here, but you really need to get out more often.'

'How long you been workin' the Six-Four, Boots?' Rimple winked at his partner. 'What I heard is that your mama gave birth in the muster room.'

Boots stood up. Rimple and Crudup had a valid point. To a large extent, the Sixty-Fourth Precinct defined the limits of his working life. He had little interest in the wider cop world outside its boundaries.

'The fuckin' duel?' Crudup said, his small eyes narrowing. 'The one that took place on the rooftop?'

'I did hear something about that,' Boots admitted, 'but I don't recall the details.'

Crudup glanced at his watch, then at the door. He was late, but the story was too good to resist. Finally he grinned. 'What I'm gonna tell you, it comes from the co-pilot of a police chopper, a sergeant named Jimmy Dermott. He claims that he was about a mile away, comin' up on a rooftop in Brownsville, when the confrontation went down.'

'Did you say a mile?' Boots asked.

'Yeah, and even though he was lookin' through binoculars, he still can't say for certain that what he thought he saw really happened.' Crudup hesitated for a moment, then asked. 'You know what they call Jill Kelly?'

'No idea.'

'Crazy Jill. And the word is that she earned her rep long before the situation I'm tellin' you about.' Crudup again looked at his watch. 'OK, down to business. Dermott claims that the perp, a Russian named Alex Luchinski, was kneeling down when Dermott first saw him. Dermott also claims that Luchinski's hands were not cuffed and that a pistol was lying on the roof a few inches from his fingertips. Kelly was standin' about ten feet away, in uniform, with her weapon holstered and her hand by her side. Accordin' to Dermott, nobody did anything for the next five seconds, then Luchinski and Kelly both grabbed for their guns. Boots, this fight was fixed from the beginning. Jill Kelly is the best shooter on the job, only a notch or two below Olympic caliber. Luchinski was dead, shot three times, center of mass, before he got his hands on his gun.'

A respectful moment of silence followed as all three cops tacitly awarded the story legendary status, true or not.

'So,' Rimple finally said as Boots walked off toward the showers, 'what do ya think of your new partner?'

'What I think is that I like her already.'

But Rimple was not about to let the matter go, not with the punchline undelivered. 'In that case, you might wanna consider that she's got uncles, cousins and an aunt on the job. In fact, one of her uncles, Mike Shaw, is Chief of Detectives.'

Maybe Boots was expecting a super-hero, Batgirl or Wonder Woman, or perhaps a Russian shotputter whose shoulders began at her ears. Whichever, he was unprepared for the auburn-haired beauty sitting in a chair to the left of Carl Levine's desk. Jill Kelly's body was slender, her manner relaxed. Though her face was noticeably broad, her features were large enough to compensate. Her dark blue eyes were truly enormous. As unapologetic as they were penetrating, they raked Detective Littlewood from his scalp to the tip of his ankle boots.

Yo, Jill Kelly's in the house.

'What's up, boss?' Boots asked.

Levine's features sagged as he recalled the one-sided conversation he'd had with Inspector Corcoran, a conversation in which his contribution was limited to a single response: Yes, sir. But then Levine's gaze happened to fall on Jill Kelly and he was immediately cheered. If Boots couldn't take a joke, fuck him.

'As of this moment,' Levine announced, 'you're on temporary assignment to the Chris Parker task force. Your job is to locate Vincent Palermo.'

Boots looked over at Jill Kelly and winked. 'You mean they didn't find him on Metropolitan Avenue?'

'No, Boots, they didn't.' Levine gestured in Kelly's general direction. 'This is Detective Kelly. She'll be your partner for the duration.'

'And who do I report to?' Boots asked.

'We don't report to anyone until we find Palermo.'

Jill Kelly's voice was low-pitched and husky, a smoker's voice if Boots had ever heard one. Boots rubbed his hands together and smiled. 'In that case,' he said, 'we'd best get on the road.'

SIX

'You mind if I smoke?' Jill Kelly asked as Boots pulled an unmarked Crown Vic away from the curb.

'Knock yourself out.' Though Boots managed to keep his tone neutral, his heart skipped a beat when Kelly rolled down the window, then thrust her mouth into the opening as she exhaled. 'Please,' he said, 'if ya don't mind. I'm just gettin' over a cold.'

Kelly brought up the window almost to the top. 'You're sure the smoke won't bother you?'

'Better than pneumonia,' Boots replied as he drew a deep breath.

They drove in silence for the next few minutes, until Jill Kelly tossed her cigarette butt into the road. 'Do we have a plan?'

'As a matter of fact, we do. See, there's no point in looking for Vinnie Palermo. He's like a woodchuck. The first sign of danger, he goes underground.' Boots glanced at his new partner. She was leaning against the seat, her hands resting in her lap. 'What we have to do is find a pal of Vinnie's, a car thief named Pete Karakovich. They call him Peter Polack on the street.'

'You know where to find him?'

'Not for sure, not right this minute. But I do know where he'll be at six o'clock.'

Kelly glanced at her watch. 'That's five hours from now.'

'Well, we could try Pete at his mother's house where he lives from time to time. Only, if he's not there, his mom'll definitely give him a heads up, in which case we'll lose him like the task force lost Vinnie. But it's your call.'

Jill smiled. It was nice the way he'd backed her into a corner. King Kong with a brain. 'Drive,' she said. 'Maybe we'll get lucky.'

They spent the remainder of the afternoon meandering through the neighborhoods of Williamsburg and Greenpoint, hoping to come upon Vinnie Palermo or Pete Karakovich as either went about his daily business. This was the longest of longshots, as Boots knew well. Both men were car thieves who plied their trade in the wee hours of the morning. They were as allergic to daylight as vampires.

But Detective Littlewood was far from upset. First, because in the course of his career he'd put in many thousands of hours behind the wheel and he liked to drive, especially while listening to the New York Yankees pound the shit out of the Boston Red Sox. Second, because Detective Kelly filled the Crown Vic's interior with smoke and kept it that way throughout the afternoon. Between the second-hand smoke and the Tic Tacs he shoved into his mouth every half hour, his cravings remained under control. His skin didn't crawl, his eyes didn't bulge, his fingers didn't tremble.

On the other hand, Boots just knew the Yankees were starting one of those streaks where they won twenty out of twenty-five games. That he wouldn't be able to bet on the games left him in a mood that equated nicely with the onset of major depression. He could almost feel the heavy hand of fate drop on to his shoulder.

By three o'clock, when his partner headed into a coffee shop for a bathroom break, Boots could stand it no more. He retrieved his cellphone and dialed a number from memory.

'Yeah?'

'Frankie, it's Boots. I see you made bail, just like I said you would.'

'It wasn't anything you did. It was what's her name, the prosecutor.'

'Thelma Blount. Anyway, I was wonderin' what you're gonna do now?'

'What I'm gonna do?'

'If you're still . . . you know, in business.'

For a long moment, Frankie Drago couldn't speak, the words sticking in his throat before he could force them beyond his vocal cords. Finally, he drew a deep breath and blasted a succinct message past the point of constriction.

'Fuck you, Boots, right in the ass.'

'C'mon Frankie, you can't blame me for what happened.'

'You hunted me down like an animal.'

'All I did was follow a trail of evidence. The reason it ended at your door was because you did the crime. Besides, there's something else you need to think about. The position you're in, it really doesn't pay to burn your bridges behind you.'

Drago took a moment as he tried to unravel the threads. Was Boots threatening to make things worse? Promising to help in the future? Or just lying through his teeth?

'OK,' Boots finally added, 'I'm sorry for how I went about makin' the arrest. I was really pissed off because you'd been lyin' to me and because of the way the Yankees lost. But that's no excuse. I shoulda definitely conducted myself in a more professional manner.'

Boots glanced through the window, saw Jill Kelly standing by the counter while the counterman filled a pair of Styrofoam containers with hot coffee. Already wrapped, two jelly doughnuts lay at her fingertips. 'I gotta make this quick, Frankie. You need to give me a yes or no before my new partner comes back.'

'You got a new partner?'

'Yes or no, Frankie?'

'All right, Boots, I'll take your bets. But I don't see what the rush is about. The Yankees are off tomorrow.'

'I know, it's just . . .' Boots watched the door to the coffee shop open, watched Jill Kelly display a careless physical confidence with each stride as she came toward him. 'The next four games against Baltimore, two bills a game,' Boots said. 'I got a feelin' the Yanks are gonna go crazy.'

*   *   *

At seven o'clock, as planned, Boots pulled to the curb on a mostly residential block of Meserole Street just off Manhattan Avenue. 'OK, first thing,' he told his partner, 'we're in Greenpoint now.'

'Not Williamsburg?'

'No, and not in the Six-Four. But it doesn't matter because I grew up in Greenpoint. Everybody knows me here.' Boots paused as Jill Kelly rolled her eyes. Maybe, he decided, he was overplaying his familiarity with the terrain.

'Anyway,' he continued, 'Pete Karakovich's Uncle Ted owns that bar over there, Gergan's, and Pete shows up almost every night for a burger and a brew. Now even goin' back twenty years to when Seamus Gergan owned the place, the bar had a certain reputation. I'm not sayin' it's a mob joint, but you should figure that anyone in there could be dirty, and that there might be a negative reaction if we try to drag Peter out.'

'Then why don't we take him on the way in? Or if he's already there, when he leaves?'

'What do we do if he runs?'

'Chase him down and beat the shit out of him. What else?'

Boots acknowledged the common wisdom with a nod. 'Yeah, well, that's the thing, Jill. I got plantar fasciitis. You know what that is?'

'Something with the foot?'

'Exactly. The tissues under the arches of my feet have these microscopic tears, which is OK as long as I take it easy. On the other hand, if I have to run a couple of blocks, I'll be limpin' for a week.'

Jill Kelly smiled, revealing a pair of fetching dimples that contrasted sharply with the expression in her eyes. 'Why don't you just tell me what the plan is, Boots,' she declared. 'So we'll both know.'

As he began to speak, Boots remembered Frankie Drago making the same point on the night before. 'Pete's too stupid to listen to reason. I'm going to approach his uncle. Maybe Ted Brochenek's been a crook all his life, but he's smart enough to know there are times when we all have to get along, like it or not.'

'And Pete will do what his uncle tells him to do?'

'Pete idolizes his uncle. They're like father and son.' Boots pushed the door open before adding, 'I've known them both for years. Me and Ted, we confess to the same priest.'

*   *   *

Everything about Gergan's Tavern spoke of age and neglect. The booths along the west wall, the bar along the east and the tables down the center had been gouged so many times, by so many pointed objects, that every name or message had been obliterated. At the far end of the room, a pool table with a pronounced tilt was covered with worn blue felt. Winning or losing on this table depended not on a steady hand but on a precise knowledge of the many dead spots on the rails.

The dozen patrons inside the bar on the night Boots and Jill Kelly showed up were a mix of workers on their way home and disorganized, wannabe gangsters like Pete Karakovich, who sat in a booth with three other mutts. One and all, their suspicious eyes followed the two cops as they strolled to the end of the bar nearest the door. Several men offered nods, including the bartender, Ted Brochenek, but these greetings were as solemn as they were tentative. Boots and his sexy partner had come for something – that much was obvious – and they could only hope it wasn't them.

Boots watched Teddy pour shots of cheap whiskey into a pair of glasses on the bar. The glasses were set before two men wearing blue, paint-spattered uniforms. Brochenek took their five-dollar bills, said something in Polish, then fed their money into a cash register as old as the building. Finally, he sauntered over to the cops at the end the bar.

'Boots, what I can get for you?'

'How about a couple of cokes?' Boots said. 'For me and my partner.'

Teddy's eyes raked Kelly's features, but his grave expression didn't change. He drew the cokes, then returned to lay them on the bar. Boots reached for his wallet, but Teddy shook his head.

'On the house.'

Boots nodded acceptance, then let his voice drop to a near-whisper. 'Teddy, I need you to listen carefully to what I'm gonna tell you now, because it's really simple and I don't want to repeat myself. I've got to speak to your nephew. There's no maybe about it, no wiggle room, no escapin' the fact. Me and Pete, we gotta talk. You with me so far?'

Teddy's sharp cheekbones and prominent brow might have been carved from stone. 'What Peter has done?' he asked.

'Nothing. He's not wanted for anythin' I know about and he's not gonna be arrested, or even detained. But I gotta talk to him.' Boots leaned closer. Already soothing, his voice became nearly hypnotic. 'You know me, Teddy. Greenpoint's not my beat and I usually don't get involved. But this thing I wanna talk to Pete about, it's too big. I can't keep it in the family, much as I'd like to. What Pete knows, he's gotta tell me.'

'My nephew, he is not a rat,' Brochenek said.

'This doesn't come as news to me, but nobody's got a choice here. Pete has to talk to me.'

'What you are saying, Boots?'

'I'm saying that if we don't come to an understanding, right this very minute, I'm gonna drag your nephew out of that booth, take him to the precinct and sweat him until he talks. And if he resists my invitation, I'll beat him down as well. In fact, I'll beat him until he cries.'

Brochenek didn't doubt, for a second, that Boots would carry out the threat. Still, he resisted. 'How I am asking Peter to wear a jacket? Better he should take beating.'

The jacket Teddy referred to was a snitch jacket. If Pete left with Boots, Gergan's clientele would conclude that he was cooperating with the police and spread the word to his criminal associates, thus ruining his reputation.

'I don't deny what you're sayin', Teddy. Pete's a stand-up guy, and destroyin' his credibility wouldn't be fair. So, here's what I suggest. If you promise me that you'll convince Pete to cooperate, my partner and I will return to the Crown Vic we're drivin' and wait for Pete to join us. That way, nobody knows nothin'.'

Boots paused for a moment, waiting for Brochenek to make up his mind, but then decided that the bartender needed another push. 'Teddy, you ever watch those *Lord of the Rings* movies?'

'My little boy loves these films.' Brochenek twisted his mouth into a circle. 'Precious. My precious. Bring to me my precious.'

'That's it.' Boots remembered to smile. 'Now, you recall the giant eye that came out whenever Frodo put on the ring?'

'Yes, Eye of Mordor.'

'Exactly, the Eye of Mordor.' Boots straightened up. 'Well, that eye, Teddy, that evil fuckin' eye, right now it's fixed on Boots Littlewood. You hear what I'm sayin'? It's fixed on Boots Littlewood and it's not gonna turn away until he tells it what it wants to know. I'm mentionin' this so you'll appreciate the gravity of my situation. Just like Pete, I got no way out.'

SEVEN

'That was great,' Jill Kelly observed as she and Boots waited in the Crown Vic. Kelly was seated behind the wheel, with Boots in the back, huddled against the door furthest from the curb. 'The Eye of Mordor?' She shook her head in wonder. 'And to think the jerk swallowed it.'

Boots said nothing for a moment, content to stare through the back window at Christine's, a Polish diner on Manhattan Avenue. A small group of men had gathered in front of the restaurant to smoke cigarettes as they quietly conversed. Only one of them was known to Boots, Mark Dupont, a violent felon newly released from prison. Boots made a note to mention Dupont's name to his snitches, maybe get a line on the man's current activities. A pure psychopath, Dupont was driven by an inner rage over which he had little control.

'Jill,' he finally said, turning back to his partner, 'with all due respect, I gotta disagree with you.'

'About what?'

'About the Eye of Mordor. Right now, lookin' at you and knowin' your uncle is the Chief of D, I feel like I'm under a microscope. I feel like my performance is gonna be weighed and measured.'

Kelly's laugh was richer than Boots would have predicted, and more disconcerting. 'Trust me on this. Nobody pulls my strings. But seeing as how you checked me out, I can understand why you'd want to be rid of me.'

'You and the task force both.'

Gergan's front door opened at that moment and Pete Karakovich stepped through. Tall and rangy, Karakovich wore a short beard that rapidly thinned as it climbed toward his sideburns. He scratched that beard as he first looked to his right, away from the Crown Vic, then slowly to his left. Finally, he jammed his hands into the pockets of his navy pea coat and walked toward Manhattan Avenue, coming to a stop next to the car. Ever cautious, he glanced back at Gergan's before opening the door and throwing himself across the seat, his clear aim to render himself invisible to passers-by.

Unfortunately, his head landed, face down, in Detective Littlewood's
rather generous lap.

'Pete,' Boots said, 'I didn't know how much you cared.'

Karakovich leaped up, cracking the top of his head into the roof
liner. He looked at Boots through glassy eyes for a moment, then
scrunched down until his head was again below the window. As if
responding to a signal, Jill Kelly started the car and headed down
the block.

Boots maintained a careful silence as Jill piloted the Ford through
several intersections, continuing on until the street dead-ended at
the East River. As always, this industrial section of Greenpoint was
deserted at night. Boots watched Karakovich straighten when Jill
shut off the headlights and cut the engine, watched the man's head
swivel from side to side as he resigned himself to the facts on the
ground. Whatever transpired in his immediate future would be
neither observed nor interrupted.

'Whatta we doin'?' he asked without looking directly at Boots
or his partner.

'We're havin' a conversation, Pete,' Boots said.

'About what?'

'About your associate in crime, Vinnie Booster.'

At the sound of his buddy's name, Pete's left leg began to
dance and he wiped his tongue across his front teeth several
times, emphasizing a small overbite. That Vinnie had confided
in him, as he'd confided in Frankie Drago, was obvious at a
glance. Still, Boots didn't prompt the man. Being a relatively
successful car thief didn't change the fact that Pete was borderline
retarded. Leaning on him before he worked through the variables
would only slow him down.

'What about Vinnie?' Karakovich finally asked. 'What'd he do?'

Boots shook his head. 'Don't bust my balls.'

At a loss, Karakovich turned to Jill Kelly, perhaps in search of
a little feminine compassion. Though Boots couldn't be sure exactly
what Pete discovered in Jill's flat stare, it could not have been
compassion because the man shuddered before looking away.

'Goddamn it,' he said.

'Don't go there,' Boots instantly replied.

'What?'

'Don't take God's name in vain. Not in front of me.'

Having markedly increased the number of variables at play, Boots wasn't tempted to interrupt the long silence that followed. He waited patiently until Karakovich said, 'Is this about the cop who got killed?'

Boots answered the thief's question with one of his own. 'You and Vinnie, you're workin' together, right?'

'Yeah, but not around here. I swear. Vinnie was on his own that night.'

'I believe you, Pete,' Boots said, 'but I need to find Vinnie and I think you can understand why.'

Pete shook his head and his gaze dropped to his hands. 'I ain't no snitch,' he said.

'I know that. I know you're a stand-up guy. I really do. But there are three things you need to think about very carefully. First, I'm not askin' you to testify against Vinnie, so there's no reason why your name should ever come up. Second, your Uncle Ted already explained the facts of life, so I won't bother to repeat 'em. Third, if this is all you have to tell me, you should've stayed inside Gergan's. Because I've got hold of you now and I'm not lettin' go until I find your partner.'

Pete surprised Boots at that point by changing the subject. 'Vinnie's scared,' he said. 'He thinks the cops're gonna try to put the shooting on him.'

Boots decided to keep the message simple. 'Where is he, Pete?'

Karakovich's mouth went into virtual spasm as he sought an escape hatch that didn't exist, until he finally admitted there was no way out, for him or Vinnie. Then he let his head rock from side to side for a moment, before saying, his voice almost a moan, 'He's shacked up with a crack whore on Maujer Street.'

They drove south into Williamsburg, then west, past the elevated Brooklyn–Queens Expressway, to within a hundred yards of the English Kills, an especially foul canal that wandered through the Brooklyn Union Gas works. Like much of Williamsburg, Maujer Street was a mix of low-rise factories and small residential buildings set cheek by jowl, as though competing for space. On this particular block, in this most undesirable corner of the community, industry had won out. Only a single tenement rose above the surrounding warehouses.

'Check it out,' Pete said as Jill cruised past. 'On the third floor.'

Boots looked up in time to glimpse a silhouette behind a tattered sheet covering a side window. The silhouette belonged to a man – that much was obvious – but it wasn't enough. Boots waited until Jill turned the corner and pulled to a stop before tossing his cellphone into Pete's lap.

'Get Vinnie on the phone, make some kind of excuse for callin'. I wanna be sure he's in the apartment.'

Pete thought it over for a moment, then said, 'If you go bustin' in there right after I call, Vinnie's gonna figure I set him up.'

'True enough,' Boots countered, 'but you gotta look at the big picture. If I'm holdin' your hand when I knock on Vinnie's door, he'll *know* you set him up.'

'A couple of things we need to work out,' Boots told Jill Kelly. By then, Petr Karakovich had completed his performance and was headed off to parts unknown. 'Vinnie Palermo, the minute he knows there's a cop at his door, he'll climb out the fire escape, no hesitation. This is an asshole who runs first and thinks later. That means somebody has to be around back, waitin' for him.'

Though her expression didn't change, Kelly eyes grew noticeably colder. 'You think I can't handle him?' she asked.

'Not at all. I'm just askin' you not to kill him.'

Again, Jill's laughter, as genuine as a child's, caught Boots off guard. 'OK,' she said, 'I get the picture. I'll only wound him.'

'You won't have to because he's a non-violent type and he's not gonna resist. You should keep in mind, the guy's six inches shorter than you and skinny as a rail.'

Boots popped the trunk, got out of the car and went around to the back. Though it was extremely cold for April, with the temperature hovering at the freezing mark, he took off his overcoat and folded it carefully before laying it down. Jill Kelly was less fastidious. She stripped out of her leather coat, tossed it on top of her partner's, finally closed the trunk.

'There's one other thing that needs sayin' and I'm gonna say it now.' Boots turned to his partner. 'Vinnie Palermo didn't kill Chris

Parker. I know that's true because Vinnie doesn't have the balls to stomp a cockroach. In fact, I'd be willin' to bet my life savings that he's never carried a gun in his life.'

'That's it?'

'No. Vinnie's a professional car thief and we both know that professional car thieves don't carry guns because they don't wanna do the extra time if they get caught.'

'Done now?' Kelly was no longer smiling.

Boots shook his head. 'Once we have Vinnie safely detained, Inspector Corcoran's gonna dump my ass in a hurry. I don't mind, bein' as I never wanted any part of him from the beginning. But then Corcoran and his task force are gonna have to deal with a big temptation.' Boots ticked the items off on his fingers. 'Vinnie was at the scene. He was in the process of stealin' a car. He's a career criminal. He's got a long-standing cocaine habit. Stir those four ingredients into the pressure cooker and it's fifty-fifty that Corcoran takes the easy way out. This kind of case – a cop killing – it makes careers and it breaks careers.'

'Not my career,' Kelly replied, 'but I'll keep what you said in mind. Now, we agreed that Vinnie will go out the fire escape the minute a cop knocks on his door?'

'Without doubt. One of us will have to be waiting in back.'

'And that has to be me, right? Being as your feet aren't up to a chase?'

Boots nodded sadly. 'Just do me a favor, OK? Once you put your hands on Vinnie, he'll give up. So, let me repeat myself: Please don't kill him.'

'And why would I do that, Boots?'

Though Jill's tone was so cold that Boots shivered, he made his point. 'Because if Vinnie Booster were to die tonight, given all those factors I pointed out, the case'll be closed by tomorrow morning.'

Kelly's breath hissed between her teeth. For just a moment, Boots was sure she'd take a swing at him. But then she spun smartly on her right heel and headed off down the block.

EIGHT

Boots watched Jill Kelly thread her way between piles of debris as she negotiated a narrow alley that separated the tenement from a chain link fence topped with razor wire. Nothing in her body language, in the set of her shoulders, the swing of her hips or her stride, indicated the presence of fear, or even apprehension. If anything, she seemed eager. Boots smiled as a stray notion rippled through his mind. While he could easily imagine himself in bed with Jill Kelly, imagine a hard, take-no-prisoners fuck that left the bedclothes in tatters, he couldn't imagine them exchanging a tender kiss afterward.

Boots continued to watch until Jill passed the far end of the building and disappeared into the darkness. Then he clipped his shield to the lapel of his jacket, withdrew his weapon and went to work.

The crime drop in New York over the past three decades is the stuff of legend, with homicide rates now hovering at levels associated with the golden era of the early 1960s. Even neighborhoods long associated with mindless violence – Harlem in Manhattan, Fort Greene in Brooklyn, the South Bronx – have become safe enough to attract yuppie enclaves. Nevertheless, there are still pockets in this city, sometimes only blocks long, sometimes limited to a single block, even a single building, where the bad old days are well preserved, like exhibits in a museum. That this particular tenement, the one Boots faced, had failed to get with the new program was obvious at a glance. The vinyl siding had peeled away along the seams and now projected outward like the half-erect quills of a porcupine. The window frames, crusted over by a century of intermittent repainting, appeared to be covered with bubbling mold. An elaborate cornice, heavy enough to crush a tank, had come loose at the building's western edge and threatened to crash into the street.

Inside the narrow lobby, Boots headed for the rear of the building, then started up the stairs. The soles of his boots crunched over debris with every step. Crack vials? Broken glass? Cockroaches thick enough to form a carpet? Detective Littlewood didn't pause to speculate – for him, this was familiar terrain. Still, he was careful not to brush against the walls or the banister as he climbed to the third floor. The pitter-pat of cockroach legs scurrying beneath his shirtsleeve was an aspect of the terrain with which he was also familiar.

Boots finally positioned himself beside the door of an apartment running along the eastern side of the building. Curling his hand into a fist, he hammered on the door three times, putting some effort into it.

'Vinnie,' he shouted, 'it's Boots Littlewood. Get your ass out here and do it now. Don't make me say it again, Vinnie. Get your ass out in this hall.'

Boots pounded on the door three more times, repeated the verbal message, then retraced his steps. Given the near-darkness and his fragile feet, he took the stairs as quickly as possible, hustling down the alley only to discover that his partner had the situation well in hand. Jill was sitting astride Vinnie Booster, whacking away at his shoulders with a spring-steel sap.

At that point, as he holstered his weapon, Boots had a vision of himself undercutting Kelly's authority, say by yanking her off the unresisting Palermo. But she stood as he approached.

'How's the feet?' she asked.

'So far so good.' Boots grabbed Vinnie by the shoulder, pulled him up, then slammed his fist into the man's abdomen. Palermo stumbled backwards before crashing to the ground.

'What was that about?' Jill asked.

'You show me yours, I'll show you mine.'

'You wanna know why I smacked Vinnie?'

'Yeah.'

'You don't run from cops, Boots, especially this one. It shows contempt and we can't have that. Plus, I fell in the slime and tore my pants. I'm gonna have to toss the whole outfit.' Kelly folded her arms across her chest, the sap still dangling from her fingers. 'Your turn,' she said. 'Why'd you hit him?'

'Simple, Jill. Vinnie's my snitch and he held out on me. We can't have that, either.'

*   *   *

'I didn't do it,' Vinnie said for the fourth time. 'I swear I didn't do it. I never shot nobody in my life.'

Jill Kelly raised a hand to slow him down. 'All right, Vinnie, we get the message. You didn't shoot anybody. Now, can we please move on?'

They were sitting in the Crown Vic, Boots behind the wheel, his partner alongside, Palermo in the back. Palermo's hands weren't cuffed because he was a witness and not a suspect, at least officially. Nevertheless, Boots spelled out the man's constitutional rights.

'Listen to me close, Vinnie,' he announced. 'You don't have to talk to us if you don't want to, and you can have a lawyer. But if you do talk to us, whatever you say is strictly on the record. You're not gonna be able to change your story later on.'

Boots expected Kelly's quick glance to be malice-filled. Instead, he found her merely curious.

'No,' Vinnie said, 'I trust you, Boots. You always played it straight with me in the past. If I gotta talk to someone, I figure it should be you.' He paused long enough to fill his lungs. 'I mean, you don't have to tell me that I fucked up. I know I shoulda come to you right away. And I swear that was exactly what I was gonna do. But when I found out the hit was on a cop, I got scared.'

'Scared that you'd be blamed?'

'Yeah, and I was scared of the shooter, too. That was some cold shit, man. One in the back, one in the head.'

Vinnie's eyes drifted up and to the left as he searched his memory banks. Then he was off and running. The story he told confirmed Frankie Drago's, but there were a number of additional details: Vinnie had entered the Nissan shortly before one o'clock; the Nissan's alarm had briefly sounded when Vinnie unlatched the door with a slim jim; Chris Parker had driven to the meeting in a Grand Cherokee; the shooter's back was to Vinnie at all times.

The only description he could offer was of an average-sized man wearing a navy pea coat and a watch cap that covered most of his head, face and neck.

As Boots drove to the Six-Four, he used the rear-view mirror to keep an eye on Vinnie Booster. Palermo seemed almost cheerful now that he'd come clean, as if he no longer had a care in the world. Unfortunately, in terms of his penal interests, his story could only have been more disastrous if he'd confessed to the murder. Vinnie knew the make and model of Chris Parker's car, a detail that had never been released to the press – beyond any doubt, he'd been there. The car alarm also hurt him. Wasn't it possible that the alarm had attracted Parker (who was, after all, a cop) and that a deadly confrontation had followed? And wasn't it convenient that Palermo hadn't seen the shooter's face? That the only alternative to himself was a silhouette?

It was ten o'clock when the trio walked into the Six-Four. The first order of business was to place Vinnie Palermo in an interview room and instruct him not to leave. Then Kelly used her cellphone to report the successful completion of her mission.

'Inspector, we've got him in custody.' She listened closely for a moment, then said, 'Got it,' before hanging up. Finally, she turned to Boots and offered her hand. 'Boots, it's been great working with you.'

'Are you telling me that my expertise is no longer required?'

'Afraid so.'

A few minutes later, Lieutenant Carl Levine summoned Boots to his office. 'You did good work, Boots. Not that Corcoran will ever give you credit.' He waved Boots to a seat, took a pint of Wild Turkey bourbon and a pair of plastic cups from the drawer of his desk, poured each of them a short jolt.

'To the bosses,' he said, forgetting, for the moment, that he himself was a boss.

'May they live long and prosper.' Boots downed his shot. 'So, that's it? I'm done?'

'Corcoran will be here in an hour. You'll want to have your fives ready. That way, the task force won't have an excuse to revisit the Six-Four.'

Levine was right and Boots knew it. The task force would be certain to reserve all credit to itself, so the smart move was to feed the beast, then move on.

Boots went to his desk and started writing. He included every detail of his confrontations with Frankie Drago, Pete Karakovich and Vinnie Palermo in a series of DD-5s. Ordinarily, this was a task he enjoyed, this imaginary war of wits he played with defense lawyers as he tried to give them as little help as possible. Not this time. Each sentence, as far as he could tell, was another handful of dirt bouncing off the lid of Palermo's coffin. To anybody who didn't know him, the man looked guilty as hell. He had motive, opportunity and almost three weeks to dispose of the means.

Just as Boots finished up, Corcoran entered the squad room, shortly followed by his running dogs from Homicide, Artie Farrahan and Thelonius Tolliver. Corcoran wore a black overcoat, probably cashmere, which he'd thrown over his broad shoulders in a manner usually associated with dead Italian gangsters. When Boots approached, he turned away, leaving Boots to hand his paperwork to Detective Farrahan.

'You gonna try to put this on Palermo?' Boots asked.

In his mid-forties, Artie Farrahan had a full head of jet-black hair that he combed across his forehead, leaving only a couple of inches of skin showing above his eyebrows. 'Why? Did Palermo do it?'

'No, he didn't, Artie, but in this particular case, I don't think his innocence will protect him.'

From inside Levine's office, Corcoran's voice rang out. 'Detective Farrahan, we're waiting.'

Farrahan smiled before turning away with a shrug. Homicide or not, he was a bit player.

Still, Boots was unsatisfied. Instead of leaving, he waited for Jill Kelly to emerge from the bathroom. 'I have a couple of questions before you join the party,' he announced, blocking her path.

'Shoot.'

'First thing, if there was a confrontation before Vinnie shot Chris Parker, how did Parker get shot in the back?'

Kelly's full mouth expanded slightly. 'Maybe Palermo got the drop on Parker, but didn't have the balls to look into his eyes when he pulled the trigger. So he made Parker turn around.'

Undeterred, Boots responded with a second question, and a third, and a fourth. He wasn't going to get another chance at this. 'Think about it, Jill. If Parker suspected that Vinnie was stealing a car, why was his weapon still in his holster, his badge in his pocket and his overcoat buttoned? And if Parker wasn't displaying a weapon, why didn't Vinnie just run away? What was his motive for murdering a cop?'

'Boots, you should've been a defense lawyer. You've got the knack.'

The remark was obviously designed to end the conversation, only Boots didn't take the hint, not even when Kelly walked away.

'You've seen the case file,' he called to her retreating back, 'which makes you one up on me. So, what's the official reason why Parker, who lives thirty miles away on Long Island, was in Williamsburg at one o'clock in the morning on his day off?'

As Boots watched his ex-partner retreat, an anomaly he hadn't considered popped into his mind. The Altima that Vinnie stole on the night Parker died was registered to a man named Rajiv Visnawana, who resided in Jackson Heights, a Queens neighborhood ten miles away. So, what was Rajiv doing in Williamsburg at one in the morning? Especially as there were no immigrants from the Indian subcontinent living in the area.

NINE

Boots entered the Sixty-Fourth Precinct at two o'clock on the following afternoon, two hours before the start of his tour. He greeted the desk officer, then headed for the weight room to complete the workout he'd begun on the prior morning. There he found Sergeant Craig O'Malley and his long-time driver, Boris Velikov, known to one and all as the Bulgarian. Both these men augmented their weightlifting with injected steroids. Boots knew this because they'd offered to juice him up. Perhaps, if he was fifteen years younger, he would have been tempted. But these days the weight room was more about slowing the rate of attrition.

'Yo, Boots, you're the best, man,' O'Malley cried out when Boots made his appearance. Craig was seated on a workout bench, his right elbow on his thigh, doing curls with a forty-pound dumbbell. 'Come down to Sally's tonight. The drinks are on me.'

'Ya got the mother-fucker,' Velikov added with a grin that would have made Dracula tremble. After years of juicing, Boris tended to speak in threat-like grunts.

'Could you repeat that?'

'Godda mother-fucker,' the Bulgarian repeated.

'I guess you didn't see the press conference,' O'Malley added.

'What press conference?'

O'Malley's right arm pivoted at the elbow, from full contraction, to full extension, to full contraction. 'The one the bosses threw at noon. Where they announced the arrest of a cop killer named Vinnie Palermo.'

Boots reached into the pocket of his trousers for his Tic Tacs. He filled his mouth, then lay down on the mat and hooked his legs beneath a bench. Boots hated doing sit-ups. Not only did they leave him panting, but his waist never seemed to get any smaller.

'Everybody knows it was you,' O'Malley added. 'You're the one who found Palermo.'

All three worked out for the next half-hour, exchanging little more than grunts, until O'Malley and Velikov decided to call it an afternoon. Boots stopped them as they headed for the showers.

'You ever hear of a mutt named Mark Dupont?' he asked. When both men shook their heads, he continued. 'Dupont's been upstate for six years on a rape charge, but he's back now. I saw him last night. Guys, Dupont's the real deal, a genuine bad boy, and I'm lookin' for an excuse to violate his parole.'

'You got a mug shot?' O'Malley asked.

'I'm gonna print some up after I finish my workout. But I gotta warn ya, just in case you should run into him, Dupont's a born cop fighter. He won't go down easy.'

Boots watched Velikov and O'Malley exchange a look of keen anticipation, thinking that not only did their shoulders begin at the tops of their ears, but the veins in their necks were as thick and juicy as night crawlers.

After a shower, Boots went directly to the squad room where he endured the congratulations of his fellow detectives while he pulled up Dupont's mug shot and printed two dozen copies. Although more than a hundred uniformed officers were assigned to the Six-Four, in Littlewood's experience only a select few had more than a passing attachment to the craft of policing. The rest confined their ambitions to the magic pension and the lifetime medical benefits that came with it.

His task completed, Boots carried the photos to the first floor and distributed twenty copies to various cops as they emerged from the muster room, including O'Malley and Velikov. He made the same pitch to each. Dupont was a violent criminal; his entire life was about mayhem of one kind or another. If they could please mention him to their snitches, maybe get a line on his current activities, Boots would be ever so grateful.

Boots followed the last of the cops he briefed out to the sidewalk in front of the precinct. It was just after four o'clock and the sun was headed for the horizon. Still, the day was warm enough for Boots to shrug out of his coat and store it in the trunk of an unmarked car before heading off.

From the Six-Four, Boots drove to Our Lady of Mount Carmel, a Roman Catholic church on Havemeyer Street in a mostly Italian section of Williamsburg called the Northside. Mount Carmel was familiar ground. Boots had attended the primary school, served as an altar boy, been baptized and confirmed at Mount Carmel. He knew most of the priests by their first names and only confessed to a Franciscan monk named Leonzo Gubetti. It was Father Gubetti he went in search of, trying him first in the rectory before tracking him down in the church's vestry. Boots was hoping to get in and out in a hurry, but when he finally came face to face with the priest, he found the monk's gaze sharp and accusing.

'Who have you been speaking to?' Boots asked.

'Connie Palermo,' the priest replied.

Boots stepped into the room. 'Vinnie's the reason I showed up this afternoon. That and I want to confess. What with Easter coming on Sunday, I figure I'll get it over with.'

Father Gubetti liked to play the jolly friar, and he was perfect for the part, with his bald dome, broad belly and florid complexion. But not this time. This time he was pissed and no mistake about it.

'Ah, yes, Boots Littlewood's annual confession. Everything should come to a stop – ba-boom – because Detective Littlewood is finally ready to confess.'

'Leo, if you don't stop busting my chops,' Boots threatened, 'I'm gonna walk out the door. In which case, you'll never know what happened to Vinnie.'

The priest slid a purple stole off a hangar, kissed it, then settled it on his shoulders. 'Threatening a priest? A heinous sin requiring immediate atonement lest you perish unexpectedly and be consigned to the bowels of hell. Follow me, child.'

Boots sighed. 'I can't wait to hear the penance.'

Father Gubetti led Boots to a small office where he set a pair of straight-back chairs face to face. Boots wasn't crazy about this arrangement, having grown up with the anonymity implied by the deeply shadowed confessional and the screen separating priest from penitent. But it was a different church now, growing more informal every day, a process that had begun with the end of the Latin mass. Brooklyn Catholics had yet to forgive the Vatican for that foray into the vernacular. If they'd wanted to be Protestants, their reasoning went, they'd have backed Martin Luther during the Reformation.

Boots kicked it off with the easy part: his temper, with which he'd been struggling for many years. Although Frankie Drago figured prominently in the list of offenses he presented, the bookmaker was far from alone.

Father Gubetti listened carefully until Boots finished, then asked the obvious question: 'Have you been trying to control yourself? Have you made an effort?'

'Well, that's just the point. It's easy to say you won't lose your temper when you're calm. But then . . .' Boots looked down at his hands, then up at Gubetti. 'Some of these assholes, Leo, they're lucky I don't kill 'em. And I think you know what I mean.'

The priest managed a weak smile. He'd been pistol-whipped by a mugger in 2004. A day later, when he regained consciousness, his first thoughts were of personal revenge. He still couldn't recall the incident without becoming angry.

'Go ahead, Boots,' he said.

This time, when Boots looked down at his hands, he didn't raise his eyes. 'What I'm gonna tell you next, about a drug dealer named Carlos Malaguez, happened about three months ago. Malaguez was wanted for second-degree assault and he'd done a disappearing act. I'd been tryin' to run him down for several weeks, with no luck, until I finally got a call from the victim's sister, who was also Malaguez's cousin. She told me that Carlos was stayin' at an apartment on India Street. What I should have done at that point was notify the lieutenant and request back-up. But I didn't. Instead, I found the patrol car assigned to that sector and drafted the two uniforms inside.'

As he organized his thoughts, Boots ran a finger beneath his tie, from his throat to the top of his vest, then touched each of the vest's pearl-gray buttons. Finally, he began to speak, his voice distant, as if he was witnessing his own story.

'Malaguez was dead. Of a drug overdose, the way it turned out. Even standing in the hall, you could smell him. One of the uniforms wanted to kick the door in, but there was no point. I sent down for the super and a set of keys. Leo, the stench when I opened that door was enough to knock you on your ass. And you can trust me on this, those two patrolmen were pathetically grateful when I told them to wait outside while I secured the residence.

'Carlos was lying on the couch when I walked into the apartment. He was swollen up double, his skin almost black. I figured he'd been dead for at least three days, but I could've been wrong. The apartment was very hot. Anyway, I didn't bother with him. There was a scale and a set of works on a coffee table, along with several grams of what looked like heroin. When I saw the dope, I knew Carlos hadn't been robbed, knew it right away. That's how come I decided to search the apartment instead of waitin' for a warrant. You hear what I'm sayin', right? I knew what I was gonna do, assuming I got lucky, and I didn't stop myself.'

Leo Gubetti regarded Boots for a moment: the gray suit, the vest, the ankle-boots. Unlike Frankie Drago, Father Leo believed that he understood the man beneath the suit. 'And did you get lucky, Boots?' he asked.

'Yeah, in a drawer in the bedroom dresser. I found a couple of ounces of dope and a roll of money. I didn't count the money. I just put it in my pocket.'

'And the heroin?'

Boots sniffed. 'I left it where it was. What'd you think?'

'All right, don't get on your high horse. How much money are we talking about?'

'Forty-five hundred.'

'Was this the only time since your last confession?'

'The only time, and the only opportunity.'

Gubetti ran his fingers through the gold fringes at the bottom of his stole. He liked Boots Littlewood, as did almost everybody who knew him, and he believed Boots to be a good man, though flawed and oftentimes weak. The temptation was to forgive him because you knew that he was trying. But enough was enough.

'You know, Boots, my forgiveness is not God's forgiveness.'

'What's that supposed to mean?'

'In order to be forgiven, you have to resolve not to sin again.

This is not something I can judge. I'm talking about your sincerity. God, on the other hand, is not likely to be fooled. As you said about your temper, it's easy to avoid sin when there's no temptation at hand.' Father Gubetti paused long enough to let the message penetrate. 'Next time you confess, Boots, I want to hear that you fought the good fight, that you made a serious effort to resist temptation. If not, I can't offer you absolution.'

Boots smiled. 'Ya know, I heard there's a Polish priest at Saint Stanislaus doesn't speak a word of English.'

TEN

B oots wrapped up his confession with an act of contrition while Father Gubetti formally absolved him of his sins. That done, the priest took off his stole and draped it over his knees.

'Would you like a glass of wine?' he asked.

'No thanks, I have to get back to work soon.'

'You're on the clock?'

'Sue me.'

'What if there's a serious crime? What if there's a murder?'

'You been watchin' too much television. There's only been one homicide in the Six-Four this year – Chris Parker's. Not only wasn't that my case to begin with, but a task force had already been formed by the time I came on duty the next day. Plus, the lieutenant has my cellphone number. If he wants me, he'll call.'

Boots scratched at his ear, thinking that he'd have to see a doctor, get the wax flushed out. If not, he'd soon be halfway to deaf. 'About Vinnie. I need some help here. I need to know what my obligations are.'

Gubetti repressed a smile of intense satisfaction. 'Go on, Boots. Bring me up to date.'

'It's hard to know where to begin. Remember, I didn't drag Vinnie into this mess. Vinnie's name was mentioned by . . . by a certain third party. Once that happened, it was just a matter of time.'

'Until?'

'Leo, when a cop's killed, every other cop takes it personally. That means the pressure on the task force would've been intense, even if the media ignored the whole incident.'

'Which, of course, it didn't.'

Boots nodded, then said, 'I wasn't assigned to the task force that investigated Parker's murder until after a certain accused felon decided to save his ass by naming Vinnie Palermo.'

'You're saying you didn't play any part here?'

'No, I played a part. My job was to find Vinnie.'

'That's it?'

'Yeah, but I didn't stop there. Being as I was a hundred percent sure Vinnie didn't shoot Parker, I read him his rights, even though he was still a witness at that point. Then, when the schmuck didn't take the hint, I made my opinion regarding his innocence clear to anybody who'd listen.'

Gubetti absorbed the following silence while he considered a response. First of all, he told himself, do no harm.

'Tell me,' he finally said, 'from a practical standpoint, is there anything you can do to help Vinnie?'

'I don't know. Probably not, since I don't have access to the case file. But I've got a hunch about something. If I recanvas the block . . .' Boots rose to his feet. The nicotine demons had the pitchforks out and his first instinct was to begin pacing the room. But he held himself in check. Gubetti was staring up at him, a worried look in his eyes.

'This morning, Leo,' Boots said, 'when they held the press conference announcing the arrest of Captain Parker's murderer, the Mayor of New York and the Commissioner of Police were both standing at the podium. From what I heard, the pair of them looked very happy. Now what do you think those two egomaniacs are gonna do if they have to announce that a mistake was made? If they have to admit that the man they accused of murdering Chris Parker is innocent? Not on some technicality, but that he actually didn't do it?'

This time, Gubetti responded immediately. 'They'll blame the messenger,' he said, 'which means you.'

'The good news is that messengers aren't killed any more. The bad news is that they can still be punished. And these are people who have the power to punish. My ex-partner on the task force is the Chief of Detectives' niece.'

They went at it for another fifteen minutes, most of their conversation centering around a single question: What did Boots Littlewood owe to a thief like Vinnie Booster? Ordinarily, both quickly agreed, nothing. But this particular situation was far from ordinary. Not only was Palermo facing life without parole, but the real killer would go free if Vinnie was convicted. Plus, the Six-Four was Boots Littlewood's turf. To a certain extent, as he understood it, all who lived within its boundaries came under his protection. Even mopes like Vinnie Palermo.

Nevertheless, Gubetti was insistent. 'There's no religious doctrine that requires you to intervene, not unless you're angling for sainthood. On the other hand, you've got to live with yourself.'

Some five hours later, after finishing his tour, Boots walked into his father's two-family home on Newell Street in Greenpoint. The frame house wasn't much – a three-story, flat-roofed cube sided with blue vinyl – but it was Andy Littlewood's pride and joy, as it had been Margie Littlewood's when she was still alive. The tiny yards in front and back were immaculately tended, the path, steps and sidewalks had been recently swept, the trim around the door recently painted.

The just-married Littlewoods had come to New York from Belfast, Northern Ireland, in 1958. Penniless Catholic refugees, they'd scrimped for years to buy their house, accumulating the down payment dollar by dollar, paying off the mortgage check by check for thirty years. Andy Littlewood had made the last payment only two months before his wife's death, an achievement they'd celebrated with a small party.

As Boots later realized, the Littlewoods' party wasn't about the mortgage. Andy Littlewood had finally vanquished a hunger that had driven him for most of his life. Between Social Security, his pension check and his tidy nest egg, Andy would never want for anything he actually desired, not for the rest of his life. He appeared content these days, a man without serious regrets, a man who'd lived up to his own expectations. Andy had his poker buddies on Monday nights, his bowling buddies on Thursday nights and a Jewish girlfriend named Libby Greenspan.

'Irwin, is that you, laddie?' While Andy Littlewood's Belfast accent had been sharpened by many years of living in a neighborhood dominated by Polish-Americans, his national origin was still obvious.

'Yeah, it's me, Dad.' Boots draped his overcoat and suit jacket over a chair, then walked into the kitchen. He took a beer from the refrigerator and carried it into the living room. There he found Andy Littlewood sitting in an overstuffed chair. A few yards away, a biography of Lou Gherig played on a flat-screen television.

Boots didn't waste any time. It was late and he was tired. He explained his predicament in detail, then shut his mouth without bothering to ask his father's opinion. Andy Littlewood loved to give advice. The problem would be slowing him down.

But Andy surprised his son this time. 'You're not after owin' Vinnie Palermo a fuckin' thing,' he said after a moment.

'And Chris Parker?'

'What about him?'

'Do I owe anything to Chris Parker? Like justice, for instance?'

'Wake up and smell the roses, Irwin. Chairman Mao killed millions of people and he died in his bed, like Josef Stalin before him.' Andy Littlewood settled back in his chair for a moment, then again turned to his son. 'Whatever you decide to do, please don't throw it in their faces.'

'You talkin' about the bosses?'

'That I am, lad. Find a way to go around them, to defeat them without their ever knowin' they've been to battle.'

Early the next morning, much earlier than Boots would have liked, he retrieved his car, an ancient Chevy Impala, and headed out to the Six-Four. He made two stops on his way, the first at a candy store where he restocked his Tic Tac supply, the second at a bakery on Bedford Avenue where he purchased a box of doughnuts. He passed one of the doughnuts to the desk officer, Sergeant Gantier, when he got to the house, then carried the rest into the squad room. It was nine thirty by that time and the day-shift detectives were going about their business. They stopped momentarily when Boots showed his face, to greet him and snatch up a doughnut, then quickly returned to work.

Left to himself, Boots approached a civilian clerk, requesting that he use the squad's computer to pull up, then print a copy of Rajiv Visnawana's driver's license. Rajiv was the owner of the car Vinnie had stolen. That done, Boots stared down at the man's unsmiling face for just a moment. With his pudgy cheeks, liquid brown eyes and soft chin, Rajiv looked weak. But appearances could be deceiving, especially when it came to the immigrants now dominating many of the city's neighborhoods. They'd brought their cultures with them, very different cultures to be sure, and it was mistake to judge them by appearance alone.

Boots carefully folded the copy, then slid it into an envelope before heading back to his apartment where he showered and shaved. As he loaded the coffee maker, he tried to reconcile the different impulses pulling at him. Despite the expensive suits and ties, Boots had never been so vain as to believe himself important, not in the greater scheme of things. He was not a mover of mountains or a shaker of worlds. Only in this obscure, outer-borough precinct, seemingly as far removed from Manhattan's glitz as the plains of Kansas, did he have any noticeable effect on his surroundings. And maybe not even here.

The scratch of a key turning in the apartment's outer door distracted Boots. 'That you, Jackie?' he called.

'Yeah.' Carrying a manila envelope beneath his arm, Joaquin Rivera strode into the kitchen a moment later. He opened the envelope and removed a dozen sheets of paper joined by a red paperclip.

Boots poured himself a cup of coffee, poured another for Joaquin, carried them to the table, finally sat down. As he filled his mouth with Tic Tacs, he struggled to repress an argument beginning to form in his mind. Quitting cigarettes, this argument went, is hard enough, even under the best of conditions. That's why most people, including Boots Littlewood, make a number of unsuccessful attempts before they get the job done. What the quitter needs, even more than a strong will, is good timing. Would even the most heartless Puritan demand that a soldier in a war zone stop smoking? Or a woman in the midst of a bitter divorce? How about when a child's gravely ill? Or when you're threatened with the loss of your economic life?

Joaquin stared at the man on the other side of the table. Unlikely as it seemed, Boots looked bigger in a t-shirt and jeans than he did in his fancy suits with their padded shoulders. His upper arms were as thick as footballs.

'Your suits,' Joaquin finally said, 'they're really costumes.'

'One more cryptic remark, Jackie, and you're goin' out the window. You've been warned.'

Joaquin laughed, then took a sip of his coffee. 'What's the matter,

Boots, you don't wanna give up any trade secrets?' He waited for
his father to smile before continuing. 'Anyway, you asked me to
check out a cop named Chris Parker?'

'Any luck?'

'One mention in the years before he was murdered. In a *New
York Times* profile of the detectives in the Lipstick Killer
investigation.'

That got Littlewood's attention. In the summer of 2001, the Lipstick
Killer had murdered four women, igniting a media frenzy that ended
abruptly when Jules Cosyn confessed to the crimes. If Boots remembered right, Cosyn had been declared unfit to stand trial after a week
of intense examination by the state's psychiatrists.

Boots pointed to the stack of papers. 'All that for one article?'

'The story about Parker's on top. The rest of it's about the investigation and the trial.'

Joaquin pushed the sheets of paper across the table and Boots
glanced down at a photograph on the top sheet, a line of detectives
posed before the wall of a brick building. Among the five faces, all
male, Boots recognized four: Artie Farrahan, Mack Corcoran, Chris
Parker and Lenny Olmeda, currently Inspector Corcoran's personal
assistant. Boots ran his finger across the photo's caption until he
found the name of the fifth cop: Patrick Kelly.

'Is there a problem?' Joaquin finally asked.

Boots took the stack of papers, carried them to the trash can on
the other side of the room, raised the lid, dropped them inside.

'Not any more,' he said.

ELEVEN

A t two thirty that afternoon, after his vaunted ability to nap
at will failed him entirely, Boots stood at the corner of Berry
and South Fourth Streets. Before him, a mural covered
the side of a single-story warehouse. Sponsored by the New York
State Office of Alcohol and Substance Abuse, the mural depicted
the evils of tobacco. Smoking infants, smoking children and
smoking adults were on display, along with a collection of

phantasmagoric figures, including a skeleton, a devil and a smoking rat. At the bottom, a row of open graves revealed sickly green coffins.

Sponsored or not, this was graffiti art, the figures crudely drawn, the message simple. Still, Boots couldn't help but wonder if the mural was counter-productive. The sight of all those suffering smokers only fueled his desire for a cigarette. Plus, his eyes were drawn to a figure at the center of the mural. While every other adult, male or female, was recognizably black, Latino or Asian, this man was definitely white. Multi-armed and middle-aged, his blue eyes were swollen by thick, horn-rimmed glasses. A heading painted across his forehead in capital letters made his role clear: TOBACCO INDUSTRY.

The sound of a tapped horn caught Boots's attention and he turned to find Sergeant Craig O'Malley staring at him through the rolled-down window of a patrol car.

'Hey, Boots, whatta ya doin'?'

'Protecting and serving,' Boots replied. 'In my own unique way.'

'Fuckin' right,' Boris Velikov said. He was seated behind the wheel, the top of his head brushing the car's roof liner.

'We ran into your boy,' O'Malley continued.

'Which one?'

'Mark Dupont.'

'Did he put up a struggle?'

That brought laughs from both cops. 'We tossed him, but he came up clean.'

'What'd he say?'

'He demanded to know why we violated his constitutional rights. Could ya believe that?' O'Malley tapped the steering wheel with his fingertips. 'Anyway, I gave him your regards.'

'Did he know who I was?'

'Yeah,' Velikov interjected, 'and if he said what he said about *my* mother, I woulda killed him.'

Boots watched the cruiser drive off, then turned back to the job at hand. He was standing on the corner where Chris Parker had been gunned down, perhaps on the exact spot. He tried to visualize the unfolding events Vinnie had described, beginning with Parker's Jeep as it turned on to the block. But he couldn't get the images right. There'd still been a foot of snow on the ground then.

Boots got back into his car and took up the paperwork he'd

rescued from the garbage pail after his failed attempt to catch a nap. That attempt had been thwarted by Vinnie Palermo, whose clueless features jumped into Detective Littlewood's consciousness every time he closed his eyes.

'No,' Vinnie had said after Boots spelled out his constitutional rights, 'I trust you, detective. You always played it straight with me in the past.'

And what Boots Littlewood should have said was, 'Vinnie, if you trust me, then take this advice to heart. Keep your big mouth shut.' But he hadn't. He'd let Vinnie confess.

Boots took out his cellphone and called the Six-Four's general information number. The duty officer, Sergeant Gilbert Gantier, answered on the third ring.

'Sixty-Fourth Precinct,' he growled. 'How can I help you?'

'Sarge, it's Boots.'

Gantier's tone softened upon learning that his caller was not some asshole civilian out to bust balls. 'Hey, Boots, thanks for the doughnut.'

'No problem.' Boots cleared his throat. 'Lemme pick your brain for a minute. What do you know about a cop named Patrick Kelly? He served on the Lipstick Killer task force.'

'What about him?'

'I want to know if he's the same Patrick Kelly who was murdered a year later.'

'That's him. He was killed in Sunnyside, in his own home with his daughter watchin'. Nobody went down for it, either.'

'You remember anything else?'

'Anything else? Boots, where've you been all your life? The Chief of Detectives was Pat Kelly's brother-in-law.'

'And Pat Kelly was Jill Kelly's father?'

'Yeah, Crazy Jill Kelly.' Gantier hesitated before adding a final comment, his tone clearly admiring. 'The bitch is a fuckin' psycho. What I heard, the SWAT team dumped her because she capped a perp without getting permission.'

Boots closed his eyes for a minute, then said, 'Thanks for the help, Gil. I owe you one.'

'In that case, the next time you buy doughnuts for the house, put in a couple of crullers. I got a thing about crullers. You could buy me for life with a fresh-baked cruller and a hot cup of coffee.'

*　　*　　*

Boots flicked through the newspaper articles he'd retrieved from his garbage pail, articles covering the short-lived career of the Lipstick Killer, then tossed them on to the back seat without reading a word. What happened to Patrick Kelly was none of his business.

He looked out through the windshield, letting his eyes run up and down the street. Despite the architecture – a mix of warehouses and apartment buildings – the short block was entirely residential, the businesses long ago converted into lofts. That was good news because every window on the other side of the road offered a clear view of this corner.

Ten years before, when the surrounding blocks were almost entirely Hispanic, Boots would have known at least a few of the residents. Not today. This little section of Williamsburg had been overrun by two waves of refugees from Manhattan. The first was an assortment of artists, hippies, punks and anarchists made home-less when Giuliani emptied the Lower East Side squats. The second, once the freaks made the neighborhood safe for Caucasians, was a plague of yuppies who quickly drove up the prevailing rents until most of the bohemians packed their bags and moved on.

But if Boots didn't know a soul, he did have one advantage. The young professionals who now lived in this section of Williamsburg were sons and daughters of the middle class, raised to support their local police. The hippies and anarchists, by contrast, had refused to give him the time of day. He was as much their enemy as Mr Tobacco, the middle-aged white man in the mural.

Boots glanced at his watch, then took out a set of glass rosary beads once owned by his mother. According to Catholic tradition, Christ's earthly body perished at three o'clock in the afternoon. Observing this moment on Good Friday had been drummed into Boots by the nuns at Mount Carmel and he had vivid memories of his mother kneeling in the kitchen, rosary in hand.

As for Boots Littlewood – who had the background and temerity to wonder how those gathered around the cross knew it was three o'clock, since they presumably didn't have watches – he felt that praying a rosary was the least he could do, half-assed Catholic that he was.

Boots looked down for a moment at the crucifix dangling from the end of the rosary, at the tiny figure, neck bent, slumped as far down as the nails that held Him would allow, then started to pray.

He didn't pray for anything in particular, didn't ask for any special favors. Boots didn't believe in a God who granted favors. For Boots, it was more like *Ask not what your God can do for you; ask what you can do for your God*. It was His show, after all.

Bad for Vinnie Booster. Bad and getting worse. By the time Boots reached a four-story tenement at the end of the block, some three hours later, he'd been treated to only two stories. The majority of the citizens he interviewed were awakened by the army of cops and paramedics who responded to the scene, not by the gunshots. Only four individuals rushed to their windows in time to bear witness. They told identical stories: two gunshots, a double-parked car, a body on the sidewalk, a car driving away. They knew nothing about a third party, a shooter on foot.

Worst of all, each of them had been interviewed by Corcoran's task force, and each was prepared to testify against Vinnie Palermo.

Boots was tempted to call it quits. The reeds on which his hopes now hung were as slender as hairs, relying as they did on his belief that men recognize the sound of their own car alarms, and the hope that Rajiv Visnawana was in an apartment with a view of the unfolding homicide. Visnawana's after-the-fact behavior had been odd enough to merit attention. In the ordinary course of events, he should have reported the loss of his car to the army of cops who showed up ten minutes later, or maybe called 911. Instead, he'd walked nearly a mile, entering the Six-Four to file his complaint at one thirty. That meant he'd left Berry Street only minutes before the first officers responded at one fifteen, while the body was still lying on the sidewalk.

Boots stood in front of the tenement, his back to the street, and looked through the small window in the outer door. The layout was common to most New York tenements. A tiny foyer led to a narrow hallway that curved around a steep flight of stairs. Once upon a time, this building had housed the very poor, if not the destitute. Now, condominium apartments in this walk-up sold for a quarter of a million dollars. The corridor's stone floor gleamed, the stairs were carpeted and the locks on the inner and outer doors were state of the art.

Boots pushed the intercom button for apartment 1A. A moment later, a woman's voice, accompanied by a wave of static, said, 'Yes?'

'Police, ma'am.'

'You'll never take me alive.' A brief silence was followed by a guffaw. 'Hey, are you really a cop?'

'Detective Littlewood. Now, if you'll just buzz me in . . .'

Another laugh. 'My momma taught me better than that. I think I'll come out and take a look at you.'

A figure appeared in the lobby a moment later, a woman carrying a wine glass. Boots raised his shield and smiled. When the woman opened the door, he stepped inside.

'Detective Littlewood.'

'Aggie Dowd.' She sipped at her wine. 'What can I do for you?'

'I'm here about the homicide that occurred on March twentieth.'

'You're wasting your time.' Dowd raised a hand. 'I took a sleeping pill at eleven that night, and I left a fan running to block out the street noise. I didn't know there was a murder until the next day.'

Boots nodded agreeably. He was inside now and he might as well do the building. 'Tell me,' he said as he reached into his pocket, 'do you know this man?'

Dowd glanced at the photo, then up at Boots, the malicious smile she displayed for his benefit so nasty that he couldn't help but return it.

'I think you'd better come inside, detective. This is a long story and I need a refill.'

TWELVE

When Aggie Dowd lit a cigarette from a burning stub lying in a glass ashtray, Boots thought he'd died and gone to heaven. The small living room fairly reeked of nicotine, as did the fabric of the upholstered chair on which he sat. He watched Aggie pour herself a glass of wine, then hold up the bottle.

'You on duty?'

'Not so you'd notice.'

The glass Dowd passed Boots was smudged around the rim, but he didn't object. 'Are you celebrating?' he asked.

'I am.'

'May I ask what?'

'After eighteen months of trying, I managed to get my ex-boyfriend canned.' Aggie Dowd stared at Boots for a minute, then took a long drag on her cigarette. 'OK,' she said, 'you ready for the one-million-dollar question?'

'Fire away.'

'Say you have a neighbor named Henrietta Penn, who takes out ads in the *Village Voice*, ads in which she proclaims herself Ms Henrietta, Hoyden of Humiliation. Say she doesn't go to work in the morning, but has men over to her apartment, usually two a day, one in the afternoon and one at night. Now, for the million dollars, what do you think Ms Henrietta does for a living?'

'You're alleging that your upstairs neighbor is a prostitute?'

'Me and the other residents, we've been trying to get her out for a year.'

All along, Boots had been wondering exactly what Rajiv Visnawana was doing in Williamsburg at one o'clock in the morning. Now he knew. He took a business card from his billfold and laid it on the coffee table. 'Cutting red tape is my specialty. Don't hesitate to call. As for Henrietta, I can't throw her into the street, but I promise to slow her down. Now, tell me about the man in the photograph.'

Fifteen minutes later, Boots climbed to the second floor, his heart happy, thinking that maybe God does answer prayers after all. He knocked on the door to the front apartment, using the heel of his hand. According to Aggie Dowd, Ms Henrietta's first client of the evening was present in the apartment.

Boots knocked again, harder this time, pounding with the side of his fist. 'Police, open the door.'

'I'm coming,' a woman's voice responded. 'I'm coming.'

Still on its safety chain, the door fell back a few inches and a face appeared in the gap. Free of make-up, the face had blond hair and blond eyebrows, a broad jaw beneath extremely narrow lips, and small eyes the color of summer haze.

'What do you think you're doing?'

'Unlatch the chain.' Boots flashed his tin. 'Right now.'

'You have no right . . .'

'Ms Henrietta, you don't open this door, I'm gonna kick it down your throat.'

Henrietta Penn scrutinized Boots for a moment, her eyes so probing that Boots knew, at once, that she was familiar with the criminal justice system. That would make it easier, there being no annoyance more extreme, in his experience, than the blather emitted by civilians who knew their rights.

Henrietta unhooked the chain and stepped back. Pushing forty, she wore a leather thong and a black bustier trimmed with stainless-steel rings that jingled when she folded her arms beneath her enhanced breasts.

'Where's the john?' he said.

Boots was standing in a tidy, middle-class living room: slip covers on the couch and the chairs, silver drapes in the windows, bookcases against the walls.

'You'll have to excuse me,' Henrietta said, 'because I don't know the rules here. Am I allowed to ask you what you want with me before you search my apartment? Or do I have to wait until you're finished?'

'March twentieth, Rajiv Visnawana.'

Boots crossed the living room, walked the length of a short hallway and threw open the door. Directly ahead of him, a naked man was clamped to a cross. Though his jaw twitched repeatedly, the man could do no more than moan. Somewhere along the line, the Hoyden had jammed a rubber ball into his mouth, then secured it with a latex gag tight enough to produce welts.

Boots stopped dead in his tracks. It was Good Friday, the day Jesus died to save the souls of the world's unrepentant scumbags, and here were two of the most unrepentant having a grand old time transforming Christ's Passion into a sexual charade. Boots felt the tectonic plates of his equilibrium slide, one over the other, felt the magma well up through the resulting cracks and fissures to invade every nerve in his body. His hands curled into fists and his hair rose on end as he considered how long it would take him to rip the john free of the cross without opening the clamps beforehand.

Behind him, Boots was vaguely aware of Henrietta Penn's voice: 'Don't, don't, don't.' Before him, the john's eyes were bulging out of his head, assuming a bullet-like shape that echoed the shape of Ms Henrietta's breasts. As Boots watched, the man began to cry.

Boots recoiled for a second time, hesitating just long enough to remember his promise to struggle against the demon of anger, the promise he'd made to God when he confessed his sins. If he bloodied this jerk, he wouldn't be able to take Communion on Easter Sunday.

Boots turned on his heel and brushed past the Hoyden. 'Get him the fuck out of here.' He continued on into the living room where he threw himself down on a chair. Boots was hoping his anger would dissipate by the time he and Henrietta were alone in the apartment. Instead, following a logic of its own, his anger morphed into an overwhelming desire for a cigarette. He looked around the room for an ashtray, but was apparently in a no-smoking zone.

'Shit,' he said. 'Shit, shit, shit.'

Boots didn't raise his head until Henrietta Penn closed the door behind the rapidly departing john and turned the locks. Henrietta was now wearing a plain, terry-cloth robe over the Hoyden of Humiliation outfit. The robe fell to her heels, emphasizing her broadening beam.

'Why'd you do that?' Boots asked.

'That?'

'I'm talkin' about the cross. It's Good Friday.'

Henrietta took a seat across from Boots and laid her hands in her lap. 'First thing, it's not my fantasy. It's the client's. Second thing, I'm putting my daughter through law school. Making my clients' perverted dreams come true is how I do it.'

'But it's your cross, Henrietta. Nobody forced you to have it here. And you definitely didn't have to use it on Good Friday.'

Henrietta finally lost her temper, an indiscretion she felt she could afford, given that she had something the cop wanted.

'They call it consenting adults, detective, and the only illegal part is the exchange of money. So, if you don't like what I do for a living, don't come busting into my apartment without a warrant. Then you won't know.'

Boots crossed his legs and sat back, affording Henrietta a moment to enjoy her little victory. Then he dropped the hammer. 'No more johns in the apartment,' he said. 'Do out-calls, set up shop somewhere else, I don't care. But if you continue to turn tricks in this building, I'm gonna have a series of hard conversations with a few of your customers. Eventually, I'll bust you.'

'Turn tricks? Is that what you said? Well, check this out – if you were as good a cop as I am a sexual artist, you would've come to me about Rajiv a long time ago.'

Unable to dispute this assertion, Boots decided to stay on message. 'Listen close to what I'm tellin' you, because I'm not making an empty threat. No more sexual artistry in this apartment. You don't shut down, I'll send you to prison.'

'Look . . .'

'Don't waste your breath. I'm not askin' for any promises. Now, tell me about Rajiv.'

Seemingly unfazed by this turn of fortune, Henrietta leaned forward. 'I have a little problem,' she announced. 'My clients expect total confidentiality. Hardly surprising, right, considering what they ask me to do? So, it would definitely hurt my business if word got around that I had a big mouth.'

Boots laughed. 'Are you askin' me to protect your reputation?'

'In return for my telling you what happened that night.'

'Oh, I see. Like, a deal?'

'Exactly.'

Boots leaned forward, closed his eyes for a moment, then let them snap open. 'I can visualize the scene pretty well, but I'm havin' trouble with the motivation part. Since you're gonna tell me everything that happened on March twentieth at one o'clock in the morning, and you're gonna do it now, the deal seems a bit one-sided.'

Henrietta smiled for the first time. 'Can't blame a girl for trying.' When Boots didn't respond, she flicked at her lower lip with a two-inch fingernail. 'Right, here goes. There's not that much to tell, anyway. Me and Rajiv are lying on the bed, recovering you might say, when his car alarm goes off. Right away, he jumps out of bed and waddles across the room as fast as his pudgy legs will carry him. The alarm stops just as he gets to the window.

'"My automobile," he keeps saying, "they are stealing my automobile. This is infamy. This is infamy." Then I hear the two gunshots, maybe three seconds apart. Boom! Boom! Real loud, right across the street. Rajiv puts his hands on his head. He spins back to face me, spins back to the window. Me, I have a live-and-let-live philosophy. I don't want to know anything and I stay right where I am on the bed while Rajiv gets dressed and leaves.'

Boots searched the woman's pale eyes. Was she lying? Many whores were pathological liars. They never told the truth about anything. 'Rajiv didn't describe what he saw?'

'He didn't say anything . . . No, wait, he did ask me a question. He asked me for directions to the precinct.'

'And he left before the police responded to the gunshots?'

'Right. I heard the sirens a couple of minutes after he ran out the door.'

Boots filled his mouth with Tic Tacs, chewed thoughtfully, then swallowed. 'When the detectives originally canvassed the neighborhood, what did you tell them?'

Henrietta sighed. 'I told them I didn't see anything. Which is the truth. But I never mentioned Rajiv.'

'Well, being as I'm a generous guy, I'm gonna give you chance to make up for that omission. I want to know everything there is to know about Rajiv Visnawana.'

'Does that include his predilections?'

Boots grin flicked on, then off, but failed to register in his eyes. 'Everything you did, Henrietta, and everything he asked you to do. And if there were props involved, I wanna see them, too.'

THIRTEEN

On Saturday morning, as Boots stood before the bathroom mirror, toothbrush in hand, he resolved to banish Vinnie Palermo for the remainder of the weekend. Easter was about family, about the food that would be shopped for today and cooked tomorrow, about taking Communion, about the guests Andy, Libby and Boots had invited to dinner. Vinnie Palermo would just have to tough it out for the next forty-eight hours, if not the next forty-eight years. Boots had yet to tell anyone of his conversation with Ms Henrietta. He could still walk away.

Boots took his own advice, immersing himself in the holiday. Most of Saturday was spent in his father's company, on a shopping expedition that took them from Veniero's bakery in Manhattan to a butcher in College Point. On Sunday morning, he and his father

walked to church, along with hundreds of their neighbors. Mount
Carmel was packed, every seat in every pew taken. The Dragos
were there – not only Frankie and his mother, but a small army of
cousins, nieces and nephews. Vinnie Palermo's Aunt Connie made
an appearance, too. Boots tried to avoid her and her notorious temper,
but he did make eye contact once, as he approached the altar rail
to receive Holy Communion. *Occhio malvagio* was what he discovered in Connie's gaze. The evil eye, carried from Sicily and preserved
through the generations. Boots absorbed the blast without reacting.

Dinner began at three o'clock in the afternoon and stretched into
the evening. Joaquin attended, accompanied by his on-again-off-
again girlfriend, Polly Boll. Father Gubetti also brought a guest,
Sister Mary Dennis who'd once caught Boots stealing a Snickers
bar from the Mount Carmel cafeteria. The outraged nun had dragged
Boots off to the confessional and Father Edward Cano, who was
equally outraged. Stealing from church was stealing from God. Did
Boots think he could cheat the Lord? If so, he should leave the
church now, become an atheist. Omniscience was one of God's three
great powers. Nothing escaped Him.

If the lecture was tough to take, the penance meted out by the
priest shook Boots to the core.

'The Fifth Commandment demands that we honor our fathers
and mothers. You have dishonored yours today, a sin you somehow
overlooked in your confession. It's best they should know and your
sin will not be forgiven until you tell them.'

Eleven years old? Telling your mom that you're a thief? Your
dad? Revealing the fact at the dinner table? The surprising part was
that Boots wasn't reformed by the experience. Though he never
again stole anything from Our Lady of Mount Carmel, he didn't
exactly become honest.

But Sister Dennis was an old woman now, her back humped, her
eyes filmy. She contributed little to a conversation dominated by
Andy and Father Leo, her thoughts as veiled as her eyes.

Boots let the talk wash over him. He'd dreamed of Jill Kelly on
the night before and he was thinking of her now. As erotic as it was
brief, the dream had occurred in the early stages of sleep. Boots
stood against a concrete wall, nude, an apple balanced on his head.
Thirty feet away, peering through the sights of a .40 caliber Browning
automatic, Jill Kelly was decked out in full SWAT-team regalia.

Boots had awakened to find himself fully erect and desperately in need of a cigarette. No surprise in either case. Yet, in the moments before he drifted back to sleep, his thoughts had turned to the slaying of Patrick Kelly. Jill had witnessed her father's murder, had watched him die. Boots imagined his own father murdered. What would he do? No, the better question, the shorter list, was what he wouldn't do.

Coffee was just being poured when Boots's cellphone went off. He let the call jump to his voicemail, but the phone rang for a second time a moment later. Resigned, he walked into the kitchen. His boss, Lieutenant Levine, had this number. Maybe something had come up that needed Detective Littlewood's attention. Maybe Vinnie Palermo had been miraculously released. It was Easter Sunday, after all – a day for miracles.

'Hey, Boots, it's Craig O'Malley. We got your boy.'

'Say that again, sarge?'

'Mark Dupont. A couple of hours ago. He tried to shoot the Bulgarian.'

'Tried?'

'The gun misfired somehow. An H&K nine millimeter. The lab has it now.'

Boots looked over his shoulder, at the swinging door between himself and his family. It was five o'clock in the afternoon on Easter Sunday, but O'Malley and Velikov were out on the street, looking for trouble. Boots didn't have to ask why. The job was their family, the only family they had or wanted.

'Did you kill him?' Boots asked.

'Nah, but the Bulgarian was mighty pissed off, especially when Dupont made like a rabbit. Boris, it takes him a while to get goin', but he's pretty fast once he throws fourth gear. After about a block, he rolls over Dupont like a tank over a mouse. Boots, you shoulda been there.'

That night, with all their guests gone, Andy and Boots settled down to watch a Yankee game recorded on the DVR that afternoon. Since neither knew the outcome, their expectations were high and they were not disappointed. The Yankee bats came alive in the first inning, all of them, from Brett Gardner who led off to Russell Martin who batted ninth. It took three spectacular fielding plays to get the Orioles out of the inning with a six-run deficit. For all intents and purposes, the game was over.

Boots let his chair recline. It would be so easy, he thought, to fall into a routine he'd chosen for himself a long time ago. The baseball season was just starting and he had the whole summer and much of the fall ahead of him. Listening to the games as he made his appointed rounds, collecting from Frankie Drago when he won, paying off when he lost, busting mutts like Mark Dupont – this is where the profoundly unambitious Detective Littlewood found his comfort zone.

Plus, there was Rose Orlac. Rose was the widow of a life-long Yankee fan. She owned a pair of reserved seats to all the weekend games. The same Rose Orlac who threw him unmistakable signals whenever their paths crossed at Mount Carmel.

'Irwin?'

'Yeah, Dad.'

'We had a grand time this afternoon, did we not?'

'We did at that.'

'I only wish your mother was here to see it.'

Apprehensive, Boots looked at his father. At one point, following Marge Littlewood's funeral, Boots had feared that Andy wouldn't survive. But Andy Littlewood was smiling.

'Do you think of her often?' he asked his son.

'Yeah, I do.' Boots jerked his chair upright. 'Especially on the holidays.'

Andy nodded once. 'Libby wants us to marry. She's a good woman. Not like your mother, but . . . Irwin, I don't want to spend the rest of my life alone, but I can't help feeling that I'm betraying Margie in some way.'

Was his father asking for his approval? Boots didn't know, but he wasn't about to venture an unrequested opinion.

'Does that mean you think Mom's sitting on a cloud, watching everything you do? That she's holding you to some standard?'

'No, not exactly. But the Church tells us that families will reunite eventually. That's all well and fine, lad, but having two wives presents a bit of a difficulty.'

Boots laughed. 'If that's the case, you have to feel sorry for old Genghis Khan. He had a thousand wives.'

FOURTEEN

On Monday morning, a few minutes before noon, Boots parked his Chevy in front of the Calcutta Palace, an Indian restaurant on Seventy-Fourth Street in the Queens community of Jackson Heights. It was raining hard, the roiling gray sky seeming low enough to scrape the car's roof. Boots slid his restricted parking permit on to the dashboard, but remained behind the wheel as he reviewed the tactics he intended to use against Rajiv Visnawana.

One of three partners, Rajiv was day manager of the Calcutta Palace and would be inside the restaurant until at least six o'clock. Boots knew this because he'd been to Rajiv's home and spoken to Indira Visnawana, Rajiv's wife. Indira was eager to offer assistance when Boots flashed his shield and told her that he had a line on her husband's stolen Nissan.

Boots watched the windshield fog over, listened to the steady pounding of the rain, the hiss of tires, the blare of horns as an endless procession of cars and commercial vehicles negotiated the two-way street. Running north from a pair of the busiest subway stations in Queens, the block was lined on either side by Indian-owned businesses. Sari shops, bakeries, restaurants, jewelry stores with hundreds of gold chains massed in their showroom windows, chains as thick as the detective's thumb, chains as thin as a hair.

Finally, Boots slid the door open, stepped out and raised an umbrella before retrieving his briefcase. Always a step behind, he'd been overdressed on Friday and he was underdressed now. Winter was making a comeback. Given the slightest encouragement, the rain would change to sleet by noon.

As he came through the front door of the Calcutta Palace, Boots folded the umbrella, shoved a handful of Tic Tacs into his mouth and took a look around. The restaurant's decor was strictly industrial, exposed duct work on the walls and ceiling, pipes criss-crossing at right angles, a fan large enough to exhaust the air inside the Midtown Tunnel. There were no multi-armed gods and goddesses in little niches, no tablas, no sitar, no beaded lamps. The Indian population of Jackson Heights, large enough to support the local restaurants and shops, wasn't into kitsch.

'One?'

The woman who approached Boots was tall and slender, with thick black hair that fell to her shoulders. Her eyes were large, her mouth generous, her nose long and proud, her cheeks smooth as satin. She held her chin high, and her smile, though obviously professional, was nonetheless enticing. In place of the traditional embroidered sari, she wore a white suit over a lavender blouse.

'I'm looking for Mr Visnawana.' Dutifully, Boots opened his billfold to expose his shield. 'I need a few minutes of his time.'

'And what did my father do now?'

Boots reacted to the seductive quality in her tone with an involuntary smile. 'It's about his car,' he said. 'The one that was stolen.'

'Well, I hope you found it. He's been going on about that car for weeks.' Her smile widened briefly as she pointed to a corridor on the other side of the restaurant. 'Across the room, down the hall, the door marked "office". Right now, he's paying bills, so he won't mind being interrupted.'

Boots never got an opportunity to judge Rajiv Visnawana's mood. The minute he flashed his shield, Rajiv's expression changed from merely curious to studiously neutral. Evidence of a guilty mind, no doubt.

'I'm from Grand Theft Auto,' Boots announced, letting his briefcase drop to the floor, 'following up on the loss of your car. How'd it work out with the insurance?'

'Half of what my vehicle is worth. This is what they call Blue Book value.' Unlike his daughter's, Rajiv's English was heavily accented. His voice flew up and down the scales, seeming as erratic as the flight of a moth. 'They are thieves, criminals. I have been robbed twice again.'

'Sorry to hear that. If there's anything I can do . . .'

'No, there is nothing. I am as helpless as a baby in the hands of these fiends.' His equilibrium more or less recovered, Rajiv ended the sentence on a note of confidence. 'Now, how can I be helping you?'

Boots looked down at the floor. 'This is embarrassing, Mr Visnawana, but it seems like we lost some of the paperwork related to the theft of your car and we need to go over the details again.

Now, I know your car was parked on Berry Street, but would you mind telling me when you first noticed it was missing?'

'After midnight.'

'How long after midnight? If you can't remember exactly, make an estimate.'

'Twelve fifteen.'

'And you reported it missing at . . . Wasn't it about one thirty?'

Visnawana's eyes widened slightly. His lie had backfired and now there was a gap he'd have to account for. 'Yes, approximately then.'

'So, where were you when you first noticed that your car wasn't parked where you left it?'

'I was visiting a friend.'

'On Berry Street?'

'Yes. I had occasion to look out the window and I found my vehicle gone.'

'At twelve fifteen?'

'Perhaps closer to twelve thirty. I am not remembering exactly when it was.'

'OK, tell me what you saw.'

'I saw my car was not there.'

Boots grinned, a flicker that instantly died out. 'What did you do next?'

'I put on my clothes and went to report my loss.'

'You didn't call nine-one-one?'

'That number is for emergencies only. This I have been told.'

'OK, I won't argue the point. You probably would have been directed to the precinct anyway. So, where did you go after you left your friend's apartment?'

'As I have already said,' Rajiv grumbled, 'I went to the station, to report the loss.'

'I know what you said, Rajiv, and I'm not doubting you. But the Sixty-Fourth Precinct is only a ten-minute walk from Berry Street. Even if it took you another ten minutes to get out of your friend's apartment, there's a forty-minute gap unaccounted for. Now, just tell me what you did for those forty minutes and I'll be on my way.'

Rajiv was ready this time. 'I was not in my own neighborhood and I became lost,' he answered.

'There, you see? Was that so hard?' Boots started to turn away, then spun on his heel. 'Wait a minute,' he said, 'there's one thing I forgot to ask.' He opened the briefcase, taking his time, then removed an object. Shaped like a miniature lava lamp with a handle instead of a base, the object was generally referred to, by the trade, as a butt plug.

'Tell me, Rajiv, have you ever seen this before?'

As he watched Rajiv's coppery skin go gray, watched his eyes widen, his lips twitch, his forehead and the space above his upper lip become speckled with little drops of sweat, Boots recalled a phrase from the Bible, something he'd read long ago: *For that which I greatly feared has come upon me.*

He reached out to grasp Visnawana's tie, to pull the man forward. 'What do you think your beautiful, sophisticated daughter would say if I showed this to her? What do you think your wife would say if I convinced Ms Henrietta to give her a call?' Boots hesitated, but Rajiv, though his lips trembled, didn't speak. 'Ya know, what I figure, half the thrill has to come from the fear of gettin' caught. I mean, ya hump a street whore, maybe catch a blow job, it's something a wife could forgive, as long as you wore a condom. But nipple clamps? Cock screws? Latex masks? Foreign objects jammed up your ass? I mean, even if you promise never to do it again, even if you keep that promise, Indira's gotta know that she'll never be the object of your fantasies. As for your daughter . . .'

'Please, officer.'

'Please? Listen to me, you cocksucker. You witnessed the murder of a police officer and didn't come forward. Not only don't I have any sympathy for you, I'm placing you under arrest for the crime of filing a false police report. You got the right to remain silent and the right to a lawyer. Or you got the right to step up, even at this late date, and tell the fuckin' truth.'

FIFTEEN

Rajiv and Boots were still out of sync. That was made clear when Rajiv shook his head as though trying to rid his ears of water, then declared, his tone accusing, 'You are not from Grand Theft Auto.'

Boots folded his arms across his chest, remembering all the

reasons why he disliked the public he was sworn to defend. A hardened criminal would already be negotiating a deal. But then, he consoled himself, a hardened criminal wouldn't make a very persuasive witness.

'What you have to figure,' Boots explained as he stepped away, giving Rajiv a little space to recover, 'is that you're gonna come clean, sooner or later. That's because you'll be forced to testify under oath before a grand jury. If you don't tell the truth, it's perjury. Remember, I've already spoken to Ms Henrietta and I know you were lookin' out that window when the shots were fired.' Boots spread his hands apart and smiled. 'Also, you should remind yourself that nobody in law enforcement cares what you were doin' when you saw what you saw. The state's interest here is Chris Parker.'

Boots watched a light dawn in Rajiv's eyes. Sure, he'd been punched around pretty good, but he was still on his feet.

'What will I say . . . to my family? Why I did not report this witnessing before?'

'I been thinkin' about that, Rajiv, and here's my advice. Tell Indira that you were at the apartment of a man you met in the restaurant, a man who offered you some gold jewelry at a fantastic discount. You didn't speak out earlier because you were afraid the jewelry was stolen, but now your conscience is bothering you. One thing for sure, as long as you're straight with me, I have no interest in the lies you tell your family.'

Rajiv's eyes blinked rapidly for a moment, then he let the air out of his lungs in a great huff. 'I saw the man who fired this gun only from behind. Believe me, this is the whole entire truth. I am not able to identify this man.'

'Do me a favor. Just take a deep breath and tell me what happened.'

'All right, I am lying on the bed and I hear a car alarm go off. I know this is my car, so I dash to the window. There I am seeing that someone is inside my car and they are trying to start it. Then another vehicle, a Jeep, drives on to the block and parks. A man gets out and I'm wondering if he's Henrietta's . . . Well, I don't know who he is, but when he gets to the sidewalk, a second man steps away from a building – I didn't see him before – and shoots the first man twice.'

'Then what?'

'Then he runs around the corner.'

'Anything else?'

'Yes, as I come out through the door, I am seeing my car driving away.'

Boots squelched an urge to recite a prayer of thanksgiving as he reached into his briefcase for a yellow pad. 'OK,' he said, 'let's get the truth down on paper. After that, we'll take a ride into Brooklyn where you'll repeat your story as many times as necessary. Myself, if I was in your position, I'd try to be consistent.'

Lieutenant Levine's features seemed to melt as he read through Rajiv Visnawana's signed statement, a statement that confirmed those of Vinnie Palermo and Henrietta Penn. By the time he finished, he looked like an English bulldog with a head cold. Sorrowful didn't even begin to describe his demeanor – not to Boots, who'd anticipated the worst.

'Bottom line, boss, Palermo's innocent,' Boots said when Levine finished.

'Only until proven guilty.'

'What's that supposed to mean?'

'It means the car Palermo stole was tracked to a chop shop in Queens over the weekend. It means blood evidence found on the car's dash has been matched to Chris Parker's blood type. It means the media is being informed even as we speak.' Levine laid his hands on the desk and allowed his weight to come forward. 'It means that I'm the asshole who gets to throw a monkey wrench into Inspector Mack Corcoran's well-oiled machine. Trust me on this, Detective Littlewood, Inspector Corcoran will not be happy.'

'I know that, boss. That's why I waited so long before I went looking for a witness. But what I figure now, as long as I'm in the shit, I'm gonna have a good time. It's not every day you get to trash an inspector's dreams of promotion.'

'Oh, great. Boots Quixote. And lucky me, I get to play Sancho Panza.'

Boots wasn't buying into the guilt trip. He'd made any number of compromises over the years, but letting an innocent man go to prison was a line he'd never crossed. To cross it now would change the way he felt about himself. That was the conclusion he'd come to and he hadn't been able to shake it, though he'd tried. Still, Boots felt enough sympathy for his boss to offer him a way out.

'Why don't I take Rajiv directly to Brooklyn North and hand him over to the task force myself? I'll tell 'em I found the witness on my own, which is the truth. You had nothin' to do with it.'

His offer promptly accepted, Boots drove a complaining Rajiv to Borough Command, led him up a flight of stairs, finally sat him in a chair.

'Don't worry,' he said, 'it'll be over before you know it.'

Of all the lies Boots told Rajiv Visnawana, this was the most blatant.

Only a single desk in the small office housing the Chris Parker task force was occupied when Boots arrived, that of Detective Second Grade Thelonius Tolliver. Tolliver was cleaning out his desk. Either the task force was being downsized or Tolliver was being dumped.

'What's up, Boots?' Tolliver asked.

Once again, Boots repeated his story, this time adding a number of details relating to why and how he'd gone about locating Rajiv Visnawana. He emphasized Henrietta Penn's statement as well, and admitted that she was a whore, though he somehow failed to mention her area of expertise.

Boots leaned back in the chair when he finished. Tolliver's expression hadn't changed, which didn't surprise Boots. A large, dark-skinned man, Tolliver had the map of Africa written on his face – his lips were full, his nose flat, his eyes obsidian. On the street, he was often mistaken for the sort of black male who haunts the dreams of white suburbanites, a trait he'd used to his advantage a decade before when he was assigned to the Anti-Crime Unit. Nowadays, he favored black turtle-neck sweaters that made his thick neck appear even thicker.

Thelonius Tolliver listened to Detective Littlewood's tale. Then, without saying a word, he pulled out his cellphone and walked away. Thirty minutes later, Inspector Corcoran, with Artie Farrahan trailing behind, swept through the squad room and into his office.

As neither man looked in his direction, Boots settled down to wait, his thoughts naturally turning to Lieutenant Sorrowful's revelations. One thing sure, if DNA testing matched the blood found in the Nissan to Chris Parker, the state's overall strategy would have to include discrediting Rajiv Visnawana. Either that or virtually admit that the blood evidence was planted.

'Hey, Boots, what're ya doing?'

Boots looked up to find Artie Farrahan walking toward him. Farrahan wore a beautifully fitted jet-black overcoat and a flame-red scarf.

'Just sittin' here,' Boots replied.

'I'm talking about with your fucking career, dummy. We got this jerk, Palermo, dead and buried.'

'You seem pretty sure of yourself.'

The accusation hung between them for a moment. It would take a DNA match to bury Vinny Booster, and the testing process was ongoing.

'What I don't understand,' Farrahan said, 'is why you give a shit about a skell like Vinnie Palermo. His whole life, the only thing he's done is steal other people's property.'

'Stop right there, Artie. Think about what you just said. The only thing Vinnie's done is steal. Meantime, you're gonna put him on trial for murdering a cop.'

'So what? Ya know, Boots, you got a hard head. That's why you been stuck in the Six-Four all these years. You never mastered lesson number one. You never learned to see the big picture.' Farrahan stood up and brushed off his coat. 'Corcoran wants you in his office,' he said. 'Now.'

'What in goddamned hell do you think—'

'Lemme stop you right there, Inspector. The blasphemy? I'd rather not hear it. I have religious objections.'

Brooklyn North's detectives had long ago hung the nickname 'Schoolmaster' on Mack Corcoran. And he had the look, no doubt about it. The craggy face, the austere mouth, the pinched nose, the oversized, wire-rimmed glasses that partially obscured his brown eyes. Looking into those eyes, Boots had to wonder if concealment wasn't the whole point. Corcoran's eyes were as dead and empty as those of a man blind from birth. And that was pretty amazing, because in every other way, from the flush in his cheeks to the way he straightened his shoulders, the man's entire body projected a swelling rage. Even his wig had shifted to one side.

'Get out,' Corcoran finally said. 'Get out before I shoot you.'

Boots gave it a couple of beats, until the hesitation became a dare, looking for any faint glimmer of life in Corcoran's eyes. But there was no life to be found there, and no hope for Vinnie Palermo, either. Or for Rajiv Visnawana, who would soon be taught a painful lesson: Never trust a cop.

SIXTEEN

Shoulder to the wheel. For the remainder of that week, Boots arrived at the Six-Four on time and worked his tours enthusiastically. On Tuesday, he helped Narcotics track down Spiros Condraconis, wanted for selling cocaine out of the Grand Street Diner. On Wednesday, he handled three robberies committed within an hour of each other near the western boundary of the precinct. As these robberies all took place within a few blocks of Bushwick Avenue and the perp displayed a knife each time, Boots drew a pair of assumptions: the mugger was local and a drug addict.

Ear to the ground. Boots spent the final hours of his tour putting the word out to his snitches. If his assumptions were correct, he'd be cuffing the perp within a week. Or so he was vain enough to believe.

Thursday was devoted to interviewing burglary victims. Though Boots couldn't do much for these folk, he maintained a properly sympathetic demeanor as he took their complaints, even when they berated him for the NYPD's failure to protect their property. He stopped by the local shops in Greenpoint and Williamsburg, too, the ones that provided him with a professional discount from time to time. These were stores owned by people Boots knew well and he put his request boldly.

'If anybody should come by askin' questions about me, especially if those anybodies are cops, give me a call.'

'You in trouble?'

'Not yet.'

It was that 'not yet' that stuck in Detective Littlewood's craw as the week drew to a close. He'd not only been looking over his shoulder and to both sides, he'd been looking straight up in the air. Just in case the other shoe was dropping.

Too much. That's what he tried to tell himself. He just wasn't that important to men like Chief of Detectives Michael Shaw and Inspector Mack Corcoran. The problem was that he couldn't make himself believe it.

On Friday, as Boots was about to call it a week, his cellphone rang. He answered on the third ring.

'Detective Littlewood.'

'Yo, detective, it's Flint Page.'

Boots nodded to himself, the wheels already turning. A small-time crook, Jimmy 'Flint' Page was a legendary snitch. He snitched for money, for a competitive advantage, to stay out of jail, for revenge. He snitched so much, and to so many cops, that Boots had come to wonder if the man didn't have a rare psychological disorder that compelled him to snitch. Like Vinnie Palermo was compelled to steal cars.

'What's up, Flint?' Boots's tone was businesslike. Flint Page was a self-styled actor. If you didn't keep him on track, he'd go on forever.

'Man, you don't sound too happy to hear my voice. And me, I have some excellent news for you.'

'Like what?'

Flint's voice grew sly. 'You remember last Wednesday, all that crazy knife shit up on Bushwick Avenue?'

'Yeah, I—'

'Yo, detective, I gotta book. Call you later.'

Boots spent the last hour of his tour waiting for Page's call. When it didn't come, he silently cursed himself for not running Page down while he was on the clock. Now he would have to do it over the weekend. Nevertheless, Page was not first on his Saturday morning schedule. In fact, as Boots rang Frankie Drago's bell at ten o'clock in the morning, his anticipation of the next few minutes was so keen that he forgot Page altogether. And not even when Mama Drago opened the door was he distracted.

'Boots.'

'My condolences about Angie,' Boots said. 'Is Frankie in?'

'You, you, you *mascalzone*, you traitor, you dare to come my house? *Tu puzzi.*'

Boots nodded agreeably. Mama Drago was old school when it came to family. She'd defend her son if he was a serial killer.

'I need to see Frankie, Mrs Drago,' he repeated. 'It's business.'

Frankie Drago chose that moment to make an appearance. Though not a tall man, he towered over his diminutive mother. 'Ma, why don't you go upstairs?'

Before complying, Mama Drago assaulted her son with a burst of Italian that reddened his ears. Frankie watched her climb to the second floor, then released an involuntary sigh. His life had turned into a horror show, no doubt about it. The monsters just kept coming.

Frankie led Boots into the kitchen. Even taking the short odds, Boots was up more than five hundred dollars. And it would have been a lot worse if the Yankees' relievers hadn't blown last night's game. Reluctantly, Frankie opened a small tin box next to the sugar bowl and counted out Boots's winnings.

Boots took the wad of bills Drago offered, recounted it, then shoved it into his pocket. 'So, how's it goin', Frankie? You holdin' up?'

'Not so's you'd notice. I had to give my fuckin' lawyer ten grand up front and he's lookin' for another twenty-five. When I mortgaged the house, Ma went nuts.'

Frankie opened the refrigerator and took out a quart of orange juice. 'You want?'

'No, thanks.'

Drago filled his glass and carried it over to the kitchen table. 'I shoulda called you right away, Boots, right when it happened. Before I did anything else. I shoulda trusted you.'

Boots shuddered. Where had he heard that before?

'See,' Frankie continued, 'it's the part about Angie bein' alive for two hours after she fell that's killin' me. My lawyer claims it shows evidence of intent. I told him a hundred times that I thought she was dead, but it doesn't cut any ice, even if it's true, even if I testify. The jury's not gonna believe me.'

'Yeah, well, I've been meanin' to talk to you about that.' Boots tried to smile, but never quite got there. 'Angie didn't live for two hours. She most likely didn't live for two minutes. Your lawyer will know that as soon as she gets the autopsy report.'

Frankie Drago observed a moment of stunned silence as he juggled a pair of conflicting emotions. He was definitely pissed-off, and rightly so, but there was this little drop of hope that kept expanding. Maybe this time the clutched straw would keep him afloat.

'Are you sayin' you lied to me?'

'Yeah.'

'Why?'

'Cops always lie, Frankie. We're encouraged to lie. We get rewarded for lyin'.'

Drago considered this for a moment, then said, 'If you have to testify at my trial, what then? You gonna play it straight?'

'What I oughta do is hang you by your balls. Not for what you did to Angie. No, I should hang you for what you did to Vinnie Palermo. The way it looks now, Vinnie's gonna die in prison.' Boots stood up. 'Put me down for a two bills a game until I let you know otherwise. As for Angie, I haven't made up my mind yet. The way it is, I'm already givin' you a break. I could have told Connie Palermo that you were the one who ratted on her nephew.'

Boots was in the Key Food supermarket on McGuinness Boulevard, comparing heads of romaine lettuce and escarole, when his cellphone rang. Across the way, her cart halted beside a table loaded with plum tomatoes, Rose Orlac fiddled with a plastic bag, trying to separate the ends. She glanced over at Boots and smiled.

'Littlewood,' Boots said into the phone as he returned her smile.

'Yo, detective, wassup?'

'You tell me, Flint. It's your dime.'

'Yours too, my man. You're on a cellphone. You pay comin' and goin'.'

'Right, and I'm also busy. So let's get to it.'

'Man, what is it with you today?'

'Come to the point, Flint. You're callin' on my day off.'

'Your dime, your day off. What I should do is hang up.'

'Yeah, but then I'd have to look for you, which would piss me off more than I'm already pissed off.'

Page cleared his throat. Reared in a Bed-Stuy housing project, he'd come up the hard way, yet had acquired enough sophistication to mingle with the bohemians and the yuppies in their little enclave along Bedford Avenue. He used his panache to market drugs to these end-users, mainly powder cocaine and marijuana.

'For a fact, I know the brother pulled those rip-offs on Wednesday.'

'The brother?'

'A Dominican brother, OK? I mean, ain't we all brothers?'

'And sisters,' Boots responded. 'So, what's your interest, Flint?'

'Money. Otherwise, I got no dog in this fight.'

Boots smiled. 'Fifty bucks. That's what the name's worth to me.'

'How do ya know that? If you ain't heard it yet?' Page went on before Boots could respond. 'Lemme tell ya, this player I'm gamin' here? He's crazy evil. Attica? Clinton? Greenhaven? He's done time in every one of 'em. Slice up your face soon as look at it.'

'Is that the real reason you want him off the street? Is he lookin' to slice up *your* face?'

Flint chose not to answer the question. 'Three bills,' he said. 'And you doggin' me at the price.'

Eventually, Boots and Flint settled on a figure, $150, a place, Flint's girlfriend's apartment on Richardson Street, and a time, ten o'clock that night. Though Boots made a valiant attempt, he was unable to persuade Flint to talk now and let him pay later.

Boots shut the phone down. Rose Orlac was on the checkout line and there were several customers standing behind her. As Boots watched, she shook out her blond hair, then bent forward to empty her cart. Instantly, as though someone had thrown a switch, a guy one line over riveted his eyes to her ass, his evaluating gaze so direct as to border on the socially unacceptable. Boots was hoping the man would say something rude so he could intervene, but the man looked away when Rose straightened.

Boots turned away as well, headed for the dairy counter. He would see Rose Orlac at church tomorrow, at which time he would make his interest known. Unless, of course, through some miracle, he ran into Jill Kelly first. According to Sergeant Gantier, Jill had once been on the SWAT team. Maybe she still had her equipment.

Ten hours later, Boots parked his Chevy on Richardson Street, several doors away from the address supplied by Flint Page. Unlike its closest neighbors, the building in question was not a tenement. Boots knew its six stories to house thirty-seven apartments, counting the super's in the basement, knew there would be a lobby on the first floor instead of a narrow corridor leading to the stairs. He knew because, just a few years before, he'd had a girlfriend named Monica Charon who lived in the building.

Down the block, a group of teenagers danced to the Boricua rap pouring from a boombox. The boys were decked out in the latest hip-hop fashions, the girls in jeans tight enough to be a second skin. Across the street, four older men sat around a folding table, enjoying the warm weather and a spirited game of dominoes. When Boots pulled to the curb, the old men checked him out, instantly made him for what he was, then returned to their game.

Boots settled back on the seat. He was in no hurry. The Yankees and the Orioles were playing out the ninth inning and he was ten minutes early. If the Yanks won – which they were very likely to do, being up six runs – the week would be off to a good start.

The game concluded a few minutes later with a soft line drive to Alex Rodriguez at third base. Boots shut down the engine, then swung the door open. Out of uniform, he wore khakis and a sweat-shirt in lieu of a three-piece suit, running shoes instead of boots. His off-duty weapon, a .32 caliber Seecamp, was tucked into a holster on his right ankle.

Eyes flicked to him as walked along the sidewalk, the dominoes players, the kids, faces in the windows, a man walking a pitbull on the other side of the street. Though Boots did not pass within fifty feet of any of these individuals, he could smell their collective relief when he turned left, pulled open the door to Page's building and stepped into a small foyer. Ahead of him, the interior lobby was well lit and clean.

Boots rang the buzzer for 5D and got an immediate response.

'Yo.'

'Open up, Flint.'

'Yowzah, boss.'

Inside, Boots crossed the lobby to the elevator. As he waited for it to descend, the front door opened and a man walked inside. The man was in his twenties, wearing a wife-beater t-shirt. He looked at Boots, repressed a double-take, finally decided to use the stairs.

Boots was still chuckling as he came out of the elevator to discover Page standing in the hallway, a door open behind him. Page wore a silky, hot-orange basketball uniform, the top large enough to fit a man twice his size, the shorts descending to mid-calf. A spider's web of delicate chains, which might or might not be gold, encircled his throat.

'Somethin' funny?' he asked.

Now that he had the man cornered, Boots wasn't above slipping in a casual zinger as he walked into the apartment. 'You joinin' the circus, Flint?'

But Jimmy 'Flint' Page didn't rise to the bait. Instead, he closed the door behind Boots an instant before the overhead light went out.

Boots reached automatically for the nine-millimeter normally holstered behind his right hip. He was momentarily confused when his hand came up empty, but then remembered the Seecamp strapped to his ankle. An instant later, something hard and unyielding crashed into his forehead.

He hit the floor, barely conscious, blood already pouring into his eyes. The beam of a flashlight thrust out at him. It moved along his body from his feet to his head, then back to his chest. A kick followed, to the side of his face, then another to his hip, then another and another. Instinctively, he began to crawl on all fours, scuttling along like a crab. The flashlight moved with him, the feet, too. How many feet? How many attackers? With his eyes now filled with blood, he had no idea. Nor did he think he could get to the Seecamp. But submission wasn't an option, either.

Boots turned suddenly and lunged backward. Purely by luck, the fingers of his left hand caught a hunk of fabric. He clamped down hard, locking his hand into a fist, then levered himself to his knees and drew his attacker toward him, all those years in the weight room finally paying off.

A pair of fists hammered at the back of his head, but he ignored them, as he ignored a kick to his ribs. Blindly, relentlessly, he swept the area in front of him with his free hand, back and forth, until his arm finally encircled a leg. Then he brought his left hand down to meet his right and twisted with all his strength.

The scream that followed was very loud, very shrill, and Boots drank it in as he spun in a half-circle to face the flashlight beam. His face was covered in blood now, blood soaked his eyebrows and eyelashes, blood filmed his eyes each time he blinked. But there had to be a hand attached to that flashlight, and if he could reach that hand, take the flashlight away, use it for a weapon . . .

Boots was so lost in his calculations that he never felt the gun when it was pressed to the back of his head. He heard it, though, heard the hammer ratchet back, and he froze. A second later, through a haze of red, he saw something long and black whip across the flashlight's beam. Instinctively, he made an attempt to raise his shoulder, but it was too late. The club hit him on the side of the head just above his ear and he dropped to the floor, face first, unable even to break his fall.

SEVENTEEN

For the first twenty-four hours following the assault, Boots moved freely through a universe where time had three dimensions, like a fish swimming through a sea as dark as it was vast. He felt no anxiety, no fear, not even a sense of mystery. He was just there, in the sea, swimming.

Though he saw nothing, Boots occasionally became aware of sounds, the somehow reassuring beep of a heart monitor, a television playing at a distance, the squeak of rubber-soled shoes, voices near and far, male and female. But he was unable, or perhaps unwilling, to place these sounds in sequence, much less in context. Once gone, they were instantly consigned to memory, a flat and slippery mirror that offered no purchase whatever.

At one point, a female voice announced, 'I'm just going to flush your foley, Mr Littlewood.'

At another, a male voice confidently declared, 'In the greater scheme of things, the cranial injuries he suffered are mild. He'll come around as soon as the swelling inside his skull recedes, probably tomorrow.'

Boots didn't know to whom these statements were made, or even if they were made at the same time, though he found it odd that he felt no discomfort, physical or psychological. But one phrase – 'in the greater scheme of things' – did fascinate him, and he eventually applied this idea to Father Gubetti, whose voice came to Boots midway through an Our Father.

'. . . *dimitte nobis debita nostra sicut et nos dimittimus debitoribus nostris.*'

A former altar boy, Boots easily translated the Latin: Forgive us our trespasses as we forgive those who trespass against us. This was old news and Boots didn't scrutinize the words, or ask himself why his old friend was praying in Latin. But he knew, in the greater scheme of things, there was to be no forgiveness. Of that he was certain.

Andy Littlewood was equally unforgiving. 'You're no listener, Irwin Littlewood, not as boy or man,' he declared, his tone bitter. 'Tell me, when you rammed your thick skull into the wall, were you hopin' the stone would crack? Or were you expectin' Joshua to bring the wall down with a blowin' of horns?'

Perhaps, Boots thought, after his father drifted away, I did hope. Perhaps I did expect the wall to crumble. The admission didn't trouble him. Nothing troubled him, not even visitations by each of the principal actors in the drama that had laid him low. Their voices swam up, crossed his path, continued on: Jill Kelly, Frankie Drago, Lieutenant Sorrowful, Vinnie Palermo, Inspector Corcoran, Flint Page. Boots noted their comings and goings without curiosity. There was no rush, not when he could move through time, side to side, up and down, backward and forward. No, there was always plenty of time when there was no time at all.

For the first ten seconds after Boots awakened, he simply continued on, unruffled, untroubled. But then his flesh turned on him, the pain seeming to rush into his consciousness from every cell in his body. He groaned as his left eye finally popped open, and for the first time he was confused. He tried to raise a hand to touch his right eye, unleashing another barrage of pain that left him nauseated.

'Boots?'

Joaquin Rivera's voice came from the right and Boots slowly turned his head to fix him with his left eye. He started to speak, only to realize that there was something in his throat, a tube that ran through his nose. Still, he managed a few words.

'If I would've known it was gonna hurt this much,' he whispered, 'I woulda stayed in a coma.'

Joaquin laughed, then said, 'I'll get the doctor.'

Boots was unconscious before either returned, but this time, now that he knew the pain was out there, his mind was not untroubled. Nevertheless, he clung to a basic perception. There was no rush. He had all the time in the world.

An hour later, he opened his eyes again to discover a man next to his bed. The man wore a white lab coat and was young enough to be his son.

'Doctor . . .'

'Detective Littlewood? I'm Dr Chang. Are you finally with us?'
Boots ignored the upbeat tone. 'My right eye. I can't see.'

'That's because it's swollen shut. Do you need anything for pain?'

'Yeah. And this tube in my nose . . .'

'The naso-gastric tube was inserted as a precaution. It'll come
out tomorrow morning.' Dr Chang leaned forward to shine a light
into his patient's good eye. 'Now, do you know where you are?'

'In the hospital.' Boots managed to raise a hand. 'How long have
I been here?'

'You came in last night – Saturday, at eleven o'clock, a little less
than twenty-four hours ago.'

'And what's the damage?'

'We've taken multiple CAT scans of your brain and we don't
believe that you'll suffer any long-term neurological deficit from
your injuries. In addition, you have three broken ribs and extensive
soft tissue damage, but these, too, will heal completely over time.
Unfortunately, the damage to your right eye is more problematical.
We'll have to wait until the swelling recedes before we can evaluate
your vision.'

Dr Chang glanced at his watch, then nodded to a nurse who
entered the room. 'We'll talk again in the morning.'

Boots watched the nurse fit the point of a syringe into a port on
his IV line, then depress the plunger. The wave of pleasure that
swept through him was as brief as it was powerful. His good eye
fluttered and he came close to achieving a genuine smile before he
drifted away.

He smiled again, even while he slept, when he happened on a
word that perfectly described the way he'd been gamed by Flint
Page: elegant. The hang-up on the first call, as if Page had been
interrupted by some villain who couldn't know he was talking to
a cop, allayed any suspicions Boots might have entertained. And
the second phone call – the banter, the bargaining – was even
more convincing. Flint had played his part well, right down to the
orange basketball gear and the gold chains. There hadn't been a
single false note.

Nevertheless, elegant or not, the bad guys had made an error in
judgment. They'd spared his life.

*   *   *

Boots woke up the following morning to find Lieutenant Sorrowful in a chair by the side of the bed. Levine skidded to the edge of the seat when Boots opened his eyes.

'Boots, you OK?'

'Never better.'

'The doc says you're gonna be all right.'

'Fuck the docs. Is it Monday?'

'Yeah, it's Monday morning, eight o'clock.'

'Did the Yankees win yesterday?'

'What?'

Boots gathered himself. His throat was on fire, rubbed raw by the tube running down into his stomach. 'The Yankees . . .'

'Yes, the Yankees won.' Levine's small mouth worked itself into a tiny frown. 'Do you remember what happened to you?'

Boots leaned back and made a show of it, letting his tongue work over his lips and his good eye jump to the ceiling before returning to Levine. Then he lied through his teeth. 'The last thing I remember was entering an apartment on Richardson Street. That was about ten o'clock on Saturday night.'

'Well, you got worked over real good. In fact, what the docs said, if you hadn't crawled out of that apartment and knocked on a door, you might not be talking to me. Without treatment, you could've definitely died.'

'The way I feel at this moment, I'd have been better off.'

Levine's chuckle was strictly for the record. 'Look, Boots, this is important. If you were injured in the line of duty, you'll be on full pay until you heal up. You should take that into—'

'I went to Richardson Street to meet Flint Page. Page claimed to know who pulled off the robberies last Wednesday.'

NYPD regulations demand that all confidential informants be registered with the Department. For any number of reasons, including the personal safety of the informant, the rule is largely ignored. But Flint Page was an exception. He'd ratted on so many of his pals, to so many cops, he had no more confidentiality to protect. Every detective in the Six-Four, including Lieutenant Sorrowful, knew his name.

'Perfect,' Levine said, 'now you're on easy street.'

'Easy street?'

'Boots, with your injuries, you could stay home for the rest of the year.'

EIGHTEEN

Levine's exit was shortly followed by the arrival of Andy and Joaquin. Boots looked into his father's eyes, found regret, fear, reproach and relief. Without the energy to address any of these, he turned to Joaquin, who seemed angry.

'Get me a mirror,' he said.

'Boots . . .' Andy Littlewood thrust himself into his son's line of sight. 'I don't think . . .'

'Jackie,' Boots repeated, making an effort to get the words past his swollen throat, 'get me a mirror.'

Joaquin left the room, returning a few minutes later with a small mirror borrowed from one of the nurses. Boots peered through his one eye at the tiny image in the glass. For a moment, he began to drift, but then he refocused long enough to take an inventory. His right eye looked as if somebody had stuck an egg in the socket. The lids were barely visible, and both eyes were the malignant red of a disfiguring birthmark. In addition, a pair of serious wounds extended across his forehead and along the right side of his skull, lacerations that had been closed with too many stitches to count. One side of his head had been shaved as well.

Boots was still taking inventory when Dr Chang entered the room. 'You weren't all that beautiful to begin with,' he observed.

'Thanks.'

'You're welcome.' Chang began to draw the curtain around the bed. 'Now, if you'll excuse us,' he told Andy and Joaquin, 'I'm just going to remove this tube from Mr Littlewood's nose.'

'How about the one in my dick?'

'That's called a foley catheter. I'll remove it when you can sit up on your own, with your legs draped over the edge of the bed. Would you like to try that now?'

Boots made a valiant attempt to rise to a sitting position. He tried first with his abdominal muscles, but the pain in his ribs and back stopped him cold. He tried next to roll on to his side, then to use his hands and arms, but it wasn't happening. Finally, he dropped his head to the pillow, his face and hair slick with sweat.

Dr Chang pointed to the chair currently occupied by Joaquin. 'A couple of hours from now, the nurses will put you in that chair. It's going to hurt, Mr Littlewood, so I'd advise you to take your pain medication. The less pain you have, the more you'll move around. The more you move around, the faster your recovery.' Chan closed the curtain, then rubbed his hands together. 'Now, let's get to work.'

The naso-gastric tube running through Detective Littlewood's nose and down into his stomach was held in place by a single piece of adhesive twisted into the shape of a butterfly. When Dr Chang deftly tore this adhesive away from the bruised and swollen tissue beneath it, Boots felt as though his skin had caught fire. Despite his best intentions (and his carefully nurtured self-image), he howled like a baby. Apparently unsympathetic, Chang next drew the NG tube from his patient's stomach, up through his esophagus and out through his nose. By the time he finished, Boots was whimpering.

'You ready for those pain meds?' Chang asked.

Boots was, in fact, eager for his pain meds, and he continued to be eager as the day wore on. Nevertheless, when an orderly transferred him from the bed to a gurney prior to a CAT scan, and when a pair of nurses got him out of bed, walked him around the room, then sat him in a chair, his body shrieked in protest. He would be a long time healing.

The remainder of the afternoon passed in a blur. Boots was visited by a neurologist who restated Chan's prognosis, and by an ophthalmologist who took no more than a step into the small ICU cubicle, but was nevertheless optimistic.

'Try not to worry,' she advised before heading back the way she'd come.

Already worried, he rang the nurse for his pain meds, then, once they were delivered, promptly fell into an image-saturated trance. He drifted for a time, again in a parallel universe devoid of apprehension. But he was more active now, and he skillfully manipulated these images, placing them in various relationships, one to the other, as he probed for a hidden treasure.

'Detective, are you awake?'

In the time it took Boots to realize that he'd been spoken to, the question was repeated: 'Detective, are you awake?'

Ah, yes, perfect, Boots thought. When the man gave you a job, you did it, the condition of a beat-to-shit detective somebody else's problem. Boots knew he was dealing with another cop even before he opened his good eye.

'Lenny Olmeda,' the cop said, flashing a detective's shield. 'You remember me.'

'Of course, you're Inspector Corcoran's secretary.'

'Attaché,' Olmeda corrected.

'We're gonna have to make this quick, Lenny. I feel like I was run over by a truck.'

'Yeah, check it out. My job's to find the truck.' Short and stocky, Olmeda's full cheeks were pitted with acne scars and he sported a *bandito* mustache that curled around his mouth in a manner likely to draw a reprimand if he was still on the street. 'Can I call you Irwin?' he asked.

'Boots,' Boots replied affably, though he was certain that Olmeda was fully aware of his nickname. 'Everybody calls me Boots.'

Olmeda took out a little notebook and balanced it on his knee. 'All right, Boots, why don't you tell me what happened?'

Boots repeated the story he told Levine that morning. The robberies early in the week, Flint Page's two phone calls, walking into the apartment. Then nothing.

'Well, you're a big help.' Olmeda's smile lifted his mustache until it splayed out along his cheeks. 'Being as you're on the job, I thought you'd have a little more consideration, maybe throw me a grounder.'

'Sorry.'

A silence followed, one Boots was not tempted to break. Finally, Olmeda said, 'Can you think of anyone who'd want to do this to you?'

'I been workin' on that, sarge, and the only name that pops up is Mark Dupont.'

'Who?'

'Mark Dupont. He's a knucklehead I spotted in Greenpoint a couple of weeks ago. I encouraged the uniforms at the Six-Four to find an excuse to violate his parole. I wanted him off the street.'

'Did they succeed?'

'They did, and he knows I was behind it. Dupont's sittin' in Rikers, but he definitely has the muscle to reach out. If I was you, that's where I'd look first.'

'What about the skell who set you up?'

Boots laughed for the first time that day. 'Yeah, that'd be great. You got four or five years with nothing to do, spend it lookin' for Jimmy Page.'

Boots passed the rest of the afternoon alternately watching television and entertaining visitors. The visitors were fellow cops at the Six-Four, other detectives and a few uniforms, including Craig O'Malley and the Bulgarian, Boris Velikov. When O'Malley asked him what happened, he told them the same basic story he told Olmeda, though he left Mark Dupont out of it.

'Flint Page? I always made the guy for a pussy.'

'Looked me right in the eye when I came out of the elevator. In fact, the last thing I remember is Flint Page holding the door to the apartment.'

For a moment, Boots was certain the Bulgarian, who'd worked himself into a frenzy of outrage, would start drooling. But Velikov surprised him.

'Fuck findin' Page,' he told Boots. 'That jerk-off never woulda did what he did if he was gonna stick around.'

'True enough, but I'm hopin' you'll do me a favor anyway.' Boots turned slightly to focus his functioning eye on O'Malley. 'The way I read it, Page most likely had a good reason to skip town before I came into the picture. Maybe you can check it out, prove me right or wrong.'

Velikov's grin lifted his taut cheeks, narrowing his black eyes still further. 'I know somebody who knows Page real good,' he told Boots, 'a scumbag who likes to beat on his wife. We been to this asshole's house five times in the last six months, but every time we bust him, his wife's too scared to testify.' He looked over at his partner. 'I'm talkin' about that Armenian.'

'Manuk Grigoryan?'

'Yeah, Grigoryan. I think I'm gonna ask him first.'

'Good idea,' Boots concurred, 'but, for now, why don't we just keep this between ourselves.'

At six o'clock, a few minutes after Velikov and O'Malley cleared the room, Boots was taken for another walk. The walking itself was not a big deal. Raising himself to a sitting position, swinging his legs over the edge of the bed, shifting forward until he slid off – this was the bad news. Once he got his weight over his feet, the pain was bearable.

Boots was just beginning a second circuit of the nursing station when Lieutenant Carl Levine walked on to the unit. Grinning, Levine did a mock double-take.

'What next, the hundred-yard dash?' he asked.

'Bataan Death March is more like it.' Boots winked at the aide who stood by his side. 'Marcy threatened to withhold my sponge bath if I didn't get out of bed.'

Marcy smiled. 'One more time, Mr Littlewood.'

Boots shuffled forward, with Levine to his left and the railing to his right. Neither spoke until Boots was safely back in bed and they were alone. Then Levine asked, 'What's up with the eye?'

'Don't know, lou. It's kinda wait-and-see. But my brain's not fried, which is very good news considering how hard I was hit.' Gingerly, Boots touched the row of stitches on his forehead. 'The docs say I'll have to see a plastic surgeon if the scar's too thick. Maybe I'll get a tummy tuck at the same time, or have my ass liposuctioned. You know, restore my youthful figure.'

Levine responded to this little tirade with a slow, empathetic sigh perfectly in keeping with his Lieutenant Sorrowful persona. 'I'm on the clock,' he explained. 'I gotta get back soon.'

'Yeah, I know, and I should've raised this particular matter when you came before. Only I was too weak and I had that tube in my throat.'

'Hey, it's all right. Just tell me what's on your mind.'

Boots turned to fix Levine with his left eye. 'Well, boss, the good news, from your point of view, is that even though you sold me out to Corcoran, I'm probably not gonna kill you.'

Levine rose out of his chair as though levitated by the hand of God. 'Boots—'

'Don't bother, lou. It's been a long day and I'm not in the mood for any bullshit. Corcoran asked you to keep an eye on me and you did it. Otherwise, those petty rip-offs on Bushwick Avenue would never have to come to the attention of anybody at Borough Command.'

For once, as he searched for the right response, a counter to the hurled accusation, Levine's face became animated, his lips and nostrils twitching, his eyebrows rising and falling.

'Boots,' he finally said, 'you don't even remember what happened in that apartment. You told me so, yourself.'

But Irwin 'Boots' Littlewood did remember. He remembered every element of the attack, including the club that hit him for the second time. That club had passed through the beam of a flashlight, becoming visible just long enough for Boots to be certain it was a nightstick.

'Who's limping?' Boots asked.

'What?'

'At Borough Command. There's somebody down there who's limping. If you don't know who it is, find out.'

'Look, Boots, I'm your superior officer. You don't tell me what to do. I'll overlook it once, in light of what happened, but—'

'That's what you shoulda said when I first accused you, boss. Now it's too late. Did I ever tell you that I went to college for a couple of semesters?'

'No.'

Boots cleared his throat, trying to work up a little moisture. It felt as if somebody was in there with a blow torch. Still, he wasn't about to be deflected. He'd begun rehearsing this speech when he asked his father to call Levine and he had it just the way he wanted. 'I took classes at John Jay, in their criminal justice program, when I first came on the job. I was thinking about the sergeant's exam and I knew I'd need some college credit. Anyway, I don't remember all that much, but part of one lecture definitely stuck with me.'

'Boots, are you crazy?'

'Wait, hear me out.' Boots dropped his head to the pillow and stared up at the ceiling. 'Professor Rabin said that men live by a code of honor in any society where they can't go to the state for justice. That's because unless they draw a sharp line, unless they make it clear that anybody crossing that line is in for a fight, they're gonna definitely be victimized. Well, lou, this is one of those cases where the line has been crossed, but the victim can't dial nine-one-one and let the cops get justice for him. He has to get it for himself.'

Boots waved off Levine's attempt to speak, even that gesture causing him to gasp. Pain meds soon, he told himself. Pain meds, dinner and the Yankees. Three cheers for modern medicine.

'For what it's worth,' he continued, 'I don't blame you. I was the one makin' all the trouble, but your neck was on the line, too. Only it's gotta stop now. Understand?'

Levine was standing alongside the bed. Despite his hangdog expression and his generally sluggish disposition, he was a powerfully built man, while Boots, of course, was helpless. But Carl Levine didn't have the inborn courage to take his bluff to the limit, not when Boots was right, so he took the easy path and tried to plead down the charge.

'For what it's worth, I had no idea what they were gonna do,' he told Boots.

'For what it's worth, I believe you. Now, if you know who's limping, tell me.'

'Artie Farrahan. When I saw him at Borough Command, he was using a cane.'

Boots fished for the call button and rang the nurse's desk. When his call was answered, he asked that his pain meds be delivered. The nurse on the other end promised to do so at the earliest opportunity, after which Boots thanked her, then switched on the little TV hanging over the foot of the bed.

'You don't mind,' he told Lieutenant Sorrowful, 'I'm gonna take my Percocets and watch the news. I'm hurtin' everywhere.'

As he watched Levine retreat, Boots suddenly realized that he'd been awake for two days and he hadn't had a single craving for a cigarette. He wondered if maybe Farrahan and company had knocked the addiction out of him, perhaps through some subtle damage to the brain's addiction center. Boots wasn't sure that human brains actually had addiction centers, but he could always hope.

NINETEEN

Boots got out on the street within days of returning home. The effort cost him, but he wanted to be seen before his bruises disappeared. The resolutely working-class neighborhood in Greenpoint where his father lived had been stable for a century. Predominantly Polish, with substantial Italian, Irish and Latino minorities, everyone knew everyone else. This excessive familiarity, as Boots had long ago admitted, was a mixed bag. Feuds, within and between families, went on for generations. Over the decades, they'd been the immediate cause of many an assault and not a few homicides. Insularity was another nasty consequence of long-term stability. Outsiders were instantly mistrusted.

It was this last that Boots intended to use to his benefit. Accompanied by his father on a beautiful morning in late April, he shuffled down Newell Street, leaning on a cane. As expected, Jenicka Balicki, Newell Street's acknowledged matriarch, had already set up lawn chairs next to the entranceway to her home. In a purple housedress and a yellow sweater (the housedress flowered, the sweater striped), she was sitting between Dorota Niski and Fianna Walsh. Boots had known these women, in their eighties now, for all of his life.

'What's up with the face?' Fianna demanded.

'He got jumped,' Andy explained. 'By persons unknown.'

'What was he doin'?'

'He was, Fianna, my love, attemptin' to right a wrong.'

The three women regarded Boots for a moment. Like most working-class people of their generation, they had mixed feelings about cops. Finally, Jenicka Balicki said, her accent still thick after sixty years in Brooklyn, 'Eh, what do I do?'

Boots quickly translated the sentence – Jenicka was asking if she could help. Boots pointed to his eye, the lids of which were now several millimeters apart, a development that made his appearance even more ghoulish.

'I need another eye,' he explained. 'I need a lot of other eyes. So, if you notice any strangers hangin' around, I'd appreciate a call to me or my father. Also, if you see any trucks parked on the block that don't belong here.'

'Trucks?' Jenicka's green eyes, seemingly without lashes or brows, fixed on Boots. 'Only in trucks there are cops.' She raised a finger. 'I see this on the television. No criminals are there in trucks. In trucks there is only stakeout.'

Jenicka's companions nodded agreement and Boots was forced to admit the possibility that his enemies were fellow cops. As this was his aim from the beginning, he did so cheerfully. These women, all widows, lived on neighborhood gossip. Gossip was what kept them alive. Gossip kept them out of nursing homes. Gossip and a rock-hard determination to die in their own beds.

His back was covered.

*   *   *

By the end of the second week, Boots was certain that Corcoran was ignoring him. As long as he was a good boy, there were to be no more attacks.

The swelling on his face was almost gone, his bruises all but faded. His cracked ribs were another matter. Ribs flex with every breath – they can't be rested and they're a long time healing. Boots would be in pain for at least another month. Even worse, though his right eye was open and he was seeing well, his upper lid drooped noticeably. He was having headaches, too, in his right temple. The doctor was non-committal. Maybe Detective Littlewood's complaints would get better on their own, maybe not, but an eyelid can be raised with a little surgery and the headaches were infrequent and not debilitating.

'I'd say,' the doc told him, 'that you got off lucky.'

Meanwhile, between the droopy lid and the healing scar, thick as the veins on the Bulgarian's neck, he looked like a Prohibition-era villain. All he needed was a fedora and a tommy gun.

Boots dumped the Percocets ten days later, his pain diminished, if not vanished. By that time, he'd fielded calls from Detective Lenny Olmeda and Sergeant Craig O'Malley. Olmeda's came first. He phoned at ten o'clock in the morning to assure Boots that the investigation was ongoing and that everything possible had been done. When asked to describe his efforts, he complied without hesitation.

'Mark Dupont's lawyered up,' he explained, 'so we can't talk to him. But we'll be speakin' with some of his criminal associates. Believe me, we're not gonna let this go.'

Sergeant O'Malley called on Boots at home, knocking on Andy Littlewood's door at eight o'clock in the evening. Boots was sitting in his father's living room at the time, watching the Texas Rangers pound the crap out of a succession of Yankee pitchers. He was glad for the interruption.

'Where's the Bulgarian?'

'I left him in the car. He's been actin' weird lately.'

This was a road Boots was afraid to travel. He quickly changed the subject. 'What's up?' he asked.

'The story on Flint Page is that he was a suspect in a homicide.'

'I've known Page for a long time and I never made him for a killer.'

'Maybe he wasn't. This was a drug deal in Bed-Stuy that went bad and there were a lotta people in the room. The word I'm gettin' is that Homicide turned up a witness who claimed that Flint pulled the trigger. That don't mean it's true.'

Boots nodded in agreement. 'Any sign of Page?'

'None. Page is either in the wind or in the river. Now me, if I had to pick, I'd pick door number two.' O'Malley turned to leave, then looked back at Boots. 'I been talkin' about your situation with Boris. We don't like the way you got fucked around, so if we can do something, let us know.'

A month into his recuperation, on a Wednesday morning, Boots journeyed to the Manhattan offices of Thomas Galligan, the private investigator who employed Joaquin. Galligan wasn't a PI in the popular sense – he never left his office, nor did he customarily do business with the general public. Instead, he limited his activities to computer investigation, and his clients to lawyers and corporations. Galligan's specialty was uncovering hidden assets.

Galligan was standing behind his assistant's desk when Boots walked into the office, whispering something through the ink-black hair that covered her ear. Without changing expression, he raised his head to carefully examine his visitor's drooping eyelid and still-livid scar. Boots took advantage of the silence to perform an examination of his own. Galligan was short, soft and slovenly. He wore a cheap shirt, a cheap tie and a cheap brown suit, each article at least a size too big for his bony frame. Teased and heavily moussed, his brown hair rose a good four inches from the top of his scalp, a wispy wave that only made his small features smaller. This was especially true of the man's eyes, the pupils of which were shrunken to mere pinpoints. He was clearly stoned.

'Are you . . .' Galligan scratched his hip.

'Boots Littlewood,' Boots said, offering his hand.

'Tommy Galligan.' Without introducing his assistant, Galligan led Boots into a large room. 'This is where the work gets done,' he announced.

Four desks in the front of the room, arranged to form a cross, held computers, monitors, keyboards and a variety of peripheral devices. Behind them, a well-worn pool table dominated the remainder of the space.

Ignoring the pool table, Boots pointed to the computers. 'What can you do with them?'

Galligan let his weight drop back on his heels. Time for the sales pitch. 'All public records,' he began, 'including births, marriages, divorces, land transfers, law suits and criminal records. Memberships in organizations, from the Rotary Club to the Carpenter's Union to the Book of the Month Club. Any mention of the subject on almost any media: the Internet, television, newspapers or magazines, in books, in academic journals. I can get you the schools the subject attended, from kindergarten forward. And as for phone numbers and Social Security numbers – hell, if you've got a number, it's out there somewhere and I'll find it.'

Galligan paused for breath. Most of the clients he pitched interrupted at this point, to express amazement or outrage, but Littlewood just stood there, his encouraging smile firmly in place.

'I can supply the names and addresses of the subject's closest neighbors,' he continued, 'where the man works and approximately how much he earns. I can also assemble a consumer profile, using data mined from warranty forms. Cars, major appliances, high-end electronics, like that.'

This time, when Galligan paused, Boots spoke up. 'And all this is legal?'

'Absolutely.'

'We need to talk.'

Galligan winked, then led Boots into a cluttered office. He was still smiling when he closed the door behind them and took a chair on the far side of a battered partner's desk.

'Let me take up the issue of financial records. I might as well, because it always comes up later.' He scratched at the side of his neck and shifted his weight. 'Let's just say there's a black market in information out there, a network. I can tap in, but it doesn't come cheap.'

Boots took the only other seat in the room, on a wheeled office chair. 'I want to investigate an inspector in the NYPD named Mack Corcoran. I want you to concentrate on a two-year period.'

'What about financial records?'

'No, let's keep it legal for now. But I want to know everything else there is to know.'

Galligan leaned back in his chair. 'Two grand,' he said. 'As long as you're not askin' me to do anything illegal.' He smiled as broadly as his small mouth would allow. 'You understand, the databases I use – ChoicePoint, Seisint, LexisNexis – they don't let you run wild through their computers. They charge by the database and you want everything.'

Boots stared at Galligan for a moment, then suddenly wheeled his chair around to Galligan's side of the desk and pulled the top drawer open. Quickly, he shuffled through the pens, the Post-it pads, the discarded mouse, the tangle of cables.

'What are you doing?'

'Simple, ya junkie fuck. You're stoned out of your mind and I'm searchin' for your works. And when I find them . . .' Boots closed the top drawer, then drew open the drawer beneath. 'Hey, what's this?' He held up a small automatic handgun. 'You got a permit for this, Tommy?'

'You have no right—'

Boots shook his head vigorously. 'Don't give me any bullshit about rights. I happen to know that you charge your best customers a thousand dollars for this search we're talkin' about. I know because Joaquin told me. What made you think you could get away with disrespectin' me? How could you be so stupid?'

Galligan extended his hands, palms out, but Boots was not ready to make peace.

'Roll up your sleeves.'

'Look . . .'

'Don't argue, just do it.'

'OK, I admit it. You made me for a junkie. You're a regular Sherlock Holmes. Now what?' He wiped a sheen of perspiration from his forehead before adding, 'I can't believe I'm gettin' squeezed like this.'

'That's because you're naive about the criminal justice system.' Boots laid Galligan's weapon on top of the desk. 'Now, first, you're gonna knock down that two grand to five hundred. Second, you're gonna answer a simple question, and I sincerely advise you to think twice before lyin' to me. Is Joaquin usin' dope?'

The surprised look on Galligan's face told the story before he uttered a sound. 'Never. The kid's square.'

'Then what is he doin' here? Why did you hire him?'

'City College has a placement office for students lookin' for work. I called them and they sent Joaquin. End of story.'

Galligan breathed a sigh of relief when Boots fished out a roll of bills. In fact, he commonly ran this search for two hundred dollars, a figure Joaquin could not have known. The cop was scary, but he'd guessed wrong this time.

'Originally,' Galligan said as he accepted payment, 'I hired Joaquin because he was cheap and willing to work part-time. But it turns out the kid's a genius at mining data. Like I already said, these outfits are set up to make you spend as much as possible, so if you're not efficient, you're gonna be out of business in a hurry. Joaquin, he's better than I am, and that's a high compliment.'

TWENTY

F ive weeks after leaving the hospital, Boots made his way to the basement of his father's house. He walked through the laundry room and into a smaller room at the back, carrying with him a bucket filled with soapy water, an assortment of sponges and a package of throwaway dust cloths. For a moment, he simply eyeballed the dumbbells, plates and bars scattered about the room. Then he went to work.

Boots had begun lifting weights in high school, when he was a scrawny freshman hoping to make the baseball team. He kept at it after he met his goal, often accompanied by his neighborhood buddies, including Frankie Drago, until he finally graduated. Following high school, Boots spent three years in the Army – as far as he could remember, he never gave weightlifting a second thought. It was only when he discovered the weight room in the bowels of the Six-Four that he started lifting again. Of course, he had practical reasons for the hours he spent pumping iron. The streets could be very unforgiving – size and strength not only gave you an advantage if you had to fight, they often deterred violence before it happened. And there were networking opportunities as well. The regulars accepted him once he proved himself to be a serious lifter, including a detective-sergeant named Steve

Guardino. It was Guardino who first recommended Boots to the Detective Bureau, acting as his rabbi.

And there was still another benefit, a less tangible benefit to be sure, but a benefit nonetheless. Tai Chi for knuckleheads: this was how Boots eventually came to understand his hobby. As the ritual played out, his focus tended to narrow, his judgment sharpen. This effect had only increased over the years, especially when he turned away from the goal of improvement, when he eased back on the weights and allowed himself to be guided by the internal rhythm of the workout. And Boots definitely felt that he needed guidance. He'd reviewed the profile of Mack Corcoran amassed by Tommy Galligan and found nothing out of order; the only item of interest was Corcoran somehow qualifying his son, who had cerebral palsy, for Medicaid.

Boots spent the entire morning cleaning the room. Then he ate lunch, strapped his ribcage with an ace bandage and worked out for thirty minutes. Barely able to rise from his bed the next morning, he was in pain for most of the afternoon. Nevertheless, he went back downstairs every other day until he gradually assembled enough puzzle pieces to map out a series of short-term goals. Now it was up to his ribs. When he finished a workout free of pain, he'd be ready.

He was just about there a week later, when Joaquin showed up.

'You busy?' Joaquin asked.

'Actually, I been wantin' to talk to you.'

Except for the ace bandage, Boots was naked to the waist. Again, Joaquin was struck by his size, and by how much smaller he looked in a suit and vest. But the costume wouldn't do Boots any good now. Between the scar and the eyelid, the man was fucking gruesome.

'So, what's up with your recovery? Galligan told me that you and him worked out a deal.'

'That's somethin' else I wanna talk about. Do you know he's a junkie?'

Taken off-guard, Joaquin's pale cheeks reddened. 'I never caught him with a spike in his hand, but it's pretty obvious. Sometimes, in the late afternoon, he nods out in his chair.'

'You're not afraid it'll rub off on you?'

'Boots, I only work for the guy, and part-time at that. What he does with his life isn't my business. Only don't get the idea that Galligan's a street junkie. Tommy's makin' money hand over fist.'

'Gimme a break. You could buy the jerk's wardrobe at a thrift shop for thirty-five cents.'

'That's his Elvis Costello look. Galligan wants to believe that he's some kind of outlaw.'

Boots considered this for a moment, thinking that maybe there was more to the PI than he'd first thought, that maybe he'd have to renegotiate his original negotiation.

'Galligan said that you're a genius at the work.'

'He went further than that. He offered me a full partnership.' Joaquin stared at a massive barbell, its plates seeming as big as manhole covers. 'I was really tempted because I think I could triple the volume within a couple of years.'

'How so?'

'Boots, gimme a one-word description of Galligan's set-up.'

'Shithole.'

'Exactly. Corporate clients expect a little show, a little hi-tech glitz. Shitholes with rock-and-roll outlaw bosses don't impress them. What I'd do, if it was up to me, is put twenty computers in that room, put 'em in little niches against the wall, and set 'em to humming when I brought clients in. See, information brokers discount for high volume, so the more business you do, the lower your costs. Meantime, Galligan loses clients as fast he brings them in.'

'So, you turned him down.'

'Yeah.'

'Was it the dope?'

'That was part of it. But there's also the illegal searches. Boots, the guy's makin' money in a business with a tremendous potential for expansion. He doesn't have to do anything illegal. Meanwhile, if he gets caught, it's bye-bye license. Now, why would he take that chance?'

'Because he's an asshole?'

'Word up.'

Boots slid a t-shirt over his head and pulled it down. The pain in his side was minimal now, more the expectation of pain than pain itself. 'What about the sleaze? Invading people's privacy?'

'Does privacy give a spouse the right to hide assets in a divorce case? Does it give someone the right to defraud a bank? Or to lie on a resumé? Or to avoid a judgment rendered by a jury? And keep in mind, Boots, the information is already out there. All we do is collect it.'

Suddenly, Boots grinned. 'Well, if that's the way you feel, you oughta take Galligan up on his offer. The man's weak, Jackie. If you lean on him from time to time, he'll mostly be a good boy. And if he's not? A year from now, after you get to know the customers, you can muscle him out.'

Boots made one more stop before putting his initial tactics into play, at the home of Vinnie Palermo's Aunt Connie. He arrived at noon, having walked the ten blocks without any discomfort. For a moment, he stood outside the narrow, two-story home, so much like his father's. Then he took a deep breath and knocked on the door.

'Well, you got a pair of balls, showin' up here.'

'That's right, Connie, and I'd appreciate you not bustin' 'em. Lemme in for a minute. I need to talk to you.'

Connie Palermo stood in the door with her hands on her hips. Twice divorced, she was in her early sixties, a thickly built woman with the piercing eyes of a winged predator.

'Hey, *strunz*, check it out. You don't tell me what to do.'

Boots shifted her out of the way and walked through the door. 'Ya know,' he said, noting that his little move had been pain-free, 'it's Vinnie's own fault. I read him his rights, even though he was only a witness at the time. It's a lot more than I'd do for anybody else.'

Connie followed him into the living room, her jaw trembling with righteous anger. 'He trusted you, Boots. That's why he said what he said. Vinnie thought you'd protect him.'

Boots rubbed at the scar on his forehead as he contemplated the price he'd already paid for Vinnie Palermo's big mouth.

'How's he doin'?'

'Vinnie?'

'Yeah, Vinnie.'

Connie plopped down on a white, sectional couch. 'He's havin' a hard time, Boots. Vinnie's not strong enough for Rikers Island.'

'If that's the case, he shouldn't have been out stealin' cars.'

Connie Palermo's eyes spewed fire. It was all Boots could do not to flinch.

'Get out of my house, Boots. You don't, I swear to God, I'll make you hurt me.'

Boots ignored the outburst. 'I wanna send Vinnie a message. For his ears only. If you talk it around, especially to Vinnie's lawyer, it's gonna work against him.'

For a moment, Connie didn't move at all, and Boots knew he'd taken her off-guard.

'What are you saying?' she finally asked.

'Tell Vinnie to hang on. It might still work out.'

'Yeah, you mean that?'

'Yeah, I do.'

TWENTY-ONE

On Monday, June 14th, two months after he was attacked, Boots found himself sitting in a car on Fresh Pond Road in the Queens community of Ridgewood. It was nine o'clock at night and he was waiting for Detective Artie Farrahan to emerge from the Pink Rose, a small neighborhood bar. The city was in the grasp of an early heatwave, the temperature in the mid-eighties, the humidity above seventy percent.

Boots wanted a cigarette so bad that he could hardly sit still. This was one of those times, he knew, when it was just as well that he had no access to nicotine. If he hadn't already tried a dozen times in the past few months, he would have searched beneath the seats for a mislaid pack.

The Chevy was parked in the shadows of a gnarled sycamore that towered over the row of houses on the block. Boots had the radio on, despite the obvious need for stealth. The Yankees were playing the Orioles at Camden Yards, one of the league's smaller parks and a feasting place for New York's sluggers. Granderson and Montero had already parked the ball in the right field seats, while Robinson Cano had lined a hanging curve ball off the center field wall that came within six inches of leaving the park. In fact, the game would've been over by the third inning if only the Yankees' pitching had held up. Unfortunately, the Orioles had jumped all over Ivan Nova in the bottom of the second, pounding out nine hits before Joe Girardi called in Hector Noesi to put out the fire.

Boots waved at a mosquito that buzzed his left ear. An instant later, he felt the insect land on the back of his neck. He slapped down hard, but his skin began to itch before he withdrew his hand. Hoping this would be the only race he lost tonight, Boots said a little prayer.

The Chevy was facing away from the Pink Rose, so that the driver's door opened on the street. With the bulb in the overhead light removed, Boots was able to leave the door slightly ajar without attracting attention. He was scrunched down behind the wheel, with the seat all the way back, his eyes glued to the rear-view mirror.

As the minutes ticked away, his thoughts were inevitably drawn to the recent past, to the long period of waiting. The delay had been forced on him by his injuries, and it wasn't only his ribs. For the first few weeks, he couldn't put two thoughts together. Yet he'd somehow managed to function. He'd shored up his flanks and thrown his enemies off the scent. Proof of the last had come only a short time before. Rather than track down Artie Farrahan, Boots had simply waited outside Brooklyn North for the man to emerge, then followed him. Farrahan had barely glanced in the mirror on the twenty-minute drive to Ridgewood.

The door of the Pink Rose opened and Boots jerked his eyes to the rear-view mirror. The tall blonde who emerged looked both ways before strolling off in the opposite direction. Boots watched her for a moment, then let his eyes drift to a crescent moon just visible on the horizon. Screened by the haze and a layer of thin clouds, the moon had no distinct edges, its light seeming to bleed into the atmosphere. On the radio, John Sterling described Noesi's mastery of the Oriole line-up.

Boots lowered the volume and settled in to wait. A half-hour passed, then another, but the delay only helped to settle him down. Nor was he unduly affected by the Yankee's narrow defeat, though he found the post-game wrap-up a depressing mix of bullshit and excuses. The Yanks had lost because Joe Girardi had a fixation with not yanking pitchers early. Joe wanted to build their confidence, or so he claimed, especially with the younger pitchers. Boots couldn't see it, not with all that money on the table. Shut up and pitch was the way he felt as he turned off the radio.

At ten fifteen, Artie Farrahan emerged from the Pink Rose. Alone, he limped toward Boots, weaving as he came. Boots waited patiently, until Farrahan tried to yank a cigarette from a crumpled pack and stumbled, dropping to one knee. Then Boots slid his fingers into a pair of leather gloves, opened the door and slid out into the street.

Crouched beneath the window line, he closed the door without latching it. His heart was pounding now, and he had to will himself to ignore the adrenaline pumping through his veins, to open his ears, to listen. Fortunately, Detective Farrahan provided unwitting assistance. He sang as he came – 'Danny Boy', in a surprisingly sweet falsetto.

Boots dropped down to peer beneath the car at Farrahan's shiny-black loafers, cursing to himself when they came to a stop behind the rear tire. A second later, a cigarette dropped to the sidewalk, emitting a tiny cloud of red sparks. Farrahan made several attempts to extinguish the smoldering butt, the sole of his shoe first coming down on one side, then the other. Finally, he moved on.

When Farrahan reached the front fender, Boots rose from his crouch and came around the trunk, gathering speed as he turned on to the sidewalk. Stealth, of course, was not a realistic possibility for a man his size. As Boots knew he would, Farrahan heard the footsteps pounding toward him. He had just enough time to execute a wobbly half-circle, to register what was about to happen, before Detective Littlewood's shoulder crashed into his chest.

Farrahan fell backward, his head striking the concrete with an audible thunk. Barely conscious, he made a feeble attempt to unbutton his jacket, to reach for his weapon. But then Boots was on top of him and the best he could do was raise a hand and beg.

'Boots, please, please.'

Boots recalled his own attempt to survive. No mercy had been show him then. He would show no mercy here. He yanked Artie Farrahan to his feet, propped him up against a parked car and drove his right fist into Farrahan's side, over and over again, until something finally cracked. Then he shifted the assault to Farrahan's face and hammered away. Blood was running now, from the back of Farrahan's scalp and from his crushed nose. Still, Boots didn't stop until the man's eyes closed and he went limp. Then he took

Farrahan's pulse, finding it strong and regular, before dropping him to the pavement.

As he walked back to his car, Boots experienced a single moment of buyer's remorse. If he was wrong, wrong about everything, he'd be in jail by morning. On the other hand, if he was right, Jill Kelly would come knocking on his door, cigarette in hand. Not a bad gamble when he thought it out. Not bad at all.

TWENTY-TWO

B oots was in his kitchen at ten o'clock on the following morning, cleaning the trap beneath the sink, when his father came into the room. By then, Boots had read all three New York newspapers and watched the news on every channel, broadcast and cable. No mention had been made of Artie Farrahan.

'You were right,' Andy Littlewood said. 'She's here.'

'Jill Kelly?'

'Cobalt eyes. Carries the map of Ireland on her face?'

'That's her.' Boots looked down at his greasy hands. 'Why don't you park her in the living room, tell her I'll be out in a minute?'

Boots soaped his hands before turning on the water in the sink. For several seconds, the drain ran freely, but then little jets of muddy water began to fill the basin. Boots cursed silently. It would take him the better part of the afternoon to pull the trap and clean it out.

Boots dried his hands, then went to meet his guest. He had a greeting all prepared, something light: 'Hey, what's a nice girl like you doing in Greenpoint?' But the words stuck in his throat when Jill Kelly's eyes dug into his. Boots held her gaze long enough to assure himself that he wasn't intimidated, then laid a small ashtray on the end table to her left.

'You wanna smoke, feel free.'

Boots Littlewood's living room might have been designed by a decorator from the Salvation Army. Though he had the money to refurnish (and Libby Greenspan was eager to assist), Boots liked his home the way it was. The mismatched end tables, the glass coffee table with the chip in the corner, a worn sofa, a Queen Anne chair, a pair of recliners, one blue, one black – all arranged to face a fifty-inch, flat-screen television.

Boots took a seat on the couch, stationing himself as close to the ashtray as possible.

'I've been expecting you,' he said. The statement was meant to challenge, but Jill's gaze didn't waver. Boots smiled. 'So, how's Artie?'

'Farrahan claims that he doesn't remember a thing.' Kelly wore an off-white linen jacket over white slacks and a navy blouse just a shade darker than her eyes. She tugged on the jacket's lapel. 'I made a bet with Uncle Mike when you originally got jumped. I bet you wouldn't take it lyin' down.'

Boots assumed that Uncle Mike was Michael Shaw, Chief of Detectives. 'I might've let it go, if they hadn't marked me. But I'll still take that as a compliment.'

'Which is how it was meant.' Jill fished in her pocket, finally pulled out a pack of Virginia Slims and a lighter. Taking her time, she lit up and drew the smoke into her lungs. 'So, tell me, Boots, how did you know?'

Boots took a deep breath when Jill Kelly exhaled, even though she blew the smoke away from him. 'You wouldn't be wearing a wire, would you?' he asked.

Kelly opened her jacket to reveal a Browning nine-millimeter tucked into a polymer holster on the left side of her belt. Designed to facilitate a quick draw, the holster had a backward rake that tilted the weapon toward her right hand.

'You wanna search me?'

'Desperately,' Boots cheerfully admitted. When Jill laughed, he continued. 'Now, the question you're askin', if I read you right, is how I knew I could get away with assaulting Artie Farrahan.'

'And how you knew I'd show up.'

Boots leaned forward, dropping his elbows to his knees. 'I expected Corcoran to come after me when I turned up Rajiv Visnawana. You know about Rajiv?' He waited for Kelly to nod, then continued. 'I was afraid Corcoran would have me transferred to eastern Queens or the northern Bronx, or convince IAB to open a file, or maybe even bring me up on charges, try to bust me back to patrol. But a physical attack? It never crossed my mind. I walked into that apartment as innocent as a baby.'

'I'll bet you grew up pretty quick.'

'Not really. In fact, my first thought – when I could think again – was kind of admiring. I never figured Corcoran to have the balls. It took a while before I realized that attacking me was an act of desperation.'

'What made you change your mind?'

'The risks, Jill. I kept askin' myself why Corcoran took all those risks when he could have operated behind the scenes. Keep in mind, anything might have gone wrong. They might've been seen, coming in or going out. Or I might've sensed the trap, or gotten to my gun and shot one of them. As it was, I managed to hurt Farrahan enough for the injury to show up later on.'

'The limp? That was you?'

'Yeah.' Boots turned his head into the smoke when Jill ground her cigarette into the ashtray. The scent hit his brain like a phero-mone. 'What I finally decided was this. First, Corcoran didn't use the job to teach me a lesson because he couldn't. Second, he couldn't because somebody was protecting me. Third, that somebody was Michael Shaw, Chief of Detectives, brother-in-law of Patrick Kelly. See, I already knew that Olmeda, Corcoran, Parker, Farrahan and your father served on a task force set up to investigate a serial killer. And I also knew that your father was shot to death a year later.'

Boots paused, waiting for Jill Kelly to flinch. She didn't. 'Corcoran might not have been swift enough to figure this out beforehand. Myself, I think he was a victim of his own ego. But I'm sure he understands by now. We're locked out of the criminal justice system and neither of us can call the cops. The explanations would be too damning. That's why Artie clammed up.'

Jill considered this for a moment, then said, 'So, what do you want from me?'

'What I want is Vinnie Palermo out of jail.'

'In that case, you and Uncle Mike are in sync.' Jill brushed her hair away from the side of her head. 'I know it's impolite to ask, but you wouldn't happen to have a cup of coffee to spare? I've been up all night.'

This was exactly what Boots had been hoping for. He led Jill Kelly through the kitchen to a sink half-filled with greasy water. 'Looks like we'll have to go out. I don't know about you, but I'm hungry anyhow.'

The plan was to drive to a restaurant thirty minutes away in Park Slope, with the windows up and locked. But Jill Kelly disappointed him.

'Forget the coffee; I have to get some sleep,' she said as she returned to her chair. 'I had a long talk with Uncle Mike before I came by. He gave me a list of items that I'm supposed to keep to myself, including his part in the play. But me, I like to lay things out. That's why I'm a crappy detective.' She paused long enough to light another cigarette. 'So let me say this. I'm not Uncle Mike's dog, though he does his best to keep me on a short leash.'

'Why?'

'Because the Kellys have been players in the NYPD for generations. Because Michael Shaw hitched a ride on the Kelly reputation when he married into the family. Because he now claims to be the family patriarch, and family patriarchs consider independence, especially on the part of females, an abomination unto God.'

Boots took a deep breath. The windows were shut and the room was filling with smoke. Maybe he could stretch the conversation out all afternoon. 'Were you at home,' he asked, 'when your father was shot?'

Jill blinked, then grinned. 'See, right there. You waited until I was distracted, then pushed one of my buttons. I'm not subtle enough for that. And the answer to your question is yes, I was there, in the house.'

'And that's why you came to my house? Your father?' Boots crossed his legs. He was wearing a pair of ratty jeans and a white t-shirt washed so many times it was nearly transparent. His drain-clearing outfit. 'I'm not tryin' to confront you, Jill, but if you're not workin' for your uncle, you have to have another reason for knockin' on my door. I want to know that reason.' He smiled. 'For obvious reasons.'

Jill Kelly folded her arms beneath her breasts. Boots had flipped the conversation on its head. She'd come expecting to put him through his paces and he was the one holding up the hoops. Watch him, she told herself, and don't underestimate him. Never assume that you know what he's thinking.

'The investigation went on for eighteen months,' she finally said. 'Detectives grilled every felon my father arrested, going back two years. Every family member and every friend of the family was interviewed.'

'I take it nothing turned up?'

'Not a single viable suspect.'

'But you're somehow connecting his death to his work on the Lipstick Killer task force.'

Kelly remained quiet for a moment. Then she changed the subject. 'We'll have a new Mayor next year,' she said, 'because our current Mayor is term-limited. A new Mayor means a new Commissioner. Down at the Puzzle Palace, the Chiefs are drooling over the prospect. Think about it. These men have spent their entire working lives moving up the ladder. They passed the sergeants', lieutenants' and captains' exams. They received advanced degrees from prominent universities. They were promoted from Captain, to Deputy Inspector, to Inspector, to Deputy Chief, to Chief. Boots, the only up from Chief is Commissioner.'

Andy Littlewood took that moment to enter the apartment. He slowed momentarily when he caught sight of Jill Kelly holding a cigarette. Andy hadn't allowed a cigarette to be smoked in his own apartment since the day he quit fifteen years before. Finally, he came forward and laid a tray on the glass table in front of the couch. The tray bore a carafe of coffee, two mugs and several slices of carrot cake.

'My son warned me,' he said, his brogue thick enough to be peat, 'not to call you a lass. But by all that's holy, when I look into your eyes, I can find no other words.'

'Thanks for the coffee.'

Andy Littlewood's smile wavered for a moment, then vanished. 'Well, then, I can see you're busy.'

Jill continued on as though they'd never been interrupted. 'Now, here's the thing. Uncle Mike would sell his soul to be named Commissioner, but he's not an idiot – no Chief of D has ever made it to the top. But Uncle Mike's willing to settle for second best, which is his job. He wants to remain Chief of Detectives after the changeover.'

'And Mario Polanco is how he plans to do it?' Boots asked. Mario Polanco was Chief of Internal Affairs.

'Exactly. Polanco is one of the hopefuls and Uncle Mike's been his running dog for years. If Polanco's named Commissioner, Michael Shaw remains Chief of D. It's that simple.'

'What's Corcoran's connection?'

'Corcoran's rabbi is the Chief of Department, Eamon Gogarty, who has more political connections in New York than the Mayor. He's everybody's favorite. Polanco's hoping to bring Gogarty down a peg.'

'And how do I fit in?'

'When Vinnie Palermo's arrest was announced, Eamon Gogarty and Mack Corcoran were both standing on the platform, along with the Mayor and the Commissioner.'

'So, if Vinnie's cleared, the blame will fall on Polanco's rivals.' Boots took a second to add up the columns. 'Are you telling me that Michael Shaw doesn't want me to look at his brother-in-law's murder? He's willing to let that go?'

'Listen and learn, Boots. If Michael Shaw had to choose between his own interests and the interests of God Almighty, he wouldn't hesitate for a minute. And he won't hesitate to feed you all the rope you want, then hang you with it if you fail to advance those interests.'

'In that case, you better hope I know what I'm doin', because the way I'm gonna set things up, Mike Shaw won't be able to hang Boots Littlewood without also hanging Jill Kelly.'

Jill crossed her legs, noting Boots Littlewood's gaze flick to her thighs. 'Why don't we get down to business,' she said. 'Tell me what you want.'

TWENTY-THREE

Boots had a list of demands all ready to go, a list he'd been preparing for weeks. He was about to begin with the items at the top of the list when his house phone rang.

'Boots, it's Fianna Walsh speakin'. You remember when you asked us to watch for the cops? Well, there's one sittin' right down the block.'

'In uniform?'

'No, but we talked it over and Jenicka's sure. The guy's definitely watchin' your house.'

'When did he show up?'

'Right after your . . . your little visitor.'

Boots was still smiling when he re-entered the living room. Boots beaten up? Cops on the block? Little visitors? Even the heaven to which Fianna and the ladies fully expected to ascend couldn't be more joyful than this.

'Problem?' Jill asked.

'Yeah, we've got an uninvited guest sittin' in a car up the block. Time for a little walk.'

'What do you plan to do?'

'Show you off.'

'Is that the price? Jill Kelly as your protector?'

Boots ignored the jibe. 'Actually, the price is a lot higher. First thing, I want to be returned to active duty, but I don't want to report to anyone but you. And no paper trail, either. I keep my notes to myself until such time as I decide to release them. Otherwise, I'll work things out on my own.'

A pair of roses blossomed in Jill Kelly's cheeks. Irish roses, no doubt, roses of Killarney. 'What else?'

'The case files on the Lipstick Killer, Patrick Kelly and Chris Parker, along with any relevant IAB files, and time enough to study them. After that, you get to watch my back on the street. The way I understand it, you've got the eyes of an eagle and the balls of a wolverine.'

This time Jill got the message. A spank on the ass, a pat on the head. 'If your only goal is to liberate Vinnie Palermo, what do you want with the other files?'

Boots shook his head. His demands were non-negotiable. 'You don't mind, I'm gonna head for the bedroom and change my clothes. I was raised in Greenpoint and I have to meet neighborhood standards.'

Now Kelly was laughing. 'Neighborhood standards? Boots, you better look in the mirror. Because if your face is the neighborhood standard, it's time to emigrate.'

Lenny Olmeda's eyes jumped back and forth, from Boots to Jill, as he watched them approach. He was wondering which of the two was actually in charge. The question was answered when Boots leaned into the window, his face close enough to count the fading stitch-marks on his forehead. Olmeda braced himself. Corcoran's instructions were succinct: Find out what he wants. Lenny Olmeda could only hope it wasn't a pound of his flesh.

'I was just coming to see you, Boots.'

'What about?'

'The case, man. I came about the case. It looks like you were right. The rumor on the street is that Mark Dupont—'

'Forget it, Lenny. Mark Dupont had nothing to do with what happened to me. I only said that to buy a little time. Now, listen close to what I'm tellin' you. Me and Jill are gonna walk around the block. If you're still parked here when we get back, I'll do to you what I did to Artie Farrahan. Plus, you should tell your boss that if he sends somebody else, I'm going to assume that individual means to do me harm and act appropriately.'

Boots straightened up and turned to face his partner. Jill Kelly was standing a few feet to the left, seeming entirely at ease except for a single detail, a detail only a cop would notice. Though her shoulders were relaxed and her arms hung at her sides, she was grasping the hem of her linen jacket with the thumb and forefinger of her left hand. If she needed to reach her weapon, of course, she'd have to get her jacket out of the way.

'So,' he said as he led her up the block, 'I heard you're a great shot. Where'd you learn?'

'My father was big on self-protection. I was ten when he enrolled me in a class at the range in Sunnyside. I took to it right away.'

'Why do you think that was?'

Jill glanced over her shoulder as Olmeda pulled away from the curb and headed down the block. 'I'm not a big fan of psychiatry,' she told Boots. 'To my mind, the examined life's not worth living. But I'll tell you this, there's a lot to be said for being really good at something. After I came within ten points of making the Olympic team last year, my self-esteem went through the roof.'

Boots watched Jill light a cigarette, carefully gauged the direction of an intermittent breeze, finally dropped a step behind her. From this position, he could observe the rise and fall of her buttocks without her catching him at it. To his experienced eye, they appeared as confident as the rest of her.

'I was never that good at anything,' he said, 'but I once hit a baseball four hundred feet. That was in a PAL championship game. Talk about a sweet spot. It felt like I hit a golf ball.'

'Did you win?'

'Win what?'

'The game.'

'No, we lost.'

Jill wiped the sweat off her forehead. 'Sorry to hear that.'

Forty-eight hours later, Boots got what he wanted: a mountain of paper that he and Jill carried to an unused bedroom in his apartment. The Lipstick Killer task force had included nearly a hundred cops investigating four homicides. Apparently, they'd toiled night and day, conducting thousands of interviews which now filled several dozen boxes. The paper generated by the year-long Pat Kelly investigation filled a dozen more. Chris Parker, by comparison, was the neglected orphan, two boxes sufficient to contain the entirety of the investigation into his death.

'Hope you brought your reading glasses.'

'Gimme a break. I just turned forty. I can read without glasses.'

'Sorry. The scar – it makes you look older.'

'Now who's pressing buttons?'

They were standing on opposite sides of a wooden desk, both grinning, both sweating. 'I realize it's not my place to ask,' Jill said, 'but what do you plan to do with all this?'

'Find a place to begin.'

'And how long will that take?'

'A couple of days? A couple of weeks? I only know we can't afford a lot of dead ends, there being only the pair of us. Of course, you could make both our jobs a lot easier.'

'Me?'

The corner of Jill Kelly's mouth slid a few millimeters to the left. A smile? A sneer? Boots maintained a neutral expression as he continued. 'Your father was murdered six years ago and you've been out for revenge ever since. This I can tell just by looking into your eyes. And I don't blame you. If it was my father, and I had to look at his body—'

'Get to the point, Boots. I don't want to hear any more bullshit.'

'OK. Why did you suddenly show up at Brooklyn North after Parker was killed? Why were you assigned to the case? Is there anything you need to tell me that I won't find in the files?'

'Boots, it's like I already said. Uncle Mike sent me to keep an eye on Corcoran.'

'Now who's bullshitting?'

This time Jill's smile was quick and genuine. 'Well, that's my story,' she declared, 'and I'm stickin' to it.'

TWENTY-FOUR

B oots got busy within minutes after Jill Kelly's departure. He had no intention of spending weeks, or even days, working through the files. If the answers were buried somewhere in the mass of paper filling the room, Jill and her uncle, the Chief of Detectives, would already know it. But that didn't mean there was nothing to be gained, no questions to be answered. First, there was the need to impress Jill with his diligence when next she visited his humble home, and to deceive her if necessary.

Boots spent the next three hours examining the Chris Parker files. He found no trace of Rajiv Visnawana's statement, nor any mention of the Hoyden of Humiliation. Instead, the paperwork documented a thorough neighborhood canvas, including six statements given by individuals who'd also testified before the grand jury. The statements were uniform in nature: two shots fired, a dash to the window, a car pulling away, a body on the corner.

After skimming the witness statements, Boots quickly reviewed the autopsy report which included a dozen photographs. One photo especially caught his attention. Chris Parker was positioned on his back prior to the beginning of the autopsy, staring up at the camera through his open right eye. His left eye was an empty socket, the bullet fired into the back of his skull having chosen this point to exit his body. A second exit wound appeared six inches to the left of his navel, and what appeared to be a third wound crossed his right hip. But when Boots took a closer look, the gash on Parker's hip was a healed scar sunk deep into the underlying muscle. It looked as if his flesh had been gouged.

Boots replaced the autopsy report, then turned to an unmarked folder tucked away at the rear of the box. Inside, he found a single sheet of Internal Affairs Bureau stationery. He read it quickly, then read it again. A drug dealer from the Brooklyn neighborhood of Bedford-Stuyvesant named Maurice Selman, facing serious federal time, had claimed that Chris Parker was extorting money from his operation. The item had been routinely forwarded to Internal Affairs by the FBI, though no proof was offered, and IAB had routinely opened a file, but made no effort to follow up.

On one level, this was less than nothing. Vague accusations against cops assigned to Narcotics Division are an everyday occurrence. But two things caught Boots's attention. First, the allegation had been made six years before, within a few months of Patrick Kelly's murder. Then there was Maurice Selman, a legendary drug dealer well known to New York cops. Selman had been shot down shortly after his release from prison, probably by a rival named Elijah 'Maytag' LeGuin. Cock of the walk in the Bed-Stuy projects, LeGuin had earned his street name as an eight-year-old when he drowned the family cat in a washing machine.

Boots turned next to the thirty-seven boxes containing the Lipstick Killer files. Reading through them was clearly beyond his capacity and he limited his attention to three items: the crimes scene photographs, the statement given by Jules Cosyn following his arrest and a profile worked up by Detective Adam Khouri, the NYPD's Quantico-trained profiler.

Boots took the crime scene photos into the living room and spread them out on the floor, separating the four scenes. Then he crawled from one to another in search of any indication that all four murders were not committed by a single individual. He found none. The crime scenes were as uniform as they were depressing. Each of the women had been strangled in a public space – two on stairwells, one as she entered her apartment, one in a basement laundry. The attack on the woman entering her apartment was the most telling. Her killer might simply have pushed her through the open doorway, then taken the time to enjoy himself, or at least to conceal her body. Instead, she was found lying across the threshold, fully clothed, her face smeared with her own lipstick.

Like Boots, Adam Khouri had made much of this particular attack in concluding that the perpetrator was disorganized and severely delusional. Many other factors supported this judgment. Though he placed no great faith in profilers, Boots could see them clearly. Each of the women was killed in a blitz attack that left her dead within two minutes. There was no sign of the sadistic behavior associated with organized serial killers like Ted Bundy, nor was there evidence of a sexual motivation. All the victims were fully clothed when discovered, and the lipstick marks (which the media had made so much of) were limited to random smears with the victims' own lipsticks. In fact, there was no indication that Cosyn had brought anything with him to the crimes scenes – no restraints, no weapons.

The subject, Adam Khouri wrote in his summary, *is a white male in his mid- to late twenties. He will have been diagnosed a paranoid schizophrenic in early adolescence and have a long history of institutional care. Although he sometimes lives with his parents, he is currently homeless. Just as he has no plan of attack before an assault, he will have no plan of escape afterward. Look for him to linger within a block or two of a particular crime scene for several hours. He will be dirty, disheveled and confused when approached, but he will speak to investigators if properly handled. Under no circumstances should he be exposed to stressful interrogative techniques. If pressed, he is likely to retreat into his paranoid delusions. If allowed to proceed under gentle questioning, he will eventually reveal his motive for the homicides.*

Boots was about to check the profiler's final prediction by examining Jules Cosyn's statement when he heard a knock on the door.

'Hey, Boots, open up. My hands are full.'

Libby Greenspan to the rescue. It was past seven and Boots hadn't eaten since breakfast. He opened the door to find Libby holding a tray loaded with lasagna, mesclun salad and a small loaf of seeded Italian bread.

'Your father says I'm supposed to stay with you until you eat.'

'Does he?' His mouth already filling with saliva, Boots took the tray and set it on his coffee table.

'Myself, I don't think you need a mother.'

Boots picked up the knife and fork on the tray. 'What're you saying, Libby?'

'Your father and I have been talking about marriage. I think he already spoke to you.'

'He did.'

'Andy tells me you didn't have much to say.'

'My opinion wasn't asked for.'

'Well, I'm asking now.'

Boots carried a chunk of lasagna to his lips, pausing a moment to let the steam drift into his nostrils. 'How old are you, Libby? Forty-four? Forty-five?'

'Forty-seven.'

'Well, my father's sixty-seven.' Boots looked directly into Libby's hazel eyes. She was a good woman, quick to smile and full of energy. As far as he could tell, she didn't have a mean bone in her body. 'Right now, Dad's healthy. In fact, I'd have to say he's rejuvenated since he met you. But down the line, that's all gonna change. I don't know how long it'll take – maybe five years, maybe ten. But however long it is, one morning you'll wake up and realize that you've gone from wife to nurse. You'll realize that the last of your good years will be spent caring for Andy in his bad years.'

Libby shook her head. Somehow, she hadn't expected Boots to get right to the point, the one she'd been thinking about for the past two months. Stupid of her, to be sure.

'I love Andy,' she said. 'Beyond that, I can only say this: I'll never desert him, no matter how bad it gets. And I know Andy will never desert me. Remember, the difference in our ages doesn't mean that he'll go first, or be the first to get sick.'

As Boots returned to his dinner, he remembered that Libby, an only child and childless herself, had no close relatives. 'You know it's gonna be a church wedding, right? You'll be married by a Catholic priest?'

'Followed by a Jewish ceremony at home.'

'Well, I can't say I know much about Jewish ceremonies, but if you want, when you walk down the aisle at Mount Carmel, I'll walk beside you.'

Libby's eyes welled up, as Boots had known they would. She reached out to touch his hand.

'Boots Littlewood,' she said, 'you are such a prick.'

The impending union of Andy Littlewood and Libby Greenspan fled Detective Littlewood's mind before Libby reached the bottom of the stairs. He turned on the Yankee game, which was in the third inning, and muted the sound. Then he retrieved Jules Cosyn's

recorded statement, which ran to forty pages and was every bit as
delusional as Khouri had predicted. Here, Boots was greatly aided
by the efficiency of the task force. Passages that bolstered the state's
assertion that Jules had confessed were highlighted. Most of these
involved references to the malevolent female deity who plagued
Cosyn's days. This deity, who bore many titles, including the Great
Whore of the Seven Systems, generally lived on Venus, but had
been recently kidnapped and taken to Saturn where the planet's
rings were actually her chains. For reasons unexplained, Jules Cosyn
had facilitated the kidnapping and was now the target of the Great
Whore's minions. These lesser demons appeared to be ordinary
human females but were actually soul-sucking vampires. Killing
them was the only way Jules could secure his personal survival.

Satisfied, Boots returned the files to their appropriate boxes. Jules
Cosyn fit Adam Khouri's profile as if designed for no other purpose,
virtually every element falling into place. Twenty-six years old,
Cosyn had been diagnosed a paranoid schizophrenic at fourteen,
been in and out of various institutions, lived on and off with his
parents, been within a block of the last crime scene when first
approached by investigators.

Bottom line, the Lipstick Killer investigation was righteous and
there was no reason to suppose any connection between that investigation and the death of Patrick Kelly.

Boots glanced at the clock as he retrieved the Kelly files. It was now
approaching eleven o'clock. He'd been at it for more than twelve
hours and he had hours to go. He considered retreating to his bedroom,
catching a few hours' sleep, but decided to continue. He had plans
for the following day and he would have to be out early. There wasn't
all that much to review anyway. The small task force assigned to
the investigation had stuffed the file with paper, almost all of it
interviews with relatives, friends and co-workers, none of whom had
anything to contribute. The exceptions were three statements given
by independent witnesses, and the statement given by Jill Kelly.

Although provided by individuals unknown to each other, two of
the statements were as similar as they were brief: somewhere between
six twenty-five and six thirty, both witnesses heard 'what might have
been gunshots' coming from the general direction of the Kelly home.
The statement by the third witness, who lived around the corner, was

more elaborate. She'd first observed a car, a Toyota, parked in front of her home at four o'clock in the afternoon. As her own car was in the driveway, she was hoping the Toyota would be moved before her husband came in at seven thirty. From time to time, she'd parted the curtains in her front window to check, but it wasn't until the conclusion of the nightly news at seven o'clock that she'd looked out to watch two men drive away 'in a big hurry'. One of these men, she'd added when pressed, 'might have been' wearing a ski mask.

'Well, I know he had on a knitted cap, but it seemed like it was pulled down too far, like it was covering his neck and his ears.'

The times didn't match up – the shots at six thirty, the getaway at seven. Not that it mattered all that much. The first two witnesses had gone about their business after hearing the shots. It was Jill Kelly who'd finally called the police.

Suddenly, Boots realized that he didn't know the final score of the Yankee game. The TV had been on the whole time, but he'd been too absorbed in the files to even note the highlights. Jill Kelly's statement in hand, he tuned his set to a cable sports channel, discovering, after a few minutes, that the Yankees had coasted to an easy victory over Toronto. A-Rod and Jeter had both gone deep, while Jeter had made a spectacular play on a foul ball that would be featured in highlight reels across the country. That left the Bronx Bombers in front of the Red Sox by two games, and Boots Littlewood up three hundred dollars for the week.

Triumphant, Boots dropped on to the couch and read the statement given by Jill Kelly, then a pre-law student at Fordham University. Amazingly brief, it could only have been the product of an intervention by one of her well-placed relatives. Otherwise, the simple possibility that she was the shooter would have led to a thorough grilling instead of the terse recitation she'd offered to Detective Lenny Olmeda.

My father picked me up at school and we drove directly home. We came into the house somewhere around a quarter to seven. I came in first. I heard my father lock the door, then I heard the shots. I knew what they were right away, but I couldn't make myself turn around. I was crying and I kept calling, 'Daddy, daddy?' Then I finally ran into the kitchen and dialed nine-one-one.

TWENTY-FIVE

Boots didn't know exactly what excuse he was going to make until he pulled to a stop before the Staten-Island home of Anita Parker, Chris Parker's widow, and noticed a 'For Sale' sign on the front lawn. It was too good to be true, but he wasn't complaining. Luck, good and bad, played a part, sometimes critical, in any investigation.

He got out, stretched and looked around. Except for a second-story addition over the garage, Parker's small colonial was as nondescript as any of its neighbors. Nothing about the house spoke to his alleged corruption, and neither did the Toyota mini-van parked in the driveway or the above-ground pool in the back yard.

Boots climbed the few steps to the front porch, slid a tricycle off to one side and rang the bell. The woman who answered had done everything possible to disguise her grief. Anita Parker's make-up was carefully applied, her dark hair tumbled evenly about her shoulders, her rose-pink blouse was freshly ironed. Nevertheless, her face was all bones and hollows, and the sooty pouches beneath her pale eyes were too dark to conceal. When Boots displayed his badge, she flinched, as if anticipating more bad news.

'Hi, I'm Boots Littlewood. I was part of the task force. They used me to find Vinnie Palermo.'

'Oh, I see. Lenny Olmeda mentioned you.'

Boots took a deep breath. 'I've been wantin' to pay my respects, but I had a little accident and I never got a chance. Then I heard you were putting your house up for sale and I figured now or never.'

As far as Boots could tell, Anita Parker's smile was genuine. He watched her back through the door, then followed her into a living room cluttered with toys.

'How many?' He gestured to a playpen.

'Three. And you?'

'One. He's in college.'

'With what they charge for tuition, I don't know whether to offer condolences or congratulations. Anyway, I've got a pot of coffee going. If you have time for a cup, I'd like to hear about what you did.' She paused to brush her hair away from her face. 'I don't know why, but knowing about the investigation, about what happened, makes it better. At least for a while.'

Settled in a chair at the kitchen table, Boots went on for the next ten minutes. He was good at telling cop stories and Anita, a cop's wife, seemed eager to listen. She even broke a smile when he described himself limping into the back yard to find Jill Kelly whomping on Vinnie Palermo.

'You know,' she said when Boots wound it up, 'there's a question I've asked Lenny Olmeda a number of times, but I can't seem to get a straight answer. Do you mind if I ask you?'

'Not at all.'

'What was Chris doing by the Williamsburg Bridge at that hour of the morning?'

Boots sipped at his coffee as he weighed his response. He saw no reason, at this point, to add to Anita Parker's misery. 'My guess is that he was meeting a snitch, but nobody knows for sure.'

Anita's response was quick. 'My husband commanded a narcotics unit. He didn't work in the field.'

'Maybe the snitch would only talk to him, or maybe the snitch was so high-level he couldn't be trusted to a subordinate. Anyway, you're asking the wrong man. I'm a precinct detective and I was only assigned to the job for a couple of days. The task force used me to find Vinnie after he went to ground and that was it.'

'But Palermo confessed to you first, isn't that right?'

Though Vinnie's statement was actually a claim of innocence, Boots nodded agreeably. 'So, tell me, when are you planning to move?'

'Tomorrow.'

'Tomorrow?' Boots glanced around the kitchen. Not a single item had been packed. 'You've got a lot of work ahead of you.'

'I'm going to let the movers pack me up. It's expensive, I know, but . . .' Her mouth curled into a sneer as she folded her hands and laid them on the table. 'The ironies keep piling up. Chris and I were living on credit cards before he was killed. Now, between the insurance and his pension, you could even say that I'm wealthy. Anyhow, I was raised in Buffalo and I still have family there.' She smiled and spread her hands apart. 'Everybody tells me I have to get on with my life, but somehow New York doesn't seem like the right place to start.'

Anita glanced at the clock on the wall. 'I need to get busy. Movers or not, I have a lot of work to do. But thanks for stopping by.'

Boots raised a finger. 'I had another reason for coming over this morning,' he admitted.

'And what's that?'

'Well, my father and I have a house in Greenpoint. We've been living there for a long time, but the neighborhood's changing. Not only are the yuppies movin' in, the Mayor wants to line the East River with high-rise condominiums. It's gonna be like starin' out through a row of teeth. Me and my dad, we think it's time to make a change.'

Anita Parker smiled. 'You want to buy the house? It's a fine house.'

'I don't deny that for a minute, but I still have to check it out, maybe come back with my father. I already copied down your broker's phone number.'

'Sounds great.' Anita rose. 'Feel free to look wherever you want. I'll be upstairs, packing the kids' clothes. We're driving.'

A few minutes later, Boots counted his blessings for the second time that morning when he discovered a double-hung window in a first-floor guest room. Concealed from outside observers by an overgrown lilac bush, the window was a burglar's delight. Boots took a handkerchief from an inner pocket and covered his fingertips before parting the curtains to flip the window's lock. He stood there for just a moment afterward, until he'd fashioned an internal map that led out to the street. Then he quickly retraced his steps, entering the front room to discover the unmistakable fragrance of a burning cigarette wafting down from the second floor. If this keeps up, he told himself as he climbed the stairs, I'm gonna have to stop on the way home, buy a lottery ticket. Because luck doesn't get any better than this.

Two hours later, after a careful inspection of the Parker house that carried him from the attic to the basement, Boots finally drove away. He had a long trip ahead of him, out to the 111th Precinct in Bayside, an upscale neighborhood in eastern Queens. As expected, the ride was all metal, asphalt and soot, from the Verranzano Bridge to the Gowanus Expressway, to the Brooklyn–Queens Expressway, to the Long Island Expressway, to the Clearview Expressway. Although traffic was heavy from beginning to end, Boots remained patient, guiding his Chevy into the left lane, moving right only at the interchanges. He kept an eye on the rear-view mirror as he went, and made a series of maneuvers when he got off at Northern Boulevard, speeding up, slowing down, turning corners without signaling. When he was absolutely certain that he wasn't being tailed, he double-parked in front of the One-Eleven.

Twenty minutes later, Detective Thelonius Tolliver, formerly of the Chris Parker task force, emerged to find Boots Littlewood standing at the curb. Tolliver nodded to himself, then hunched a pair of heavily muscled shoulders as he walked straight up to Boots.

'I like the look,' he said, jerking his chin toward Boots's injuries. 'Gives your face character.'

Boots smiled. 'Thanks for caring.'

'So, what'd you come here for?'

'Guidance.'

Tolliver laughed. 'You want a guide, ask an Indian. Me, I'm not Sacajawea.'

'I was hopin' you'd be pissed off.' Boots returned Tolliver's smile. 'At what?'

'At bein' transferred from Homicide out to the sticks.'

'Ah, I get it. But you made a little mistake. I wasn't demoted. I asked for the transfer.'

Boots nodded thoughtfully. 'In that case, let me buy you a drink. To celebrate.'

'Here's to you, Thelonius.' Boots raised his glass. 'The first man in the entire history of the NYPD to voluntarily quit the ultra-prestigious Homicide Division.'

They were sitting in El Matador, a Mexican restaurant on Thirty-Ninth Avenue. Boots found the decor overdone, too many sombreros and blankets, too many saddles embossed with silver buckles, too many capes and swords. Still, El Matador had one shining virtue. It wasn't a cop bar.

Boots watched Tolliver sip at his scotch and milk. The man's face was composed, as always, and it was impossible to tell what he was thinking. 'Can I make an educated guess?' Boots finally asked.

'About what?'

'About why you're in Bayside.'

Tolliver shook his head, the gesture slow and deliberate. 'You got a family, Boots?'

'Yeah, a son. He's pretty much grown-up now.'

'I wish I could say the same. Me, I got five dependent kids and an old lady with rheumatoid arthritis. You hear me, Boots? I got a sick wife and five children and no dog in this fight.'

'Is that why you came to Queens? Because it's quiet?'

'Give this man a cigar. Burglaries. Auto theft. No overtime. I put in my hours and go home to what really matters.'

'Then let me appeal to your detective's curiosity. Listen to my educated guess. Tell me if I'm bein' an asshole.'

Tolliver raised his glass. 'It's your dime, Boots. Guess away.'

'OK, my gut tells me that in the course of your investigation you discovered that Chris Parker was dirty and that you decided to remove yourself from the scene because you didn't know who else might be dirty. Corcoran? Farrahan? Olmeda? They were Chris Parker's old buddies.'

'That's good. You must've gotten your hands on Parker's file.' Tolliver saluted with a meaty hand, then leaned across the table. 'What do you want from me, Boots?'

'Guidance, like I already said. I can put Corcoran, Parker, Olmeda and Farrahan together, but I don't know who else is out there. Or if there's anybody I can trust.'

Though Tolliver's nose was broad and his mouth large, his face was dominated by a pair of round cheeks that bulged from either side of his face. He scratched at those cheeks as he pondered his options. 'I'm a good cop,' he said. 'I never took a penny in my life.'

'That's why it gets to you when you see another cop with his hand out.' Boots drained his Corona. He'd already decided not to stop talking unless Tolliver got up and walked out. In his experience, a man with a conscience could always be worn down.

'You've had a look at the Parker file – that right?' Tolliver asked.

'Read it from cover to cover.'

'So you know that Maurice Selman accused Parker of extortion.'

'Yeah, but Selman's dead.'

Suddenly Tolliver leaned forward, his voice dropping to a near whisper. 'What about a dealer named Elijah LeGuin? Was his name mentioned?'

'Maytag LeGuin? I didn't see a word.'

'Well, three different informants connected Parker to LeGuin, so the fact that LeGuin's name doesn't appear in the case file oughta tell you something.'

'It tells me why you left Homicide,' Boots replied. 'And I don't blame you.'

Tolliver finished his beer and stood. 'It's been swell, Boots.' He stretched out his hand, gesturing with his chin at Boots's forehead. 'And for what it's worth, I'm wishin' you luck. After what happened, I know you won't back off. But me, I have other priorities, so what I'm suggestin' is this. You want a guide, go speak to LeGuin, who knows where the bodies are buried. Maybe, if you ask him real nice, he'll draw you a map.'

TWENTY-SIX

Boots shoveled the last of the pancakes on to a plate, handed the plate to Joaquin, then turned back to the stove. He dropped a chunk of butter into the pan and waited for it to melt before adding ladles of pancake batter. 'Go easy on the syrup,' he said without turning around.

'Please, Boots, tell me we're not gonna do the weight thing at nine thirty in the morning.'

'You're sayin' that your weight's not on the rise?' Boots turned down the burner, then slid a spatula under one of the pancakes. Not quite.

'Actually, I don't recall bringing the subject up.'

Joaquin cut through his stack with the edge of a fork. Boots was right – he'd gained ten pounds over the past couple of months. And, yes, just like Boots told him when he was fifteen, he'd be struggling with his weight for the rest of his life. Thanks for reminding me, prick.

'I've been thinking over what you said the other day, about taking Galligan's offer. He wants seventy thousand for half the stock, ten up front.'

Boots stifled a groan. There was no way he could raise ten grand without taking a loan from the credit union, or, even worse, approaching his father.

'Nothing to say?' Joaquin asked.

'Are you sure you can make a living?'

'Going in, I'll draw a grand a week, plus half of the profits at the end of the year. Assuming we make a profit after we finish with the banks.'

'The banks?'

'The business needs to expand and remodel. It'll take cash.'

'What about school?'

'I've already spoken to the administration. They'll let me take a leave of absence for the fall semester.' Caught up in his own thoughts, Joaquin leaned forward. 'I'm enrolled in two courses over the summer and I'm committed to working thirty hours a week for Tommy Galligan. By the time September rolls around, I should have a pretty good idea of where the business is going. If I'm not satisfied, I can always re-enroll at NYU.'

Boots added syrup to his pancakes and began to eat. 'There's somebody I want you to check out,' he said. 'Elijah "Maytag" LeGuin, a drug dealer. I might have to take him off the street, but I don't want it to happen at one of his spots. I want it to go down somewhere quiet.'

'Why's that?'

'Because he'll most likely feel obliged to display his contempt for authority if his pals are watching. Besides, LeGuin is at least two steps removed from day-to-day operations and I could be lookin' for months. What I think, he's got a hidey-hole, a house or an apartment, somewhere he goes to get away from the pressure. The property might be in his name, in the name of his sisters or brothers if he has any, or his mother or father, or even a girlfriend. How much would it cost me to find out?'

Joaquin's grin spread from ear to ear. Boots would come up with the ten grand. Of course he would. But he'd expect a lifetime of freebies in return.

'How fast do you need this, Boots?'

'Like yesterday.'

Boots finished his breakfast, then headed off to the bathroom to shave. When he returned, he found Jill Kelly huddled over a mug of black coffee. Joaquin was seated across from her, grinning like a smitten twelve-year-old.

'Are you a cop?' Jill asked.

'No, I'm a student. Which reminds me. If I don't get myself in gear, I'll miss my first class.'

'Don't let me keep you.' Jill turned to Boots, a quizzical smile playing at the corners of her lips. Breakfast dishes? Latino and gringo? The age difference?

'It's a good thing you came by, Jill,' Boots said. 'I've been going crazy with those files.'

Joaquin poked his head into the kitchen. 'Nice meeting you,' he said to Jill Kelly. 'Boots, I'll get back to you in the next couple of days.'

Boots shot Joaquin a hard look. He and his son had a deal. One cooked and the other cleaned up. While Boots didn't mind Jill thinking he might be gay, housewife was another story.

'You gonna tell me?' Jill asked.

'About what?'

Jill watched Boots run a line of detergent over the dishes in the sink, then turn on the water. Of his sexual orientation, she had no doubt. Gay men don't strip you naked with their eyes.

'About your friend.'

'Jackie's my son.'

'I was just gonna say that. The resemblance is unmistakable.'

Boots refused to be provoked. 'There's no great mystery to it,' he said without turning around. 'Go back eleven years. I'm in the Six-Four, bullshitting with the desk officer, when this kid walks into the house. His clothes are halfway to rags and he's dirty, too, and scared out of his mind. The way he approaches us, it's like a pigeon approaching somebody tossin' crumbs on the sidewalk. He comes forward, turns back, comes forward again. Finally, I ask him what he wants. His mother, he tells me, is back in their apartment, dead from HIV, and he doesn't know what to do.'

Boots dried his hands, then took a seat at the table. 'It turns out the kid has no relatives to take him in. That means foster care, which is only a half-step from prison. Me, I do what all cops do. I hand him over to the social workers and try to put him in the past. Only I can't forget how alone the kid looked, how helpless, like he was standin' right on the edge, starin' down into the pit, like he was ready to give up, to let himself fall. And me, Jill, I had it easy when I was a kid. I never worried for one second about havin' a place to sleep, a roof over my head, food on the table, parents who loved me. Meanwhile, this kid, he's been nursin' his mother alone for the last six months, thinkin' that if he loses her, he'll be on the street.' Boots tapped the side of his nose. 'I became his foster parent first. A couple of years later, I adopted him.'

Jill spun her coffee mug between her palms. The son-of-a-bitch had snuck up on her again. If she didn't jump his bones soon, she'd end up with an inferiority complex. 'You're not lying, are you?'

'Catholic honor.' Boots drew a cross over his heart. 'But, really, it wasn't a big deal. I enrolled Jackie in Mount Carmel and walked him to school on the first day. When he got to the door, I told him, "I can give you a place to live, put clothes on your back and food on the table, but I don't have time to mold your character. You have to do it on your own. Sink or swim."'

'I assume he got the message.'

'He's a student at NYU.' Boots experienced another moment of regret. NYU student sounded a whole lot better than sleazebag PI. 'But enough with the soap opera. Jill, am I wrong to assume that you've been all over these files?'

Jill answered without hesitation. Maybe she was getting used to it. 'No, you wouldn't. I've been reading them for the last three years.'

'Then let me ask you about Jules Cosyn and the task force. Did you find anything wrong with the investigation, any detail out of place?'

'Boots, I personally interviewed the profiler and the shrink who examined Cosyn before he was declared unfit to stand trial. There's no doubt he killed those women.'

'And no reason to believe the investigation itself led to your father's death.'

'I know where you're headed.' Jill tossed her hair back.

'Where's that?'

'After the task force closed the investigation, the boys went to Brooklyn North Narcotics, with Mack Corcoran as the unit commander.'

Boots slid his chair a little closer to the table. He hadn't known about the boys going to Narcotics, though it made sense. The Chiefs who ruled the Puzzle Palace would have been overjoyed by the arrest of Jules Cosyn – serial killer investigations commonly ran on for years. Rewarding the detectives on the task force with choice assignments was par for the course.

'Now, when you say "the boys", are you including your father?'

'My father, Corcoran, Parker, Olmeda and Artie Farrahan.'

When Jill Kelly lit a cigarette, Boots, though he fetched an ashtray, barely reacted. The nicotine demons were visiting him less often these days. 'You know,' he said, 'there's a question I have to ask you.'

'Was my father dirty?' Jill was staring directly into Boots's eyes, her own eyes marble-hard. 'See, I know about the IAB thing on Parker. And I know certain snitches connected Parker to Maytag LeGuin.'

Boots let it ride for a couple of beats, then said, 'I had to ask the question, Jill, because it was too obvious to leave out there. That doesn't mean you have to answer.'

'Yeah, I know.' Jill drew on her cigarette, sucked the smoke deep into her lungs, held it for just a second before releasing her breath. Finally, she looked away. 'I can't be objective about my father,' she said, 'but I can tell you this. Dad's finances were examined by a task force and he came up clean. Plus, there was no estate. Except for the pension, he pretty much died broke.'

Boots nodded, then leaned back, giving Jill some space. 'What I'd like to do, unless you have a better idea, is take a look at your father's house and the surrounding neighborhood. Your mother still lives there, right?'

'I live there, too.'

'Even better.' Boots rose, walked to the hall closet and took his shoulder harness off the shelf. He shrugged into the harness, then into a corduroy sports jacket. The fit, he noted, was a little tight. If he didn't start working out again, he'd have to cut calories.

'You ready?'

TWENTY-SEVEN

Boots would never know exactly when he became aware of the van. To be sure, the Ford Windstar entered his field of vision even before it turned on to the block, when it was still in the intersection. But he was too distracted to notice. First, there was Jill Kelly striding alongside him, the sunlight reddening her auburn hair. Then there was the caressingly warm June day and a steady breeze that riffled the branches of an oak planted long before his birth. Fianna Walsh and Jenicka Balicki didn't help either. They were sitting in lawn chairs on the other side of the street, measuring Boots and his little visitor with greedy eyes.

Nevertheless, there were dead giveaways and he should have noticed. Antennas sprouting from the van's roof like the shafts of spears, tinted windows dark enough to hide the occupants, the steady scratch-scratch of a rap tune playing at high volume, a throbbing muffler audible from a hundred yards away.

But he didn't notice, not until the van suddenly accelerated, its tires chirping on the asphalt. Then everything jumped into focus, producing a kaleidoscopic overlay of details: the rear window coming down, the muzzle of a shotgun, the face of a black man, a shot from behind him, a splash of blood inside the van, the shotgun jerking up an instant before discharge, chunks of brick falling to the side-walk as the van raced off.

And Jill Kelly saying, 'Shit.'

Boots turned to find Jill in a shooter's stance, the barrel of her Sig-Sauer pointing to the sky. 'If it wasn't for the old ladies,' she explained, 'I would've gotten the driver, too.'

Across the road, Fianna Walsh and Jenicka Balicki bore identical expressions: mouths agape, eyes bulging, nostrils flared.

Boots closed his eyes and silently repeated the numbers and letters on the Ford's license plate. He didn't want to write them down, not yet. From behind, he heard Jill on her cellphone, giving her uncle a heads-up. When she finished, she tapped Boots on the shoulder.

'Look, you didn't discharge your weapon, so there's no reason you have to be here when the first units arrive.'

Suddenly, Boots realized that his hand was resting on the grip of his automatic. He was relieved. At least he'd made it that far. He watched Jill holster her weapon. Her shoulders were relaxed and she held her head to one side, a quizzical smile on her lips. Only her blue eyes betrayed the turbulence just beneath the surface. They appeared to have shattered, each tiny shard reflecting its own light.

'Spell it out, Jill,' he said. 'What did massa tell you?'

'Massa?'

'Sorry. Uncle Mike.'

Jill laughed that same girlish laugh. 'This is what I get for saving your life?'

'Call it a good-faith beginning.'

Sirens wailed in the distance, a pair at least. 'Go upstairs,' Jill said. 'Let me handle the details. Later on, you'll give a statement.'

'That's it?'

'Don't volunteer anything. If you're asked, we were working a cold case.'

'Your father's murder?'

'Yeah, my father's murder.' Jill smiled. 'By the way, you didn't happen to catch the plate number of that van, did you?'

'Jill, I don't even know if the van *had* a plate.'

The first thing Boots did upon entering his apartment was write down the Windstar's license plate number. The job turned out to be something of a challenge. His fingers began to tremble when he picked up the pen, slowly at first, then faster, until his entire hand was twitching. He had to draw the six characters one stroke at a time, willing his hand to move across the page. He was just finishing when his father opened the door and stepped inside.

In no mood for a lecture, Boots looked up Craig O'Malley's number, then jabbed at the keypad of his cellphone. It took three tries to get it right.

'Sarge? It's Boots.'

'Boots, what's doin'?'

'What's doing is that someone just tried to kill me.' This wasn't

strictly true. Jill Kelly might well have been the target, Boots
Littlewood the innocent bystander.

'Tried to kill you?'

'Don't worry, you'll hear all about it. This'll make the papers for
sure. But I need something in a hurry. I need you to run a plate
for me before the assholes from IAB show up.'

'Let's hear it.'

Boots read off the six letters and numbers he'd written in his
notebook, then waited impatiently until the information was
retrieved. Finally, despite the shakes, he printed a name and address:
Isabella Amarando, 212 Groton Street in Forest Hills.

Boots put the phone away, then turned to his father. 'I want you
to pack a bag and stay with Libby until it's over.'

'And how long will that take?'

'I don't know, Dad, but men who fire shotguns from moving
vehicles don't hesitate to kill family members. It's not a chance we
need to take.'

'And you'll also be leavin'?'

'As soon as the bosses are done with me. You understand, if you
stay, you'll be the only game in town.'

Andy laid his hand on his son's shoulder. 'I take your point,
Irwin. But I want you to promise me that you'll be careful this time.
If I lost you . . .'

Boots looked down at his trembling hands for a moment, then
said, 'Cross my heart and hope to die.'

At eleven o'clock, two investigators knocked on the door. Both
were captains, one from the Chief of D's office, one from Internal
Affairs. They took Boots's statement in thirty minutes, their manner
so affable Boots felt himself part of some grand scheme. The show
was now being run from police headquarters, also called the Puzzle
Palace, not from Brooklyn North. Corcoran was locked out and
Boots was included. Praise the Lord and pass the chicken.

At one o'clock, after surrendering her weapon and being debriefed,
Jill Kelly was summarily dismissed. She clung to the edges of the
investigation for a short time, watching a flock of white-suited CSU
cops perform a grid search. She didn't know exactly what they were
looking for, but she found the effort somehow comforting. It was
so well defined, so manifestly sane, crawling around with a pair of

tweezers, looking for a piece of fluff. The only problem was how you'd explain it to the kids.

Jill finally turned away when she was certain she was unobserved. She climbed the steps to Andy Littlewood's front door, then the stairs to Boots Littlewood's apartment. She wasn't surprised to find the door unlocked and Boots standing just a few feet away. If his hands were as quick as his mind, he would've gotten off the first shot. Jill closed and locked the door behind her, then turned to face a pair of gray eyes as hard as granite. Boots was looking at her as though she was prey.

Without conceding exactly who would devour whom, Jill gathered the lapels of her jacket and spread them apart to reveal her empty holster. She stood there for a few seconds, then said, 'Look, Boots, the shooting board confiscated my weapon. I'm completely helpless.'

Boots wrapped his fingers in Jill Kelly's blouse and yanked her into his arms. Or perhaps she simply jumped into his arms the minute he touched her. The way she clung to him, like a monkey to a tree, he couldn't be sure. Then his hands tightened over her buttocks, tightened hard, and his lips found the hollow in her throat. Her responding moan buckled his knees. He stumbled to the bedroom and laid her down on the bed. Quickly, despite his still-trembling fingers, he unbuttoned her blouse and stripped off her pants, leaving her in matching black bra and panties.

For a moment, he could do no more than stare down at her. The sheet-smooth belly, the curve of her hips, the midnight-blue eyes that stared up at him as he shrugged out of his jacket and took off his shirt. The miracle was that some small part of his rational mind was still alert. Telling him that he was in it now, in the shit for sure, and there was no going back.

As for Jill, she had only one moment, if not of fear, at least of apprehension. She was on the bed, naked, her legs apart, and Boots was dropping toward her, Godzilla with a hard-on. But then he was inside her and her legs were curled over his hips and they were moving together and none of it mattered. She was riding the Oblivion Express. If necessary, she would ride it all the way to hell.

Boots distinctly remembered a former lover saying that if a man couldn't make a woman sweat, what good was he? By that measure,

Boots supposed that he was good enough. He was lying on his side, staring down at Jill Kelly's slick breasts, his predictions come true. The bedding was in tatters and they'd yet to exchange a tender, post-coital kiss.

'What are you thinking, Boots?'

'Don't tell me you're looking for reassurance.'

'Actually, I decided to have you the day you walked into Levine's office. It really messed up my plans, you finding Vinnie Palermo so fast. I was still looking for an excuse to run into you when you got your ass kicked. After that, I decided to lay off, see what you'd do about it.'

'And you liked that you saw?'

'The scar? The droopy eyelid? How could I resist?'

Boots ran his hand from Jill's throat, over her breast and down to her thigh. Crazy Jill Kelly? How about Psycho Boots Littlewood? It'd been what, three minutes, and he was already stirring. The woman was as addictive as crack cocaine.

'C'mon,' she said, 'tell me what you're thinking.'

'I'm thinking of Dante's *Inferno*, of the words written over the gates of hell, which Brother Dominick drummed into the heads of all his tenth graders.' Boots slid his hand down between her legs. 'Abandon hope, all ye who enter here.'

Jill Kelly was still laughing when Boots covered her mouth with his own. Needless to say, his kiss was anything but tender.

TWENTY-EIGHT

Frankie Drago couldn't believe his luck. Boots Littlewood standing in the doorway, a garment bag draped across his shoulder, a suitcase hanging from his left hand. Saying, 'Frankie, I need a place to hang out.'

'Sure, Boots. Abso-fuckin'-lutely. Come right in.' Frankie stepped back to let Boots pass. 'But one thing you might wanna think about. If you have to ask how much it costs, you can't afford it.'

Boots dropped his bag on the living-room floor. 'You hear about what happened?'

'Yeah, Jenicka phoned my mom a couple of hours ago. I heard your partner saved your life.'

'Don't go there, Frankie.'

Drago grinned as he retrieved Boots's luggage and led him down the hall to a bedroom at the back of the house. He gave Boots a chance to settle down, then said, 'My lawyer got the autopsy report on Angie. Just like you said, she died instantly. Now I'm thinkin' I could beat the charge altogether.'

'Only if you have the balls to take it to trial.' Boots sat on the edge of the bed. It was too soft. He tested a pillow. Also too soft, plus it was a feather pillow and he was allergic to feathers.

'You got a point there,' Drago conceded. 'I got some big choices ahead of me.'

'What's the state offering?'

'If I plead to second-degree manslaughter, I'll get three years. If I go to trial and I'm convicted, it'll be ten years before I get a parole hearing.' Frankie shook his head in disgust. 'It ain't fair, Boots. Why should I be punished for exercisin' my right to a trial? If three years is a reasonable punishment for what I did to Angie, why should I have to do an extra seven because I wanna plead innocent?'

Boots was constantly amazed by how often people used the word fair, how they could bend it to fit whatever argument they happened to be making. In fact, the sharks who ran the system were being extremely kind to Frankie Drago because he'd thrown Vinnie Palermo into their feeding tank. Fair had nothing to do with it.

'So,' Boots said, 'whatta ya hear from Vinnie?'

'Vinnie?'

'He hasn't called? I'm surprised. You and him go way back. Plus, he was a guest in your home when he incriminated himself.'

Drago folded his arms across his chest. God, he hated this man. 'Yeah, Vinnie called.'

'So, how's he makin' out?'

'What can I say, Boots? Vinnie's been inside before. He's survivin'.'

'What about you, Frankie? What are you doin'?'

'For Vinnie?'

'Yeah?'

'I been sendin' money orders to his account, enough to keep him in candy bars and toothpaste. I can't think of any other way to help him. The prosecutors already told my lawyer they wouldn't need me to testify at his trial, so even if . . .'

Frankie suddenly drew himself up. He was holding Boots Littlewood's marker, not the other way around. 'What about when you testify at Frankie Drago's trial, Boots?' he asked. 'What are you gonna say then?'

'That depends on the skills of your attorney. But I'll tell ya this, whatever I say is gonna be the truth.'

'Except for the part about not givin' me a Miranda warning?'

Boots looked past Frankie's shoulder, into a dusty mirror on the far wall. No longer livid, the scar on his forehead was healing nicely. Not so his drooping eyelid. Sometimes, in the morning, it was as if he was peering beneath a drawn window shade.

'Except for that, Frankie. Except for that.'

Boots settled down in the living room after dinner, with Frankie Drago for company and a beer at his elbow. The Yankees were playing the Mets, Mike Pelfrey against CC Sabathia, a match-up that definitely favored the Yankees.

'Frankie,' he said as the Yanks took the field, 'I'm gonna be goin' out later. If you've got an extra set of house keys, I won't have to wake you up at three o'clock in the morning.'

Drago lit a cigarette. 'Ya know, Boots, this is my house, not a . . . a headquarters.'

'I hear ya, but I have to do this thing at night. There's no other way.'

The game was still close in the fifth inning when Pelfrey let Brett Gardner and Derek Jeter reach base with one out. That left him to face Alex Rodriguez. Almost against his will, Boots found himself drawn into the confrontation. These were men who did not like to lose, especially in front of a packed house with five million people watching on television. He could see it in Pelfrey's eyes when he looked in for the sign, in A-Rod's bat as he took his practice swings. He could see that they spoke with the same voice: Not thy will, but mine. When Gardner stole third on the first pitch, Boots knew that it didn't matter. Nor did it matter when Jeter stole second on the eighth pitch. It didn't matter until Pelfrey finally made a mistake on the tenth pitch, an arrow-straight, waist-high fastball over the outer half of the plate, the one A-Rod had begun praying for while he was still on-deck.

Twenty seconds later, Rodriguez was standing on third base, accepting congratulations from Larry Bowa, the third base coach, while Pelfrey, who'd already exceeded his pitch count, was headed for the dugout. But the move came too late for the New York Mets. The floodgates were open now and the Yankees poured it on over the next two innings, opening an eight-run lead.

Impatient when the game began, Boots found himself grateful now. He liked to see his options laid out clearly, like laundry on a line. Boots could remember his mother hanging laundry, especially in the spring when she threw open every window to 'rid us of the smell of winter'. Boots suddenly wished he could rid himself of Jill Kelly, then instantly took it back. As his father might say, she was grand, her every move a dare. And she was right about saving his life, too. As Boots remembered it, the diameter of the shotgun's muzzle was wide enough to cover his entire face.

'Boots?' Frankie asked when the last out was finally recorded shortly before eleven.

'Yeah, Frankie?'

'Suppose my lawyer asks you if it could've happened with Angie the way I said it happened when I spoke to that prosecutor. What're you gonna say?'

'Your statement to Thelma Blount isn't admissible. If you recall, it was off the record.'

'C'mon, Boots. Don't bust balls.'

Boots rose and stretched. 'If I'm asked, I'll say that I know you shoved Angie, I know that she fell back into the stairway, I know that she died when she hit her head on the basement floor. As to what was goin' on in your mind when all this happened? I'm not a psychic.'

Frankie Drago wasn't satisfied. 'But what if he asks you if you think it's possible that Frankie Drago didn't mean to kill his sister, or even hurt her.'

'What will I say?' Looking into Frankie's eyes, Boots knew the question had little to do with the legal system. Frankie had yet to forgive himself – most likely he'd never be free of the guilt, no matter how many times he confessed to the priests at Mount Carmel. 'First thing, your lawyer has to put the question more precisely. He has to ask me if there's any physical evidence provin' you intended to inflict death, or any major injury, upon Angie. And just for the record, that you deliberately killed your sister by pushin' her down a flight of stairs never crossed my mind. It's too stupid, even for you.'

With his radar on full alert, Boots walked the several blocks to where he'd parked his car. The streetlights seemed brighter, the shadows deeper, the lights of oncoming cars blinding. He struggled to be aware of everything going on around him, the traffic, silhouettes in the windows, Ferdie Salise walking a poodle so old and fat its legs shook when it squatted to pee. Boots heard airplanes passing overhead, helicopters running up and down the East River, doo-wop music from an apartment three stories above his head, the Platters doing their signature tune, 'The Great Pretender'.

Boots didn't believe he could be traced to Frankie Drago's, but his car was another matter. The buckshot meant for his body had slammed into the bricks a mere ten feet above his head. Relative to human flesh, brick is very hard, yet the chunk gouged from the face of the tenement was big enough to hold a grapefruit.

When a meandering drive through the neighborhood failed to uncover a tail, Boots detoured over the Williamsburg Bridge, to a garage on Houston Street that catered to cabbies on a 24/7 basis. A flash of his badge and a twenty-dollar bill got his Chevy on a lift ten minutes after his arrival. Using a borrowed drop light, he checked the undercarriage, from front to rear, in search of a tracking device. His approach was as systematic and meticulous as all those white-suited cops Jill Kelly had watched earlier in the day. When he was satisfied, he had the car brought down, then inspected the trunk and the engine. Nothing.

'So, what else can I do for you?' the mechanic asked. 'Maybe a quick oil change?'

'Nope, I'm good to go.'

Boots found himself with mixed feelings as he headed off to Anita Parker's Staten Island home. He could operate without looking over his shoulder for oncoming bullets, at least for the present, and that was all to the good. But the scales had shifted. More and more, it seemed to him that Jill Kelly had been the primary target when that shotgun appeared in the van's window. And what was he gonna do about that? Except jump into bed with her at the earliest opportunity. Greedy as any fat-cat CEO.

TWENTY-NINE

Within a minute of climbing through Anita Parker's unlocked window, Boots was thoroughly tested. He was in the dining room, now emptied of its furniture, when the overhead light came on. This was a lucky break as it turned out, but at the time Boots felt his heart jump into his mouth, looking, maybe, to desert the sinking ship. Nevertheless, his head swiveled, to the right and the left, covering the empty room, and his gun was in his hand before he'd taken a breath.

The light in question, Boots realized after a few seconds, was on a timer. The timer would switch the light off and on several times each day, as other timers would turn other lights off and on. The goal was to frighten burglars and vandals by simulating the activities of a family in residence. In fact, timers are an aid to burglars, as these were to Boots. Now any light in the house could be turned on without attracting the attention of meddlesome neighbors.

Boots started in the attic and worked his way down. He'd been all over the house only a day before without uncovering anything out of place on the upper floors. Still, he methodically searched each room, all those years of experience coming into play. By the time he reached the basement, he was able to concentrate on the problem at hand without a nagging fear that he'd missed something. If Chris Parker had a hidden stash upstairs, it wasn't in a closet or along the baseboards or behind any cabinet or beneath a trap door.

With the house cleaned out by the movers, the basement seemed empty: a few makeshift workbenches, plastic water pipes, an oil burner, a washer and dryer in a small laundry room. Not so on the day before, when every nook and cranny was taken up by Chris Parker's woodworking tools.

Still permeated by the pungent odor of wood shavings, the basement had been Parker's retreat, the place he came to be alone. If he was going to hide something in the house, something he didn't want even his wife to know about, this was where he'd put it. Still, the basement had been so cluttered that if not for Anita Parker,

Boots might never have uncovered the anomaly. Anita had spoken at length about her home's many advantages, seeming, once she got started, unable to stop. Boots had listened patiently, aware that she was cataloguing her memories, not pitching real estate. Anita remembered completing the addition over the garage, replacing the roof, remodeling the kitchen, preparing a bedroom for their first child, upgrading the furnace in the basement.

'We replaced the furnace two years ago,' she'd said. 'The system we installed was top of the line. It uses half the fuel that the old system used and it doesn't clank every time it shuts down.'

When Boots had finally reached the basement, he'd made a cursory inspection, then stood before the new furnace for several minutes before he put his finger on what was bothering him. A sheet-metal duct running above a long workbench wasn't connected to the new heating system on either end, though one end rested against the furnace. Had the contractor who installed the new system left the duct behind? Had Chris Parker taken advantage?

Boots had been about to find out when Anita came thumping down the stairs, a laundry basket cradled in her arms.

'It never ends,' she'd said.

Boots gave the end of the duct resting against the furnace a tug, moving it far enough to get his hand inside, but found nothing. He walked calmly to the other end, twenty-five feet away, and focused the beam of his flashlight along the inside. About half-way down, a small shadow blocked the light. Boots twisted the flashlight to angle the beam into the shadow which then became a black shopping bag.

The duct was made of box-like segments, press-fit into a single unit. Boots separated the two segments at the center by holding them against his body, then yanking in opposite directions. They came apart easily, one end dropping down to release the bag. Boots could tell by the sound the bag made when it hit the concrete floor, the muffled ker-chunk, that there was money inside.

Something over twenty thousand dollars, as a quick count revealed, more than enough to set up Joaquin. Boots found himself wishing that Father Leo was in the room so he could kick the priest's ass from one wall to the other. Yeah, the commandment says, Thou shalt not steal. But if the money didn't belong to Boots, who did it belong to? Who was he stealing from? Anita Parker? On the grounds that her husband had extorted it, fair and square? Or maybe the city or the state? Or how about Maytag LeGuin? What would Maytag say if Boots walked up and handed him a bag of money?

'This is yours, I believe.'

Boots shook his head in an effort to erase the entire train of thought. He let the money fall to the floor, then retrieved the only other item in Parker's stash – a DVD in a jewel case. Boots examined the disc for a moment, but there was no label to indicate its contents, which he found encouraging. Parker would not have taken such pains to conceal a few hours of video shot at a family celebration.

Boots slid the DVD into his pocket, then dropped to his knees and stuffed the cash into the bag. It was time to get out and he knew it. Still, for the length of a drawn breath, he continued to stare down at the stacked bills. He wanted them so bad. He wanted them more than anything they could hope to buy, and he couldn't shake off the notion that only a chump would leave them behind.

Boots released his breath, shoved the money into the bag and the bag into the duct, and finally pressed the segments together. Whoever's money it was, it wasn't Boots Littlewood's money. That was how you knew, or so the nuns had explained way back when. Plus, there was Father Leo's threat to withhold absolution. If Boots ignored the priest, he might as well quit going to church altogether.

It was well after two o'clock when Boots turned the key in Frankie Drago's door. He tiptoed through the living room, down the hall and into the bathroom. Fifteen minutes later, he was asleep. This was a trait for which Boots could take no credit. Except for those rare occasions when his conscience troubled him, he was able to drop off at will.

Boots slept deeply for several hours, then fell into a series of dreams centering around his mother. In the years since her death, Boots often dreamed of Margie Littlewood, dreams in which he and his mother might be any age, in which they skipped from season to season, setting to setting. He walked beside her in the Bronx Zoo, watched her prepare dinner on a snowy day, swam next to her in a YMCA pool.

In his dream on this night, Boots sat beside his mother in a wooden pew at Mount Carmel. He felt her thigh pressed against his own, smelled the flowery perfume she wore to church. He rose with her, sat with her, knelt with her, sang with her. So happy he could barely contain himself.

And then, without transition, Margie Littlewood was no longer beside her son. She was at the front of the church, beyond the altar rail, in her coffin, and she wasn't coming back, never, no matter how much he wanted to see her again.

Boots awakened in a panic. He swung his legs over the edge of the bed and put his face into his hands. Even now, when he entered his father's apartment, he sometimes heard, very faintly, his mother call out his name.

Fully awake, Boots took a shower, then retrieved the DVD and headed for the kitchen, drawn by the odor of onions browning in olive oil. When he came through the door, Frankie Drago was breaking eggs into a mixing bowl.

'Boots, I been wantin' to talk to you.' Drago added salt, pepper and chopped garlic, then whisked the eggs into a froth before pouring them over the onions.

'What about?'

'What do you think?' This time Frankie was prepared. No more evasions.

'About that question I suggested your lawyer ask me?' Boots's grin flicked on and off.

'Yeah, that one. And no more bullshit. I wanna know what you're gonna say.'

'Well, Frankie, should your mouthpiece ask me if there's any physical or circumstantial evidence provin' that you intended to kill Angie, I'm gonna say no. But you could've figured that one out for yourself.'

'How so?' Drago folded the omelet, then cut it in half.

'Because no evidence that you intended to kill your sister exists. Of course, that doesn't mean you'll be acquitted. Remember, I'm just one little arrow in the state's quiver. That's why I'm gonna give you a piece of advice. The prosecutor will raise a question of his own – a very important question which you're gonna have to answer convincingly if you hope to walk away relatively unharmed.'

'And what question would that be?'

'Why was your basement door open, exposing a steep and narrow staircase with a concrete floor at the bottom end? My father doesn't leave the door to the basement open. In fact, nobody I know leaves the door open. So why did Frankie Drago's basement door happen to be open when he happened to shove his sister through it?'

THIRTY

B oots ate his omelet standing up. He was annoyed by Drago's ingratitude. The issue of the open door would play a far more important role in the bookmaker's trial than Boots Littlewood's testimony. But Frankie Drago was pissed off because Detective Littlewood had rained on his freedom fantasy. Par for the course. Boots took Chris Parker's DVD out of his pocket and held it up.

'You have a player for this?'

'What's on it?'

'I don't know, Frankie. That's why I need the player.'

Drago led the way into the living room, handed Boots a remote control, then slid the disc into his DVD player. When Boots didn't ask him to leave, he dropped into a chair and lit a cigarette.

The disc opened on an outdoor scene in a neighborhood that might be found in any of New York's outer boroughs, a block of five-story apartment buildings and two-family, attached homes, brick, brick and more brick. There were parked cars on both sides of the road, a half-dozen pedestrians going about their business, a Con-Ed crew digging up the street.

The scene remained static for a few seconds before a car – a blue, late-model Volvo, driven by a woman – glided into view. The Volvo came to a stop next to a Toyota, then attempted to parallel-park. The effort was comical, the Volvo's rear tires pounding the curb several times before the car again pulled up alongside the Toyota and the driver got out. Bundled up in a puffy, down jacket, she walked directly to the camera, reaching out as she came.

The camera tilted down for a moment, then righted itself to reveal Chris Parker striding toward the Volvo. He spun on his heel to offer a brief smirk, climbed in, finally parked the car with practiced ease. Fade to black.

The Bronx Zoo followed. Parker or his girlfriend striding along various paths, watching various animals, eating hotdogs, eating cotton candy. All sunshine and smiles.

After ten minutes of sightseeing, Boots pressed search and was rewarded with Parker and pal on a sandy beach. Both wore bathing suits, the contrast between the pair so extreme Boots couldn't ignore it. The woman – a girl, really, in her early twenties at most – was thin enough to be the victim of a wasting disease. Her skin was sallow, the undersides of her eyes dark and heavy, the muscles of her legs and arms slack. Next to the toned and tanned Chris Parker, she was small enough to be a child, an effect emphasized by the pink barrette that held her brown hair in place.

'What, you're into home movies now?' Drago asked.

'That's Chris Parker. That's the man Vinnie's accused of killing. I found the DVD in a heating duct.'

'Yeah? So what?'

'So there has to be something on it that Parker wanted to keep hidden. If not, why hide it?'

Boots pressed search again, his persistence this time resulting in a pay-off of sorts: Chris Parker on a king-sized bed with a thirtyish blond, both naked, going at it for all they were worth.

Another press of the search button produced a second woman between the sheets with Chris Parker, then a third and a fourth, none of them the girl Boots had seen in the earlier footage.

Boots shut off the DVD player. 'Frankie, you better go upstairs, tell your mother not to come down. If she sees this, she might get the wrong impression.'

'Good thought.' Drago ground out his cigarette, then rose. 'I gotta take Mom to church anyway, and after that I'm gonna head for Silky's. Be a lotta business today, what with the Mets playin' the Yankees for the last time this season. You wouldn't wanna place a bet, would ya – give me a chance to get even?'

Boots shook his head, his mind already turning back to the video. He waited for Drago to leave the room, then laid the remote control on a table and stared at the half-smoked butt in the ashtray with frank desire. If his cravings were more infrequent now, they were no less powerful. He got up, sat down, his eyes jumping across the room as though seeking an escape hatch. Boots found Drago's resolutely early-American furnishings somewhat unnerving. Wing chairs and a three-seat couch with an unnaturally high back, American-eagle lamps with black shades, Washington crossing the Delaware on the wall behind the television. Every single piece, Boots knew, including a factory-frayed Betsy Ross flag, had fallen off the back of an eighteen-wheeler. Another day, another truck, and Frankie would have surrounded himself with chrome, glass and leather.

Boots was trying to decide if he needed to review the entire DVD. Parker's reason for hiding the disc was obvious enough. What Boots had discovered was a kind of trophy wall – here the head of an ibex, there a gazelle, there an impala. The private journal of a man addicted to sex. Though Boots was a strong believer in the concept of consenting adults, he very much doubted that the women on the DVD had consented to being taped. Still, no matter how despicable Parker's conduct, he wasn't around to punish and there was no sense in getting worked up. There were other things to consider, like maybe some of the women in Parker's videos were married and he was using the videos for blackmail. As a motive for murder, blackmail would definitely suffice.

When Boots heard the front door close, he crossed to the window and watched Frankie and his mom head off to Mount Carmel. Boots usually accompanied his father to mass when he had Sunday off. But not today. Today, Andy was in Astoria, driven from his home by his son's bullshit.

Boots fetched a spiral notebook and a pen from his room, then returned to his chair and made a few notes about what he'd seen. When he finished, he knew that he had to review the disc. All of the video was shot in the same room through two cameras, positioned on the front and back walls. These cameras had a zoom capacity which could only have been implemented by a third party, and unless Parker was chronically quick on the trigger, the footage had been edited down. These factors, and the near certainty that the video had been shot over a long period of time, led to a simple conclusion: Chris Parker had maintained a private hidey-hole, a place where dreams come true, his own little Shangri-La. Finding that garden of Eden would be priority number one for Boots Littlewood.

*   *   *

Boots dragged his chair to within a few feet of the television, then used the remote to start the DVD player. A moment later, the Volvo glided into view. Boots was hoping to get a plate number off the car. When that didn't happen, he paused the disc, then concentrated on the setting. Boots was assuming the scene had been shot close to Parker's hideaway and he wanted to remember the block when he came upon it. Finally, his eye settled on a five-story apartment building near the far corner. Flanked by two-family homes with sunken garages, the building's white brick and featureless architecture made it the closest thing to a landmark.

Boots restarted the disc, then settled back to endure thirty minutes of zoo and beach before he caught a break. The particular footage he watched had been shot from the passenger seat of a car with the camera focused on Chris Parker. Boots watched for street signs, business signs, anything to place the car at a particular location. He was almost ready to give up when the car slowed to a stop at a red light and Parker gave the camera a playful shake. The lens zoomed out, hesitated briefly, finally pulled back.

Boots reversed the disc, then made three attempts before he managed to freeze the image at just the right moment. The camera was now focused on a small plaque mounted beside the door of a frame house. The plaque was easily read: A. Gubenkian and Son, Attorneys at Law. Better yet, after the light changed, the car drove for less than a mile before turning on to a street with a white apartment building at the end of the block.

Boots leaned back as the scene shifted to the bedroom and Chris Parker's sexual exploits. He told himself to put aside his distaste, that he'd seen far worse in his time, that reviewing the entire contents of the disc was a job that had to be done and there was nobody else to do it. Plus, the room was dark and the focus poor. Parker had not so much recorded his triumphs as created a way to resurrect them in his memory.

Fortunately, the disc's many segments were short, most around five minutes, with abrupt transitions as Chris and his partners skipped from position to position. Boots had the DVD set to run on double time, which made the whole thing even jerkier. At times, the mattress bounced up and down like a dinghy in a hurricane.

After a while, Boots realized that some of Parker's love partners were common prostitutes, which made the whole business even more pathetic. He began to grow bored at that point, his mind wandering away from the action, but then he saw the face of his partner, saw Jill Kelly naked against a stack of pillows, beckoning Chris Parker forward, smiling that enigmatic smile, eyes sparkling with excitement.

In an instant, as if the pieces had only been waiting to jump into place, Boots knew everything. He shut off the DVD player, then stared at the blank screen until he heard the front door open. Mama Drago returning home.

Boots glanced at his watch to find that an hour had gone by, an hour in which he'd asked himself a single question: What am I going to do? An hour in which he'd been unable to form a single coherent response, though he did conclude that he was truly and irrevocably fucked.

THIRTY-ONE

The Yankee game was playing on the radio and Boots knew they were behind, though he didn't know the score. He was parked in a nondescript neighborhood in the Brooklyn community of Bensonhurst, five minutes from the Verranzano Bridge leading to Staten Island. Outside, the sky was rapidly filling with dark-edged clouds, the string of perfect June days about to end, but he was as unaware of the weather as the ball game. Boots was feeling sorry for himself. Talk about your bad breaks. Talk about your dumb decisions. Boots had volunteered to brace Frankie Drago, figuring he was familiar with the bookmaker's little quirks. How could he predict that Drago would name Vinnie? That Vinnie would be charged with murder? That Crazy Jill Kelly would land, feet first, in the middle of his contented little life? Even thinking about her, he felt himself stiffen.

Boots sighed, then glanced across the street at a baby in a stroller. The girl was staring directly at him, her gaze as intrusive as a slap in the face. Boots looked back at her, wondering what she was trying to decide. She was too young for language, too young to be guided by experience, yet her stare was all-consuming.

Maybe she was trying to understand how a grown man could be such a complete asshole.

The self-accusations were still flying when the woman Boots awaited stepped from the white-brick apartment building. She looked in both directions, then walked directly toward him. Boots might have gotten out at that point, but he remained where he was, his mind kicking into high gear. Though he was too preoccupied to know it, his gaze was even more intense than that of the child across the street. And, like the child, words played no part in his calculations. Only a sense – derived from her bent posture and a heavy sweater that hung below her hips, from the way she stared down at the sidewalk, from her slow and hesitant gait – of how to proceed.

Be firm, but gentle, he told himself as he withdrew his shield and opened the door. Be her daddy.

Be her daddy? Not unless her daddy had a scar on his forehead and one eye halfway closed. When Boots stepped into her path, the woman raised a hand to her mouth and began to quiver.

'Excuse me, Miss.' He placed his shield directly in front of her face, the better to block her view of his own. 'My name is Detective Littlewood and I need to speak with you.'

'Me?'

'Tell me your name.'

'Madeline Gobard.' Up close, she wasn't unattractive, just unhealthy. Her brown hair was lifeless, perhaps even dirty, her eyes dull, the whites yellowed. 'Did I do somethin' wrong?'

'I don't think so, Madeline. But we need to talk.' Boots held up the disc, trying to keep it simple. 'We need to talk about this DVD. And about Chris Parker.'

Madeline pulled the sleeves of her sweater down over her trembling hands. 'Do I gotta move?' she asked. 'I don't have no place to go.'

'How old are you?'

'Eighteen.' She ran her fingers through her hair, which fell right back over the sides of her face. 'I didn't have nowhere to live when I hooked up with Chris. Chris gave me a home.'

Boots nodded agreeably. Like so many of the men and women he dealt with, nature had left Madeline woefully unprepared for survival in the modern world.

'All right,' he said, 'first thing, we're going to inspect your apartment.'

'It ain't really mine.'

'Then you have nothing to worry about.' She didn't resist when Boots took her arm. 'Why don't you give me the keys?'

Chris Parker's living room might have been plucked from a department store showroom. A couch and matching side chairs, end tables supporting green ceramic lamps, a tall bookcase filled with popular novels. A large vase sporting a flock of cranes and a school of leaping fish rested on a cabinet by the window. Across the way, a Bose stereo surrounded a flat-screen TV with a built-in DVD player. Boots stared at the television for a moment. He wanted to put his foot through the screen, but knew, if he did, Madeline was likely to jump out the window.

'Is this where Parker watched his home movies?' Boots asked.

Madeline had yet to raise her eyes from the floor. 'Yes,' she said.

'And what did you do while he indulged his fantasies?' The words were out before Boots realized that the last thing he wanted to know was the answer to this question. 'Scratch that. Let's see the rest of the apartment.'

The bedroom Madeline led Boots into was dominated by a familiar king-sized bed. Boots looked to the corners of the room, found the pin-holes at the junction of walls and ceiling.

'Chris was very strict,' Madeline declared without being prompted. 'I did whatever he said.'

'Did you want to?'

'No.'

'Then why?'

'My mother dumped me out when I was seventeen, so I had to live on the street. That was very hard. People hurt you on the street. Sometimes they hurt you bad.'

'Why did your mother ask you to leave?'

When she responded after a moment's consideration, Madeline's inflection was ruler-flat. 'Her boyfriend was makin' a move on me, ya know. Comin' into the bathroom when I was in the shower. Comin' into my bedroom when I was gettin' dressed. She said I was leadin' him on.'

Boots sighed. He wanted to hate her, but it was impossible. 'Where did Chris sleep?'

'He usually didn't stay over.'

'Where did he sleep when he did stay?'

'On the bed.'

'And you?'

'Sometimes with him, when he wanted me. The rest of the time on the couch.'

Boots nodded, then walked into the second bedroom. Aside from a large table dominated by a computer and various bits of peripheral hardware, the room was empty. Boots traced a pair of cables that ran up the wall, then across the top of the room to a closet. He opened the closet to find it, like the room, almost empty.

'You have to push,' Madeline said.

'Huh?'

'On the back.'

'Show me.'

Madeline walked into the closet and gave the wall a shove. A concealed door popped open to reveal an extremely narrow space. Parker's carpentry skills were much in evidence here.

Boots stepped into the small space behind the closet. He had to duck to get through the door, then turn sideways to fit into the makeshift room. To his right, a pair of small monitors, each with its own controller, rested on a shelf. There was no ventilation in the room, and no place to sit down.

'Whose name is on the lease?' Boots asked.

'Chris's.'

'And who's been paying the rent since he died?'

'I have.'

'How?'

Boots stepped out of the closet and turned to face Madeline, the mistake she made beginning to register. Already hooked at the corners, her mouth fell still further. Boots put his hand on her shoulder.

'Chris is gone, Madeline,' Boots said as he guided her into the living room. 'I'm your only hope now. It's me you have to please.'

The tone of voice, the look in his eyes, the gentle touch. If only his cellphone hadn't begun to ring, the effect would have been as empathetic as Susan Sarandon praying for that twisted killer in *Dead Man Walking*. But the toneless trill, almost insect-like, ruined the performance. Disgusted, Boots took out his cellphone.

'Yeah.'

'Hey, Boots, was I such a disappointment?'

'Jill?'

'I mean, I've been rejected before, but moving out, that's a bit extreme. You could've just sent me a note.'

Boots's laugh was a little too sharp and Madeline backed away. Though Boots didn't try to hold her, he gestured toward the couch and she sat without protesting.

'Don't take it personally, Jill, It's just that I'm allergic to lethal projectiles.'

'So, how do I find you?'

'You're doin' it right now. But there's a question I've been wantin' to ask you.'

'Why don't you come over tonight – say about eleven – ask it then?'

Boots didn't reply for a moment. Not that he was in any doubt. In fact, the thrills would begin with him getting from his car to her door without being shot.

'Didn't you say you lived with your mother?'

'My mother's a drunk, Boots. She'll be passed out long before you get here.'

Madeline was up and moving as Boots shoved the phone into his pocket. She crossed the room to the cabinet beneath the window and opened the door to expose a small safe.

'What you want's in here.'

'Is it locked?'

'Yes.'

'Do you know the combination?'

'It's written on a piece of paper.'

Boots ground his teeth in frustration. 'Get the paper and open the safe.' After a second, he added, 'Please.'

A few minutes later, Boots was looking at the contents of the safe: a stack of DVDs on a shelf, a pile of money on the bottom, a small ledger beneath the money.

Boots pointed to the cash. 'This how you've been payin' the rent?'

'Yes.' Madeline was standing to one side, her arms folded across her breasts.

'What about the DVDs? Are there any more in the apartment?'
'Not that I know about.'
'There are no more safes, no more false closets?'
'No.'

Boots took up the ledger, found it handwritten in some sort of code. There were dates, figures and a series of names: Goose, Pedro, Carlos, Ricardo. Without Parker to unravel the code, the ledger didn't amount to much, not as evidence. But it would provide a rough estimate of LeGuin's payoffs. That would be important later on.

'All right, Madeline, what I'm gonna do is leave this money so you can keep paying the rent.' Boots stopped when Madeline burst into tears. Talk about disabilities. What Madeline needed was support. What she'd likely find, when the money ran out, was a series of men who'd exploit, then discard her.

Boots went in search of a tool box, certain the handy Chris Parker wouldn't be without a basic collection of household tools. He found what he was seeking under the sink and hauled it, along with the DVDs, into the second bedroom. Though far from computer literate, Boots knew that anything on the DVDs was also on the computer's hard drive. He was tempted to destroy the hard drive on the spot, but contented himself with the discs, cutting them into slivers with a pair of tin shears.

'Madeline, can you operate the whole system?'
'How do ya mean?'
'I want to know if you can make a DVD?'
'Yeah, ya just click and the computer does it for ya.'
'What about sound? Why was there no sound on the DVD I had?'
'The bed squeaked.'
'What?'
'The bed squeaked real loud and you couldn't hear anything else. So Chris recorded with the volume off.'
'Can you turn it on?'

Madeline's eyes clouded with suspicion. As far as she knew, Chris Parker's system had a single purpose. 'What do I gotta do?'
'Only one thing, and then I'll be on my way, at least for the present. I want you to help me shift some furniture.'

THIRTY-TWO

Boots dashed the two blocks between the nearest parking space and Jill Kelly's modest row house through a cold, pelting rain. Though he was aware of the potential for threats against his life, he failed to keep an eye out for would-be assassins. There was no point. Carried by a sharp wind, the rain was blowing into his eyes and it was all he could do not to stumble over cracks in the sidewalk. Fortunately, the door opened as he tore up the steps and then he was inside with Jill Kelly, her ice-blue t-shirt and lace-trimmed panties commanding the whole of his attention.

'Boots, you're all wet,' she said, smiling that amused vampire smile, the one that said *Welcome to my castle.* 'I think you'd better get out of your clothes right away. Otherwise, you'll catch your death.'

Boots did as he was told, letting his wet garments drop, one at a time, to the carpet. Finally, he stood naked in front of her.

Jill's smile dissolved as she laid her hand on his chest. When she could feel his heart beating against her palm, she leaned forward to lightly pinch his nipple with her teeth. His heart kicked up a notch and she backed away.

'I hope you were right about your mother,' Boots said.

Now Jill was grinning. The son-of-a-bitch had blindsided her again. 'Do you think we should put your clothes in the dryer now? Or later?'

Boots answered her question with one of his own. 'Would you catch an attitude,' he asked, 'if I ripped that t-shirt off your body?'

'Yeah, I would.'

'I was hoping you'd say that.'

Boots knew it was more than a bad case of the hots. And there was nothing he could do about it. Free will be damned; he was helpless. Boots felt as if he'd been tapped on the shoulder, been delegated. But to do exactly what? To protect Crazy Jill Kelly from herself? Talk about your suicidal impulses. Boots glanced at the clock. Three in the morning and the room smelling of tobacco and sex, Jill asleep alongside him, snoring lightly. From somewhere in the basement, Boots could hear the dryer turning.

Boots turned when Jill rolled on to her back. Relaxed in sleep, she was even more beautiful, and he thought, just for a moment, that he recognized the woman she might have been. Her face was Irish-pale, her auburn hair nearly black in the darkened room. Her relaxed shoulders and opened hands left her frail and vulnerable. Across the top of her breasts, a spray of pale freckles attracted his mouth like magnets. Boots resisted their pull, not because he feared waking Jill, but because Jill had emptied his pockets and he couldn't get hard again if he used a splint.

Boots laid back on the pillow and closed his eyes. A few minutes later, he fell into a sleep from which he emerged after four dreamless hours. Jill was shaking him, and none too gently.

'C'mon, Boots,' she said, her tone matter-of-fact, 'you gotta get out before my mother comes down.'

Boots sat up and rubbed his eyes. 'Ya know, Jill,' he said, 'it would have been kinder if you'd dressed yourself before makin' that request.'

'What's the matter, Boots, you didn't get enough last night?'

'I did get enough last night, but it's morning now.'

'And time to go home. Your clothes are on the chair.' Jill slipped into a bathrobe. With no realistic expectation of success, she was hoping to bum-rush Boots out the door without having that serious conversation.

Boots slid his feet over the edge of the bed, then grabbed his clothes and stumbled into the bathroom. He relieved himself, washed his face with brown soap that smelled like incense, finally took a moment to stare at himself in the mirror. Neither his damaged eye nor his scars, he reminded himself, had anything to do with Jill Kelly. If there was a war, it was between Mack Corcoran and Boots Littlewood. Jill was an ally.

Nevertheless, when Boots emerged from the bathroom, he led with a question that was certain to provoke an evasive response.

'Tell me what happened on the day your father was killed.'

'Did you read the case file?'

'I did.'

'Then you know.'

Boots had expected Jill to become angry, but her eyes were mild. She'd anticipated the question.

'Fine, so let me see if I've got the facts straight. When you heard the shots, you became so terrified that you couldn't bring yourself to turn around. Thus, you not only failed to observe the shooter, but you can't be sure there was only one man involved. That about it?'

'Like I said, Boots, my statement speaks for itself.'

'What about your mother? What happened to your mother's statement?'

'She didn't give a statement because . . .'

'Because she passed out before you and your father came home. I get it, Jill. I get that you don't trust me.'

Jill Kelly walked Boots to the front door. It'd been a long time since she'd felt this way about a man. She pulled him into a kiss that rolled on until they were both out of breath.

'Say, Boots,' she said as she opened the door, 'you wouldn't want to tell me where you're stayin' these days. As long as we're talkin' trust.'

The smile Boots flashed was as bright as it was brief. 'I wouldn't, Jill. But I will say this. The bedroom is perfect. The ruffled spread, the pleated curtains, the stuffed dog, the *Sesame Street* puppets, the pink sheets. Just perfect.'

Boots went back to Frankie Drago's long enough to shave, shower and change his clothes. Then he headed off to Astoria, to Libby Greenspan's, for an early lunch. Outside, a pale sky was veiled by thin clouds and it was much cooler, more like April than June. Boots took the scenic route, over the Pulaski Bridge and across western Queens. There was plenty of traffic, but he didn't mind the leisurely pace. He was thinking about Jill Kelly, imagining them a hundred and fifty years ago in a small Arizona town, the only law in the county. Wouldn't they be surprised, the bad guys in their black hats, when they squared off against Crazy Jill at ten paces? Just in case, Boots put himself in a second-floor window with a shotgun.

When Boots walked into Libby's apartment, Joaquin was sitting at the dining-room table. Before joining him, Boots accepted a kiss from Libby and a hug from his father.

'You do that thing for me, Jackie?' he asked.

'I might've.'

Boots noted a familiar spark in Joaquin's eye. The kid had pulled off something slick and couldn't wait to talk about it. 'So, let's hear the story.'

'First, Elijah LeGuin's mother is deceased, his father unknown and he's never been married. He has two siblings, younger sisters, both in the military. One is stationed in Iraq. She's a major. The other one's a captain. She's in Texas. They didn't seem likely candidates for what you wanted, but I searched for property listings in both their names, and in their brother's name. *Nada.* Then I thought about what you said, about how LeGuin might use a girl-friend to front for him. All well and good, but how do I find her if she's not legally tied to LeGuin?'

Libby came out of the kitchen with a carafe of coffee and a couple of mugs. When she laid them on the table, then turned away, Boots said, 'I take it you've already heard this story.'

'Twice,' Andy said from inside the kitchen.

Joaquin blushed and Boots made an effort to look away. 'Go ahead, Jackie. I didn't mean to interrupt.'

Joaquin filled his mug, then his father's. 'I ran a limited search through New York City birth records going back three years. The limitation I chose was paternity. I wanted to know whether LeGuin had fathered any children. If the search had come up negative, I would have extended it to five years and included New Jersey, maybe Pennsylvania. But I got lucky right away. Elijah LeGuin is the father of two children by a woman named Isabella Amarando. She owns a three-bedroom condo on Groton Street in Forest Hills.'

Boots made the connection instantly. Isabella Amarando was the registered owner of the Ford Windstar used in the drive-by. Unable to contain himself, Boots marched off to the bathroom, where he called Craig O'Malley. Could they meet this afternoon, at the sergeant's convenience?

'Four thirty, same place as last time.'

Lunch started out well, considering the tension. Boots knew that all assembled, especially Andy, wanted to learn something of his activities. An estimate, at the very least, of when the family could return home. Boots told them nothing, as he struggled with his impatience. Events were speeding up and he needed to get out in front.

But the silence was too much for Andy Littlewood and he decided, at the last minute, not to respect his son's privacy. He had too much at stake here. 'Father Leo,' he declared, 'says to tell you that you're in his prayers.' When Boots didn't respond, he added, 'Father Leo thought you might want to come by for confession.'

'Tell him my soul is still pure from the last time.'

A self-professed atheist, Joaquin laughed. 'I think my father's in love,' he announced as he bit into a pickle. 'And having seen Jill Kelly, I can understand why.

But he couldn't, of course. Joaquin didn't know the first thing about Crazy Jill. Boots calmly bit into his sandwich. He was comforted by the thought that he could never have her. Even if things worked out, she would eventually move on.

'She's beautiful, that girl, and blazin' hot,' Andy said. He glanced at Libby, noted her frown, finally echoed his son's thoughts. 'But she's all wrong for you, Irwin. She's not a woman you can possess, no more than you can hold fire. All you can do is dance in her flame and hope you're not consumed.'

Boots was initially pleased when his cellphone began to trill. First, because the time when he'd have to respond to his father was rapidly approaching. Second, because he hoped it was Jill Kelly. He carried the phone into the kitchen before answering.

'Boots, it's Levine,' Lieutenant Sorrowful said.

'What's up, lou?'

'Lenny Olmeda, he's dead. Shot down in his apartment. His cleaning lady discovered the body. I'm calling to give you a heads-up.'

'When did this happen?'

'Preliminary estimate, last night between seven and ten o'clock.'

Boots took a second to think it over, then said, 'The shit's gonna hit the fan now.'

'The bosses are trying to keep a lid on things. Public Information is talking about a possible suicide.'

'Who's investigating?'

'The Chief of D's office.' Levine paused to take a breath. 'What you have to think here, Boots, is that somebody's eventually gonna knock on your door, ask for a minute-by-minute account of your movements during the relevant time frame.'

Boots grinned to himself. He had an airtight alibi for the relevant time frame. He was playing hearts with Frankie Drago and his mother. Boots imagined explaining his relationship with a known bookmaker accused of killing his sister.

Oh yeah, me and Frankie, we go way back.

At which point an IAB team would lead him into a courtyard, put him against a wall, ask him if he wanted a last cigarette.

THIRTY-THREE

'**N**ice lobby.'

Boots turned to Boris Velikov, who exhibited a loopy smile beneath glassy eyes. According to O'Malley, the Bulgarian's antidepressant level had recently been nudged upward.

'Yeah,' Boots said for lack of something better, 'high-class all the way.'

In fact, there was something about the lobby that struck him as empty. Maybe it was the aspiration: the red rug, the flocked wallpaper, a gilded chandelier that would have been at home in a whorehouse. From outside, the ten-story, eighty-unit building was no more than a collection of rectangles. But luxury was the name of the game in the new millennium. Everybody wanted to be on the next rung, and if you couldn't make it in real life, you could always plaster the lobby with oil paintings dark enough to pass for respectable.

The building's obligatory doorman rose to his feet and came toward them. A middle-aged Latino, he wore a double-breasted maroon jacket with gold piping and a pair of epaulets worthy of an admiral in the Kaiser's navy. On his face, an uh-oh expression rose suddenly, deflated just as suddenly when the three giants revealed their badges, finally blossomed once more as he considered the implications.

Boots proffered Maytag LeGuin's mug shot. 'Is this man in apartment eight-F?'

As Boots spoke, Velikov moved to the doorman's right, O'Malley to his left, polar bears surrounding a beached seal.

'Yes,' the doorman said. 'This man is in Ms Amarando's apartment. Do you wan' me to announce you?'

'Do you want me to beat you to a pulp?'

'No.'

'That's good. Now, tell me who else is up there.'

'Please, I only start my shift one hour ago, at ten o'clock. I see Mr LeGuin go up aroun' ten thirty.' He shrugged. 'Who else might be there—'

'Amarando, she get a lot of traffic?'

'I don' un'erstan' wha' you askin' me.'

'I wanna know if drugs are being dealt out of that apartment. I wanna know if Ms Amarando gets visitors of a certain type.'

The doorman's head swung from side to side. 'Ms Amarando, she's a very quiet lady. Her sister comes sometimes, and her mother. But she don' make no trouble.'

Boots positioned himself to one side of the door, then knocked lightly. He was hoping to remove LeGuin without disturbing the neighbors. There was no response and he knocked again, this time a little harder. Finally, a woman's voice from inside: 'Who is it?'

'Police,' Boots said. 'Open the door. We have a search warrant.'

This was true. Boots did have a warrant, which he'd spent many hours securing, but it was for Isabella Amarando's Ford Windstar, not her residence.

Boots heard Isabella whisper to someone – an exchange of advice, no doubt. Finally, she said, 'Slide the warrant under the door.'

'Open up, Isabella. Or we'll bust our way inside. No bullshit. I mean now.'

'Awright, awright.' The door opened a few inches. The safety chain was still on. 'Lemme see the warrant?'

Boots held it up for Isabella's inspection, turning after a few seconds to the last page and the judge's signature. 'Make it easy on yourself. There's no reason to get the neighbors involved. Remember, your children live here.'

From inside the apartment, a male voice said, 'Open the damn door.'

Boots was inside the apartment, his weapon drawn, an instant after Isabella released the chain, forcing her backwards and on to her butt. Maytag LeGuin was sitting in a chair fifteen feet away. Boots locked his weapon on LeGuin's forehead. This man had tried to murder him, to end his life, whether or not the dealer was inside

the van. Boots again heard the roar of the shotgun, then a shower
of brick on the sidewalk behind him, as if the events were ongoing.
He felt time slow down, and the absolute certainty that he wasn't
quick enough to defend himself burst into his consciousness like a
shroud. If it hadn't been for Jill Kelly . . .

Boots felt the desire to kill LeGuin ripple through his flesh, felt
it leap into the tip of his right forefinger, the one resting on the
Glock's trigger. What would it take? Three pounds of pressure? You
could produce three pounds of pressure merely by accident, right?

LeGuin's eyes were darting about, from Boots's scar, to his half-
closed eye, to the barrel of his gun. 'Hey, man,' he said, 'no reason
to get crazy here.'

The dealer's speech hinted at his British origins, the effect jarring
enough to slow Boots down. Still, Boots had to ask himself if putting
a round in LeGuin's skull wouldn't do wonders for his post-traumatic
stress. Surely, the remedy would be more effective than handing
LeGuin over to the state. Boots thought of Jill Kelly, of her all-too-
evident stress. Jill would delight in this little adventure, no doubt,
and nothing would have made Boots happier than to have Jill with
him at that moment. But it was clearly impossible.

'Anybody else in the apartment?' Boots asked.

'My children,' Isabella responded.

'Where are they?'

'In their beds, asleep.'

'No one else?'

Isabella's mouth opened, then shut.

'Remember,' Boots said, 'we've got a warrant.'

'Elijah's cousin, Malcolm,' she said. 'He's sick in his bed.'

Boots glanced at O'Malley. 'Check it out. I need a moment with
Mr LeGuin.'

'No problem.'

Maytag LeGuin didn't protest when Boots pulled him off the couch,
spun him around and cuffed his hands behind his back. In his early
forties, LeGuin had the sad eyes of a prizefighter suddenly grown
old in the ring. Still, he met Boots's gaze evenly.

'You know who I am?' Boots asked.

'No.'

'I'm the man you tried to murder two days ago.' Boots gave it a couple of beats, then said, 'What would you do, Maytag, if you got your hands on somebody responsible for a shotgun bein' fired at your head? What would you do if you had such a man in your power?'

LeGuin had a sharp nose and chin, both of which he emphasized by tilting his head up. 'You can't put my hands on no shotgun. Two days ago, I was in Jersey City.'

Boots pressed the barrel of his Glock against LeGuin's forehead. 'You say that again, I'll kill you.' As far as he could tell, he meant it.

'Yo, Boots, you better come check this out.'

Boots turned to Craig O'Malley. Like his partner, O'Malley wore a leather jacket that would've been appropriate on a mob wannabe. 'What's up, sarge?'

'Guy in the bedroom's been shot.'

'Bad?'

'See for yourself.'

Boots recognized the boy instantly. The face in the van's window, the face behind the shotgun. He'd never have thought it possible if asked beforehand, but the round face and protruding front teeth seemed as familiar as the images he carried of his own mother.

Still in his teens, the boy's face was pouring sweat and his breathing was labored, the phlegm rattling in his lungs. He had a badly infected entrance wound high up on the right side of his chest. The injury itself did not appear life-threatening, but the whole room smelled of rot.

'You waitin' for him to die? That what it is?' Boots had LeGuin by his left arm. He squeezed down as he asked the question. 'That what you're hopin', Maytag? You hopin' he'll die with your kids in the next room? Maybe they could watch you cut up the body, learn a few life lessons?'

Boots glanced at the Bulgarian's face. The loopy smile was gone, replaced by a rage so blind that Boots had to suppress a smile. Not for the first time did he remind himself never to get on Velikov's bad side.

'You sent this kid to kill me,' he continued. 'Now you're gonna let him die. Tell me somethin', how'd you like it if we dragged your ass upstate and handcuffed you to a tree? How'd you like it if we taped your mouth shut and left you there?' Boots jerked his head toward Velikov. 'You think my partner would have a problem with that?'

LeGuin picked his words carefully. He didn't think Boots would follow through, but he wasn't absolutely sure. Boots would already be dead if their positions were reversed. Meanwhile, Elijah LeGuin hadn't even been arrested. Was that good or bad news? He didn't know. But he was sure that Boots wanted something more than revenge.

'Malcolm took a bad turn this afternoon. I was thinkin' about callin' nine-one-one 'bout the time you arrived.'

Boots lifted a wallet from the top of a small bureau. He found a driver's license and a Medicaid ID card inside, both issued to Malcolm Sutcliffe, age nineteen. He put the license in his shirt pocket, then turned to Isabella.

'Where's the van?' he asked.

No more than five feet tall, Isabella stood with her hands on her hips, the very picture of defiance. 'If you're talkin' about my Windstar, it was stolen on Friday night.'

'You report the theft?'

'Yeah.'

'When?'

'Sunday morning. That's when I went out to look for it.'

Boots was about to ask how she knew the van was stolen on Friday if she didn't notice it missing until Sunday, but then he glanced at LeGuin. Maytag wasn't worried about the van, which would have Malcolm Sutcliffe's blood in it. That meant the vehicle had already been destroyed.

'OK, here's the plan. I'm gonna make a phone call, after which I'm takin' Maytag out of here. You, Isabella, the minute the door closes behind us, will call nine-one-one and have Malcolm carted off to the hospital. I'll be outside until the ambulance arrives, just to make sure. Keep in mind, if I want to, I can have your kids taken away. You think I'm lyin', just try me.'

Boots turned and walked back to the living room. He consulted a small notebook, then punched a series of numbers into the key pad of his cellphone. Madeline Gobard answered on the second ring.

'We're on the way,' Boots said.

THIRTY-FOUR

nspector Murad Najaz pointed to the DVD in Boots's hand. 'How long?' he asked.

'Three hours.'

Boots and Najaz were in a small office within the larger suite of offices comprising the headquarters of the NYPD's Detective Bureau. Earlier that morning, only a few hours after the DVD was completed, Boots had reached out to Jill Kelly's uncle, Michael Shaw, Chief of Detectives. Inspector Najaz was as far as he'd gotten.

'What will I learn if I watch it?'

'A mid-level cocaine and heroin dealer named Elijah LeGuin will admit to paying off Mack Corcoran, Lorenzo Olmeda, Arthur Farrahan and Christopher Parker for ongoing protection. LeGuin will also admit that he orchestrated the attempted murder of Detective Jill Kelly at the request of Mack Corcoran.'

Najaz folded his thick arms across his even thicker chest. Well over six feet tall, his size alone produced what the bosses referred to as command presence. Najaz was a black man, raised in Brooklyn by parents who'd converted to Islam when Muhammad Ali became a Muslim.

'Any of this admissible?' he asked.

'No, but combined with other information, it opens avenues of investigation almost certain to bear fruit.'

'Like what?'

Boots ticked the items off on his fingers. 'Malcolm Sutcliffe, the boy who fired a shotgun at two police officers on Saturday morning, and who was wounded at the scene, is presently recovering in Elmhurst General Hospital. One of his intended victims, meaning myself, observed him in a neutral setting and is prepared to identify him in court. Sutcliffe was left to die by Maytag LeGuin and now has every reason to cooperate with the authorities. In addition, the registered owner of the Ford van used in the shooting is the mother of LeGuin's two children. Her freedom can be traded for LeGuin's cooperation.'

'All right, enough.' Najaz's forefinger traced a little circle. 'Start it up.'

A moment later, Elijah 'Maytag' LeGuin's head and torso filled the screen, the close-up so extreme that when he turned to the right or the left, as he did from time to time, a chunk of his head left the frame. Boots had instructed Madeline carefully. Under no circumstances was Boots Littlewood, seated at the other end of a small table, or O'Malley and the Bulgarian, who'd positioned themselves along the wall, to become visible.

'Is what they say about you true, Maytag?' Although distorted by the distance between the speaker and the microphone in the wall, the disembodied voice clearly belonged to Boots Littlewood.

'True. I got two eyes, two ears, two feet, two arms, two legs and two balls. What else you wanna know?'

'I want to know,' Boots persisted, 'if you put cats in washing machines when you were a kid. That's part of your rep. It helps make you what you are. I just wanna know if it's true?'

'Yeah? Straight up? Because what I'd like to know is if you still fuck your daughter in the ass.'

The screen went blank for a few seconds, then LeGuin reappeared. Though his face was unmarked, his short-cropped hair had been pushed to one side, revealing a scar over his right ear.

'You tried to kill me,' Boots said, 'but I've only treated you with respect. How do you explain that?'

'You kidnap me, beat me down, then call it respect?'

Boots laughed out loud. 'Count yourself lucky that I don't actually have a daughter.'

After a moment, LeGuin chuckled. 'I sometimes lose my temper, let my rap get all crazy. But that bullshit with the cats? I hate that like I hate that name – Maytag. Swear on my sainted mum, I never threw her cat into no washin' machine. Those were her gerbils I washed.'

Both men laughed a little too long, neither apparently wanting to be the first to stop. Finally, Boots said, 'OK, let me repeat the question I asked you a moment ago. Now, I'm gonna elaborate a little, but that's just my way, so don't mind me. It's still the same question.'

A short silence followed, then Boots started up. 'Two days ago, I was standin' on the sidewalk in front of my own home, mindin' my own business, when a van registered to Isabella Amarando, the mother of your children, turned on to the block. The van came to within thirty feet, then a boy named Malcolm Sutcliffe rolled down the window and aimed a shotgun at my face. If my partner hadn't wounded Malcolm, what was left of me would be lyin' on an autopsy table in the morgue. Now, that's a lot of provocation, Elijah. That's enough provocation to make a man crazy for revenge, yet I haven't shown you any disrespect. I want you to tell me why that should be so. And while you're at it, ask yourself about Captain Parker and Sergeant Olmeda. Ask yourself what happened to them. What happened and why.'

Seconds turned into minutes as LeGuin prepared his response. He began to speak several times, his mouth opening, then closing again as he reconsidered. Finally, he said, 'You got anybody stupid in your family? You got anyone just naturally chumps out, like it's in his blood?'

'My family and everyone else's.'

'Well, let's say this, sometimes you tell Stupid to do one thing and Stupid does another. Then it's on your head.'

'You talkin' about Malcolm?'

LeGuin's knee began to jump. 'I'm talkin' about tellin' Stupid, "Just follow the bitch. See where she goes, what she does." But Stupid ain't got the self-control of a hungry rat. Stupid wants to represent. Stupid wants to be a gangsta. He listens to them beats and thinks it's for real.'

When LeGuin stopped speaking, Boots patiently turned him around. 'That's fine, Elijah, but it doesn't answer the question. Why am I treatin' you with respect?'

Najaz signaled Boots to stop the video. A detective for thirty years, he was the co-author of a textbook on the craft of interrogation. He knew that Boots was seeking to establish a rapport with LeGuin before asking any pointed questions. Though often effective, the technique was time-consuming.

'Tell me where you're headed?' he asked Boots. 'Maybe we can skip some of the boilerplate.'

'I want to convince LeGuin that Corcoran is out of the picture. The payoffs come to me from now on. In return, I'll overlook the attempt on my life.'

Najaz laughed. 'You're right,' he admitted. 'The tape can definitely not be presented in a court of law.'

*   *   *

It took forty minutes before LeGuin answered the question, and only after Boots posed it as a hypothetical. If a person unknown had done all the things LeGuin did, and if cops unknown were still respecting him, what did that mean?

'If all those ifs you just said was true,' LeGuin declared, 'then the dude would figure the cops wanted somethin'.' His head did a slow dance, chin swiveling up and to the left. He'd broken through a barrier, one self-erected, and on some level he knew it.

'And what do you think those cops would want, Elijah?'

They again circled the block, Boots probing, LeGuin evading. Quick-witted, the dealer might even have believed that he was holding his own. In fact, he was gradually shedding his defensive posture. His shoulders dropped and his fingers uncurled as he slouched in the chair, legs crossed at the knee.

Finally, Boots slapped the table. 'Why don't we look at this another way? Pretend you're directin' a movie and the actor playin' the cop asks you to explain his motivation. What would you tell that actor?'

LeGuin's emotions played across his face. His lips moved almost continually, tightening down, pursing. He kept his eyes averted for the most part, but the glances he threw Boots were pointed. Boots was offering him a way out. If he accepted it, they could pretend to be entrepreneurs negotiating a business deal. This was definitely preferable to handcuffed and helpless, but LeGuin had been around for a long time and he had a nose for traps. On the other hand, there was that moron, Malcolm, who'd hold out for maybe ten seconds before spilling his guts.

'I don't wanna slow your roll,' he finally said, 'but I can't pay double. I can't pay Corcoran and pay you, too. You got to take the man off my back.'

'No problem.'

LeGuin recoiled. 'See, right there I gotta ask myself if you're full of shit.'

'Why's that?'

'You remember a player named Maurice Selman? Came up before me? He was capped around six years ago.'

Maurice Selman was the dealer who'd accused Corcoran of extortion. 'Yeah,' Boots said, 'I know who he is.'

'Well, it was Corcoran's people who offed him.'

'How do you know that?'

'Man told me straight to my face. I don't come across, he'll do to me what he done to Maurice. Plus, Maurice wasn't the only one.'

'There were others?'

'Told me he killed a cop, too. Way back when.' LeGuin closed his eyes for a second, then looked down at the floor. They'd been at it for an hour. 'I ain't disrespectin' you. I ain't sayin' you're soft. But Corcoran . . .' LeGuin raised his head to stare across the table. 'Tell you this, he's gonna cap that bitch or die tryin'.'

'And what bitch would that be?'

'Jill Kelly. All my life, I never knew a man to hate a woman like that.'

THIRTY-FIVE

Boots paused the DVD, then leaned back in his chair. 'That's the breakthrough. After that, me and Maytag became partners.'

'Did he add anything important?' Najaz waved the question off. 'Scratch that,' he said, pointing at the DVD player. 'Are there any other copies of the disc?'

'One.' After the job was complete, after O'Malley and Velikov left to drive LeGuin home, after a fumbling Madeline Gobard produced a pair of DVDs, Boots had opened the computer, extracted the hard drive, then smashed it to pieces with a claw hammer. No record of Jill Kelly and Chris Parker's tryst now existed. Or so he hoped.

Najaz jerked his receding chin at the TV screen. 'You were good,' he declared, 'very good. Too good to be doing what you've been doing all these years. So, why were you never promoted? Why are you still a detective, third grade?'

'Beats me,' Boots returned.

As the silence built, Najaz realized that Boots was playing him the way he'd played LeGuin. Najaz found this turn of events amusing. 'And why is it,' he needled, 'that you're still working down in the . . . What's that precinct again?'

'The Six-Four.'

'Right, the Six-Four. How did it come to pass that a man of your talents spent his career as a squad detective in Brooklyn?'

'Most likely because I have a low tolerance for bullshit.'

Najaz laughed out loud. 'That would do it,' he admitted. 'Now, is there anything more that I need to see?'

Boots pointed the remote at the screen and pressed search. 'Yeah, one last bit. It's not long.'

LeGuin's hands were moving – small, palms-up gestures to illustrate the various points he made. He spoke directly, without hesitation, his truthfulness apparent at a glance.

'When Corcoran come to me with that bullshit – go out and kill a cop – I got so pissed I wanted to ask him why he didn't do it his own self. But Corcoran, he don't appreciate back talk, so what I did was play him for time. I put Malcolm and another boy to watch Kelly, figurin' the right opportunity would never come and it'd all blow over. But Malcolm ain't too good at thinkin' ahead. He sees you and Kelly walkin' down the street and he just has to bust a move, just can't control hisself. Never mind there's witnesses on the street. Never mind he's ridin' in a vehicle can be traced back to Isabella. Man, if I even dreamed the boy was packin' heat, I woulda bitch-slapped him across the room.'

'I believe you, Elijah. And like I already said, I'm willin' to forget the whole thing. It's over, right?'

'Far as I'm concerned, it was over before it started. But Corcoran, he ain't under my control. Last time I spoke to him, he said he put out another contract on Kelly. Said he put it with someone who wouldn't fuck it up. Said it was her or him.'

Boots didn't object when Najaz retrieved the disc. 'I got one more thing you might want to look at, inspector.' He took a small book from his briefcase and offered it to Najaz. 'This was Chris Parker's ledger. I don't know if it'll do you any good – it's in code – but here it is.'

Najaz accepted the slim volume. 'I suppose there's only one more question to ask.'

'Before you report?'

'Yeah, before I report.'

'So, let's hear it.'

'What do you want?'

'The murder charges against Vinnie Palermo dismissed.'

Najaz nodded to himself. He'd been sure that Jill's white-hat assessment of Boots was purely fanciful, like much of what Crazy Jill told her uncle. Not so.

'Hang tight, Boots, this might take a while.' Najaz rose to his feet and walked to the door. 'And one thing you might consider while you're waiting. No matter what Jill may have told you, Michael Shaw loves his niece. He wants to protect her.'

'If he can?'

'If he can.'

Boots remained alone in the small room for the next forty-five minutes. On the verge of leaving several times, he managed to check himself. Boots wanted out of the Puzzle Palace, wanted to be away from men he considered terminally ambitious. His need of them pissed him off, and he was still simmering when Chief of Detectives Michael Shaw walked into the room.

Instinctively, Boots rose to his feet, a priest before the Pope. That pissed him off, too, as did Shaw's first words: 'Sit down, Boots. Sit down.'

Tall and reed-thin, Shaw had one of those Irish faces that shed color as the years go by. His skin was porcelain pale, his feathery hair gone beyond gray to white, his blue eyes as pale as water. He fixed those eyes on Boots, his tiny mouth expanding into a smile.

'Is there an implied threat to your visit?' he asked.

'I'm giving you what Jill told me you wanted. In return, I'm asking you to drop murder charges lodged against an innocent man by a team of bent cops.'

Shaw remained standing. He was waiting for Boots to flinch, but didn't really expect that to happen. Nevertheless, he gave it another try. 'I'm asking again. Is there a threat here?'

'A threat? Chief, the only reason I came here today is because I'm hopin' against hope that I won't have to prove Vinnie innocent by arresting Parker's actual killer.'

That was enough for Michael Shaw. He shifted his weight to his right leg and rubbed his aching hip, his demeanor softening.

'I'm getting old, Boots. My days blur, my youth is fast becoming

the rock I cling to. For some reason, I need to make sense of it.'
Shaw took a step toward the door, then stopped. 'There was no
sweeter child than Jill Kelly. And no child who loved her father
more. Patrick Kelly was everything to his daughter – father and
mother, parent and guardian. He put food on her table and washed
the dishes afterward. He tucked her into bed. He bought her First
Communion dress.'

Shaw's pale eyes retreated as the blood rose suddenly to inflame
his cheeks. 'And beautiful she was, detective, as she walked to the
altar, an angel with a smile bright enough to banish despair itself.
I tell you this because I know you love her. Because even a blind
man could see it. Jill's life was ripped apart when her father was
killed. You think you can repair her, but you can do no such thing.
The best you can do, the most you can hope for, is to protect her.'

It was a good speech, Boots decided, lots of man-to-man sincerity,
lots of doomed Irish-poet sentimentality, lots of puffed-up Irish
blarney. Listening to it was the price he had to pay and he didn't
begrudge the cost – if the Chief had expected applause, Boots's
hands would already be moving. But the Chief had missed the point,
missed it altogether. Boots did not think he could repair Jill Kelly.
Nor did he want to. He wanted Crazy Jill the way she was and he
couldn't wait, now that he was done with the Puzzle Palace, to track
her down. He looked up to find Chief Shaw with his hand on the
doorknob.

'Despite what you may think, there are limits to what this office
can accomplish. I can't, for instance, now that Mr Palermo's been
indicted, wave a fairy's wand and have him released. But if it's any
consolation, I don't believe he murdered Captain Parker and I'll do
what I can to free him . . .'

'But?'

Shaw's sliver of a mouth expanded briefly. 'You have Inspector
Najaz's phone number. Use it whenever you want. In the meantime,
take care of my niece.'

On the following afternoon, with no word from Jill, Boots drove his father and Libby Greenspan from Astoria to Brooklyn. Home again. That evening, they had a modest celebration, an Italian dinner also attended by Joaquin, Father Gubetti and Frankie Drago.

The bookmaker's presence was more than a gesture of gratitude. Boots was informing the neighborhood that Angie Drago's death was an accident, at least in his opinion. Whatever lingering doubts Boots may have had were finally dispelled that morning. As Boots was packing his things, Frankie presented him with a pair of receipts issued by Dave Molitor, a local carpenter who took odd jobs.

The door leading to the Drago basement could not have been open when Angie was pushed. It could not have been open because the door wasn't there. Molitor had taken it down in order to repair the frame after a hinge ripped away two weeks before Angie's death. Boots knew Molitor well enough to be sure he wouldn't fake the receipt to help Frankie Drago. He also knew the man worked cheap and did good work, but was an unreliable drunk. Most likely, he'd taken Frankie's down payment to the nearest bar.

The talk at dinner was dominated by Father Gubetti, who sat on the board of the Greenpoint–Williamsburg Preservation Society. An ad-hoc organization, the society was created to fight the city's plans for the East River waterfront between the Williamsburg Bridge and Newtown Creek.

The administration's scheme had undeniable benefits. For example, the heavy industry along the East River, most of it long abandoned, would be replaced by a multi-use esplanade. Though old enough to remember the days when Domino Sugar and the Schaefer Brewery supported hundreds of neighborhood families, the priest did not object to the esplanade, which would include a good bit of park land. Domino and Schaefer had been closed for decades. They weren't coming back, nor were dozens of other businesses fronting the river. Leaving the infrastructure to rust and crumble wasn't to anybody's advantage. No, the problem, for Gubetti, was that the city's plan would allow private developers to line the area behind the esplanade with high-rise, high-end residential towers. Ten thousand apartments would be constructed, ten thousand apartments selling for a million dollars and up. The beginning of the end for working-class Greenpoint and Williamsburg.

'The system,' Leo announced over a dessert of miniature cannolis, espresso and anisette, 'has abandoned us. Our elected representatives welcome us into their offices. They smile, smile, smile, and they ask for our votes. Yet their plans somehow ignore every suggestion we make. I tell you, these politicians and the men who run them have sold their souls to a false god. The marketplace cannot substitute for conscience. Efficiency does not make a callous act virtuous.'

Boots enjoyed the sermon, though he didn't contribute. Going all the way back to his childhood, he could not remember a time when some group wasn't 'taking over the neighborhood'. Blacks, Puerto Ricans, hippies, yuppies, liberal judges, conservative judges – and now the filthy rich. For Boots, forty years of Armageddon was enough.

After dinner, Boots nominated himself and Leo Gubetti to clean up. He waited until he and the priest were alone, then got right to the point, taking a manila envelope from the top of the refrigerator.

'There's a statement from an eyewitness and a DVD in here. If I'm not around to do it myself, I want you to make copies of both. Send one set to Vinnie's lawyer, spread the rest between as many reporters as you can.'

'I thought you said you were safe?'

'Call it a sin of omission, but I only claimed that Jill Kelly was the target on Saturday afternoon.'

'Ah.' Gubetti flashed his tiny monkish smile. 'So, then, what you're now saying, if I understand correctly, is that any future peril in which you find yourself will be entirely of your own making.'

Boots handed Gubetti a towel. 'I'll wash, you dry,' he said.

Four hours later, at eleven o'clock, when Jill finally called, Boots felt as if he'd been yanked into another dimension. There was his family world – the wine, the liqueur, plates of food passed around the table, the priest's sermon, the Yankees who were in the tenth inning of a scoreless game. And then there was the Crazy Jill Kelly world, into which he was instantly sucked when he heard her voice. Reality times ten.

'Boots?'

'Yeah.'

'Where are you?'

'Home.'

'Home?'

'That's right. It turned out, the other day, they were after you, not me.' Boots drank in Jill's laughter; he absorbed it. 'What's funny?'

'You never stop surprising me, Boots. So, are you up for a visit? I'm ten minutes away.'

'Yes, Jill, I'm definitely up.' Boots tone was more-or-less resigned.

'Then why don't you describe, in loving detail, the various perverted acts I'll be made to perform once you have me in your power?'

'Any other time, I wouldn't hesitate, but right now you need to keep your eyes on the rear-view mirror. This is no joke. Corcoran's going to kill you if he can.'

Boots finally looked up to see that the game was over. The Yankees had lost in eleven innings, one–nothing, stranding fourteen runners in the process. He picked up the remote and shut the set down, the Yankees' travails instantly behind him. Only that morning, he'd decided to pick up a can of whipped cream on the way back from Astoria, then forgotten about it. Now he didn't have time to run out.

Jill Kelly marched through the door wearing an off-white pants suit over a matching blouse sheer enough to hint at the black bra beneath. She put a finger to Boots's lips and said, 'Tell me later.'

What they made could not be called love, not by any dictionary definition of the word. Jill was strong and tall, and Boots was forced to use his own strength against her, to lock her hands above her head while she contained him with her hips and thighs. They were both sweating by the time he changed the terms of the debate, rolling on to his back, pulling her astride him. He watched her shake out her wet hair, thinking it was her show now, unsurprised when she made the most of the opportunity. Jill began to ride him, her travel at first only an inch or two, then lengthening slowly until he was barely inside her, finally plunging down to unleash a wave of sensation that spasmed through his body. Jill's eyes had turned inward by then – what they looked at, Boots could not imagine. She was flushed, from her scalp to her shoulders, and her mouth hung open, her tongue visible on her lips. When Boots took her breasts in his hands, she folded her own hands over his and pressed down hard, her eyes suddenly opening as she said his name, just once, before she exploded into orgasm.

'Boots.'

THIRTY-SEVEN

Encouraged by Jill, Boots managed to postpone the inevitable through a quick shower, which they took together, then a second, slower odyssey, this one more deliberate. But time marches on, and flesh fails. Suddenly, they were lying beside each other, their shoulders and knees touching, and the inevitable could no longer be postponed.

'How do you know,' Jill began, 'that I was the target on Saturday?'

Boots felt the ground shift, a fissure open. This was going to be very bad. If not for her leaving her gun in the other room, there was even a chance that he'd come out dead. He laid his hand on her thigh just above her knee.

'I had a long conversation with Maytag LeGuin.'

The story that followed was true in every respect, though it left out a number of details. Velikov and O'Malley became hired help, Madeline Gobard's existence was never mentioned, Chris Parker's hideaway was reduced to 'somewhere private'. On the other hand, Boots described the scene at LeGuin's Forest Hills apartment in detail; Malcolm Sutcliffe's wound, Isabella Amarando and her family, how easily they could be exploited. Finally, he turned to his conversations with Shaw and Inspector Najaz.

'When they got around to asking me what I wanted,' he concluded, 'I told them straight out. The murder charges against Vinnie Palermo have to be dropped.'

'Did you threaten them?'

'Your uncle asked me that identical question, asked me twice: was I threatening him?'

'What'd you answer?'

'That I hoped with all my heart that I wouldn't have to prove Vinnie innocent by arresting Parker's actual killer.'

'And who would that be?'

'That would be you, Jill. You executed Chris Parker. Lenny Olmeda, too.'

Jill lit a cigarette, forcing Boots to go in search of an ashtray. He finally settled on a chipped saucer which he carried into the bedroom. Jill took the saucer and laid it between them on the bed.

'How'd you find LeGuin?' she asked.

'I traced him through the plate number on the van.'

'Ah, I remember. That's the plate number you told me you didn't get.' Jill took a drag on the cigarette, releasing the smoke in a thin line. She watched the smoke until it splashed against the ceiling, then said, 'Does that mean you knew all along? Knew that I was Killer Jill, not Crazy Jill?'

Boots drew a breath. 'Chris Parker recorded your sexual encounter, yours and a couple of dozen others. I know this because I found a DVD when I searched his house. You were on it.'

Jill flicked the ash at the end of her cigarette into the saucer. 'So what? I was in a cop bar on a Saturday night when Chris walked in. We had a couple of drinks, Chris wasn't bad-looking, I was in the mood. If he turned out to be pervert, it's not my problem.'

Boots ignored the entire statement. He had to get it out there, but he couldn't bring himself to say the words. Instead, he spoke about his search of Chris Parker's house. The temptation, he explained, had been irresistible, what with Parker's connections to Maurice Selman and Maytag LeGuin, and the house being empty. He'd been hoping, even expecting, to prove that Chris Parker's murder was related to his corruption. That would be enough to get Vinnie off the hook. Instead, he'd found the DVD.

'Did you get off?' Jill asked when Boots finally ground to a halt. 'Watching me perform?'

'What I did was destroy every disc in that apartment, and the computer's hard drive, too. I can't say that Parker didn't brag to his pals, but at least there's no physical evidence.'

'Evidence of what?'

'Evidence of why you waited six years to take your revenge.'

Jill's thoughts whirled through her mind, autumn leaves on a windy day, dancing just out of reach. For now, she could only watch them. The problem was Boots Littlewood. It'd been so long since she'd wanted a man for more than sex; she didn't trust her emotions. Nor, for that matter, did she trust Boots. Maybe, as things now stood, he wasn't prepared to reveal 'Parker's actual killer', but there were no future guarantees. Boots was obsessed with Vinnie Palermo. If pushed to the wall, she didn't know what he'd do. Most likely, he didn't know, either.

'The six years,' Boots continued, 'that's what threw me off.' He sat up, then leaned against the headboard. 'If you were out for revenge, why wait so long? The answer is obvious now that I know you were intimate with Parker. You had to wait because you didn't know the identities of the men who killed your father and . . .'

Boots hesitated for a few seconds, his courage almost failing him again. Finally, he said, 'The men who killed your father, then raped you.'

A shudder tore through Jill's body. Suddenly, she wanted to dress, to cover her nakedness, but it seemed to her that any move she made would be an admission of some obscure and undefined guilt. Unable to remain still, much less frame a response, she finally pulled herself to her knees, then punched Boots in the mouth.

Boots saw the punch coming, but didn't try to block it, or even move out of the way. The blow hurt him and he had to take a moment to clear his head.

'Besides yourself, there were three witnesses to your father's murder.' Boots swiped at a trickle of blood from the corner of his mouth. 'Two of them heard a pair of gunshots around six thirty, but took no action. The third saw two men, one of whom possibly wore a ski mask, drive away at seven o'clock. Since each of the witnesses was firm about the time, I simply assumed that what the last witness saw was unrelated to the case. How else to account for that missing half-hour?'

Jill sat back on her heels. 'Is there a point here?' she asked.

'In the case file – Chris Parker's – there's a photo of his body lying on an autopsy table. I don't remember why I looked at it. I'd reviewed the ME's report by then and knew the cause of death. But I did look, Jill, and what I noticed was a very long, very deep scar on Parker's hip. You saw that scar when he raped you six years ago. You saw it again in his bedroom shortly before you killed him.'

So, there it was, her secret, out in the open, and now her freedom was on the line. Although Jill Kelly did not fear death, incarceration was another matter.

'Assuming you're not lying,' she said, 'when you said you destroyed the DVDs and the hard drive, you knew you were destroying evidence in the murders of two cops. Is that right?'

'Yeah, I knew.'

'Why'd you do it?'

Jill was entirely unprepared when Boots took her by the shoulders and pressed his mouth to hers. Though she found the taste of his blood intoxicating, she neither resisted nor surrendered. She was sure Boots felt that he'd undressed her completely, that her soul was now as exposed as her body. Wrong again, but she appreciated the gesture enough to set him straight.

When Boots released her, she rose to her feet. 'Don't worry, Boots, I'm not going for my gun. I'm looking for a bathrobe.'

'Are you cold?'

Jill leaned over to grind out her cigarette. 'Just naked,' she said.

Boots watched Jill struggle with an oversized flannel bathrobe, one that fit him loosely. For Jill, it was like wrapping herself in a kimono. Meanwhile, he was feeling more and more naked himself.

'Let me see if I've got the whole picture.' Jill sat down in a rocking chair, his mother's rocking chair, carried from Ireland and passed down to Boots as an heirloom. 'We start with Jill Kelly, young and innocent, a student at Fordham University, filled with the hopes and dreams appropriate to young women of her age and station. Then, in a space of thirty minutes, the youth, the innocence, the hopes and the dreams come crashing down – she is raped within sight of her father's body. Shamed and humiliated as she is by her defilement, she can't bring herself to speak the unspeakable, not to the street cops who appear first, or to the hardened detectives who follow. So she clutches her secret to her heart and holds her tongue. Months pass, then years. She quits school, becomes a cop, her great secret all the while corrupting her heart and her soul until she's fully transformed. Until she becomes Crazy Jill Kelly.'

Jill smiled. 'Have I got it right? Is that the sequence you imagine, Boots?'

Unable to produce a verbal response, Boots reached down to draw the sheet to his waist. Jill's laughter ran straight down into his heart.

'What I knew,' she continued, 'even while it was happening, even while Parker slammed into me, was that the brand of justice offered by the state just wasn't gonna be good enough. That's why I kept the rape to myself. Now, I'm not saying that I wasn't humiliated, or that I wasn't ashamed. I just knew that pointing out my assailant in a courtroom wouldn't cleanse me of shame and humiliation, that what rape victims usually find in a courtroom is more shame and more humiliation.'

Boots watched Jill light another cigarette. 'Cleansed by blood,' he said, 'that was option number two, right?' He gave her a chance to reply. When she didn't, he said, 'Well, did it work? Are you cleansed?'

'If by that you mean restored to something I never was, then the answer is no. But when I search my conscience, as I have a number of times, I can't find an ounce of regret.'

THIRTY-EIGHT

Jill crossed her legs and began to rock slowly, her eyes criss-crossing the room. At first, Boots suspected that she was looking for a bug of some kind, but she surprised him.

'This room,' she grinned, 'it's really you. The family photos on the bureau, the signed baseballs, the corduroy bedspread, the battered furniture. It's oak, right?'

'I don't know. I bought the set from Teddy Marks before he went to prison. It was in better shape then.'

'No cigarette burns?'

Boots looked down for a moment, then shook his head. 'Are we done?'

'No, Boots, we're not.' Jill began to rock a little faster as she organized her thoughts, her eyes turning inward. When she finally began to speak, her voice was more tentative, as though she'd never before conducted this particular review of the facts.

'I joined the cops,' she explained, 'when it became obvious that my father's case wouldn't be closed with an arrest. My plan, before that, was to have a short conversation with whoever got charged. I wasn't overly worried about the direction this conversation might take because I had five years of simulated combat experience behind me. But nobody was arrested, and Uncle Mike not only refused to let me see the case files, he made sure nobody else in the family did, either. Keep in mind, there are thirty-one Kellys on the job, ranking officers among them. Our ties to the NYPD go back a hundred years.'

Jill hesitated, closing her eyes briefly. Despite the bravado, she looked somehow older to Boots, and very tired.

'You don't have to do this,' he said.

Her eyes jumped open. 'I didn't unlock the door, Boots. You did.'

Chastened, Boots simply waited for her to begin speaking.

'On the day I was promoted to detective, Uncle Mike finally gave me the case file. He told me it was complete and I bought the lie. Uncle Mike can be very persuasive. Did he play the kindly grampa for you, Walter Cronkite in a uniform?'

'Yeah, he was good.'

'As usual.' Jill tugged on the sleeves of the robe as she folded her arms beneath her breasts. 'Here's a fact you can take to the bank: I received my gold shield only because of my connections. I'm possibly the worst detective in NYPD history. I have no patience and all that bullshit with hair and lint drives me crazy. But I worked hard. I reinterviewed anyone whose name appeared in the file, including Corcoran, Olmeda, Farrahan and Parker, and I spent fifteen months working on a list of violent offenders arrested by my father. I got nowhere, of course, absolutely nowhere. That's because a piece of the puzzle, the only piece that mattered, had been withheld by kindly Uncle Mike. That piece, an IAB file, was given to me by a Kelly about six months ago, a cousin who grew up with my father. It seems that Patrick Kelly was already working for Internal Affairs when he was placed on the Lipstick Killer task force. Corcoran was dirty. Farrahan, Parker and Olmeda, too. My father's job was to get the proof.

'It's still hard for me to describe the way I felt when I read that file. I had them, Boots. Finally. Call it rebirth, the phoenix rising. Call it whatever you want, but there was no going back. The only thing I needed to know after that was which one raped me. I wanted to begin with the worst offender in case I got caught right away, then climb the ladder of culpability.

'Gut instinct, Boots. I chose Parker because of the way he stared at my breasts when I first interviewed him. Women get used to being eye-fucked by men. It's just one of those things you can't do anything about, like men being stronger. But Parker had the eyes of a true pig. His lust surrounded him like a force field.'

Jill slowed down long enough to smile. Boots's eyes were pinned to hers, his gaze so penetrating it took all her will not to flinch.

'I have to admit, Boots, that events took a very erotic turn when I stripped away Chris's pants and saw that scar. Parker was lying on the bed, no doubt thinking, "I'm gonna fuck the bitch I raped six years ago." I was standing a few feet away, thinking, "I'm gonna fuck the scumbag I intend to murder." Now, what could be hotter than that?'

When Jill stopped abruptly, Boots released his breath. All along, he'd been hoping that Jill's discovering Parker's scar was an accident, the result of a chance meeting, a stirred memory. Not so.

'You want to hear how I lured Parker to Berry Street? It's a funny story, I promise you.'

Resigned, Boots simply said, 'Yeah.'

'After that night, I kept Parker at arm's length. He was eager to go again, very eager, but I put him off without actually turning him down. Then, one night, I called him on his cellphone. I think I caught him at home, but I'm not sure. I told him that I had a long-term fantasy I wanted to act out. Can you guess the fantasy, Boots?'

'You wanted to play the part of a hooker.'

'Street whore is the way I put it to him, street whore turning a car trick. If he would drive to Berry Street and wait a couple of minutes, I'd come walking down the sidewalk, appropriately dressed, and we'd negotiate the cost of whatever services—'

'Enough, Jill.'

'Enough? What's the matter, Boots, you squeamish? You want to go in the bathroom and vomit?'

Boots slid his feet over the edge of the bed and sat up. He reached out for Jill's hand, but she pulled away.

'Right on that corner, there's a building, a converted warehouse with a recessed doorway that turns to the left. I was in there when Vinnie Palermo showed up. I couldn't see him, but I heard a car alarm go off, then a door open and close. Chris arrived a moment later, before I could leave. I should have stayed put, what with a witness only a few yards away, and I knew it. But there were all those memories. Like the gunshots that killed my father, like Parker knocking me to the floor, like Parker ripping off my pants, then my panties, like Parker forcing my legs apart. Boots, once you start down that road, self-preservation becomes irrelevant. I was wearing a knit cap, a navy pea coat and black jeans. I tucked my hair under the cap, turned up my collar and stepped out behind Chris when he got out of the car. As you can imagine, I'd fantasized this scene many times in the past, and there'd always been a final exchange. You know, a few snappy lines, a little back and forth. But when the moment came, I found myself speechless. So I decided to send the rest of the boys a message. I put one round in Chris Parker's back, then another in his head. Then I walked away.'

For his part, Boots was just glad to be done. He'd expected the worst, but he was still breathing air and Jill was sitting across from him. As far as he could tell, she wasn't about to go anywhere. Boots wasn't fooled by Jill's bravado. Her eyes, when she told her story, had darkened almost to black, the light they projected no more than sparks in a night-time sky. Life had smacked her down. Her scars were as visible as his own.

As for Parker, Boots could not bring himself to care. Even as a boy, he'd recognized, as did all his friends, the difference between personal revenge and telling the teacher.

'Do you think your uncle knew?' he finally asked.

'Knew what?'

'Knew who killed your father, and why.'

Jill slid the rocker forward. 'Knowing and proving aren't the same thing. Except for street rumors, there was no evidence that

Corcoran and the boys were even dirty. I wasn't a hundred percent sure myself until I saw the scar on Parker's hip.'

Boots nodded to himself. Corcoran's rabbi, Eamon Gogarty, was highly placed. Michael Shaw would never start a war with Gogarty, not without the sort of rock-solid ammunition Pat Kelly had been trying to obtain at the time of his death. Suddenly, Boots realized that Michael Shaw was using him to accomplish what his brother-in-law couldn't. Boots was now Shaw's point man, like it or not.

'Tell me about Olmeda,' he said.

'Olmeda was the one who held me down.'

'How do you know that?'

'He confessed.'

'Right before you killed him?'

'Right before.'

Boots smiled as he found himself imagining Father Gubetti hovering above them. Revenge is a crime in the State of New York. But is it a sin? Most likely, the priest would invoke Jesus instructing the faithful to love their enemies, a command that apparently fell on deaf ears. Boots Littlewood had never met a single man or woman who even liked their enemies. Not one.

'Boots?'

'Yeah?'

'I asked you a question.'

'I'm sorry, I drifted a bit.'

'I asked you what you wanted. From me.'

Boots stared at Jill as he searched for an answer. She seemed astonishingly beautiful at that moment, beautiful beyond any dream of beauty. And though he knew it was utterly irrational, he couldn't shake the feeling that he'd been waiting all his life to meet her. Nevertheless, when he finally spoke, there was nothing of these sentiments to be found in his words.

'I want to help you stay alive,' he said, 'so I can keep on fucking you.'

And not even Crazy Jill Kelly had an answer for that one.

THIRTY-NINE

Early the next morning, shortly after sunrise, Boots stood before the open window in his front room. Pushed by a cool breeze, a pair of lace curtains fluttered to either side of his face. The breeze carried the fragrance of the pink roses, many hundreds of them, blooming on a trellis in Fianna Walsh's tiny yard. Fianna's trellis was the wonder of Newell Street, a source of intense pride, an event that marked the passage into summer as surely as the rising temperatures. But Boots neither smelled nor even noticed Fianna's roses. Nor did he hear the sudden blast of a fog horn out on the East River, or Ivan Pinetka's blaring television. No, after carefully checking the vehicles parked by the curb, and the rooftops across the street, his thoughts had turned inward.

Reaching far back into his childhood, Boots had always been an optimist, a believer in solutions to life's problems, major and minor. Not perfect solutions, of course – Boots wasn't a fool. He merely thought that if you took this little piece and moved it this way, and that little piece and moved it that way, and another little piece and moved it another way, you eventually reached a door marked 'Exit'. A door you were willing to open because what was on the other side didn't scare the crap out of you.

But for all Boots knew, the dicks assigned to the Olmeda homicide had already collected the evidence needed to arrest Jill Kelly. Maybe they were searching for her right now. Maybe it was only a question of who'd find her first, the cops or the assassin hired by Mack Corcoran. And even if Michael Shaw protected Jill on the first count, and Corcoran was persuaded to accept a truce, the maze continued to twist back and forth, from one dead end to the next. Boots hadn't changed his mind about Parker and Olmeda. With no sympathy for either man, he'd let God judge Detective Kelly. But that didn't mean he could let her kill anybody else, now that he was personally involved. Unlike Ms Kelly, Boots lacked the mitigating factors necessary for a pass on the Fifth Commandment.

Boots laughed to himself. *Let* her? Last time he looked, Jill hadn't asked for permission. Probably, she'd never asked for permission in her entire life. And that was the problem. You don't catch comets when your fancy boots are anchored in concrete. No matter how it turned out, he'd eventually lose her.

Well, he decided, that would be his anchor. Fuck the concrete. He would lose her. To a hired killer's bullet, to the State, if he turned her in to save Vinnie Palermo, if she put a round through his head in order to stop him. He would lose her even if murder charges against Vinnie were dropped and the possibility of happily-ever-after reared its alluring head. There was no exit at the end of this maze.

'Boots, what are you doing up so early?'

Afraid that Jill had come directly from bed, eyes swollen with sleep, stark naked, Boots didn't turn around. 'We have to leave,' he said. 'We have to get out.'

'Are you trying to get rid of me before your father wakes up?'

Jill's tone was playful, echoing as it did her perfunctory eviction of Boots Littlewood from her mother's home. Not so his reply.

'I put my family in enough danger having you here at all. Now we have to leave.'

If Artie Farrahan was unhappy when Boots Littlewood stepped into his back yard, he was utterly dismayed when Jill Kelly followed. Artie was lying on a lounger, enjoying the early sun. He wore a canary-yellow swimsuit, small and tight, a choice of attire he instantly regretted. Jill was looking him up and down, contemptuous in the way only a beautiful woman can be. Farrahan grunted against the pain in his ribs as he raised himself to a sitting position, the inner tube of flab around his waist settling below his navel.

As Boots and Jill Kelly approached, Farrahan searched for some-thing to say, some witty comment that would lift him to their level. Unfortunately, until he knew what they wanted, those words didn't exist. Finally, he settled for 'Hey, Boots.'

Boots sat down at a metal table with a folded umbrella in the middle. Without hesitation, he lifted a copy of the *New York Times*, exposing Farrahan's Browning automatic. He winked at Farrahan, then put the newspaper down.

For the next moment, Boots and Artie measured each other's battle scars – Boots's eye and forehead, a pronounced depression in Farrahan's left cheekbone.

'You gonna need surgery?' Boots asked.

'Yeah, my sinuses don't drain on that side. And you?'

'It's elective. Whether I wanna look good or not. I can see fine.' Boots lowered his chin slightly. 'So, whatta ya think, Artie? You think the eye gives me character?'

Jill Kelly watched this exchange from a chair to Boots's left. She pronounced it typical male bullshit, and instantly boring. Men couldn't be in the same room for two minutes before they started wagging their dicks. Meanwhile, the biggest dick in this room was snugged into the holster attached to her belt. It was all she could do not to execute Artie Farrahan on the spot.

Boots turned the crank in the umbrella's shaft, putting a little zip into the effort. He watched as the umbrella expanded to reveal alternating wedges of red and gold that reminded him of Farrahan's ties. The day was rapidly warming and Boots was overdressed in his customary gray suit.

'We have to stop this thing,' Boots said. 'It's gone too far.'

Caught off-guard, Farrahan took a minute to consider his options. Finally, he said, his tone wistful, 'I got a call earlier this morning from the headhunters. I've been suspended.'

Boots nodded to himself. IAB Chief Mario Polanco was Michael Shaw's ally. The boys were on the move.

'Weren't you already on sick leave?'

'Yeah, could ya believe it? Ten days ago, they were callin' me a hero. Now I'm the target of an investigation.'

Boots nodded. 'So, you can see what I'm sayin', right? We each have our own problems. This other business, it has to stop.'

'You speakin' for . . .' Farrahan couldn't bring himself to pronounce Jill's name, or even look at her.

'I'm speakin' for all concerned.'

Farrahan leaned forward, dropped his hands to his knees. 'I haven't left my house in days,' he said. 'I didn't want any part of this from the beginning. You should be talkin' to the inspector.'

'Corcoran? Well, it's a funny thing, Artie, but Corcoran's upped and disappeared. That's how come we stopped by. We're hopin' you can tell us where he is, maybe start the negotiations.'

'I got no idea where he is.'

'When was the last time you spoke to him?'

'Four, maybe five days ago. It was right after they found Lenny Olmeda.'

'What'd you talk about?'

'Whatta ya think?'

'Besides Lenny.'

Farrahan looked up and to the left, the movement so fast it escaped Jill Kelly's attention. Not so Boots Littlewood's. Artie Farrahan was censoring himself.

'We talked about Parker, too,' Farrahan said. 'Corcoran was scared.'

'Scared enough to put out a second hit on Jill?'

Another hesitation, another lie. 'He was scared enough to do anything, but—'

'You're lyin', Artie. It won't do.'

As though she'd produced it by sleight of hand, Jill's gun was out and pointing directly at Artie Farrahan's head. Boots was impressed. He'd barely seen her hand move and he'd known it was coming. Boots placed his own hand on the gun and pushed the barrel down. Farrahan responded with something between a sigh and a moan.

'Why don't you give us a little room?' Boots said to Jill Kelly.

Jill stared at Boots for a moment, then pulled Farrahan's Browning from beneath the newspaper. She ejected the clip and the round in the chamber, then stood.

'Did you wet your pants, Artie? Do you fear death? Because if you fear death, you've already lost.'

Boots watched Jill retreat to the shade of a Japanese maple, thinking her remark a bit on the cryptic side. But then he turned back to Artie Farrahan. The man's fingers were still trembling.

'That bitch is crazy,' Farrahan said.

'Actually, I think it's a clan thing.'

'What?'

'You killed a Kelly. Nobody gets away with that.'

'Boots, I swear, I had nothin' to do with Pat Kelly.' Farrahan was almost whispering now. The hair combed across his forehead was dripping sweat. 'Look, I admit I was dirty. I took the money and mostly did what I was told. But I didn't kill anybody. I'm not a murderer.'

'Did you know it was gonna happen?' Boots watched Farrahan hesitate yet again. Jill had unnerved the man. His balls were in her pocket. 'Why'd they do it?' he asked.

'Kill Pat Kelly?'

'Yeah.'

'He was IAB.'

'So what?'

'If you knew Corcoran, you wouldn't be sayin' that. And Chris Parker was the same way. Those guys thought they could get away with anything.'

Which they would have, Boots thought, if not for that scar and Chris Parker's ego. As it was, they'd bought six more years.

'Was that why Chris Parker made another move on Jill?' he asked. 'Because he thought he was invulnerable?'

'Another what?'

'Forget that.' This time, Farrahan's confusion was genuine. He knew nothing of Jill Kelly's rape. Boots murmured a silent prayer of gratitude. 'Look, I'm gonna ask you a question now and I want a straight answer. No bullshit, Artie. If I think you're lyin', I'm gonna walk through the gate, leave you to Crazy Jill.'

'Boots . . .'

'Tell me everything you know about Corcoran puttin' out a second hit on Jill Kelly.'

Farrahan swiped at his eyes with the back of his hand. His ribs hurt with every breath and the side of his face ached. He was trapped, a rat so crippled he didn't have to be caged.

'The last time you spoke to Mack Corcoran,' Boots continued, 'was after LeGuin's failure, right?'

'Yeah, a couple of days. Corcoran was pissed.'

'Pissed enough to hire someone else?'

'Yeah, he was really pissed.'

'Artie, try to concentrate. Did Corcoran hire somebody to finish the job that LeGuin botched?'

'He kept goin' on about Jill Kelly, how much he wanted to kill her, how much he hated her, how his problems were all her fault. I swear, Boots, he sounded like one of those assholes who kills his ex-wife or his girlfriend, then tells you that she brought it on herself.'

Farrahan stopped suddenly as he realized that Boots was about
to slap him. He'd already been hit by Boots and had no desire to
repeat the experience. 'Yeah, OK. Corcoran told me he was gonna
use somebody else, but he didn't tell me who it was. He just said
this guy wouldn't fuck it up. But I got an idea who it is, Boots.'

'And who would that be?'

'You understand, I'm guessin' here. I'm thinkin' what I would
do in the same situation, who I would pick.'

The words tumbled out, one after the other, without any rise or
fall in tone. Though Boots couldn't be absolutely sure, he believed
it very likely that Farrahan was telling the truth.

'So, who would you pick, Artie? If you were Mack Corcoran?'

'About six months ago, the inspector brought this kid named
Rick Bauer into Narcotics. Rick's maybe twenty-five, only been on
the job for a couple of years, but Corcoran jumped him over a dozen
other guys. Boots, you can believe me when I tell you Bauer came
with both hands out. He was dirty from day one.'

'So what?'

'Bauer was special forces in Afghanistan. From the stories he
told, I got a definite feelin' that he enjoyed the killing. Anyway, it's
not like the inspector has a directory of hitmen. It's not like he can
pick and choose. Bauer makes sense and he's available.'

Farrahan was feeling a little better now. Jill Kelly was on the
other side of the yard and Boots appeared to be in control. But then
Boots rose to his feet, his jacket coming open to reveal an old-
fashioned shoulder holster and a dangling automatic.

'If I was you,' Boots said, 'I'd consult my lawyer, then cut a
deal, maybe ask for protective custody. The alternative is to get your
ass in the wind, like Corcoran. But what you don't want to do,
Artie, is make yourself an easy target, which is what you're doin'
now. Jill's not a forgiving sort.'

'I hear what you're sayin'.' Farrahan tried to smile, but couldn't
bring it off. 'Only I know you, Boots. You're the white knight who
risked his life to free Vinnie Palermo. You won't let her kill anyone.
It's not in you.'

There it was again. *Let* her. Boots shook his head in disgust. 'Suit
yourself,' he said.

FORTY

The bullet that punched through the windshield missed Jill Kelly's head only because she turned to flick her cigarette out the window. Sitting next to her with the keys in his hand, Boots failed to process what happened, even when the headrest next to him exploded, even when Jill pushed the door open, rolled out on to the sidewalk and began running up the block. It took a second crack of the rifle, this one tearing a hole in the trunk of a Ford Taurus, before he came to his senses. And even then a good five seconds passed in which he was able to do no more than watch Jill dodge and weave, staying close to the cars parked along the curb as she flew toward the far corner.

Cursing to himself, Boots finally tumbled out of the car. His every instinct was to take cover, to call for back-up. Instead, he crossed to the opposite sidewalk, then ran after his crazy partner, his feet already hurting. Boots was hoping against hope that Jill was running away from the shooter. That didn't seem likely because she was pointing her weapon ahead of her, but hope was all he had at that point. The rest was about fear – not for his own life, but for hers. If those bullets had been meant for him, he'd already be dead.

Jill crossed the street at the corner, then sprinted the length of a short block, running alongside a fenced schoolyard. She stopped abruptly at the center of the next intersection and swept the road ahead.

'C'mon,' she muttered, 'c'mon, c'mon, c'mon. Show yourself, you prick. Show me where you are.' She was still muttering when Boots came up beside her.

'Jill . . .'

On the far side of the next intersection, a red car pulled away from the curb and headed in the opposite direction. Jill leveled her weapon, her concentration divided equally between the pressure of her finger on the trigger and the target centered between the gun's sights. Boots had to yank her hand up to catch her attention.

'What? What?'

'Do you know who you're shooting at?'

Jill turned to a small parochial school on her right, St Anselm's. She gestured to a door standing ajar. 'He came out of there. He had to.'

Boots eyes shifted to a pair of filthy windows on the second floor. Both had broken panes of glass despite the wire mesh covering them. Out in the schoolyard, the basketball court was marked by broken concrete and hoops long bent out of shape. St Anselm's had apparently been among the losers in the last round of Catholic school closings.

Jill holstered her automatic. In the distance, a siren wailed. Now they'd be tied up for hours. Now she'd have to deal with Uncle Mike. Resigned, she took Boots's arm and led him back the way they'd come. When they reached the car, she pointed to a hole in the windshield an inch below the roofline, then to what was left of the headrest.

'There's only one line of sight that could have produced that trajectory. The shooter was up on the roof of the school.'

'Now, you're telling me you calculated the trajectory while you were rolling out of the car?'

'Do you doubt me, Boots?'

Boots was grinning now. His adrenal glands were still pumping away, but Jill, except for a sheen of perspiration on her forehead, seemed perfectly relaxed. 'As a matter of fact,' he told her, 'I think you're lying through your teeth. But it does make for a good story. In fact, I'd have to say it enhances the legend to a considerable degree.'

'Well . . .'

'Well, what?'

'Well, I might have noticed somebody rise up and fire that second shot. I might even have noticed that he was firing a rifle with a four-power scope. But I was heading for the school, anyway.' Jill smiled. 'I love ya, Boots, but combat's not your thing.'

Boots raised his shield as a cruiser turned on to the block, its siren running full out. He could barely hear himself think. 'Are you still pissed about the red car?' he shouted.

'A little bit,' Jill admitted.

'Jill, you were two hundred yards away and the car was moving. Plus, you don't know who was in it.'

'Didn't you tell me, on the way to the car, that Rick Bauer was ex-military?'

'Special forces.'

'Well, that's what the military teaches its snipers. Shoot and move, which is what actually happened. And what I was hoping to do was hit the car, not the driver. I wanted to mark it, so we'd know it if we saw it again. The shot was challenging, but I could have pulled it off.'

Jill took out her telephone as two uniformed cops walked up to Boots. The older of the two nodded once, in recognition of the shield Boots displayed, then asked, 'Who's she callin'?'

'Her uncle, the Chief of Detectives.'

The cop stared at Boots for a minute, then turned to his partner. 'Rope off the whole fuckin' block,' he instructed. 'I'm gonna call the sergeant.'

The detective-captain who finally showed up to run the scene had Boots hauled off to the nearest precinct, the One-Twelve. 'Nothing personal,' he said, 'but I want you outta here before the reporters show up.'

Once delivered, Boots was stashed on a wooden bench in the squad room. Nobody told him he couldn't leave, but, except for a trip to the john, he stayed where he was. Boots watched the detectives going about their business, on the phone, taking complaints, processing the mutts and skells who came their way. It was like watching a memory. And the fact that no one paid any attention to him only added to the illusion, as if he wasn't there at all.

After a half-hour, Boots took advantage of this studied indifference to call Joaquin on his cellphone.

'Where are you?' he asked.

'Galligan's.'

'I want you to hang out there. I'll be coming by later on.'

'How much later?'

'I don't know, Jackie. And don't call me back. I'll get there as soon as I can.'

Five hours later, at four o'clock, as Boots was considering the possibility that Artie Farrahan was the assassin's primary target, Inspector Murad Najaz strode across the squad room and opened the door to the lieutenant's office. He didn't bother to close it behind him. A minute later, the lieutenant made a hasty exit. Short and balding, he yanked out a pack of cigarettes as he walked past Boots.

'Inside,' he snarled without turning his head.

Boots pulled himself up and hobbled into the office. The bottoms of his feet were on fire and he was trying to walk on his toes.

'Close the door,' Najaz said.

In full dress uniform, the inspector had apparently come from some official function. The ribbons and medals splayed across his enormous chest gleamed faintly in the fluorescent light, while the contrast between his dark skin and the bone-hard collar of his white shirt was stark enough to impress.

'You're not doing a very good job, detective,' Najaz said. 'You're supposed to be shielding her.'

'Chief Shaw could do that all by himself,' Boots said. 'All he has to do is arrest Mack Corcoran.'

The inspector's demeanor underwent a rapid transformation, from gentle to fierce. 'There's a limit, detective. A line you'd be wise not to cross. If I choose to, I can make your life a living hell.'

Boots shrugged his shoulders. 'What about LeGuin and Sutcliffe?'

'Not that it's any of your business, but the District Attorney is negotiating with both of them, and we're reaching out to Arthur Farrahan's attorney as well. Farrahan's been suspended, by the way. As for Palermo, there's blood evidence against him and he's already been indicted, but we're doing what we can.' Najaz drew a breath before settling down. 'Boots, you talk about arresting Corcoran as if that would solve your Jill Kelly problem. But even if Corcoran's charged with murder, he'll almost certainly be released on bail. At which point the game starts all over.'

FORTY-ONE

Boots limped into Galligan's at six thirty to find the Yankee pre-game show running on a computer monitor. Derek Jeter was being interviewed by a Yankee announcer named Michael Kay. Asked to predict the likely outcome of a three-game series with the Boston Red Sox, Jeter recited a laundry list of injured Yankee players. For just a moment, Boots felt a predictable annoyance. He hated excuses, especially when they spilled from the mouths of millionaires. But then his interest vanished, here and gone. He had other things to worry about.

Boots gave Joaquin a hug before getting down to business. 'Is Galligan here?' he asked.

'In his office.'

'Is he stoned?'

'I haven't checked.'

Boots looked around the cluttered reception area. Nothing had changed. 'Didn't you say you were gonna remodel?'

Joaquin smiled. 'I'm not a partner yet.'

'But soon, right?'

'Maybe.'

Boots shrugged. 'I want to find somebody's address,' he told Joaquin. 'A cop named Rick Bauer.'

'Rick? Is that short for Richard?'

'I don't know.'

'Well, can you narrow the search area? Say from anywhere on the planet to the Western hemisphere. Bauer is a very common name. There are bound to be multiple Rick Bauers and Richard Bauers out there, not to mention R. Bauers.'

Boots grinned. 'How about Thelonius Tolliver? I suspect there aren't too many Thelonius Tollivers in the New York area. See if you can get me the number of his cellphone.'

Ten minutes later, Boots was on the line with the man himself. Normally polite, this time Boots started the conversation with a direct question. 'Thelonius, when you were at Brooklyn North, did you ever run into a cop named Rick Bauer?'

Tolliver's voice was as flat as it was cold. 'I'm working. In case you're interested.'

'I just have a couple of questions. It won't take a second.' Boots paused before adding, 'I've been shot at twice in the last five days.'

'That was you?'

'Me and Jill Kelly.'

'Funny, but your name wasn't mentioned when I watched the news tonight. Kelly's either.'

'Now you understand my problem. I tell ya, it doesn't get any easier.' Boots tried for a laugh, but didn't quite get there. 'But I'm not lookin' to vent.'

'Hallelujah.'

'I was just wonderin' if Rick is Bauer's nickname, if maybe his real name is Richard Bauer.'

'Richard Aloysius Bauer.'

'Aloysius?'

'Chris Parker was Bauer's commanding officer. Whenever he wanted to speak to Bauer, he'd yell out, "Richard Aloysius, in my office." The other narcs used to tease the kid about it. But I don't see why you're askin' me these questions, Boots. I don't understand why you're askin' me instead of your partner. The way I heard it, Bauer and Jill Kelly were close at one time.'

Boots shut his eyes. More bullshit, more deception. He thanked Tolliver, then hung up. 'Look for Richard Aloysius Bauer,' he told Joaquin. 'Try the city first, then move out to the burbs.'

Galligan was peacefully adrift, his thoughts rolling gently through his mind, playful as otters in a snow bank. He was dreaming of a mega-business created by Joaquin Rivera, of revenues so great that he, Tommy Galligan, could afford to pass the remainder of his life in a drug-induced haze. Boots Littlewood's sudden appearance put the lie to that fantasy. Galligan wasn't gaining a partner. He was marrying into the mob.

'I don't have a lot of time,' Boots said. 'You've done some work for me on a cop named Mack Corcoran. Corcoran's in the wind and I want you to find him.'

'And how would I do that?'

'I don't care, as long as Jackie's not involved.' Boots took out a roll of bills, counted off two hundred dollars, laid the money on Galligan's desk. 'This'll get you started.'

'And that's it?'

In the short term, as both men knew, the best way to find Corcoran was through his credit cards, assuming he was using his cards. This was a service Galligan had performed many times in the past and his conscience wasn't overly troubled by the request. What galled him was a lecture delivered by Joaquin only a few days before. The costs of violating state and federal law, Joaquin had insisted, far outweighed any benefits. Once he became a partner, there would be no more illegal searches.

Galligan finally picked up the money and returned it to Boots. 'Risk my license to help you? Keep the kid out of it? Well, I don't want your money. What I want to know is that you're gonna be there when I need a favor.'

'Absolutely.' Boots put the cash away and stuck out his hand, thinking how much better he liked Galligan when the man was stoned. 'Any time.'

The Yankee game was playing on the radio when Boots slid into the passenger seat of Jill's midnight-green Chrysler 300. He closed the door and grinned.

'Don't tell you're a fan,' he said.

'I turned the game on for you, Boots.'

'You were that sure I'd show up?'

'I just didn't want to be surprised again.'

The Chrysler was parked on Twelfth Avenue in the Queens neighborhood of College Point, a few cars ahead of the Dodge that Boots was forced to rent after his own car was towed to an impound yard in Long Island City.

'Is that Bauer's place?' Boots gestured to a four-story apartment building.

Jill nodded. 'Third floor, in the rear. He's not home.'

'How do you know?'

'When I couldn't locate his car, I knocked on his door.'

Boots smiled. He could easily imagine Jill pounding away. Bauer was an avenue to Mack Corcoran.

'You and Rick, I hear you're acquainted.'

Jill laughed out loud, as Boots had feared she might. 'Rick had the good looks and the toned body,' she explained, 'but he didn't know anything about sex. When the chips were down, he was too weak.' She looked at Boots and winked. 'One on one, I know I can take him.'

'You know this from a single encounter?'

'More like three-quarters.'

With nothing to add, Boots watched the leaves of an ancient linden dance through the pink light cast by a streetlamp. He felt entirely comfortable in Jill's car, entirely at home. As if he didn't have a care in the world.

The Yankee game concluded a few minutes later with the Yanks on the wrong end of a five–one score. Jill shut off the radio and lit a cigarette. 'Stakeouts,' she informed Boots, 'drive me crazy.'

Boots moved his seat back as far as it would go. He liked stakeouts, the way he liked to drive slowly. This was especially true on warm nights when the streets were so quiet you could hear your partner breathing. This section of College Point was entirely residential, mostly two-family homes with a scattering of featureless apartment buildings like the one Bauer lived in. Resolutely middle-class, the Point closed down early during the week. Boots and Jill were undisturbed except for the occasional sideways glance from a citizen walking the family pooch.

For the next two hours, until shortly after midnight, they watched the neighborhood go to bed. Lights went out in living rooms and kitchens, bathrooms and bedrooms. A full moon, veiled by thin clouds, rose until it stood almost directly overhead. At the far corner, a family of raccoons scuttled across the road and began to rummage in a garbage pail. Cars turned on to the street from time to time, coming from either direction. Rick Bauer's was not among them.

'Bauer's in the wind,' Jill finally said. It was after midnight by then.

'What makes you say that?'

'Rick showed his true colors this afternoon.' Jill drew on her cigarette, flicked the ash out the window. 'See, Rick was kneeling down when he took the first shot. I didn't see it coming and it was pure luck that I moved when I did. But once I was on the sidewalk, Rick couldn't get off a second shot without exposing himself. Exposing yourself entails a measure of risk, true, but Rick still had every advantage. He had a scoped rifle. I had a handgun. He was on a roof. I was on the ground. He was stationary. I was running. But he lacked the courage to stand upright for three seconds. He rushed the shot, missed, then ran away. For my money, he's still running.'

Boots responded by wrapping his hand around Jill's head and pulling her mouth to his. His spirits had lifted the minute he saw her sitting behind the wheel of the Chrysler. 'You remember what you told Parker?' he asked. 'About turnin' a trick in the back seat of a car?'

'Yeah?'

'Well, I was wonderin' if there wasn't some kernel of truth to your little ploy, if maybe this was a fantasy that you've had, but never acted out.'

'Because I never found the right partner?'

'Exactly.'

Jill stared at Boots for a few seconds. 'And how much would you pay for me? What's my price?'

'Fifty dollars.'

'That's it?'

'C'mon, Jill, gimme a break. We're talkin' street whore, not call girl.'

They haggled briefly before reaching an agreement which, if not entirely specific, at least established the parameters. Then Jill started the car and put it in gear.

'Money first, right?' She held out her hand. 'Isn't that the way it works?'

'Absolutely.'

Boots let Jill get halfway down the block before he unbuckled her belt, then slid her pants and panties down over her hips. As he wet his finger and began to stroke her, gently at first, then more insistently, he pressed his lips to the soft hollow of her temple.

Jill's Chrysler was muscle-car all the way, its 340 horsepower able to propel its 4,000 pounds from zero to sixty in under seven seconds. Even with the driver undistracted, handling the sedan required a fair degree of concentration. As it was, the car jerked forward, tires chirping, then slowed abruptly, what with Jill's hips moving one way and her foot another. She didn't complain, though. She simply continued on until she found a quiet spot near Powell's Cove on the East River. Then she cut off the ignition and the lights.

'How do you want it?' she asked.

Boots groaned as her fingers encircled his swollen cock. 'Get in the back,' he said. 'I'll show you.'

FORTY-TWO

t was déjà vu all over again, waking in Jill's bed, Jill standing over him, saying, 'Get up.'

Without truly committing himself, Boots rolled on to his back. 'Your mother again?'

'I sent my mother to her sister's house in Yonkers.'

'So, what's doin'?'

'There's something you need to see.'

Intrigued, Boots fumbled into his clothes, made a quick trip to the bathroom, then followed Jill upstairs to a room at the back of the house. Ahead of him, early morning light poured through a double-hung window to flood three long shelves mounted on the opposite wall. The shelves were crowded with medals, ribbons and loving cups, dozens of them. Detective Kelly's glittering trophies.

Boots picked up a faded blue and gold ribbon. First place in a handgun competition open to children twelve years old and younger. He picked up another. Second place in a simulated combat competition.

'How many girls competed for this ribbon?'

'One.'

Still curious, Boots walked to the center of the exhibit, to a simple plaque.

DEADWOOD DAYS

QUICK-DRAW COMPETITION

BEST TIME – WOMAN'S DIVISION

JILL KELLY

.345

'What is that?' Boots pointed to the figure at the bottom.

'That's the time, point-three-four-five seconds.'

'A third of a second? That's what you're saying?' Boots continued before Jill could answer. 'Tell me, Jill, what did you actually do in a third of second?'

'Draw, fire, cock the weapon and hit a four-inch target ten feet away. But you should consider, the fastest man did it in a quarter of a second.'

Boots sighed. 'What do you want to show me?'

Jill pointed a remote control at a TiVo resting next to a small TV. She turned it on, backed it up, finally set it rolling forward.

Boots felt his pulse jump. The man behind the podium was Chief of Detectives Michael Shaw. To his left, Internal Affairs Chief Mario Polanco stood with his hands folded at the waist. Shaw, his paper-smooth cheeks leached of all color by the outdoor light, cleared his throat twice before announcing the arrests of Malcolm Sutcliffe and Elijah LeGuin for the attempted murder of Detective Jill Kelly.

'The case,' he announced, 'is still before the grand jury and further indictments are being sought. The principal suspects are police officers.'

With that, IAB Chief Mario Polanco approached the podium. Polanco's complexion was very sallow, almost jaundiced. His dark eyes, veiled by even darker brows, had the glitter of a zealot's, while a monk's fringe of curly hair stood away from his skull like the rim of a helmet. Boots couldn't imagine Polanco in the Commissioner's office. And how the Chief had risen as far as he had was likewise unfathomable.

After a brief review of the facts already stated by Michael Shaw, Polanco delivered a fiery sermon on the evils of corruption. Zero tolerance for corruption was, and would always be, he told the reporters, the official policy of the NYPD.

Boots stopped listening after a few sentences. The speech was boilerplate, the only important detail Polanco's refusal to name the unindicted suspects. Out of respect for their constitutional rights, or so he piously claimed. But all knew that a subsequent news conference, one that named names, would be covered by every media outlet in the city.

Boots took out his phone and called Sergeant Craig O'Malley. 'Maytag and his nephew were arrested,' he announced. 'For trying to cap Jill Kelly. We pulled it off.'

'Lemme tell the Bulgarian.'

Boots waited until Velikov emitted a grunt that was most likely appreciative. Street cops like O'Malley and his driver handle the cannon fodder, the petty dealers, the junkies. The Maytag LeGuins of this world are generally above their station.

'But there's bad news, too,' Boots said. 'Cops are gonna go down. Corcoran for sure, probably others. It was Corcoran who ordered the hit on Kelly.'

'And takin' him down is supposed to be the bad news?'

After an appropriate pause, Boots said, 'Plan to celebrate at Sally's when I finish up. The drinks are on me.'

'Number one rule of detecting,' Boots told Jill Kelly. 'Don't forget to thank the precinct cops who helped you out.'

'That's good to know. Myself, I never worked in a precinct.'

Boots flinched, but then, like an aftertaste on the back of the tongue, detected a rueful note. 'Corcoran's in his late fifties. If Farrahan gives him up and he's indicted for your father's murder, would that be enough?'

Jill was quick to respond. 'I won't be able to answer that question until I'm in the same room with him.'

'And how do you plan to accomplish that?'

'With the help of my partner.'

Boots laughed. 'When you didn't report the rape and that scar on Parker's hip, you threw away the evidence that would have convicted him in a courtroom, including DNA evidence. You threw it away deliberately. Now, that was your choice and I don't condemn you. But I'm not you, Jill—'

'Good thing, because I'm already too narcissistic.'

Boots refused to bite. 'I'm not gonna help you kill Mack Corcoran. Put it out of your mind. Send that hope to the moon.'

'What about Rick Bauer? You want me to handle him alone?'

Boots was about to say something about his presence being a liability, given the relative skills of all concerned parties, when his cellphone began to trill. He considered letting the call go over to his voicemail, but then picked up.

'It's Frankie Drago, Boots. I just got a call from Vinnie. They're droppin' the murder charge.'

'Just like that?'

'Accordin' to Vinnie's lawyer, the cops are sayin' there's a possibility the blood they found was contaminated. Don't ask me for the details. I don't have 'em and I wouldn't understand 'em if I did.'

The gears in Boots's skull began to click. Mike Shaw was giving him an excuse to back off. Jill didn't – and wouldn't – need him.

Did she know? Jill's head was turned ever so slightly to the left, her look sideways and up. She was smiling, too.

'Hey, anybody home?' Frankie said. 'You did it, Boots. You got Vinnie out. It's like a fuckin' miracle.'

'I gotta go, Frankie. Tell Vinnie not to steal any more cars.'

Boots shoved the phone in his pocket. 'The murder charge against Vinnie Palermo has been dropped,' he told Jill Kelly. When she didn't answer, he said, 'I'm gonna go.'

'Is that right?'

'Didn't you tell me that Bauer was in the wind? Besides, your uncle's after him now. After Corcoran as well.'

'What makes you so sure?'

'Because the attack took place a block away from Artie Farrahan's home; he has to be thinkin' he was Bauer's real target. You just happened to come along at the right time. Now maybe he's wrong, maybe we were followed. But Artie has Jill Kelly to worry about, too. He can't afford to let events play themselves out.'

'So, he's cooperating?'

'Yeah, and if hard-pressed, he'll implicate Corcoran in your father's murder. Add it up, Jill. Corcoran will get fifteen years on the drug charges alone. He'll get another ten for conspiring to kill you. Even if the sentences run concurrently, he'll be in his mid-seventies before he gets his first parole hearing.'

Jill surprised Boots when she stepped close enough to stick a playful finger into his navel. 'Go on, Boots. Get moving.'

'That's it?'

'That's it.'

On his way out, Boots noticed that every window was covered, and that Jill had placed a lamp before each of them. This didn't make walking through the front door any easier. He thought briefly of making his exit through the back, then took the plunge.

A gentle rain washed over him as he made his way to his car. He walked slowly, refusing to run, his fear of being afraid greater than his fear of Rick Bauer, but he let go a sigh of relief when he slid into his rented Dodge. After a moment, he started the car and got the defroster going, then slid the seat back and took out his phone.

'Inspector, it's Boots Littlewood.'

Najaz hesitated, then said, 'You've heard about Palermo? We're letting him off on the homicide, but not the grand theft auto. He's got priors, so you can expect him to do a couple of years.'

'Fine with me, inspector. Vinnie's no angel. And I wanna thank you, too.'

Najaz laughed. 'Gimme a fuckin' break.'

'All right.' Boots returned the laugh with a manly chuckle. 'I'm calling about a cop named Rick Bauer, one of the boys at Brooklyn Narcotics.'

'I know who he is.'

'Well, what I want to know is if Bauer was ever on a SWAT team.'

'With Jill Kelly?'

'Exactly.'

FORTY-THREE

Jill Kelly paused to examine her reflection in the storm door before ringing Gladys Kohl's bell. She was wearing a linen jacket the color of old ivory, white jeans and a pale yellow blouse. A mistake, she finally decided. The contrast between the light clothing and her dark red hair was too extreme. She should have balanced her look with the emerald-green slacks still in her closet. Why hadn't she noticed when she checked herself out in the bedroom mirror?

'Jill, so nice to see you. It's been ages.'

'Cut the shit.' Jill pushed Gladys back into the house, leaving the door open behind her. 'Your brother tried to kill me.'

'What . . .'

'Yesterday afternoon. He missed.'

As she walked through the foyer and into the living room, Jill's eyes moved systematically. She saw nothing and missed nothing, looking only for movement, the shadow at the corner of the eye. Finally, she took up a position with her back to the fireplace.

Gladys approached to within a few feet. 'You think you're some kind of Wonder Woman,' she muttered through trembling lips, 'but all you are, all you can ever hope to be, is a common bully.'

Jill was holding the hem of her jacket between the thumb and forefinger of her left hand, prepared to lift the jacket away from the weapon at her belt. There were three paths into the room: through an archway directly ahead of her and through doors to her right and left. Jill monitored these points without looking directly at any of them. If you focused too hard on the details, you tended to miss the big picture. That's why you developed reflexes through practice. Thinking slowed you down.

'Is he in the house, Gladys? Would you tell me if he was?'

'I'm going to call the police.'

'Good idea. Only I should warn you, they'll ask for permission to search the premises.'

'Which you plan to do without permission.'

'Actually, Gladys, I came here to cut a deal. I don't have anything against Rick. In fact, I remember our little affair as reasonably pleasant. And I don't blame him for trying to kill me. What, with the uncontrollable greed, Rick has a habit of making bad choices.'

'Is there a point here?'

The shadow came from Jill's right, a ghost image that preceded Rick Bauer into the room. Jill stepped to her left, placing Gladys Kohl between herself and the Colt Commander in Rick's hand. In her forties, Gladys was fifteen years older than her brother and probably a bit heavier; she made a good shield. Nevertheless, Rick's best chance was to shoot first and the hell with his sister. But Rick had a fondness for melodrama and it came as no surprise when he used his sister as an excuse to indulge this quirk.

'So,' Rick said, 'how have you been?'

'Still above ground. How about you?'

'I seem to have screwed up.'

'That's the greed. Once you give in to greed, your fate is out of your hands. Greed is worse than dope.'

'And you? What did you give in to?'

'Vanity.'

Jill knew, at that moment, that if she chose to, she could take Rick Bauer. He would concede the first move and he would not survive. 'I didn't come here to hurt you, Rick. You have enough trouble already.'

'Then what do you want?'

'Mack Corcoran.'

'And what happens if I don't help? Or if I can't?'

Jill stepped in close to Gladys, who'd gotten the picture by then. Her eyes were wild with fear, not least because she couldn't bring her legs to move.

'You don't wanna go there,' Jill said.

Boots was sure Jill made him. She'd driven away from her home at top speed, powering the big Chrysler into a screaming left turn before tearing off toward Northern Boulevard. Then she'd slowed to a near crawl on the long drive to eastern Queens and the community of Bayside. Boots had no choice except to match her pace, his nondescript Dodge Stratus, despite the rain, as conspicuous as a horse-drawn carriage. There was comfort in this, comfort of a sort. Jill's Chrysler was far more powerful than the Dodge with its energy-conserving four-cylinder engine. If she wanted to, she could lose him in a matter of seconds.

Boots knew where Jill was headed once they passed through Flushing. After leaving the military, Bauer had moved in with his sister and her family in Bayside. He was still living there when he applied to the NYPD, only moving to College Point a year after leaving the Academy. At least, according to Inspector Murad Najaz.

If pressed, Boots could not have explained why he was tailing Jill Kelly. True, his educated guess (based almost entirely on past performance) had been prescient. Both Jill and Rick had worked on the Manhattan SWAT team, their tenures overlapping by eight months. Rumor had it they were lovers.

Jill had lied to him again. Her affair with Rick Bauer had been far from the unsatisfactory one-night stand she'd described. But there didn't appear to be any reason to care. He was resigned to losing her, even assuming he had her now. The smart move was to back away, let Jill, Mike Shaw and Corcoran finish their game, pick up the pieces afterward. And if it was Humpty Dumpty time, if the puzzle could not be reassembled, then so be it.

But there was that tug, like someone had attached a fishing line to his brain and Jill was holding the rod, every flick pulling him further away from his old life. He needed to speak with his father, with Leo Gubetti, to be brought down to earth. Instead, he was following Jill Kelly along rainy streets, listening to the rap music blaring from a car alongside him. Boots couldn't make out the lyrics, only that the artist was repeating the same words over and over, faster and faster, louder and louder.

When he parked the car forty-five minutes later, Boots made no effort to conceal himself. He pulled to the curb fifty yards from Jill's Chrysler, then watched as Jill approached the front door of a Tudor home, paused to admire her own reflection, finally conferred with a middle-aged woman before pushing her way inside. He was encouraged when Jill left the door ajar, but stayed where he was for several minutes, listening to the rain spatter on the roof and the thump-thump of the wipers running back and forth across the windshield. His adrenals were already pulsing. Reality times ten.

Jill saw Boots first. He was coming forward slowly, but deliberately, his Glock pinned to Rick Bauer's skull. And why not? Bauer had a gun in his hand and he was pointing it at what he could see of Jill Kelly's face. Jill wanted to tell Boots that she had the situation under control, but was afraid the threat to Rick's ego would force him into action. Rick had begun to sweat, his surfer-blond hair to mat at the temples. He was so locked on Jill Kelly that he didn't see Boots until Boots was ten feet away.

'Drop the gun, Rick,' Boots said.

'I'm on the job,' Bauer returned. 'This woman broke into my home.'

'Drop the gun.'

This time Rick managed a little laugh: heh-heh-heh. 'Looks like we have ourselves a stand-off. You kill me, I kill her.'

'Drop the gun.'

Boots's single-mindedness finally drew Bauer's attention. 'And what comes next?' he asked.

'All I can promise is that I won't let her kill you. Drop the gun.'

There it was again. *Let* her. Talk about making promises you can't keep. Boots took a breath, held it for a second, then squeezed the trigger. His hands, he noted, were rock steady.

As though chasing the bits of brain and bone that spattered across an oil painting on the far wall, Rick Bauer pitched sideways. He did not pull the trigger of his Colt, nor did he let go. Although he was obviously dead, he looked, to Boots, as if he was still making up his mind.

Boots turned to Jill Kelly. She was pushing her way past a screaming Gladys Kohl, coming directly for him, her eyes as wild as he'd ever seen them.

'Crossed a line there, buddy,' she said as she took out her phone, 'and you won't be comin' home any time soon.'

FORTY-FOUR

They stashed Boots in an upstairs bedroom this time. He'd pulled the trigger and there'd be no keeping his identity from the press. The only good news was that the shooting had gone down in Queens, which left the boys at Brooklyn North out in the cold. But that didn't mean Boots was off the hook. Far from it. Line-of-duty shootings were subject to close scrutiny by a review board. Boots's gun would be examined, the scene assessed and witnesses interviewed. Maybe Gladys would remember that he'd ordered her brother to drop his weapon four times, but that didn't mean she'd tell the truth.

The room Boots was in belonged to a teenager, a boy. There were sports posters on the wall, a pile of dirty clothes topped by a pair of high-end Nikes with soles smooth enough to pass for slippers. Jammed between a closet and the foot of the bed, a weight bar with plates at either end threatened to trip the unwary housekeeper.

Boots picked up the weights. Sixty pounds; he was used to more. But he couldn't remain still and he began to work anyway. Curls, presses, pull-ups, knee bends. He'd taken a man's life; tradition dictated that he be overwhelmed by the gravity of the deed. In fact, he was obsessed with the look in Jill Kelly's eyes. Through some black magic forever unfathomable to the likes of him, Jill could live within her craziness. And if she couldn't tame the beast, she could exercise enough control to enjoy the ride.

Not so, Boots Littlewood. For as long as he could remember, he'd battled to stay on the right side of the odds. Burglars, thieves, rapists, killers. They were enough for him. He didn't need to slay dragons. He didn't want to be a hero.

Twenty minutes later, the door opened to admit Farrell Monaghan from the Detectives' Benevolent Association, Boots's free lawyer. Boots laid down the weight bar.

'Congratulations,' Monaghan said through stained teeth, 'you're a hero.'

Gladys Kohl, he continued, had not only confirmed Detective Littlewood's account, she'd also claimed that her brother forced the Kohl family to admit him on the night before. Then she'd led the investigators to Rick's bedroom where they discovered five kilos of Afghani heroin in an army duffel bag.

Boots thanked Monaghan for the information, then sent him packing. If Mike Shaw decided to screw Detective Littlewood, no DBA lawyer could stop him. Boots wondered if Shaw and Polanco had known about the heroin all along, if Jill had known. The taint from that dope would eventually rise through the ranks to engulf Michael Shaw's rivals.

Inspector Najaz showed up at noon. 'You're being promoted,' he announced, 'to detective, second grade. Congratulations.'

'Thanks.'

'Plus, you get the next two weeks off.' Najaz winked. 'To recover from the shock.'

Boots wanted to tell Najaz that he felt fine, but with the adrenalin having fled his body, the only thing he really felt was limp.

'What about Corcoran?'

'You leave Corcoran to us, Boots. We have a warrant for his arrest. We'll find him.'

'Does that mean Jill no longer needs my help?'

'Did she ever?' Najaz laid a fatherly paw on Detective Littlewood's shoulder. 'For the record, the Chief thanks you for protecting his niece this morning. But what I think is that you were more likely protecting yourself.'

And that was exactly right. Driven by the certainty that he was the slowest gun in the room, Boots had decided to counter his disadvantage by shooting first. Or, at least, that's the way he remembered the decision-making process, the way he wanted to remember it.

At three o'clock, shielded by a posse of uniformed officers, Boots was rushed to his car, then chauffeur-driven to his father's house in Greenpoint. The hope was to avoid the cameras, but the strategy backfired. When Boots saw his face on the evening news, he looked like a cringing perp.

'If you're supposed to be a hero,' Libby asked, 'why were you hiding?'

'The bosses – Shaw and his underlings – wanted to make sure I didn't speak to the reporters.'

Boots was already irritated by the penetrating glances, from Libby, from Andy, from Joaquin. What were they searching for? Signs of an imminent collapse? At seven o'clock, he went for a walk. Big mistake. Word had spread through the neighborhood. Now he was a fucking celebrity. For just a moment, he thought Jenicka Balicki was going to ask him to autograph her babushka.

He ended up at Mount Carmel's rectory, no surprise, in a room with Leo Gubetti, who uncorked a bottle of wine. This was a social visit, not a confession.

'I'm tryin' to feel something for this dope-smuggling jerk,' he told the priest, 'but I can't get there. Even his sister hates him.'

'You still seem upset.'

'Not about Rick Bauer.'

'Then what?'

'Something Jill Kelly said right afterward. She told me that I'd crossed a line and I wouldn't find my way back, not in the short term.'

'And you believe she was right?'

Boots shook his head. 'God forgive me, Leo, but I can't help thinkin' that next time it'll be easier.'

Later on, with the bottle drained, Boots finally gave voice to his real concerns, which were not for himself. 'Mack Corcoran,' he told the priest, 'is living proof that the eyes are not the windows of the soul. His are completely flat, like mirrors. Flat and empty. That's because he hasn't got a soul and there's nothing to look at.'

'Everyone has a soul.' The words were meant to provoke and Gubetti wasn't disappointed when Boots snorted in contempt. When it came to evil, cops were self-proclaimed experts. You couldn't argue with them.

'I've seen eyes like his before, Leo, seen them many a time. The men who own those eyes are beyond redemption.'

'That's blasphemy.'

Boots thought it over for a moment, then said, 'Mike Shaw's

playin' his own game. Jill, too. And me, I'm like a blind man tryin' to cross Park Avenue without a guide dog. Cars are comin' at me from every direction. I don't know whether to jump, dodge or crawl. I don't even know who's more dangerous – Shaw, Corcoran or Jill Kelly.'

Jill called at eleven o'clock that night. 'Hey, Boots, what are ya doin'?'

'Waitin' to hear your voice,' Boots admitted.

'Why didn't you call me?'

'I figured you were out lookin' for Corcoran.'

'Yeah, well, that's a problem, Boots. But it's a problem for tomorrow. In the meantime, I was wondering if you wanted to play a game.'

'Sure, what game do you have in mind?'

'Enemy Combatant.'

'And who would that be, the enemy combatant?'

'That would be you.'

'And you'd be . . .'

'The interrogator.'

Boots sighed. 'I'll bring the hood,' he said.

FORTY-FIVE

As it turned out, Boots and Jill did not play Enemy Combatant, or any other game. When Boots came through the door, he reached out to stroke Jill's cheek with the backs of his fingers and that was the end of that, the two of them doing everything at once, their own private orgy, unapologetic, taking with both hands, gimme, gimme, gimme. At one point, Boots held Jill against the wall, her feet off the ground, pinning her arms against her sides, but she continued to grind into him, lithe and slippery, no quarter asked or given.

Innocent as insects was how Boots explained it to himself, but then, afterward, Jill rose up to bestow that tender kiss once deemed unimaginable.

Boots was lying on the rug, his back beginning to itch, staring up into Jill Kelly's eyes. In the dimly lit room, they were the color of visible light at the coldest end of the spectrum. Any darker and you couldn't see them. Yet he felt somehow scorched when she finally glanced away.

'Are you going to help me find Corcoran?' she asked.

'No.'

'Why not?'

'Lines.'

'What?'

Boots answered her question with one of his own. 'Do you draw lines? Anywhere? The reason I ask is because it seems to me that you put a citizen's life at risk this morning. And I think you did it on purpose.'

'Rick's sister? That's who you're talking about?'

'Yeah, Gladys Kohl.'

Jill hesitated, then grinned. 'I wanted to find out what you'd do,' she finally admitted. 'Plus, I never liked Gladys to begin with.'

Boots had nothing to add. He got up and led Jill into the shower, let her scrub the rug fibers off his back, then watched her shampoo her hair, fascinated by the rise and fall of her breasts. When she spoke, he failed to catch the words over the rush of the water.

'Gladys set me up.'

'What?'

'Gladys set me up.' Jill turned to rinse the back of her head. 'Max Kohl is a lawyer who's about to be disbarred after pleading guilty to felony tax evasion. The Kohls have two mortgages on their Bayside property, both in arrears, and the banks are threatening to foreclose. Their only child, Adam, won't be starting college in the fall because they can't pay his tuition. Bottom line, Gladys knew her brother was in the house, she knew why, she expected to profit, she set me up. All I did was exploit a flaw in someone else's tactics.'

There was nothing to do the following morning but go home. Jill Kelly was on a set course. Better not to ask questions, better not to invite the lie. Still, she surprised him. When he kissed her at the door, she pressed the side of her face against his chest. Suddenly, Boots imagined Jill at the kitchen table, late at night, pouring over a case file, going on that way year after year. Jill had made a big concession, explaining herself. Perhaps she was making another now. Or maybe she only wanted him to locate Corcoran. That would be even more flattering, Jill assuming that he could find the man. But she didn't ask for his help, didn't even say goodbye. She let him walk through the door and closed it behind him.

At home, he found his answering machine jammed with messages from reporters. Their enterprise impressed him. They knew very well that he couldn't speak to them without permission from his superiors, but they were trying anyway. Well, at least he'd had the foresight to buy his cellphone minutes in bulk instead of signing with a big company. Boots's home number was unlisted, but a dozen reporters had gotten it. They'd have his cellphone number too if it appeared on any registry.

Boots headed to the weight room at the Six-Four after lunch. By then, he'd had enough of Libby and his father and their maddening solicitude. He couldn't sit still, either, not without Rick Bauer's silhouette popping up.

At twenty-five, Rick had seemed a boy, handsome and fit, his dirty-blond hair long enough to violate regulations. Never mind that he was a drug smuggler, that he tried to murder Jill Kelly, that he had the conscience of a cockroach. Boots Littlewood had flipped Rick Bauer's switch, from on to off, lights out, see you in hell. There was no way around the facts.

The weight room was crowded when Boots arrived. O'Malley and Velikov were present; Antoine Crudup, too. But there were no sympathetic looks, no penetrating glances from this crew. Boots needed their company and he needed room. They gave him both.

He started slowly, with the stretching exercises he usually avoided, but once he got going found that he couldn't stop. He wanted a cigarette, too. This would get better, he told himself, but then couldn't decide which 'this' he was talking about – Rick Bauer, Jill Kelly or just the nicotine. He wanted to be with Jill, sitting next to her while she filled the car with smoke.

The room gradually thinned as the four o'clock shift change drew near. Only Velikov approached Boots, and he waited until O'Malley was in the shower.

'You OK, Boots?'

'No, I'm fucked.'

The Bulgarian nodded slowly, then patted Boots on the shoulder.

'Don't worry,' he advised, 'one time I shot this asshole, I took a whole week to get over it.'

An hour later, Boots climbed to the squad room two floors above and had a civilian tech print out the photograph on Mack Corcoran's driver's license. As he watched the tech's fingers whip across the computer's keyboard, he suddenly put his own finger on a small item bobbing at the edge of his awareness. Last night, in the shower, Jill had rattled off an up-to-date list of the Kohl family's misfortunes. How did she know?

Boots made it through the weekend before he broke down and called Tommy Galligan on Monday morning. He escorted his father to church and watched the Yankees beat Kansas City, one of those games where the Bombers scored early and often.

The players seemed to grow younger as the innings piled up, kids again. Boots knew that everybody on the field had been a superstar in Little League and high school, back when the game was still fun, when you believed your talent would carry you to the Hall of Fame, believed it with all your heart. When you lived in a world free of doubt.

Those days were long gone, even for superstars like Derek Jeter and Mariano Rivera. Now, when the boys of summer stepped into the batter's box, their expressions were grim, each turn at the plate another challenge, the fans ready to jump down your throat whenever you failed. And you failed a lot, the greatest hitters who ever played the game unable to get on base more than four of every ten trips to the plate. For the average player, professional baseball was about futility.

After dinner, still restless, Boots headed off to Silky's, a bar named after the racehorse Silky Sullivan, who'd once come from forty lengths back to win a stakes race. Inside, except for a stamped-tin ceiling, Silky's was all wood: bar, floor, walls and booths. Cheaply framed photos covered every vertical surface, most of race horses in full flight. Silky's had been owned and operated by several generations of the Peck family. One and all, they fancied themselves horsemen, the Pecks, though the horses owned by the family were cheap claimers who finished up the track with astonishing regularity.

Frankie Drago was sitting in a booth at the end of the room when

Boots walked in, across from an up-and-coming gangster named Sam Golibek. Boots nodded to Frankie, then went to the bar and ordered a Jack Daniels, neat. Silky's was a neighborhood joint, still undiscovered by the swelling population of young professionals. Most of the other patrons knew him, knew also that an attempt had been made on his life and that he'd killed a man. They knew about his role in liberating Vinnie Palermo as well. That was made apparent when Sam Golibek approached him.

Golibek reminded Boots of Rick Bauer. He was young, handsome and prepared to do violence. 'What you did for Vinnie,' he said, 'it was the right thing.'

A rare moment of camaraderie between warriors from opposing camps – that was undoubtedly Golibek's intention. Call him a romantic, but he was totally unprepared for the flame that shot up into Boots's eyes, or the flush that rose into his cheeks, or the words that dropped from his mouth, one at a time, heavy as stones.

'If I'm still lookin' at your face ten seconds from now, you repulsive mutt, I'm gonna slam your nose through the back of your fuckin' head.'

FORTY-SIX

Boots did not sleep well that night and was not in a good mood when he approached the door to Galligan's offices. Nor was his disposition improved by finding the door locked, or by the hour-long wait before Galligan popped out of the elevator at eleven o'clock.

'Hey, Boots.' Galligan's watery eyes swam behind his wire-rimmed glasses like fish in an aquarium. If he was any higher, he wouldn't be able to walk. 'I was gonna call you.'

'And that's it? You don't even say you're sorry?'

Galligan unlocked the door, slithered inside, threw a light switch. 'Sorry about what?'

'About me havin' to stand in the hall for an hour. You're supposed to be running a business.'

'Only when my receptionist's not on vacation.' Galligan made a

wet sound in the back of his throat that might have been a laugh.
'Besides, late is why God made answering machines.'

As he trailed Galligan to his office, Boots swallowed the blasphemy, his anger as well. He was consoled by the near certainty
that one fine day he would have the exquisite pleasure of separating
Galligan, if not from his teeth, at least from his business.

Too pleased with himself to recognize the threat, Galligan flopped
into his chair. Business was booming, thanks to Joaquin.

'Mack Corcoran,' he told Boots. 'You said he was trying to hide,
right?'

'That's right.'

'Well, he's not tryin' too hard.' Galligan opened the middle drawer
of his desk and took out a single sheet of paper. 'Corcoran's Visa
card was used eleven times over the weekend. Breakfasts, lunches,
dinners, a movie theater, two bars and a boutique.'

'No debit card? No ATMs?'

'No.' A fringe of Galligan's hair at the top of his forehead stood
up in a little wave. He patted this fringe very gently with one hand
as he passed the list to Boots with the other. 'What difference does
it make?'

'Debit cards and ATMs require PIN numbers. With credit cards,
nobody even checks the signature.'

Boots scanned the list for the vendors' addresses: Orchard Street,
Avenue A, Avenue B, Twelfth Street, Second Avenue, all on the
Lower East Side of Manhattan. From Boots's point of view, it
couldn't get any worse. He considered strangling the messenger,
whose stoned smile never wavered.

'You owe me one,' Galligan reminded.

The Lower East Side of Manhattan, called the East Village by real
estate agents, is home to hundreds of thousands of residents. A wall
of low-income housing projects lines its eastern boundary, from
Avenue D to the river, while four- and five-story tenements prevail
to the west. The projects are dominated by Hispanics, mainly Puerto
Ricans, the tenements by young professionals, mainly white. For
the yuppies, the Lower East Side is the bottom rung on Manhattan's
ladder of success – the starting point.

The mix appears volatile on the surface – low-income Latinos
and high-aspiration Gringos – but for the most part everybody

gets along. The storefronts along First Avenue and Avenue A are dominated by trendy restaurants, those on Avenue D by bodegas, check-cashing stores and Pentecostal churches. Avenue C is the borderline.

Boots drove into this mix at noon and went to work. At three o'clock, he found the answer to the only relevant question at Azzollini, an upscale boutique that might have sat more comfortably in the affluent West Village. Azzollini marketed handbags designed by Renata Azzollini through stores in Paris, Milan and New York.

For a moment, as he gathered himself, Boots stared through the window at handbags displayed like works of art in a museum. A willowy blonde in a long skirt flowed through this exhibit, wielding a feather duster. Her movements were even more languid than Galligan's.

Boots felt as though he'd wandered into somebody else's house of worship when he opened the door and stepped inside. The bags at Azzollini began at five hundred dollars and climbed rapidly from there. Maybe it was the feathers, or the semi-precious stones, maybe the bags were actually some kind of investment, maybe they were cheap at the price. Still, Boots couldn't see Mack Corcoran forking out seven hundred bucks for a handbag while he was on the run from Jill Kelly. But he couldn't imagine Corcoran being stupid enough to use a credit card, either.

'May I help you?'

Boots displayed his shield. 'Detective Littlewood,' he said. Up close, the blonde was stunning, right down to her professional smile. 'I'm here about a handbag purchased on Saturday.'

'Any particular bag?'

'One that cost seven hundred and forty-one dollars and thirty-four cents and was paid for with a credit card.'

'Oh, right.'

'You know which one I'm talking about?'

'Except at Christmas, we only sell a few bags a day, especially in the summer when people leave town. So, yes, I do remember.'

'Does that mean you handled the transaction?'

'I did.'

Boots held up Corcoran's photograph. 'Was this the man who made the buy?'

'Uh-uh. The man who purchased the handbag was much younger.' She brought a finger to her lips. 'Do we have a problem here?'

No, the problem was Jill Kelly's, unless Boots found her before she reached Mack Corcoran.

'Please,' he said, 'describe the man who bought the handbag.'

'I can do better than describe him, detective. I have him on tape. Give me a day and I'll give you his picture.' She drew herself up. 'At Azzollini, we're serious about credit cards.'

Now what? Boots kept asking himself that question as he drove back and forth, from Houston Street to Fourteenth Street, while he sat on a bench in Tompkins Square Park, as he ate a quick dinner, while he walked the avenues, peering into showroom windows.

From the earliest days of the Republic, New York has been a magnet for the best, the brightest and the most ambitious. At first, they came from upstate and New England, the second and third sons of Yankee farmers. Today, having graduated from the right universities, they come to the Lower East Side of Manhattan from every state in the country, young professionals, men and women both, determined to bite off a chunk of the apple. None of this was news to Boots Littlewood, who was familiar with a smaller yuppie enclave in Williamsburg. But he was struck, as he made his way, by how attractive they were, these boys and the girls, and how young. When he stopped for a beer at eight o'clock, he felt entirely out of place. Conversations swirled around him, a continual buzz in a language that might have been Greek for all he understood the words. No one approached him, no one met his gaze, not even in the mirror. He was that far outside the orbit of their lives.

Boots didn't mind. In his experience, these strivers were more insular than Albanian gangsters. They hung out together, married each other, eventually moved to the burbs where they lived side by side. And that was only if they didn't scuttle back to Peoria, utter failures.

At one o'clock, Boots was still at it, driving back and forth, hoping against hope that he could head Jill off. But the area to be covered was large and there were traffic lights on every corner, so that when Boots finally located Jill's midnight-green Chrysler on First Avenue, he knew it might have been sitting there for as long as thirty minutes.

Boots pulled to the curb in front of a fire hydrant and got out. The club scene was running full tilt, with knots of smokers on the sidewalk in front of every bar, including the one alongside Jill's Chrysler. Boots approached the two men and three women, his gaze traveling from face to face as he flashed his tin. He reminded himself that he was dealing with the children of the middle class. Though they believed themselves daring, even revolutionary, respect for authority came as naturally to them as their BlackBerrys and iPods.

Boots pointed to the Chrysler, hoping, in part, to draw attention from his drooping eyelid. 'Did any of you notice the woman who parked this car?'

They looked from Boots to each other, confused, as if Boots's shield had scratched, but not penetrated, the bubble that surrounded them.

'That Chrysler,' Boots prompted. 'Did any of you happen to notice the woman who parked it?'

'I saw her.'

'Ah.' Smile firmly in place, Boots turned to a smallish girl in a tank-top and jeans. 'What time was that?' he asked.

'Five minutes ago? Ten? I noticed her because she was wearing a jacket. The jacket was, like, red suede, and she had dark red hair, and I thought, you know, that it all, like, worked. Only the outfit definitely wasn't club gear. So it was, like, very strange.'

'Did you notice where she went?'

'Is she a . . . a person of interest?'

Boots repressed a smile. 'Please, did you notice where she went?'

'She walked across the street. But, look, I don't think I can identify her. Like in a line-up.'

'You didn't see where she went after that?'

'No.'

Boots scanned the rest of the smokers. 'Anybody else?'

'I saw her, too.' The man wore a Hawaiian shirt, red and gold, over carefully torn jeans. 'I saw her get out of the car and walk across the street.'

'Did you notice which way she went?'

'No, but she did something strange.'

'And what was that?'

'Halfway across First Avenue, she stopped and looked up.'

'At anything in particular?'

'Well, I can't be sure, of course, but I think she was checking the rooftops.'

FORTY-SEVEN

Boots walked to the curb and performed his own sweep. There were five apartment buildings on the east side of the block between Ninth and Tenth Streets. The height of their roofs varied by no more than a couple of yards, so that it was possible to traverse the entire block without coming down. This would give Jill access to the doors leading to the stairwells, or to the fire escapes in front and back if those doors were locked.

Boots didn't think Jill had scanned the rooftops in search of a concealed shooter. Jill was looking for a way inside. But inside which building? Boots's eye was drawn to the five-story tenement at the southern end of the block. Except for two apartments, on the second and third floors, all the windows were covered with sheets of plywood.

Fifteen years earlier, when Boots first put on the uniform, he would have assumed the structure to be abandoned. But times had changed. Once the last tenants were out, the landlord would reconfigure the cramped apartments, then market them as luxury condominiums. Even in this weak housing market, the units would likely be sold before the contractor finished working.

Boots crossed the street and walked down the block. The metal door to the nearly emptied building was jammed between two shuttered businesses, a laundromat and a copy shop. Boots tried the door, found it locked, then peered through a window scribbled over with graffiti. The darkened hall inside was narrow, barely arms' width, the stairs leading to the second floor narrower still. It was the perfect spot for a set-up.

Impulsively, Boots rang the buzzers to every unit, all twenty, in the hope that somebody in one of the still-occupied apartments would let him in. But there was no response and he finally backed off to lean against a car parked at the curb.

'Hey, get the fuck off the car.'

The author of this request was a smallish man, no more than five-eight. Clearly drunk, his arms were splotched with fading tattoos, from shoulders to wrists.

As Boots stared at the man, he was reminded of a late-night conversation he'd had with Jill Kelly. Boots had asked her about an encounter with a Russian pimp on a rooftop in Brooklyn, an encounter that left the pimp dead. Jill's initial response, which she offered without a trace of apology, went to the heart of the matter: 'I was in a foul mood that day.'

'Did you hear what I fuckin' said?'

Boots Littlewood was in a foul mood, too, and while he didn't consider shooting the drunk, he was keenly aware of a desire to beat the crap out of him. Like most cops, Boots detested belligerent drunks.

'I'm a cop,' Boots said.

The drunk took a step forward. 'And?'

Sighing, Boots produced his shield. 'You want to move the car, say so. Otherwise, be on your way. I'm not gonna tell you again.'

Boots didn't have to. An instant later, before the drunk's alcohol-befuddled mind registered the underlying threat, the top corner of the building exploded, showering First Avenue and Ninth Street with broken glass. Boots looked up to see a tongue of orange flame leap through the window, pause for an instant, then turn upward to lick at the side of the building. A cloud of oily-black smoke followed, pouring into the night sky.

'Holy shit.'

The drunk staggered toward Boots. His face had been cut by the falling glass and there was blood running from his cheek. Boots pushed him aside, ignoring a cut that ran for several inches along his own bicep.

The screams of a woman just a few yards away seemed more compelling and Boots raked her with his eyes. When he failed to observe any injury beyond the one to her psyche, he ran to the corner, grabbed a wire trash can and carried it to the door. He could hear the fire crackling overhead, along with a steady hiss that might have signaled an eruption of steam. The flames in the windows were now white-hot.

Boots slammed the trash barrel's weighted bottom into the door's window. Made of high-impact plastic and designed to resist an assault, the window bent, but did not break. Boots retrieved the barrel and raised it again just as the door opened and an old man ran out, shortly followed by a younger man carrying an elderly woman over his shoulder. The woman looked at Boots as she came past, blinked once, then smiled.

'Thank you, sonny,' she said.

Boots pushed his way inside and started up the stairs. On the second floor, he passed a man and a woman, each cradling a young child.

'Is there anyone else in the building?' he asked.

Barely pausing in his headlong flight, the man called out, 'No.'

Boots continued on, climbing the last flight of stairs to find the apartment at the corner of the building fully engulfed. Even from twenty feet away, the heat was intense. But the fire was drawing oxygen up the stairwell and through the apartment, pushing the smoke out the windows, so that he was able to see the dancing man well enough. Suspended between floor and ceiling, the man twisted back and forth as if in agony. Then the rope around his neck gave way and he plunged to the floor.

Boots took several steps toward the flames, the hiss of the fire now a steady roar. His eyes swept the landing in search of another body and he peered into the apartment through the flames. Much as he wished it was different, he couldn't reject the evidence right in front of him. The door to the apartment would be lying in the hallway if it had been dislodged by the explosion. Instead, the door was inside the apartment, still on its hinges. Someone had been here to open it, but not the man on the rope. The man on the rope was Mack Corcoran. He'd been dead for at least a day, probably longer.

Boots took a breath, found it hot enough to hurt. His face was burning, but he inched forward anyway. He was imagining Jill trapped inside, somehow alive, and he unable to help her, just as he'd predicted. When the heat forced him to stop, his heart was seized by a cluster of emotions midway between dread and despair. The fire was pushing into the hallway, the smoke, too, and the roof above his head was surely engaged. Still, he couldn't bring himself to flee, not until the banister on the stairs leading to the roof burst into flame. Even then, he backed down the stairs, one flight at a time, convinced that averting his eyes would lead to some further catastrophe.

'Yo, Boots, fancy meeting you here.'

Boots whirled, his hand reaching for his weapon, the same weapon that had been confiscated two days before. Jill Kelly was standing in a third-floor doorway, holding a small dog, a terrier of some kind. The animal was looking up at her through adoring eyes.

'Would ya believe it,' she said, 'the fuckers ran out and left the dog behind. I heard him cryin' when I came past and thought it was a kid.'

Boots could not bring himself to utter a sound. Jill's face and body were blackened with soot, the hair on the right side of her head singed. Her eyes were as round as marbles.

'I saw it coming,' she said. 'I knew I was being set up.'

'Then why did you open the door?'

'What?'

Boots had just time enough to record the blood trickling from Jill's right ear before she collapsed into his arms.

Jill was gone before Boots reached the lobby, handed over to an onrushing firefighter who began to administer oxygen as he hustled her out the door. Seconds later, she was on her way to Beth Israel Medical Center.

Boots's first instinct was to follow, but the uniformed officers on the scene, encouraged by their sergeant, insisted that he remain. And so he did, allowing a stray paramedic to clean and dress the cut on his arm.

'If you don't get that sutured,' the paramedic cautioned, 'you're gonna have a hell of scar.'

Boots stared at the man through his drooping eye. 'Thanks for the advice.'

His medical needs addressed, Boots was approached by a detective named Lansky. Their conversation was brief. 'I'm on assignment to the Chief of D, but I can say this much,' he told Lansky. 'I was standing in the street when the explosion took place. I entered the building to help evacuate the residents. I ran into Detective Kelly on the third floor. I never reached the scene of the fire.'

'Do you wanna tell me what you were doing here in the first place?'

'I don't.'

Lansky nodded twice, then fell back on one of the ten commandments of policing: when in doubt, pass the buck. He called his lieutenant, leaving Boots to cool his heels. Najaz showed up ninety minutes later, driving a black Jaguar sedan. He was smiling as he approached Boots.

'The Chief wants a word with you,' he said.

On cue, the rear door of the Jaguar opened. Boots tried not to smile as he crossed the street and settled into the butter-soft leather. He ran a speculative finger over the wood trim.

'Sapele,' Michael Shaw declared.

'Sapele?'

'Sapele wood, also called African mahogany. Myself, I don't know how Najaz affords a car like this. I make do with a Lincoln Town Car.'

Boots closed his eyes. 'How's Jill?'

'Almost deaf, at least for the short term. But she'll go home in the morning. Thanks to you.'

Boots understood the last remark to be a reprimand. He'd been instructed to leave town, but here he was, still on the playing field.

'Did you speak to her?'

'I wrote down a few questions and she answered in a rather loud voice. It seems she went to that apartment after receiving a tip from an anonymous source.'

'Who was she looking for?'

Shaw was leaning into the shadows, yet his skin was somehow whiter than ever. His face seemed to float, as if his body stopped where the collar of his shirt began.

'Jill was in search of Mack Corcoran. Whether or not she found him will be determined by DNA comparison. The body, I'm told, was burned beyond recognition.'

Boots stared down the block. The fire was out and the firefighters were gathering their equipment. Huddled next to a step-in van, a covey of white-suited CSU cops drank coffee while they waited for the apartment to cool.

'You tried to murder your niece,' he said. 'You killed Mack Corcoran and created a false trail with his credit cards, a trail Jill followed.'

Boots allowed the silence to build for a moment, then said, 'Let me suggest a pair of scenarios. The first, to be used in case Jill survives, goes like this. Driven to madness by his hatred for Jill Kelly, Corcoran rigs a booby trap, calls Jill, reveals his location, then hangs himself.' Boots shifted in his seat. 'The alternate scenario, if she doesn't survive, is a little more complex. Here, Jill is just one

of the many detectives assigned to run Corcoran down. As a
matter of routine, she follows a money trail in the form of credit
card purchases to the Lower East Side where she uncovers his lair.
The *how* part is irrelevant, of course, since Jill isn't around to explain
herself. No, what's important is Jill's decision to confront Corcoran
without calling for back-up, a decision with fatal consequences. But
that's Jill Kelly, right? Never happy unless her toes are hanging
over the edge of the cliff.'

Boots smiled and shook his head. 'In a way,' he concluded, 'I
don't blame the family. I mean, talk about an inconvenient woman.
What will she do next week? Next year?'

Shaw's face tightened down. 'There's a limit,' he warned.

'To Crazy Jill Kelly? A limit?' Boots turned slightly. 'I used to
believe that Jill had no fear. You know, a kind of genetic defect,
like some people can't feel pain. But I was wrong, Chief. Jill likes
danger. She likes the way it feels when her life is at risk. This may
not work out to your advantage.'

Shaw waved the comment off. 'Corcoran knew he'd die in prison.
I suspect he chose the easy way out. That he also wanted to avenge
himself comes as no surprise. According to both Artie Farrahan and
Elijah LeGuin, Corcoran hated Jill Kelly.'

'Listen to me. I know Corcoran didn't use his credit cards over
the weekend. Another man used them, someone much younger. I'll
have his photograph within the next twenty-four hours.'

'But will you show it to my niece? Knowing how easily she
becomes upset? I mean, hasn't the poor girl suffered enough? Does
she really need another war?'

Though Shaw's features were in shadow, Boots detected a trace
of liar's delight in the man's tone, a smug satisfaction that hinted
of an underlying narcissism more appropriate to a preverbal infant.
Boots had run up against this syndrome before. Shaw knew he was
ruthless. Ruthlessness was what he liked best about himself.

'I used to think that all men – and a few women, it should be
admitted – were equally ambitious. As ambitious as I, myself. That's
not true, of course. There are men like you, Boots, who spend their
entire careers in a backwater precinct without ever realizing they've
missed out on the juiciest parts of a human life. In some ways, I
pity you. In others, now that my declining years approach, I find
myself envious. Contentment is beyond me.'

'Is there a point here?'

'Yes, if Jill were to buy into your theory, she'd feel compelled to do something about it. In which case, of course, you'd lose her, one way or the other. So I'm advising you to go back to your simple life in the Sixty-Fourth Precinct, to your dad and your boy, and leave Jill Kelly to me. That girl and I, we understand each other.'

FORTY-EIGHT

S lick! Slick with two exclamation points!! That's how Boots came to think of the all-out assault on the media engineered by Mario Polanco and Michael Shaw. In the weeks following the death of Mack Corcoran, Internal Affairs, with the full cooperation of the Detective Bureau, arrested twenty-seven police officers. There were press conferences every morning, Polanco at the podium, Shaw a respectful step behind. Polanco was brilliant, displaying a level of righteous indignation that would have made a Pentecostal preacher blush. In this context, his jutting brow and blade-sharp nose became assets. Mario Polanco would not be turned back in his fight to purify the New York Police Department, despite accusations of witch hunt leveled by the unions representing the many suspects. By the end of the first week, he'd earned a media nickname: Super Mario.

By the start of the second week, the news cycle had turned over. Corcoran was left behind, lost in the tumult. Corruption was now the story. Not to say that Corcoran went unmentioned. No, only that the focus had changed.

Enter Jill Kelly, hero. And why not? Jill in her hospital bed. Jill wheeled through the hospital's lobby. Jill recovering at home. Jill newly promoted. Jill nominated for a New York City Medal of Honor. Jill as tough and beautiful in her photographs as she was in person.

This was a combination the media could not, and did not, resist. The Department was forced to deny requests for interviews from a dozen celebs, including Oprah Winfrey and Ellen DeGeneres.

And, oh, by the way, the untimely deaths of Chris Parker and

Lenny Olmeda? They were likely the result of a falling-out among thieves. Polanco dropped this nugget on Friday afternoon just before the conclusion of a scheduled news conference, the information instantly lost to a succession of carefully staged perp walks.

There were no guarantees here, not for Mario Polanco and not for Michael Shaw. Yes, cleaning house was a good idea. But how did the dirt get there in the first place? Why was the filth allowed to accumulate? The arrests being made all over New York were not of allied co-conspirators. These were rogue cops operating in small, self-contained units. They'd been operating for years. So, why the delay? And why now?

Would these questions eventually be asked? Would Polanco be tainted by his own zeal? Boots didn't know. But Polanco had cracked the blue wall of silence and neither the rank and file nor the unions would support him for Commissioner. If the media turned against him, he and Michael Shaw would promptly retire when the next Mayor took office in January.

Beyond a grudging admiration for Polanco and Shaw, Boots had no real interest in the power struggle unleashed by the murder of Chris Parker. Yet he continued to watch the evening news before dinner. It was only after ten days that he admitted the truth. He was awaiting a glimpse of Jill Kelly, as though a staged appearance could substitute for the phone call she hadn't made.

On the second Friday, the kickoff to the Fourth of July weekend, Boots took himself to a cop bar named Sally's on Bushwick Avenue. There he fulfilled his promise to Craig O'Malley and Boris Velikov. The party began an hour after the four o'clock shift change and continued well into the evening.

There were two television sets in Sally's, on either end of a long bar, one playing the Yankees, the other the Mets. Boots stayed down at the Yankee end, along with a knot of diehard fans, though he did not have a bet on the game.

Boots had given up on the season, even though the Yankees were in first place. Mariano Rivera, their Hall of Fame closer, was down for the count, as was Andy Pettitte, their lefty ace. Worse still, the bottom of the batting order was mediocre in the extreme, a failure Boots laid at the door of Brian Cashman, the team's general manager.

The Yankees had failed to sign any of the available free agents over the past two years, relying instead on aging superstars who were no longer super.

The contrast with the Boston Red Sox was so extreme that Boots couldn't ignore it. 'Over the last few years,' he told Sally Hernandez, 'the Sox signed John Lester and Adrian Gonzalez. That's why they're leading the league by four games. I'm tellin ya, Sally, this is a front-office problem, Theo Epstein versus Brian Cashman.'

Boots was prepared to go on, but Sally's eyes were already glazed. Boots let his own eyes drift back to the television. On Tuesday afternoon, he would return to the Six-Four, to Lieutenant Sorrowful, to the muggers, burglars, robbers and knuckleheads who populated his working days. And if Jill Kelly was gone, gone for good, he would not mourn her.

At midnight, Boris Velikov challenged Boots to an arm wrestle. Boots looked the Bulgarian up and down, a contemptuous evaluation that brought a smile to Velikov's slash of a mouth.

'How long ya think you're gonna hold out?' Boris asked.

'Five seconds,' Boots promptly replied.

In fact, he lasted for three.

Two nights later, at one o'clock in the morning, Boots piloted his recovered Chevy over the Verranzano-Narrows Bridge, from Brooklyn to Staten Island. The night-time view of Manhattan's southern tip from the bridge's crest was normally spectacular, especially at night. But not on this July Fourth weekend. There was barely a lit window in any of the office towers. From this distance, they looked like tombstones in a graveyard.

Though he might have shaved twenty minutes off the trip to Anita Parker's home if he'd remained on the Staten Island Expressway, Boots opted for the scenic route, on Hylan Boulevard around the edge of the island. Boots was feeling, as he'd been for several weeks now, a simmering recklessness. He sensed this affliction as he might a subclinical disease. Sexually transmitted, no doubt, by Crazy Jill Kelly.

Boots had no problem with calculated risk, but reckless was not his game. He scouted the Parker house three times before he parked his car and made his way to the unlocked window at the back of the house. Once inside, he went directly to the basement and yanked the two ends of the vent apart. When the plastic bag dropped to the floor, spilling money as it fell, he sighed.

Boots had his argument in place, the one he would make to Father Gubetti in the confessional. The priest had instructed him to resist and he'd done just that. Resisted for weeks and weeks until . . . until the great Temptor overcame his resolve by insisting that the loot, like any other treasure, belonged to he who recovered it. Did the new homeowner have a greater claim than Boots? Or some workman hired to remove the vent?

The cellphone in his pocket began to trill just as Boots knelt to gather the cash. He'd forgotten to shut it off. Now it would ring five or six times if he didn't answer. He yanked the phone out, pushed the on-button, whispered, 'Yeah?'

'Hey, Boots, whatta ya doin'?'

Boots looked down at the pile of bills. Somehow, lying to Jill Kelly seemed the perfect way to kick off their post-Corcoran relationship.

'Hangin' out,' he said.

'Well, I have a question I want to ask you.'

'Ask away.'

'I want to know whether you'll still love me if I have to wear a hearing aid?'

Boots shoved the cash into the plastic bag as he carefully considered his reply. Only when he had the words right did he finally speak.

'Jill Kelly,' he said, 'I'd still love you if you wore two wooden legs and a badly fitted set of false teeth.'

'What if I took the false teeth out?'

And not even Psycho Boots Littlewood had an answer for that one.